The Best American Mystery Stories 2014

GUEST EDITORS OF
THE BEST AMERICAN MYSTERY STORIES

The Best American
Mystery Stories™ 2014

Edited and with an Introduction
by **Laura Lippman**

Otto Penzler, *Series Editor*

A Mariner Original

HOUGHTON MIFFLIN HARCOURT

BOSTON • NEW YORK 2014

www.hmhco.com

ISSN 1094-8384
ISBN 978-0-544-03464-8

Printed in the United States of America
DOC 10 9 8 7 6 5 4 3 2 1

"My Heart Is Either Broken" by Megan Abbott. First published in *Dangerous Women*. Copyright © 2013 by Megan Abbott. Reprinted by permission of the author.

"Collectors" by Daniel Alarcón. First published in *The New Yorker*, July 29, 2013. Copyright © 2013 by Daniel Alarcón. Reprinted by permission of Daniel Alarcón.

"Princess Anne" by Jim Allyn. First published in *Ellery Queen's Mystery Magazine*, November 2013. Copyright © 2013 by Jim Allyn. Reprinted by permission of Jim Allyn.

"Snuff" by Jodi Angel. First published in *One Story*, Issue No. 179. *From You Only Get Letters from Jail.* Copyright © 2013 by Jodi Angel. Reprinted by permission of Tin House Books.

"Former Marine" (pp. 1–19) from *A Permanent Member of the Family: Selected Stories by Russell Banks*. Copyright © 2013 by Russell Banks. Reprinted by permission of HarperCollins Publishers and Knopf Canada.

"Going Across Jordan" by James Lee Burke. First published in the *Southern Review*, Volume 49:2, Spring 2013. Copyright © 2013 by James Lee Burke. Reprinted by permission of the *Southern Review*.

Contents

Foreword

THE WORDS *subjective* and *subjectivity* are extremely useful. What they describe is like the blood in the veins of an editor who is forced to reject a book or story. There is an inherent insult implicit in rejection. The editor is essentially saying, *Your work isn't good enough; it doesn't measure up.* What a dreadful thing to hear! After months, or even years, of slaving over a manuscript—rewriting again and again, arriving at *le mot juste* after trying a dozen other words, even desperately resorting to a thesaurus, editing line by line, fine-tuning (comma? or semicolon?)—and finally being convinced that it is as good as it is ever going to be, you are so proud of it that you are willing to send it out to the world. To hear that it's being rejected is brutally painful.

A diplomatic editor can help lessen the blow by employing the word *subjective.* "I have no doubt that plenty of editors will feel differently about it, because of course all taste is subjective." "I'm sorry, but it's just not my kind of book—but I'm sure you understand that editorial decisions are always subjective." And so on. These aren't lies. Well, not always. There are times when the complete sentence might well be "It's just not my kind of book . . . because I like books that have a modicum of originality and that haven't been scrawled with a crayon, like this one."

As I read stories for this distinguished anthology series, I am reminded of this notion of subjectivity, because so many different kinds of stories fall into the broad category of mystery and I don't want to be overly exclusionary, selecting only a single type of story that will keep the scope of the book too narrow. Like you, and like most people, I have subjective preferences for certain styles, subjects, characters, and plot elements of fiction, to which I naturally gravitate. My taste tends to run to darker, tougher stories (probably as a counterweight to my generally happy, sunny, optimistic personality). I have never found myself enthralled by the exploits of cats or other household pets as they use their extraordinary brainpower and intuitive sense to help their somewhat dim owners solve complicated crimes, though these tales aren't much worse than books in which the police are portrayed as such dunderheads that crimes need to be solved for them by florists, hairdressers, cooks, fashion designers, gardeners, Realtors, or booksellers.

Mystery is a very broad genre that includes any story in which a crime (usually murder) or the threat of a crime (creating suspense) is central to the plot or theme. Detective stories are one subgenre, others being crime (often told from the point of view of the criminal), suspense (impending manmade calamity), espionage (crimes against the state, which potentially have more victims than a single murder), and such sub-subgenres as police procedurals, historicals, humor, puzzles, private eyes, noir, etc. I love good stories in all these forms and others.

This series of anthologies tends to be more balanced than my own range of preference by virtue of several factors. First, my colleague on every book in the series has been and will remain forever (please, Lord) Michele Slung, who does the initial reading. She examines and reads (at least partially) somewhere in the neighborhood of three thousand to five thousand stories a year, culling the nonmysteries and the truly dreadful (of which there are more than you might imagine in your darkest nightmare). She then sends me stacks of stories she feels are eligible, from which I select the fifty of which I am most fond. Her taste is more catholic than mine, and her taste is impeccable, so I am exposed to a wider range of fiction than I might normally choose to read.

The second factor is the taste of the guest editor. It is almost impossible to think that two people who read a great deal will have exactly the same taste, and that certainly has proven to be the case with all the authors who have agreed to be guest editors for this series. To be fair, however, some stories are so obviously brilliant that it would be unthinkable for anyone to fail to appreciate them. So yes, subjectivity is significant, but sometimes an accomplished writer will have the stars align so that he or she produces work that is so transcendently exquisite that argument would be either futile or puerile.

Laura Lippman, the guest editor for this volume, frequently has been on regional and national bestseller lists, both for her outstanding Tess Monaghan series and for her suspenseful stand-alone novels. She has been nominated for seven Edgar Allan Poe Awards, winning for *Charm City*. Although on a tight deadline for the delivery of her next novel, she still somehow made the time to read all fifty stories that I submitted to her and come up with a wonderful final list. As the series editor, I get to play my own game and select my own choices—a list not shared with anyone. I bring it up because I've raised the issue of subjectivity as well as the notion that some stories defy argument. Seventeen of the stories in this book were also on my list of the top twenty of the year. Of course, I am utterly flabbergasted that Laura didn't pick my other top three, but I concede that this is how we know subjectivity exists, and I have nothing at all against the three outliers.

It should go without needing to be mentioned that I'm grateful to Laura for the tremendous amount of time, energy, and thought she put into the role of guest editor, just as I am to the authors who took on the same task in the past, without whom these very distinguished collections would not be as excellent as they are (and that's not just my subjective opinion; the reviews have been nothing short of astounding ever since the first anthology was released, in 1998). My deepest gratitude continues to resonate for Lisa Scottoline, Robert Crais, Harlan Coben, Lee Child, Jeffery Deaver, George Pelecanos, Carl Hiaasen, Scott Turow, Joyce Carol Oates, Nelson DeMille, Michael Connelly, James Ellroy, Lawrence Block, Donald E. Westlake, Ed McBain, Sue Grafton, and Robert B. Parker.

There can be little as troubling as learning that I missed a great story that deserved to be in *The Best American Mystery Stories* of the year. It's happened twice that I know about. Once the story was in an author's collection that had been sent to me but never got to my desk; I learned of it almost a year later. Another story was in a literary journal that wasn't familiar to me (I can guarantee you that I know it now and it is read carefully). As a result, I engage in a nearly obsessive quest to locate and read every mystery/crime/suspense story published, living in eye-bulging fear that I will miss another worthy story. Therefore, if you are an author, editor, or publisher, or care about one, please feel free to submit a story for next year's anthology and send a book, magazine, or tearsheet to me c/o The Mysterious Bookshop, 58 Warren Street, New York, NY 10007. If the story first appeared electronically, you must submit a hard copy. It is vital to include the author's contact information. No unpublished material will be considered, for what should be obvious reasons. No material will be returned. If you distrust the postal service, enclose a self-addressed, stamped postcard and I'll reassure you that it arrived and will be read.

To be eligible, a story must have been written by an American or Canadian author and first published in an American or Canadian publication in the calendar year 2014. The earlier in the year I receive the story, the more fondly I regard it. Some knuckleheads (no offense) wait until Christmas week to submit a story published the previous spring (this happens every year), causing my blood pressure to reach dangerous levels. I wind up reading a stack of stories while everyone else seems to be partying, shopping, and otherwise celebrating the holiday season. It had better be an extraordinarily good story if you do this, because I will start reading it with barely contained outrage. Since there is necessarily a very tight production schedule for this book, the absolute firm deadline for a story to reach me is December 31. This is not arbitrary or arrogant but a product of time constraints. If the story arrives twenty-four hours later, it will not be read. Seriously.

O.P.

Introduction

THE OTHER DAY a friend tweeted, "21 years ago today I got married in Las Vegas. Best decision ever."

I replied, "But worst opening ever for a noir story."

And yet here I am, guilty of the same perky satisfaction as I contemplate the very existence of the mystery short story, much less the superb stories I had the pleasure of reading for this, *The Best American Mystery Stories 2014*. These stories, filled with mayhem and murder and darkness, make me want to dance and giggle. I'm weird that way.

The thing is, the mystery story has no practical reason to *be*. It is an unforgiving form, cutting the writer little slack. A short story is hard enough to write; a short story that incorporates a satisfying crime plot—with the requisite twists and answers but a resolution that must never be too on-the-nose—is harder still. I know from my own experience that a five-thousand-word short story can take as long to craft as twenty thousand words of a novel, but maybe that's just me. (I doubt it.) Short stories can pay well, but generally don't, and if you calculated out the hourly wage, you'd weep. The short story is, to steal one of my favorite lines from James M. Cain's *Mildred Pierce*, about as commercial an enterprise as a hand-whittled clothespin. And yet, year in and year out, *The Best American Mystery Stories* anthology attests to the abundance of good short stories out there, which are discovered among the usual suspects (*Alfred Hitchcock's Mystery Magazine* and *Ellery Queen's Mystery Magazine*), venerable publications (*The New Yorker*), literary journals (*Southern Review, Sewanee Review, Antioch Review*), and cutting-edge newcomers (*Needle*).

I tried, in reading for this series, to offer up a variety across genres and subgenres. There are straightforward whodunits here, cozy in tone if not in deed, such as "Festered Wounds" by Nancy Pauline Simpson. There is Charlaine Harris's "Small Kingdoms," where we thrill and yet shiver to the realization that a new kind of sheriff is in town. But there are also stories that come at their crimes aslant, allowing the reader to fill in the disturbing and puzzling blanks—Jodi Angel's "Snuff" and Roxane Gay's "I Will Follow You." This collection also has a sense of wanderlust that mirrors my own, ranging widely throughout the United States and reaching all the way to Antarctica in Laura van den Berg's haunting story of that title.

But why does anyone write short stories? I only know why I write them: because someone has given me a subject, a deadline, and a promise of money, although the money is the least important aspect. (See hourly wage/weeping, above.) In fact, Michele B. Slung, who has been assisting Otto Penzler with this anthology since he began editing it seventeen years ago, jump-started my stalled ambitions that way. I met her at a party in Washington, D.C., and she asked, upon learning that I was a journalist, if I would consider submitting a story to a collection of erotica she was editing.

At the time I had managed to complete only a few short stories and relatively small ones at that—wistful vignettes inspired by my time in Waco, Texas. The stories all centered on the odd emotions kicked up when an assessor for the local tax district meets his new sister-in-law, a sullen Baltimore girl. It was less *Desire Under the Elms,* more *Mild Lust at the Piggly-Wiggly.* But I had enjoyed writing those stories and been encouraged by one teacher, Sandra Cisneros, then ripped apart by her successor, a gifted short story writer who had planted a flag in the vast territory that is Texas and declared it off-limits to me, an outsider who had missed some local nuances. She wasn't wrong, but she wasn't right either. If she taught me anything, it's that a tormentor can push you as hard as a mentor.

Michele accepted my first attempt at erotica, published under a pseudonym, and asked for a second when the collection yielded a sequel. My sophomore effort required a heavier editorial hand, but I've never minded editing. (And the second story was based in Texas, although told from the point of view of a new arrival. Boo-yah, in your face, former writing teacher, who seems to have disappeared. Hey, I'm the first to admit I hold tight to my grudges. They're good fodder for short stories, for one thing.) At this point, Michele suggested that I should consider writing a novel. She never specifically told me to write a crime novel, but she did mention that women often found it easier to start a novel when they approached it through the mask of genre, pretending the task was lesser (or at least less presumptuous) than attempting the Great American Novel.

As it turned out, I had sixty pages that I had scribbled in a black-and-white composition book, about an out-of-work reporter named Tess Monaghan who couldn't figure out what to do with her life . . . Jump forward twenty years, literally. I've written nineteen novels and almost twenty short stories in that time.

I think I wrote at least two or three novels before anyone suggested I try a mystery short story. My first one, suitably enough, was for a series called *First Cases,* and it centered on Tess. And you know what? It's not that good. In fact, it's a waste of a lovely title, "Orphans Court," and a decent-enough idea. Maybe I should rewrite it someday.

But the pattern had been established. I wrote short stories if someone asked me. When I teach, I describe this as writing from external prompts, and it sounds like the antithesis of art, but that's why I like it. The approach demystifies creativity, which could do with a little demystification. Did I want to write about baseball? Sure. Golf? Why not? Cocaine? You betcha. Dangerous women (twice), jazz, cities well known to me (Baltimore, Washington, D.C.), cities not quite so well known to me (New Orleans, Dublin). Poker, spies, New York City, Sherlock Holmes. Yes, yes, yes, yes. A ghost story with a sport, a *Twilight Zone* tribute. Senior-citizen criminals. Books themselves. The only subject I ever declined was cars, and the editor hocks me to this day. I keep telling him, "Dude, I drive a Jetta. A Jetta with manual transmission, but a *Jetta.* I was not the woman for the job."

But perhaps my favorite assignment was "a box." Brad Meltzer approached me with that one, and I said sure. I was getting cocky at that point. Riding high, due for a fall. All of a sudden the deadline was two weeks away and I still had no clue what I was going to write. To complicate matters, I was teaching at Eckerd College's annual Writers in Paradise conference, which left me with virtually no free time.

Then my friend and faculty colleague Ann Hood lost her sweater. You think I can carry a grudge? Ask her how she feels about the restaurant where she left her distinctive black cardigan. We called. We went back three times. Finally I asked to see the lost-and-found box for myself, convinced that the staff had overlooked the sweater. No, the black sweater was not there. But pawing through that sad collection of left-behinds, I remembered an assignment from my early days as a reporter in Waco, Texas, when I was asked to write an article about what was in the lost-and-found boxes at summer's end. I had triumphed over the less-than-interesting findings by writing in what I imagined to be a very good imitation of Philip Marlowe's voice. (God, I hope that piece never surfaces. RIP, my Waco clips.) But now I began to imagine a more sinister version of this story, one in which a young woman who imagines herself to be sophisticated, perhaps even a libertine, discovers that she's a real piker when she comes up against a couple of good citizens from Waco, sometimes called the buckle on the Bible belt. In fact, I saw a distinctive buckle on a belt, emerging snakelike from a soft, sagging cardboard box, an item that could be linked to an unsolved murder—and the editor who assigned the story.

I have two more short stories due right now—*right now*—and I just wish Ann Hood would lose another item of clothing.

No discussion of writing short stories would be complete without a discussion of those who edit short stories. I've done it exactly once, for the Akashic Books noir series, and found it gratifying yet challenging. Sure, you want all the stories to be perfect upon arrival, but then you have to wonder if you're even doing your job. As a short story writer, I yearn to believe they're perfect when they leave my desk—but a little voice in the back of my head tells me when they're not. Some of my best experiences have resulted from very good editing. Otto Penzler, for example, once told me that a story just wasn't good enough and explained what he thought the weaknesses were. He gave me a chance to rework it; that story, "Hardly Knew Her," was nominated for an Edgar and won the Anthony Award. Since the news of the selections for this collection went out into the world, I've heard from some editors who say they did nothing—nothing!—to the chosen stories. But I suspect that some outstanding editors are standing behind these stellar stories.

So we circle back to why anyone writes short stories. One of the writers in this collection, Megan Abbott, told me that her students at Ole Miss, where she was the John and Renée Grisham writer in residence for 2013–2014, become starry-eyed over the occasional unicorn that wanders into the publishing forest—the writer who enjoys a big success with a collection of short stories. Most recently it was B. J. Novak, and George Saunders just before him, but such critically adored bestsellers are rare and almost unheard-of for those who specialize in the mystery story, such as the late Edward D. Hoch. I wonder again: Why does anyone write mystery short stories, with their exacting, exasperating demands?

I can speak only for myself. The phone rings. Actually, my e-mail box pings. Actually, it makes no noise at all, because my computer is set to mute. I'll try again: A blonde walks into my office. That's true and it happens every day, thanks to Marko at Sally Hershberger Salon. I check my e-mail, see a request from an editor. *Could you write about . . . ?* And I say yes.

Unless it's about cars.

I am grateful that the writers of this collection said yes, whether to external or internal prompts, to characters or situations that suddenly appeared, requiring their attention. Because as a reader, when I'm yearning for a short story, nothing else will do. As demanding as the form may be for the writer, it is exceedingly rewarding for the reader. Being guest editor of *The Best American Mystery Stories 2014* was like being given an enormous box of very good chocolates and asked to go hog wild. If my final selection veers to the dark ones, preferably with nuts, that's my personal taste. No, it really is—in chocolates and in stories. Dark, with nuts.

Dig in.

LAURA LIPPMAN

The Best American
Mystery Stories 2014

MEGAN ABBOTT

My Heart Is Either Broken

FROM *Dangerous Women*

HE WAITED IN THE CAR. He had parked under one of the big banks of lights. No one else wanted to park there. He could guess why. Three vehicles over, he saw a woman's back pressed against a window, her hair shaking. Once, she turned her head and he almost saw her face, the blue of her teeth as she smiled.

Fifteen minutes went by before Lorie came stumbling across the parking lot, heels clacking.

He had been working late and didn't even know she wasn't home until he got there. When she finally picked up her cell, she told him where she was, a bar he'd never heard of, a part of town he didn't know.

"I just wanted some noise and people," she had explained. "I didn't mean anything."

He asked if she wanted him to come get her.

"Okay," she said.

On the ride home, she was doing the laughing-crying thing she'd been doing lately. He wanted to help her but didn't know how. It reminded him of the kinds of girls he used to date in high school. The ones who wrote in ink all over their hands and cut themselves in the bathroom stalls at school.

"I hadn't been dancing in so long, and if I shut my eyes no one could see," she was saying, looking out the window, her head tilted against the window. "No one there knew me until someone did. A woman I didn't know. She kept shouting at me. Then she followed me into the bathroom and said she was glad my little girl couldn't see me now."

He knew what people would say. That she was out dancing at a grimy pickup bar. They wouldn't say she cried all the way home, that she didn't know what to do with herself, that no one knows how they'll act when something like this happens to them. Which it probably won't.

But he also wanted to hide, wanted to find a bathroom stall himself, in another city, another state, and never see anyone he knew again, especially his mother or his sister, who spent all day on the Internet trying to spread the word about Shelby, collecting tips for the police.

Shelby's hands — well, people always talk about babies' hands, don't they? — but they were like tight little flowers and he loved to put his palm over them. He never knew he'd feel like that. Never knew he'd be the kind of guy — that there even were kinds of guys — who would catch the milky scent of his daughter's baby blanket and feel warm inside. Even, sometimes, press his face against it.

It took him a long time to tug off the dark red cowboy boots she was wearing, ones he did not recognize.

When he pulled off her jeans, he didn't recognize her underwear either. The front was a black butterfly, its wings fluttering against her thighs with each tug.

He looked at her and a memory came to him of when they first dated, Lorie taking his hand and running it along her belly, her thighs. Telling him she once thought she'd be a dancer, that maybe she could be. And that if she ever had a baby she'd have a C-section because everyone knew what happened to women's stomachs after, *not to mention what it does down there,* she'd said, laughing, and put his hand there next.

He'd forgotten all this, and other things too, but now the things kept coming back and making him crazy.

He poured a tall glass of water for her and made her drink it. Then he refilled it and set it beside her.

She didn't sleep like a drunk person but like a child, her lids twitching dreamily and a faint smile tugging at her mouth.

The moonlight coming in, it felt like he watched her all night, but at some point he must have fallen asleep.

When he woke, she had her head on his belly, was rubbing him drowsily.

"I was dreaming I was pregnant again," she murmured. "It was like Shelby all over again. Maybe we could adopt. There are so many babies out there that need love."

They had met six years ago. He was working for his mother, who owned a small apartment building on the north side of town.

Lorie lived on the first floor, where the window was high and you could see people walking on the sidewalk. His mother called it a "sunken garden apartment."

She lived with another girl and sometimes they came in very late, laughing and pressing up against each other in the way young girls do, whispering things, their legs bare and shiny in short skirts. He wondered what they said.

He was still in school then and would work evenings and weekends, changing washers on leaky faucets, taking out the trash.

Once, he was in front of the building, hosing down the garbage cans with bleach, and she rushed past him, her tiny coat bunched around her face. She was talking on the phone and she moved so quickly he almost didn't see her, almost splashed her with the hose. For a second, he saw her eyes, smeary and wet.

"I wasn't lying," she was saying into the phone as she pushed her key into the front door, as she heaved her shoulders against it. "I'm not the liar here."

One evening not long after, he came home and there was a note under the door. It read:

> My heart is either broken or I haven't paid the bill.
> Thx, Lorie, #1-A

He'd read it four times before he figured it out.

She smiled when she opened the door, the security chain across her forehead.

He held up his pipe wrench.

"You're just in time," she said, pointing to the radiator.

No one ever thinks anything will ever happen to their baby girl. That's what Lorie kept saying. She'd been saying that to reporters, the police, for every day of the three weeks since it happened.

He watched her with the detectives. It was just like on TV except nothing like on TV. He wondered why nothing was ever like you thought it would be and then he realized it was because you never thought this would be you.

She couldn't sit still, her fingers twirling through the edges of her hair. Sometimes, at a traffic signal, she would pull nail scissors from her purse and trim the split ends. When the car began moving she would wave her hand out the window, scattering the clippings into the wind.

It was the kind of careless, odd thing that made her so different from any girl he ever knew. Especially that she would do it in front of him.

He was surprised how much he had liked it.

But now all of it seemed different and he could see the detectives watching her, looking at her like she was a girl in a short skirt, twirling on a bar stool and tossing her hair at men.

"We're gonna need you to start from the beginning again," the male one said, and that part was like on TV. "Everything you remember."

"She's gone over it so many times," he said, putting his hand over hers and looking at the detective wearily.

"I meant you, Mr. Ferguson," the detective said, looking at him. "Just you."

They took Lorie to the outer office and he could see her through the window, pouring long gulps of creamer into her coffee, licking her lips.

He knew how that looked too. The newspapers had just run a picture of her at a smoothie place. The caption was, "What about Shelby?" They must have taken it through the front window. She was ordering something at the counter, and she was smiling. They always got her when she was smiling. They didn't understand that she smiled when she was sad. Sometimes she cried when she was happy, like at their wedding, when she cried all day, her face pink and gleaming, shuddering against his chest.

I never thought you would, she had said. *I never thought I would. That any of this could happen.*

He didn't know what she meant, but he loved feeling her huddled against him, her hips grinding against him like they did when she couldn't hold herself together and seemed to be grabbing on to him to keep from flying off the earth itself.

"So, Mr. Ferguson," the detective said, "you came home from work and there was no one home?"

"Right," he said. "Call me Tom."

"Tom," the detective started again, but the name seemed to fumble in his mouth like he'd rather not say it. Last week he'd called him Tom. "Was it unusual to find them gone at that time of day?"

"No," he said. "She liked to keep busy."

It was true, because Lorie never stayed put and sometimes would strap Shelby into the car seat and drive for hours, putting 100 or 200 miles on the car.

She would take her to Mineral Pointe and take photos of them in front of the water. He would get them on his phone at work and they always made him grin. He liked how she was never one of these women who stayed at home and watched court shows or the shopping channels.

She worked fifteen hours a week at the Y while his mother stayed with Shelby. Every morning she ran 5 miles, putting Shelby in the jogging stroller. She made dinner every night and sometimes even mowed the lawn when he was too busy. She never ever stopped moving.

This is what the newspapers and the TV people loved. They loved to take pictures of her jogging in her short shorts and talking on the phone in her car and looking at fashion magazines in line at the grocery store.

"What about Shelby?" the captions always read.

They never understood her at all. He was the only one.

"So," the detective asked him, rousing him from his thoughts, "what did you do when you found the house empty?"

"I called her cell." He had. She hadn't answered, but that wasn't unusual either. He didn't bother to tell them that. That he'd called four or five times and the phone went straight to voicemail and it wasn't until the last time she picked up.

Her voice had been strange, small, like she might be in the doctor's office, or the ladies' room. Like she was trying to make herself quiet and small.

"Lorie? Are you okay? Where are you guys?"

There had been a long pause and the thought came that she had crashed the car. For a crazy second he thought she might be in the hospital, both of them broken and battered. Lorie was a careless driver, always sending him texts from the car. Bad pictures came into his head. He'd dated a girl once who had a baby shoe that hung on her rearview mirror. She said it was to remind her to drive carefully, all the time. No one ever told you that after you were sixteen.

"Lorie, just tell me." He had tried to make his voice firm but kind.

"Something happened."

"Lorie," he tried again, like after a fight with her brother or her boss, "just take a breath and tell me."

"Where did she go?" her voice came. "And how is she going to find me? She's a little girl. She doesn't know anything. They should put dog tags on them like they did when we were kids, remember that?"

He didn't remember that at all, and there was a whir in his head that was making it hard for him to hear.

"Lorie, you need to tell me what's going on."

So she did.

She said she'd been driving around all morning, looking at lawn mowers she'd found for sale on Craigslist. She was tired, decided to stop for coffee at the expensive place.

She saw the woman there all the time. They talked about how expensive the coffee was but how they couldn't help it. And what was an Americano, anyway? And, yeah, they talked about their kids. She was pretty sure the woman said she had kids. Two, she thought. And it was only going to be two minutes, five at the most.

"What was going to be five minutes?" he had asked her.

"I don't know how it happened," she said, "but I spilled my coffee, and it was everywhere. All over my new white coat. The one you got me for Christmas."

He had remembered her opening the box, tissue paper flying. She had said he was the only person who'd ever bought her clothes that came in boxes, with tissue paper in gold seals.

She'd spun around in the coat and said, *Oh, how it sparkles.*

Crawling onto his lap, she'd smiled and said only a man would give the mother of a toddler a white coat.

"The coat was soaking," she said now. "I asked the woman if she could watch Shelby while I was in the restroom. It took a little while because I had to get the key. One of those heavy keys they give you."

When she came out of the restroom, the woman was gone, and so was Shelby.

*

He didn't remember ever feeling the story didn't make sense. It was what happened. It was what happened to them, and it was part of the whole impossible run of events that led to this. That led to Shelby being gone and no one knowing where.

But it seemed clear almost from the very start that the police didn't feel they were getting all the information, or that the information made sense.

"They don't like me," Lorie said. And he told her that wasn't true and had nothing to do with anything anyway, but maybe it did.

He wished they could have seen Lorie when she had pushed through the front door that day, her purse unzipped, her white coat still damp from the spilled coffee, her mouth open so wide, all he could see was the red inside her, raw and torn.

Hours later, their family around them, her body shuddering against him as her brother talked endlessly about Amber Alerts and Megan's Law and his criminal justice class and his cop buddies from the gym, he felt her pressing into him and saw the feathery curl tucked in her sweater collar, a strand of Shelby's angel-white hair.

By the end of the second week, the police hadn't found anything, or if they did they weren't telling. Something seemed to have shifted, or gotten worse.

"Anybody would do it," Lorie said. "People do it all the time."

He watched the detective watch her. This was the woman detective, the one with the severe ponytail who was always squinting at Lorie.

"Do what?" the woman detective asked.

"Ask someone to watch their kid, for just a minute," Lorie said, her back stiffening. "Not a guy. I wouldn't have left her with a man. I wouldn't have left her with some homeless woman waving a hairbrush at me. This was a woman I saw in there every day."

"Named?" They had asked her for the woman's name many times. They knew she didn't know it.

Lorie looked at the detective, and he could see those faint blue veins showing under her eyes. He wanted to put his arm around her, to make her feel him there, to calm her. But before he could do anything, she started talking again.

"Mrs. Caterpillar," she said, throwing her hands in the air. "Mrs. Linguini. Madame Lafarge."

The detective stared at her, not saying anything.

"Let's try looking her up on the Internet," Lorie said, her chin jutting and a kind of hard glint to her eyes. All the meds and the odd hours they were keeping, all the sleeping pills and sedatives and Lorie walking through the house all night, talking about nothing but afraid to lie still.

"Lorie," he said. "Don't—"

"Everything always happens to me," she said, her voice suddenly soft and strangely liquid, her body sinking. "It's so unfair."

He could see it happening, her limbs going limp, and he made a grab for her.

She nearly slipped from him, her eyes rolling back in her head.

"She's fainting," he said, grabbing her, her arms cold like frozen pipes. "Get someone."

The detective was watching.

"I can't talk about it because I'm still coping with it," Lorie told the reporters who were waiting outside the police station. "It's too hard to talk about."

He held her arm tightly and tried to move her through the crowd, bunched so tightly, like the knot in his throat.

"Is it true you're hiring an attorney?" one of the reporters asked.

Lorie looked at them. He could see her mouth open and there was no time to stop her.

"I didn't do anything wrong," she said, a hapless grin on her face. As if she had knocked someone's grocery cart with her own.

He looked at her. He knew what she meant—she meant leaving Shelby for that moment, that scattered moment. But he also knew how it sounded, and how she looked, that panicky smile she couldn't stop.

That was the only time he let her speak to reporters.

Later, at home, she saw herself on the nightly news.

Walking slowly to the TV, she kneeled in front of it, her jeans skidding on the carpet, and did the oddest thing.

She put her arms around it, like it was a teddy bear, a child.

"Where is she?" she whispered. "Where is she?"

And he wished the reporters could see this, the mystifying way grief was settling into her like a fever.

But he was also glad they couldn't.

*

It was the middle of the night, close to dawn, and she wasn't next to him.

He looked all over the house, his chest pounding. He thought he must be dreaming, calling out her name, both their names.

He found her in the backyard, a lithe shadow in the middle of the yard.

She was sitting on the grass, her phone lighting her face.

"I feel closer to her out here," she said. "I found this."

He could barely see, but moving closer saw the smallest of earrings, an enamel butterfly, caught between her fingers.

They had had a big fight when she came home with Shelby, her ears pierced, thick gold posts plugged in such tiny lobes. Her ears red, her face red, her eyes soft with tears.

"Where did she go, babe?" Lorie said to him now. "Where did she go?"

He was soaked with sweat and was pulling his T-shirt from his chest.

"Look, Mr. Ferguson," the detective said, "you've cooperated with us fully. I get that. But understand our position. No one can confirm her story. The employee who saw your wife spill her coffee remembers seeing her leave with Shelby. She doesn't remember another woman at all."

"How many people were in there? Did you talk to all of them?"

"There's something else too, Mr. Ferguson."

"What?"

"One of the other employees said Lorie was really mad about the coffee spill. She told Shelby it was her fault. That everything was her fault. And that Lorie then grabbed your daughter by the arm and shook her."

"That's not true," he said. He'd never seen Lorie touch Shelby roughly. Sometimes it seemed she barely knew she was there.

"Mr. Ferguson, I need to ask you: Has your wife had a history of emotional problems?"

"What kind of question is that?"

"It's a standard question in cases like this," the detective said. "And we've had some reports."

"Are you talking about the local news?"

"No, Mr. Ferguson. We don't collect evidence from TV."

"Collecting evidence? What kind of evidence would you need to collect about Lorie? It's Shelby who's missing. Aren't you—"

"Mr. Ferguson, did you know your wife spent three hours at Your Place Lounge on Charlevoix yesterday afternoon?"

"Are you following her?"

"Several patrons and one of the bartenders contacted us. They were concerned."

"Concerned? Is that what they were?" His head was throbbing.

"Shouldn't they be concerned, Mr. Ferguson? This is a woman whose baby is missing."

"If they were so concerned, why didn't they call me?"

"One of them asked Lorie if he could call you for her. Apparently she told him not to."

He looked at the detective. "She didn't want to worry me."

The detective looked back at him. "Okay."

"You can't tell how people are going to act when something like this happens to you," he said, feeling his head dipping. Suddenly his shoulders felt very heavy and he had these pictures of Lorie in his head, at the far corner of the long black lacquered bar, eyes heavy with makeup and filled with dark feelings. Feelings he could never touch. Never once did he feel sure he knew what she was thinking. That was part of it. Part of the throb in his chest, the longing there that never left.

"No," he said suddenly.

"What?" the detective asked, leaning forward.

"She has no history of emotional problems. My wife."

It was the fourth week, the fourth week of false leads and crying and sleeping pills and night terrors. And he had to go back to work or they wouldn't make the mortgage payment. They'd talked about Lorie returning to her part-time job at the candle store, but somebody needed to be home, to be waiting.

(Though what, really, were they waiting for? Did toddlers suddenly toddle home after twenty-seven days? That's what he could tell the cops were thinking.)

"I guess I'll call the office tomorrow," he said. "And make a plan."

"And I'll be here," she said. "You'll be there and I'll be here."

It was a terrible conversation, like a lot of those conversations couples have in dark bedrooms, late into the night, when you know the decisions you've been avoiding all day won't wait anymore.

After they talked, she took four big pills and pushed her face into her pillow.

He couldn't sleep and went into Shelby's room, which he only ever did at night. He leaned over the crib, which was too small for her but Lorie wouldn't use the bed yet, said it wasn't time, not nearly.

He put his fingers on the soft baby bumpers, festooned with bright yellow fish. He remembered telling Shelby they were gold-fish, but she kept saying *Nana, nana,* which was what she called bananas.

Her hands were always covered with the pearly slime of bananas, holding on to the front of Lorie's shirt.

One night, sliding his hand under Lorie's bra clasp, between her breasts, he felt a daub of banana even there.

"It's everywhere," Lorie had sighed. "It's like she's made of bananas."

He loved that smell, and his daughter's forever-glazed hands.

At some point, remembering this, he started crying, but then he stopped and sat in the rocking chair until he fell asleep.

In part, he was relieved to go back to work, all those days with neighbors and families and friends huddling in the house, trading Internet rumors, organizing vigils and searches. But now there were fewer family members, only a couple friends who had no other place to go, and no neighbors left at all.

The woman from the corner house came late one evening and asked for her casserole dish back.

"I didn't know you'd keep it so long," she said, eyes narrowing.

She seemed to be trying to look over his shoulder, into the living room. Lorie was watching a show, loudly, about a group of blond women with tight lacquered faces and angry mouths. She watched it all the time; it seemed to be the only show on TV anymore.

"I didn't know," the woman said, taking her dish, inspecting it, "how things were going to turn out."

you sexy, sexy boy, Lorie's text said. *i want your hands on me. come home and handle me, rough as u like. rough me up.*

He swiveled at his desk chair hard, almost like he needed to cover the phone, cover his act of reading the text.

He left the office right away, driving as fast as he could. Telling himself that something was wrong with her. That this had to be some side effect of the pills the doctor had given her, or the way sorrow and longing could twist in her complicated little body.

But that wasn't really why he was driving so fast, or why he nearly tripped on the dangling seat belt as he hurried from the car.

Or why he felt, when he saw her lying on the bed, flat on her stomach and head turned, smiling, that he'd burst in two if he didn't have her. If he didn't have her then and there, the bed moaning beneath them and she not making a sound but, the blinds pulled down, her white teeth shining, shining from her open mouth.

It felt wrong but he wasn't sure why. He knew her, but he didn't. This was her, but a Lorie from long ago. Except different.

The reporters called all the time. And there were two that never seemed to leave their block. They had been there right at the start, but then seemed to go away, to move on to other stories.

They came back when the footage of Lorie coming out of Magnum Tattoo Parlor began appearing. Someone shot it with their cell phone.

Lorie was wearing those red cowboy boots again, and red lipstick, and she walked right up to the camera.

They ran photos of it in the newspaper, with the headline "A Mother's Grief?"

He looked at the tattoo.

The words *Mirame quemar* written in script, wrapping itself around her hip.

It covered just the spot where a stretch mark had been, the one she always covered with her fingers when she stood before him naked.

He looked at the tattoo in the dark bedroom, a band of light coming from the hallway. She turned her hip, kept turning it, spinning her torso so he could feel it, all of it.

"I needed it," she said. "I needed something. Something to put my fingers on. To remind me of me. Do you like it?" she asked, her breath in his ear. The ink looked like it was moving.

"I like it," he said, putting his fingers there. Feeling a little sick. He did like it. He liked it very much.

*

Late, late into that night, her voice shook him from a deep sleep.

"I never knew she was coming and then she was here," she was saying, her face pressed in her pillow. "And I never knew she was going and now she's gone."

He looked at her, her eyes shut, dappled with old makeup.

"But," she said, her voice grittier, strained, "she was always doing whatever she wanted."

That's what he thought she said. But she was sleeping, and didn't make any sense at all.

"You liked it until you thought about it," she said. "Until you looked close at it and then you decided you didn't want it anymore. Or didn't want to be the guy who wants it."

He was wearing the new shirt she had bought for him the day before. It was a deep, deep purple and beautiful and he felt good in it, like the unit manager who all the women in the office talked about. They talked about his shoes and he always wondered where people got shoes like that.

"No," he said. "I love it. But it's just . . . expensive."

That wasn't it, though. It didn't seem right buying things, buying anything, right now. But it was also how colorful the shirt was, the sheen on it. The bright hard beauty of it. A shirt for going out, for nightclubs, for dancing. For those things they did when they still did things: vodka and pounding music and frenzied sex in her car.

The kind of drunken sex so messy and crazy that you were almost shy around each other after, driving home, screwed sober, feeling like you'd showed something very private and very bad.

Once, years ago, she did something to him no one had ever done and he couldn't look at her afterward at all. The next time he did something to her. For a while, it felt like it would never stop.

"I think someone should tell you about your wife," the e-mail said. That was the subject line. He didn't recognize the address, a series of letters and digits, and there was no text in the body of the e-mail. There was only a photo of a girl dancing in a bright green halter top, the ties loose and dangling.

It was Lorie, and he knew it must be an old picture. Weeks ago, the newspapers had gotten their hands on some snapshots of

Lorie from her late teens, dancing on tabletops, kissing her girl-friends. Things girls did when they were drinking and someone had a camera.

In those shots, Lorie was always posing, vamping, trying to look like a model, a celebrity. It was a Lorie before he really knew her, a Lorie from what she called her "wild girl days."

But in this picture she didn't seem to be aware of the camera at all, seemed to be lost in the thrall of whatever music was playing, whatever sounds she was hearing in her crowded head. Her eyes were shut tight, her head thrown back, her neck long and brown and beautiful.

She looked happier than he had ever seen her.

A Lorie from long ago, or never.

But when he scrolled further down, he saw the halter top riding up her body, saw the pop of a hip bone. Saw the elegant script letters: *Mirame quemar.*

That night he remembered a story she had told him long ago. It seemed impossible he'd forgotten it. Or maybe it just seemed different now, making it seem like something new. Something uncovered, an old sunken box you find in the basement smelling strong and you're afraid to open it.

It was back when they were dating, when her roommate was always around and they had no place to be alone. They would have thrilling bouts in his car, and she loved to crawl into the back seat and lie back, hoisting a leg high over the headrest and begging him for it.

It was after the first or second time, back when it was all so crazy and confusing and his head pounding and starbursting, that Lorie curled against him and talked and talked about her life, and the time she stole four Revlon eyeslicks from CVS and how she had slept with a soggy-eared stuffed animal named Ears until she was twelve. She said she felt she could tell him anything.

Somewhere in the blur of those nights—nights when he too told her private things, stories about babysitter crushes and shoplifting Matchbox cars—that she told him the story.

How, when she was seven, her baby brother was born and she became so jealous.

"My mom spent all her time with him, and left me alone all day," she said. "So I hated him. Every night I would pray that he would be taken away. That something awful would happen to him. At night I'd sneak over to his crib and stare at him through the little bars. I think maybe I figured I could think it into happening. If I stared at him long enough and hard enough, it might happen."

He had nodded, because this is how kids could be, he guessed. He was the youngest and wondered if his older sister thought things like this about him. Once she smashed his finger under a cymbal and said it was an accident.

But she wasn't done with her story and she snuggled closer to him and he could smell her powdery body and he thought of all its little corners and arcs, how he liked to find them with his hands, all the soft, hot places on her. Sometimes it felt like her body was never the same body, like it changed under his hands. *I'm a witch, a witch.*

"So one night," she said, her voice low and sneaky, "I was watching him through the crib bars and he was making this funny noise."

Her eyes glittered in the dark of the car.

"I leaned across, sticking my hands through the rails," she said, snaking her hand toward him. "And that's when I saw this piece of string dangling on his chin, from his pull toy. I starting pulling it, and pulling it."

He watched her tugging the imaginary string, her eyes getting bigger and bigger.

"Then he let out this gasp," she said, "and started breathing again."

She paused, her tongue clicking.

"My mom came in at just that moment. She said I saved his life," she said. "Everyone did. She bought me a new jumper and the hot-pink shoes I wanted. Everyone loved me."

A pair of headlights flashed across them and he saw her eyes, bright and brilliant.

"So no one ever knew the real story," she said. "I've never told anyone."

She smiled, pushing herself against him.

"But now I'm telling you," she said. "Now I have someone to tell."

"Mr. Ferguson, you told us, and your cell phone records confirm, that you began calling your wife at 5:50 p.m. on the day of your daughter's disappearance. Finally, you reached her at 6:45. Is that right?"

"I don't know," he said, this the eighth, ninth, tenth time they'd called him in. "You would know better than me."

"Your wife said she was at the coffee place at around five. But we tracked down a record of your wife's transaction. It was at 3:45."

"I don't know," he said, rubbing at the back of his neck, the prickling there. He realized he had no idea what they might tell him. No idea what might be coming.

"So what do you think your wife was doing for three hours?"

"Looking for this woman. Trying to find her."

"She did make some other calls during that time. Not to the police, of course. Or even you. She made a call to a man named Leonard Drake. Another one named Jason Patrini."

One sounded like an old boyfriend—Lenny someone—the other he didn't even know. He felt something hollow out inside him. He didn't know who they were even talking about anymore, but it had nothing to do with him.

The female detective walked in, giving her partner a look.

"Since she was making all these calls, we could track her movements. She went to the Harbor View Mall."

"Would you like to see her on the security camera footage there?" the female detective asked. "We have it now. Did you know she bought a tank top?"

He felt nothing.

"She also went to the quickie mart. The cashier just IDed her. She used the bathroom. He said she was in there a long time, and when she came out, she had changed clothing. Would you like to see the footage there? She looks like a million bucks."

She slid a grainy photo across the desk. A young woman in a tank top and hoodie tugged low over her brow. She was smiling.

"That's not Lorie," he said softly. She looked too young, looked like she looked when he met her, a little elfin beauty with a flat stomach and pigtails and a pierced navel. A hoop he used to tug. He'd forgotten about that. She must have let it seal over.

"I'm sure this is tough to hear, Mr. Ferguson," the male detective said. "I'm sorry."

He looked up. The detective did look very sorry.

"What did you say to them?" he asked.

Lorie was sitting in the car with him, a half block from the police station.

"I don't know if you should say anything to them anymore," he said. "I think maybe we should call a lawyer."

Lorie was looking straight ahead, at the strobing lights from the intersection. Slowly she lifted her hand to the edges of her hair, combing them thoughtfully.

"I explained," she said, her face dark except for a swoop of blue from the car dealership sign, like a tadpole up her cheek. "I told them the truth."

"What truth?" he asked. The car felt so cold. There was a smell coming from her, of someone who hasn't eaten. A raw smell of coffee and nail polish remover.

"They don't believe anything I say anymore," she said. "I explained how I'd been to the coffee place twice that day. Once to get a juice for Shelby and then later for coffee for me. They said they'd look into it, but I could see how it was on their faces. I told them so. I know what they think of me."

She turned and looked at him, the car moving fast, sending red lights streaking up her face. It reminded him of a picture he once saw in a *National Geographic* of an Amazon woman, her face painted crimson, a wooden peg through her lip.

"Now I know what everyone thinks of me," she said, and turned away again.

It was late that night, his eyes wide open, that he asked her. She was sound asleep, but he said it.

"Who's Leonard Drake? Who's Jason whatever?"

She stirred, shifted to face him, her face flat on the sheet.

"Who's Tom Ferguson? Who is he?"

"Is that what you do?" he asked, his voice rising. "Go around calling men."

It was easier to ask her this than to ask her other things. To ask her if she had shaken Shelby, if she had lied about everything. Other things.

"Yes," she said. "I call men all day long, I go to their apartments. I leave my daughter in the car, especially if it's very hot. I sneak up their apartment stairs."

She had her hand on her chest, was moving it there, watching him.

"You should feel how much I want them by the time they open their doors."

Stop, he said, without saying it.

"I have my hands on their belts before they close the door behind me. I crawl onto their laps on their dirty bachelor's sofas and do everything."

He started shaking his head, but she wouldn't stop.

"You have a baby, your body changes. You need something else. So I let them do anything. I've done everything."

Her hand was moving, touching herself. She wouldn't stop.

"That's what I do while you're at work. I wasn't calling people on Craigslist, trying to replace your lawn mower. I wasn't doing something for you, always for you."

He'd forgotten about the lawn mower, forgotten that's what she said she'd been doing that day. Trying to get a secondhand one after he'd gotten blood blisters on both hands using it the last time. That's what she'd said she was doing.

"No," she was saying, "I was calling men, making dates for sex. That's what I do since I've had a baby and been at home. I don't know how to do anything else. It's amazing I haven't been caught before. If only I hadn't been caught."

He covered his face with his hand. "I'm sorry. I'm sorry."

"How could you?" she said, a strangle in her throat. She was tugging all the sheet into her hands, rolling it, pulling it off him, wringing it. "How could you?"

He dreamt of Shelby that night.

He dreamt he was wandering through the blue-dark of the house and when he got to Shelby's room, there was no room at all and suddenly he was outside.

The yard was frost-tipped and lonely-looking and he felt a sudden sadness. He felt suddenly like he had fallen into the loneliest place in the world and the old toolshed in the middle seemed somehow the very center of that loneliness.

When they'd bought the house, they'd nearly torn it down — everyone said they should — but they decided they liked it, the "baby barn," they'd called it, with its sloping roof and faded red paint.

But it was too small for anything but a few rakes and that push lawn mower with the sagging left wheel.

It was the only old thing about their house, the only thing left from before he was there.

By day, it was a thing he never thought about at all anymore, didn't notice it other than the smell sometimes coming off it after rain.

But in the dream it seemed a living thing, neglected and pitiful.

It came to him suddenly that the lawn mower in the shed might still be fixed, and if it were then everything would be okay and no one would need to look for lawn mowers and the thick tug of grass under his feet would not feel so heavy and all this loneliness would end.

He put his hand on the shed's cool, crooked handle and tugged it open.

Instead of the lawn mower, he saw a small black sack on the floor of the shed.

He thought to himself in the way you do in dreams, *I must have left the cuttings in here. They must be covered with mold and that must be the smell so strong it*—

Grabbing for the sack, it slipped open, and the bag itself began to come apart in his hands.

There was the sound, the feeling of something heavy dropping to the floor of the shed.

It was too dark to see what was slipping over his feet, tickling his ankles.

Too dark to be sure, but it felt like the sweet floss of his daughter's hair.

He woke already sitting up. A voice was hissing in his head: *Will you look in the shed? Will you?*

And that was when he remembered there was no shed in the backyard anymore. They'd torn it down when Lorie was pregnant because she said the smell of rot was giving her headaches, making her sick.

The next day the front page of the paper had a series of articles marking the two-month anniversary of Shelby's disappearance.

They had the picture of Lorie under the headline "What Does She Know?" There was a picture of him, head down, walking from the police station yesterday. The caption read: "More unanswered questions."

He couldn't read any of it, and when his mother called he didn't pick up.

All day at work, he couldn't concentrate. He felt everyone looking at him.

When his boss came to his desk, he could feel the careful way
he was being talked to.

"Tom, if you want to leave early," he said, "that's fine."

Several times he caught the administrative assistant staring at
his screen saver, the snapshot of Lorie with ten-month-old Shelby
in her Halloween costume, a black spider with soft spider legs.

Finally he did leave, at three o'clock.

Lorie wasn't in the house and he was standing at the kitchen
sink, drinking a glass of water, when she saw her through the
window.

Though it was barely seventy degrees, she was lying on one of
the summer loungers.

Headphones on, she was in a bright orange bikini with gold
hoops in the straps and on either hip.

She had pushed the purple playhouse against the back fence,
where it tilted under the elm tree.

He had never seen the bikini before, but he recognized the
sunglasses, large ones with white frames she had bought on a trip
to Mexico she had taken with an old girlfriend right before she got
pregnant.

Gleaming in the center of her slicked torso was a gold belly
ring.

She was smiling, singing along to whatever music was playing in
her head.

That night he couldn't bring himself to go to bed. He watched
TV for hours without watching any of it. He drank four beers in a
row, which he had not done since he was twenty years old.

Finally the beer pulled on him, and the Benadryl he took after,
and he found himself sinking at last onto their mattress.

At some point in the middle of the night, there was a stirring
next to him, her body shifting hard. It felt like something was
happening.

"Kirsten," she mumbled.

"What?" he asked. "What?"

Suddenly she half sat up, her elbows beneath her, looking
straight ahead.

"Her daughter's name was Kirsten," she said, her voice soft and tentative. "I just remembered. Once, when we were talking, she said her daughter's name was Kirsten. Because she liked how it sounded with Krusie."

He felt something loosen inside him, then tighten again. What was this?

"Her last name was Krusie with a *K*," she said, her face growing more animated, her voice more urgent. "I don't know how it was spelled, but it was with a *K*. I can't believe I just remembered. It was a long time ago. She said she liked the two *K*'s. Because she was two *K*'s. Katie Krusie. That's her name."

He looked at her and didn't say anything.

"Katie Krusie," she said. "The woman at the coffee place. That's her name."

He couldn't seem to speak, or even move.

"Are you going to call?" she said. "The police?"

He found he couldn't move. He was afraid somehow. So afraid he couldn't' breathe.

She looked at him, paused, and then reached across him, grabbing for the phone herself.

As she talked to the police, told them, her voice now clear and firm, what she'd remembered, as she told them she would come to the station, would leave in five minutes, he watched her, his hand over his own heart, feeling it beating so hard it hurt.

"We believe we have located the Krusie woman," the female detective said. "We have officers heading there now."

He looked at both of them. He could feel Lorie beside him, breathing hard. It had been less than a day since Lorie first called.

"What are you saying?" he said, or tried to. No words came out.

Katie-Ann Krusie had no children, but told people she did, all the time. After a long history of emotional problems, she had spent a fourteen-month stint at the state hospital following a miscarriage.

For the past eight weeks she had been living in a rental in Torring, 40 miles away, with a little blond girl she called Kirsten.

After the police released a photo of Katie-Ann Krusie on Amber Alert, a woman who worked at a coffee chain in Torring recognized her as a regular customer, always ordering extra milk for her babies.

"She sure sounded like she loved her kids," the woman said. "Just talking about them made her so happy."

The first time he saw Shelby again, he couldn't speak at all.

She was wearing a shirt he'd never seen and shoes that didn't fit and she was holding a juice box the policeman had given her.

She watched him as he ran down the hall toward her.

There was something in her face that he had never seen before, knew hadn't been there before, and he knew in an instant he had to do everything he could to make it gone.

That was all he would do, if it took him the rest of his life to do it.

The next morning, after calling everyone, one by one, he walked into the kitchen to see Lorie sitting next to Shelby, who was eating apple slices, her pinkie finger curled out in that way she had.

He sat and watched her and Shelby asked him why he was shaking and he said because he was glad to see her.

It was hard to leave the room, even to answer the door when his mother and sister came, when everyone started coming.

Three nights later, at the big family dinner, the welcome-home dinner for Shelby, Lorie drank a lot of wine, and who could blame her, everyone was saying.

He couldn't either, and he watched her.

As the evening carried on, as his mother brought out an ice cream cake for Shelby, as everyone huddled around Shelby, who seemed confused and shy at first and slowly burst into something beautiful that made him want to cry again—as all these things were occurring, he had one eye on Lorie, her quiet, still face. On the smile there, which never grew or receded, even when she held Shelby in her lap, Shelby nuzzling her mother's wine-flushed neck.

At one point he found her standing in the kitchen and staring into the sink; it seemed to him she was staring down into the drain.

It was very late, or even early, and Lorie wasn't there.

He thought she had gotten sick from all the wine, but she wasn't in the bathroom either.

Something was turning in him, uncomfortably, as he walked into Shelby's room.

He saw her back, naked and white from the moonlight. The plum-colored underpants she'd slept in.

She was standing over Shelby's crib, looking down.

He felt something in his chest move.

Then, slowly, she kneeled, peeking through the crib rails, looking at Shelby.

It looked like she was waiting for something.

For a long time he stood there, 5 feet from the doorway, watching her watching their sleeping baby.

He listened close for his daughter's high breaths, the stop and start of them.

He couldn't see his wife's face, only that long white back of hers, the notches of her spine. *Mirame quemar* etched on her hip.

He watched her watching his daughter, and knew he could not ever leave this room. That he would have to be here forever now, on guard. There was no going back to bed.

DANIEL ALARCÓN

Collectors

FROM *The New Yorker*

ROGELIO WAS THE YOUNGEST of three, the skinniest, the least talkative. As a boy, he slept in the same room as his brother, Jaime, and his earliest, most profoundly comforting memories were of those late nights, before sleep: the chatter between them, the camaraderie. Then Jaime left for San Jacinto, and shortly afterward, when Rogelio was eight, his father died. In the months after that, Rogelio began skipping school to spend hours walking in the hills above town. He liked to be alone. He gathered bits of wood, and used his father's tools to carve tiny animals—birds, lizards, that sort of thing—which he kept in a box under his bed. They weren't particularly lifelike, but they were surprisingly evocative, and, at age twelve, he presented one to a girl he liked, as a gift. With trembling hands and a look of horror on her face, the girl accepted it, and for the next week she avoided his gaze. The other children whispered about him whenever he came near. There was no need to hear the exact words; their meaning was clear enough. The following year, Rogelio quit school officially, and his mother and his sister agreed that there was no practical reason for him to stay in town any longer, so he left to join Jaime in San Jacinto.

Rogelio was small for his age, but tough, good with his hands and his fists. He didn't have a temper, the way his brother did. Instead he possessed an equanimity that his family found almost disconcerting. He'd been shunned all his life, or that's how he felt, and he'd grown accustomed to it. He loved his brother, looked up to him, and never worried about whether Jaime loved him in return. He could follow instructions, had decent mechanical intuition, but, unlike most of his classmates, he had not learned to read. Jaime tried to teach him, but soon gave up: the boy kept confusing his letters. More than a decade later, Henry Nuñez, Rogelio's cellmate in Collectors prison, explained to him that there was a condition called dyslexia. "How about that?" Rogelio said, but his face registered nothing—not regret or shame or even curiosity—as if he were unwilling to contemplate the ways in which his life might have been different if he'd had this information sooner.

For the first couple of years in San Jacinto, he worked on the broken-down trucks that his brother bought on the cheap. Together they would cajole these heaps of rusting metal back to life. Each machine was different, requiring a complex and patient kind of surgery. Parts were swapped out, rescued, jerry-rigged. It was as much invention as repair. When a truck was reborn, they sold it and reinvested the profits, which weren't much at first, but the brothers were very careful with their money. In a photograph from this time, Rogelio sits on a gigantic truck tire with his shirt off; he is lithe and wiry, and he wears the blank expression of a child who asks no questions and makes no demands of the world. Not a happy boy, but, given his situation, perhaps a wise one.

Eventually Jaime bought his kid brother a motorbike, the kind outfitted with a flatbed of wooden planks in front. This machine became Rogelio's source of income for the next few years; he rode it around the city, from one market to another, carrying cans of paint, lashed-together bundles of metal pipes, chickens headed for slaughter, crammed into crates stacked so high that he had to lean to one side in order to steer. San Jacinto was growing steadily, but not yet at the torrid pace that would later come to define it; Rogelio knew every corner of the city then, and years later, at Collectors, he would draw a map of it on a wall of the cell that he shared with Henry, using white chalk to trace the streets and the railroad tracks and to label the apartment he'd shared with his brother.

Henry asked him why he'd gone to the trouble.

"Because one day I'll go back there," Rogelio said.

In 1980, the year Rogelio turned seventeen, Jaime took him to a brothel near the center of town. It was the first of its kind, and had been built for the hoped-for wave of young, fearless men with money. There were rumors of gold in the hills, and the brothel's fantastical anteroom paid tribute to those stories: the walls were painted gold, as were the bar and the wooden tables and chairs. In fact, that night even the three prostitutes on display for Rogelio's choosing had followed the color scheme: one in a gold miniskirt, another in gold lace panties and bra, and the third in a gold negligee. Three little trophies, all smiling coquettishly, hands on their hips. Jaime encouraged Rogelio to pick one, but he couldn't. Or wouldn't. The moment stretched on and on, far past what was comfortable, until the girls' put-on smiles began to fade. And still the boy stood there, immobilized, amazed.

"Oh, fuck it," Jaime said finally. He pulled a wad of bills from his pocket and paid for all three.

It seems that Jaime had begun to sell more than refurbished vehicles.

When Rogelio was eighteen, he traded in his motorized cart for a small loading van and, shortly after, traded the van for a truck that he brought back to life with his own hands. The first time the reconstructed engine turned over was one of the proudest moments of Rogelio's life. Each new vehicle expanded his world. Now he was a driver; he ferried a dozen laborers down to the lowlands, men who stood for hours without complaint as the truck bounced along rutted and bumpy roads. Once there, Rogelio discovered a prickly kind of heat he'd never felt before. He liked it, and began volunteering to drive that route whenever it was available.

The following year his brother sent him in the other direction, over the range to the west, and on that trip Rogelio saw the ocean for the first time. It was 1982; he was almost twenty years old. He sat at the edge of the boardwalk in La Julieta as the fancy people of the city strolled by, confident-looking men in blazers and women in bright dresses, boys he took to be his age but who appeared to possess a variety of secrets that Rogelio could only guess at. None so much as glanced in his direction. He wondered if he looked out of place, if they could tell that he was a stranger here, or if they could even see him at all. But when he considered the ocean Rogelio realized how insignificant these concerns were. He was happy, he told Henry later, and in prison he liked to remember the hours he'd spent there, gazing at the sea.

For the next few years Rogelio drove the route to the coast, to the lowlands, and back again, carrying vegetables to the city, raw materials to the mountains, laborers to the jungle. He was a quiet young man, still a boy in some ways, but he was dependable. He began to ferry other packages as well, small, tightly bundled bricks, which he kept under the seat or in a compartment hidden above the wheel well. One or two at first, then dozens. These were delivered separately, to other contacts. Rogelio never opened them to see what was inside (though he knew); he never touched the money (though he assumed that the quantities in play were not insubstantial). He had no qualms about this work. He trusted his brother. He never considered the consequences, not because he was reckless but because what he was doing was normal. Everyone was doing it.

On the last of these trips, Rogelio's truck was searched at a checkpoint along the Central Highway, 65 kilometers east of the capital. The war was on, and the soldiers were randomly stopping trucks from the mountains to look for weapons and explosives. Rogelio was unlucky. Perhaps if he'd been more astute he could have arranged to pay the soldiers off, but he didn't. Instead he waited by the side of the road while the men in uniform went through his vehicle with great care. Rogelio had time to consider what was happening, how his life was changing course before his very eyes. Not everyone has this privilege; most of us miss the moment when our destiny shifts. Later he told Henry that he'd felt a strange sort of calm. He considered running into the hills, but the soldiers would have shot him without thinking twice. So instead he admired his truck, which he'd had painted by hand, emerald and blue, with the phrase "My Beautiful San Jacinto" splashed across the top of the windshield in cursive lettering. At least, that's what he'd been told it said. He recalled thinking, *What will happen to the truck? Will it be waiting for me when I get out?*

The soldiers found the package, and to protect his brother Rogelio said nothing about its origins. He played dumb, which wasn't difficult. Everyone—from the soldiers who conducted the search, to the policemen who came to arrest him, to his ferocious interrogators, to the lawyer charged with defending him—saw Rogelio as he assumed they would: as a clueless, ignorant young man from the provinces. All these years, and nothing had changed: he was still invisible.

Henry's route to Collectors was very different, and it began at the Teatro Olímpico, after the third performance of his controversial play *The Idiot President*. That morning one of the right-wing papers had declared the play outrageous. "It mocks our authorities and gives succor to the enemy," the critic wrote. Henry had celebrated. "Maybe now we will sell some tickets," he'd said to a friend.

But that night, after the show, there were two men in dark suits hanging about. No one paid much attention to them, least of all Henry. Then the theater emptied, the audience dispersed, and one of the men approached. "Are you Henry Nuñez?" he said.

Henry had a leather bag thrown over his shoulder, nothing inside but some dirty clothes and a few annotated scripts.

Who were these idiots, who asked inane questions when the entire theater universe *knew he was Henry Nuñez.* Who else, exactly, could he be?

They placed their giant hands on Henry. His friend and costar Patalarga emerged from backstage just in time to see what was happening. He tried to stop the men, and when he wouldn't shut up they knocked him out and locked him in the ticket booth.

Henry was held with little human contact in a mercifully clean though still unpleasant cell. He was questioned about his friends, his plays, his travels around the country, his motives, but it was all strangely lethargic, inefficient, as if the police were too bored to decide his fate. He wasn't beaten or tortured, which was a great relief, of course; he surely would've confessed to anything at the mere threat of such treatment. On the third day, Henry, still thinking, breathing, and living in the mode of a playwright, asked for a pen and some paper in order to jot down notes about his tedious imprisonment, things to remember should he ever want to write about his experience. He was denied, but even then, in his naïveté, he wasn't worried. Not truly concerned. If he'd been asked, Henry would have said that he expected to be released at any moment. His captivity was so ridiculous to him that he could hardly conceive of it. He just couldn't understand why anyone would be upset by *The Idiot President.* Had they seen the play? It wasn't even any good!

On the fifth or sixth day, when Henry was finally allowed a visitor, his older sister, Marta, appeared at the jail, representing the entire living world outside the small cell that held him — his family, his friends, his supporters. It was a burden that showed clearly on her face. Her eyes were ringed with dark bluish circles, and her skin was sallow. She hadn't eaten, she reported; in fact, no one in the family had stopped to eat or rest for five days, and they were doing everything they could to get him out. He imagined them all — his large, bickering extended family — coming together to complete this task: it would be easier to put them on shifts and have them dig a tunnel beneath the jail. The image made him smile. Marta was happy to see that Henry hadn't been abused, and they passed much of the hour talking about plans for after his release. She had two children, a daughter and a son, ages six and four, who'd both made him get-well cards, because they'd been told that their uncle was at the hospital. Henry found this amusing; the fact that the cards had been confiscated at the jail he found maddening. Marta assured him that they'd remember this little anecdote later and laugh about it.

"Why wait?" Henry said.

"Don't be ridiculous," his sister answered. But already she was suppressing a grin.

He was referring to a game they'd played as children: spontaneous, forced, meaningless laughter. With diligence, they'd perfected this skill—rolling around cackling, rubbing their bellies like lunatics, before doctor's appointments or family trips, or on the morning of an exam for which they hadn't prepared. They'd used it to get out of chores, to be excused from church. Neither recalled the game's origins, but they'd been punished for it on many occasions and had always feigned innocence. *We can't help it,* they'd both said, laughing still, tears pressing from the corners of their eyes, until their behavior had landed them in weekly sessions with a child psychologist. Even so, they were proud that they'd never betrayed each other. At the peak of the game, when Henry was ten and Marta twelve and they were as close as two human beings can be, the two of them had been able to manufacture laughter instantly, hysterical fits that lasted for a quarter of an hour or longer. Henry considered this his first successful dramatic work.

He insisted. "Why not?"

They'd been whispering until then, but now they took deep breaths, like divers preparing for a descent. The cell, it turned out, had good acoustics. The laughter was tentative at first, but soon it was ringing brightly through the jail. Unstoppable, joyful, cathartic. At the end of the block, the guards who heard it had a different interpretation: it was frightening, demonic even. No one had ever laughed in this jail, not like that. One of them rushed to see what was happening, and was surprised to find brother and sister laughing heartily, holding hands, their cheeks glistening.

The hour allotted for the visit had passed.

Leaving the jail, Marta gave a brief statement to the press, which was shown on the television news that evening. Her brother was completely innocent, she said. He was an artist, the finest playwright of his generation, and the authorities had interrupted him and his actors in the legitimate pursuit of their art. Those responsible should be ashamed of what they'd done.

The following day the charges against Henry were announced: he was being held for incitement and terrorism. An investigation was under way. Henry was informed of the accusations that morning by the same guard who'd discovered him and Marta laughing, and who refrained from making the obvious statement about who might be laughing now—a small mercy, which Henry nonetheless appreciated.

He was taken from the jail in the back of a windowless military van, with nothing to look at but the unsmiling face of a soldier, a stern man who did not speak. Henry closed his eyes and tried to follow the van's twisting path through the city. "We're going to Collectors, aren't we?" he asked the soldier, who answered with a nod.

On the morning of April 8, 1986, Henry entered the country's most infamous prison.

The day he was sent to Collectors was the loneliest of his life. Nothing he'd learned previously had any relevance anymore, and each step he took beyond the gate and toward his new home was like walking into a tunnel, away from the light. He was led through the prison complex—a vision of hell in those days, full of half-dead men baring their scarred chests, impervious to the cold. He'd never been more frightened in his life. One man promised to kill him at the first opportunity—that evening, perhaps, if it could be arranged. Another, to fuck him. A third looked at him with the anxious eyes of a man hiding a terrible secret. Two guards led Henry through the complex, men whom he'd previously thought of as his tormentors but who now seemed more like protectors— all that stood between him and this anarchy. Halfway to the block, he realized that they were as nervous as he was, that they, like him, were doing all they could to avoid eye contact with the inmates who surrounded them. At the door to the block, the guards unlocked Henry's handcuffs and turned to leave.

The playwright looked at them helplessly. "Won't you stay?" he asked, as if he were inviting them in for a drink.

The two guards wore expressions of surprise. "We can't," one of them said in a low voice, embarrassed. They turned and hurried back to the entrance.

An inmate led Henry into the block, where men milled about with no apparent order or discipline. *I'm going to die here,* he thought. It was an idea that all new inmates contemplated upon first entering the prison. Some of them, of course, were right. Henry was taken to his cell, and didn't emerge for many days.

When Henry arrived in Collectors, Rogelio had already been wait-ing more than eighteen months for a hearing in his case. Waiting, that is, for an opportunity to affirm that he was a victim, that he knew nothing about the laws of the country, that he'd never been educated, and could not therefore be held accountable.

Henry's family had tried to arrange for a private cell, but none were available. He knew that he should be grateful for what he had—many others were in far worse conditions—but under the circumstances he found it difficult to muster much gratitude. For the first few days he hardly stirred. He didn't register Rogelio's face, and he knew nothing of his new home, beyond what he'd managed to glean during that initial terrifying walk. Henry was given the top bunk, and for three days he slept long hours, or pre-tended to sleep, facing the wall. Thinking. Remembering. Trying to disappear. He didn't eat, but felt no hunger. The night of his arrest had been catalogued in his mind, divided into an infinite series of micro-events: he remembered each flubbed line of the performance, the expressions on the faces of the audience mem-bers who'd expected and hoped for better. Could any of those details be shifted slightly—just enough to alter the outcome? Was there a light revision he could make to that evening's script so that it would not end with him here, in Collectors?

During those three days Rogelio came and went, seemingly uninterested in and unconcerned by Henry's condition. But by the fourth day Rogelio had had enough. He tapped Henry on the back.

"You're allowed to get up, you know."

Henry rolled over.

"You're alive," Rogelio said.

That afternoon Henry took his first real walk through the block. He met a few people who would later become friends, or something like friends, and he saw much to remind him of the danger he was in. There were men whose faces seemed congenitally incapable of smiling, men who locked eyes with him and spat on the ground. When he shuddered, they laughed.

Rogelio wasn't talkative, but he was helpful, and he explained many things that day. According to him, Henry was lucky—it was clear that he wouldn't have to work ("You're rich, aren't you?" Rogelio asked), though almost everyone else inside did. Rogelio repaired old plastic chairs (he shared a workshop on the roof with a few other men) and made pipes out of bent metal scraps, which he sold to the junkies. The junkies were everywhere, a miserable lineup of broken men who roamed the prison offering sex or blood or labor for a fix. Rogelio wasn't proud of this work, but without it he wouldn't have survived. His brother sent money only occasionally, enough to cover the cost of the cell and little else. Otherwise he was on his own.

Neither Henry nor Rogelio owned the cell where they slept. It belonged to the boss, Espejo, who made extra money on visiting days by renting it out so that men could be alone with their wives. "Those days will be difficult," Rogelio warned. Henry would have to be outdoors all day, and in the evening the room would smell different and feel different. He'd know that someone had made love there, and the loneliness would be overwhelming.

Henry nodded, though he couldn't understand—wouldn't understand, in fact, until he lived through it himself. There was a lot to learn. There were inmates to steer clear of, and others whom it was dangerous to ignore. There were moments of the day when it was safe to be out, others when it was best to stay inside. The distinction depended not on the time of day but on the mood of the prison, which Henry would have to learn to read if he hoped to survive.

"How do you read it?" he asked.

Rogelio had a difficult time explaining. It involved listening for the collective murmur of the yard, watching the way certain key men—the barometers of violence in the block—were carrying themselves. Small things: Did they have their arms at their sides or crossed in front of them? How widely did they open their mouths when they talked? Could you see their teeth? Were their eyes moving quickly, side to side? Or slowly, as if taking in every last detail?

To Henry it sounded impossible. Rogelio shrugged.

"Remember that most of us here are scared, just like you. When I first came, I didn't have a cell. If there was trouble, I had no-where to go."

They were sitting in a corner of the yard, beneath a dull gray winter sky. The light was thin, and there were no shadows. Henry still didn't quite grasp how he had got here. Nowhere to go—he understood these words in a way he never could have before. He wrote letters to his sister, cheerful dispatches that didn't reflect the gloom he felt, or the fear. His letters were performances, stylized and utterly false outtakes of prison life. In fact he was despairing: This is what it means to be trapped. To be frightened, and to be unable to share that fear with a single soul.

"You'll get it," Rogelio said. "It just takes time."

The frenetic daily exchange of goods and services went on about them. Two men waited to have their hair cut, sharing the same day-old newspaper to pass the time. A pair of pants, a couple of sweaters, and T-shirts stolen from some other section of the prison were for sale, hanging on a line strung between the posts of one of the soccer goals. Three junkies slept sitting up, with their backs against the wall, shirtless in the cold. Henry saw these men and felt even colder.

"Where did you sleep back then?" he asked. "Before you had a cell."

"Under the stairs," Rogelio said. He laughed. "But look at me now!"

Henry did look.

His new friend had a bright smile and very large brown eyes. His skin was the color of coffee with milk, and he was muscular without being imposing. His clothes were mostly prison-scavenged, items left by departing men, appropriated by Espejo or some other strongman and then sold. Nothing fit him well, but he seemed unbothered by that. He kept his black hair very short, and wore a knit cap most of the time, pulled down low, to stay warm. These dark winter days he even slept with it on. His nose was narrow and turned slightly to the left, and he had a habit of talking softly, with a hand over his mouth, as if sharing a confidence, no matter how mundane an observation he might be making.

As if we were accomplices, Henry thought.

A few weeks later Henry saw a man being kicked to death, or nearly to death, by a mob that formed unexpectedly at the door to

Block 12. He and Rogelio stood by, horrified at first, then simply frightened. Then, almost instantaneously, they accepted the logic of the attack: every victim was guilty of something. The chatter: *What did he do? Who did he cross?* The men watching felt safer. Less helpless. A crowd gathered around the victim, but no one moved to help him.

Visiting days weren't so bad at first. Henry's family and friends took turns coming to see him, the ones who could tolerate the filth, the overcrowding, the looks from the junkies. They left depleted and afraid, and most didn't come back. The hours immediately after the visitors had gone were the most difficult of the week. It required a great collective energy to welcome so many outsiders, to put the best face on what was clearly a terrible situation. Collectors was falling apart; anyone could see that. Damp winters had eaten away at the bricks, and the walls were covered with mold. Every day new men were brought in. They were unchained and set free inside, forced to fight for a place to sleep in the already overcrowded prison. Family day, when women were allowed in, came on alternate Wednesdays and was especially brutal. By the end of the afternoon the inmates were worn out from smiling, from reassuring their wives and children and mothers that they were all right. (Fathers, as a rule, did not visit; most of Henry's fellow inmates didn't have fathers.) It wasn't uncommon for there to be fights on those evenings. As long as no one was killed, it was fine, just something to relieve the tension.

Nine weeks in, Henry felt almost abandoned. On family days he was as alone as Rogelio. Espejo rented out their cell, and in the evening, as they lay on their bunks, they could still feel the warmth of those phantom bodies. Their perfumed scent. It was the only time the stench of the prison dissipated, though in some ways this other smell was worse. It reminded them of everything they were missing. Henry had been unable to persuade any of the women he used to see to visit him, and he didn't blame them. None of these relationships had meant much to him, though at times his despair was so great that he could concentrate on any one of those women's faces and convince himself that he'd been in love. As for Rogelio, he was far from home and hadn't had a visitor, male or female, in months.

"Did you see her?" Henry asked one evening after the visitors had gone, and because Rogelio hadn't, he began to describe the woman who'd made love with her husband on the lower bunk that day. She was married to an inmate named Jarol, a thief with a sharp sense of humor and arms like tense coils of rope. Henry talked about the woman's curves, how delicious she'd looked in her dress—not tight, but tight enough. She had long black hair, doe eyes, and fingernails painted pink. She was perfect, he said, and she was: not because of her body or her face but because of the way she'd smiled at her husband, with the hungry look of a woman who wants something and is not ashamed of it. A man could live on a look like that.

Henry said, "She didn't care who saw."

He could hear Rogelio breathing. They were quiet for a moment.

"What would you have done to her?" Rogelio asked. His voice was very low, tentative.

This was how it began: with Henry speculating aloud about how he might spend a few minutes alone with a woman in this stifling, degrading space. He had no difficulty imagining the scene, and he could think of no good reason not to share it.

He would have torn off that dress, Henry said, and bent her against the wall, with her palms flat against that stupid map of San Jacinto. He would have pressed hard against her, teased her until she begged him to come in. From the bottom bunk, Rogelio laughed. He would have made her howl, Henry said, made her scream. Cupped her breasts in his hands and squeezed. *Is this why you came, woman? Tell me it is!*

Already Henry was disappearing into his own words. He had his eyes closed. The walls had begun to vibrate.

"What else?" Rogelio said, his voice stronger now. "Go on. What else would you do?"

When they finished, each on his own bunk that first time, both men laughed. They hadn't touched, or even made eye contact, but somehow what they'd done was more intimate than that. For a moment the pleasure of each had belonged to the other, and now something dark and joyless had been banished.

A week later Henry gathered up his courage and went to see Espejo, the boss, to propose doing a production of *The Idiot President* in Block 7. Espejo was a small but well-built man whose lazy grin

belied a long history of violence, a man who'd risen far enough
from the streets to relax and now controlled the block through
sheer force of reputation. If any inmate questioned his authority,
he dispensed pointed but very persuasive doses of rage. Mostly,
though, he protected his charges—there were fewer than two
hundred men in the block, and after nightfall they were in con-
stant danger of being overrun by one of the larger, more ferocious
sections of the prison. Espejo directed a small army of warriors
tasked with keeping those potential invaders at bay.

Henry was afraid of this man, but he reminded himself that as
fellow inmates of Block 7, he and Espejo were on the same side.
Espejo's cell seemed more like a comfortable student apartment,
with a squat refrigerator, a black-and-white television, and a coffee-
maker plugged into a naked outlet. Espejo kept a photo of himself
from his younger days framed above his bed. In the picture he was
shirtless, astride a majestic white horse, riding up the steps of a
swimming pool toward the camera. A few delighted women stood
behind him, long-legged, bronzed, and gleaming in the bright
sun. Everything was colorful, saturated with tropical light. A child
—Espejo's son, perhaps—sat on the edge of the diving board,
watching the horse maneuver its way out of the water. On the boy's
face was an expression of admiration and wonder, but it was more
than that: he was concentrating, watching the scene, watching his
father, trying to learn.

Henry wondered what had happened to the boy. Perhaps he'd
been shuttled out of the country, or died, or perhaps he was old
enough by now to be living in another of the city's prisons, in a cell
much like this one. There was no way of knowing without asking
directly, and that was not an option. The photo, like the lives of
the men with whom Henry now lived, was both real and startlingly
unreal, like a still from Espejo's dreams.

Rogelio had warned Henry not to stare, so he didn't.

"A play?" Espejo said when Henry told him his idea.

Henry nodded.

Espejo lay back on his bed, his shoeless feet stretched toward
the playwright. "That's what we get for taking terrorists in the
block," he said, laughing. "We don't do theater here."

"I'm not a terrorist," Henry said.

A long silence followed this clarification, Espejo's laughter replaced by a glare so intense and penetrating that Henry began to doubt himself—perhaps he *was* a terrorist, after all. Perhaps he always had been. That was what the authorities were accusing him of, and outside, in the real world, there were people arguing both sides of this very question. His freedom hung in the balance. His future. Henry had to look away, down at the floor of the cell, which Espejo had redone with blue and white linoleum squares, in honor of his favorite soccer club. One of Espejo's deputies, a thick-chested brute named Aimar, coughed into his fist, and it was only this that seemed to break the tension.

"Did you write it?"

Henry nodded.

"So name a character after me," Espejo said.

Henry began to protest.

Espejo frowned. "You think I have no culture? You think I've never read a book?"

"No, I . . ." Henry stopped. It was useless to continue. *I've already ruined myself,* he thought.

They were quiet for a moment.

"Go on," Espejo said finally, waving an uninterested hand in the direction of the yard. "If you can convince these savages, I have no objection."

Henry thanked Espejo and left—quickly, before the boss could change his mind.

Everyone wanted to be the president, because the president was the boss. Everyone wanted to be the servant, because, like them, the servant dreamed of murdering the boss. Everyone wanted to be the son, because it was the son who actually got to do the killing in the play. It was this character whose name was changed: he became Espejo.

And indeed, the project sold itself. A week of talking to other inmates, and then the delicate process of auditions. Henry had to write in extra parts to avoid disappointing some of the would-be actors. It was for his own safety—some of these men didn't take rejection very well. He added a chorus of citizens to comment on the action; ghosts of servants past to stalk across the stage in a fury, wearing costumes fashioned from old bed sheets. He even wrote a few lines for the president's wife, played with verve by Carmen, the block's most outspoken transvestite. Things were going well. Even Espejo joined in the enthusiasm. It would be good for their image, he was heard to say.

Rogelio wanted to audition too, but there was a problem.

"I can't read," he confessed to Henry. "How can I learn the script?"

Henry smiled. They were lying together on the top bunk, close, naked.

"I can teach you."

Later he'd remember the look on Rogelio's face, and the hope implicit in his own offer. Perhaps by saying these words, Henry was already imagining a life outside those walls.

When Rogelio didn't respond, Henry pressed him. "Who do you want to be?"

Rogelio thought for a moment. "The servant is the one who dies?"

Henry nodded.

"How?"

"He's stabbed in the back."

"Well, then," Rogelio said, "I guess that should be me."

When the play was performed, three weeks later, Henry paid special attention to that scene. He and Rogelio had worked on the script every night, pacing in their cell, bouncing the servant's lines back and forth until Rogelio knew them by heart, but he had insisted on practicing the death scene on his own. Out of timidity, Henry thought, but when he saw the performance he realized that he had been wrong. The entire population of Block 7 was watching: hard, fearless men who gasped at the sight of Rogelio staggering. They recognized the look of terror on his face. They'd been that man; they'd killed that man. They watched Rogelio fall in stages, first to his knees, then forward, clutching his chest, as if trying to reach through his body to the imaginary knife wound. Henry and the others, all of them held their breath, waiting, and were rewarded with a final flourish: Rogelio's right leg twitching. Espejo was the first to stand and applaud. The play wasn't even over.

Henry was released that November, thinner, older, after a year and a half in prison. He didn't say to Rogelio, "I'll wait for you." Or, "I'll see you on the outside." But he thought those things, held them secret but dear, until the day, a few months later, when two of the more volatile sections of Collectors rose up to protest conditions inside. Block 7 had the misfortune of sitting between them, and when the army arrived to put down the revolt, it too was destroyed. Henry heard the news on the radio. The men who had made up the cast of *The Idiot President* all died in the assault, shot in the head, or killed by shrapnel, or crushed beneath falling concrete walls. More than three hundred inmates from Blocks 6, 7, and 8 were killed, and though Henry wasn't there, part of him died that day too. He lost Rogelio, his best friend, his lover—a word he had never used, not even to himself. In the days after, he sometimes woke with the taste of Rogelio on his lips. Sometimes he woke to the image of Rogelio lying dead of a knife wound.

Henry mourned, even roused himself enough to participate in a few protests in front of the Ministry of Justice (though he declined to speak when someone handed him the bullhorn), but in truth the tragedy both broke him and spared him the need ever to think about his incarceration again. No one who'd lived through it with him had survived. There was no one to visit, no one with whom to reminisce, no one to meet on the day of his release and drive home, feigning optimism.

Princess Anne

FROM *Ellery Queen's Mystery Magazine*

HOWARD PICKED UP his blinking line. "Investigations Division, Jim Howard."

Silence. "Hello?"

Rough breathing. He could make out a quiet beeping in the background. "Charlie?"

"Jus' a sec," a weak voice said. Charlie Post had been in intensive care for ten days now. Howard waited as he gathered enough strength to speak.

"Lyle Collins is coming out," Post finally rasped. "My guy at Eddystone told me."

Eddystone was the warehouse of choice for Northern Indiana criminal psych patients. Howard felt a cold knot forming in the pit of his stomach.

"For Christ's sake, don't they ever die inside?"

"Coming out late this month. The report will say he's stable."

"Stable?! And what do the geniuses think did that? Sloppy Joes every Thursday?"

"Stay on'm, Jim. He's ancient history. Off the books. He'll be flying under the radar." Charlie Post coughed hard.

Howard was jammed up, in the middle of a limbo that involved moving his life and his work from the Northern Indiana Investigations Division of the state police to northern Michigan, where he was trying to land a position with the Major Case Unit of the Michigan State Police. He and Charlie Post went way back. Way back was where Lyle Collins was coming from.

"Stay on'm. I know you're spread thin. Just remember that bastard won't be able to keep it together for long. He'll be hungry."

"I'll make time, Charlie."

Howard could hear fluid bubbling in Post's throat. "Billy Ferguson used to come over Sunday nights to play hearts with the family. Sweet kid. He and Angie were a match, you know. Rare thing. Then one fine spring day he's just gone." Howard could not see the hand he lifted from the bed and waved slightly. "Just gone. Angie never got over it."

"I remember," Howard said. "You hang in there, Charlie."

"Been doin' that," he whispered. "I'm ready for somethin' else."

"I'll stop by next week."

"Better make it sooner than that."

Howard's face was grim. He was going to miss old Charlie Post.

Some people have graves in their lives from early childhood, places to visit with their families to express their love for those gone on ahead. Neither of the Lanes had a grave in their life until they moved out into the country. It came with the house and became part of the fabric of their young family.

They had bought the abandoned farm for a song. Although it was only 25 miles from South Bend, it looked like something from the heart of Appalachia. The *Deliverance* banjo-boy would have felt right at home.

Many well-heeled South Bend professionals were into McTrophy homes of the castle variety or Frank Lloyd Wright knockoffs. Derek Lane, a tax attorney on the way up, and his wife, Parveen, a working pharmacist until she became pregnant, lived simply. They liked old things. Liked to clean them up, fix them, and make them part of their world. The fact that these things were often bargains suited the Lanes perfectly. They saved their money and looked for a vintage place with character and a little land.

They had found the peeling white eyesore lost on five acres in the rolling Indiana countryside. It might as well have been on the dark side of the moon. The Realtor hadn't even bothered to put it on the website. Who would ever want to take on the work of a falling-down farmhouse with acreage that had not been tended for years? The Lanes loved it.

The couple had been inspecting the wildly overgrown grounds

near the house when they found the grave. It was tough going. Beneath an early spring canopy of towering white oak and black locust, they were engulfed by head-high scrub brush and prickly raspberry bushes. Parveen, who came from a desert country, marveled at the vibrancy of the emerging green life. First they found the lid of the cistern, took one look down into that dank, water-filled tank, and decided to have it filled in. Their baby would be here soon and the cistern was an accident waiting to happen. They found green hundred-year-old bottles and rusty tools. They found a maze of half-buried chicken-wire fences and a pile of glazed bricks with raised letters that said "Metropolitan Block," the foundation of something long since rotted away. They admired the glazed bricks and would put them to good use. They found a perfectly preserved brown jug. Then they found the grave.

The house overlooked a small hollow that fell away, rising quickly again at the edge of their property. Later they would install a large picture window so that they could look across that little hollow. They had been inspecting the brow the house sat upon when Parveen noticed a smooth spot on the ground. She thought it was the odd piece of broken brick, but when she rubbed it with her shoe she saw that it was larger than that. She scraped more away with her shoe and saw letters. The two knelt down together and with their gloved hands gently pushed away the dirt and matted leaves. Deeply and carefully carved into a thick piece of aged oak, the epitaph had a few worn letters but was clear nonetheless:

> HERE LIES PRINCESS JENNY
> Forever friends in this gentle place
> My little princess
> Gone home now to this good earth
> Sleeping now where we lived together
> And will again
> When the heavens and the oceans and the mountains
> Shall pass away

For a couple who treasured relics, nothing they might have found could have been more endearing. Parveen raised a hand to her reddening throat as Derek slowly read the words aloud in his clear barrister voice. He nodded his head approvingly and smiled. He stood up, put his hands on his hips, and looked about. They were home.

Derek took the oak marker down to his basement workshop. He cleaned out the letters with a wire brush and let the wood dry out for three weeks. He soaked the underside in black creosote and soaked the surface in boiled linseed oil. After it dried, he replaced it exactly, now essentially impervious to the elements.

Parveen gathered softball-sized fieldstones of gray and gray-ish pink and gray-black and made a semicircle around the top of the marker. She planted crocosmia with the orange-flame flowers that the hummingbirds loved and moonbeam coreopsis with their bright bursts of yellow, daisylike blooms.

Derek cleared the grounds of the forgotten homestead on week-ends and vacations, removing the chaos of brush and dropping the dead trees with his thunderous 1950s Homelite chainsaw. It all began to look parklike, a five-acre estate. They installed the pic-ture window and added an outside light. Sometimes at night they would light up the little grave and the area around it, the artifi-cial light casting shadows so differently from the moonlight. When they turned off the light, the moonlight flowed down through the boughs, blanketing the marker and the fieldstones and the flowers in a magical glow.

Derek cut logs from the steel-like black locust and made twin benches. One he placed next to the grave, the other he placed directly across on the opposite ridge close to the property line. The benches became their favorite places to sit and read and have coffee, and, finally, wonderful places to sit with baby Margaret.

Margaret arrived after Smoky, the black Lab, and Trudy, the calico cat, had already joined the family, and after the heavy lifting at the place was done. A puppy, a kitty, a blond-headed baby girl. A young, vigorous, devoted couple. What had been a forgotten and forlorn place was now bursting with life. Derek and Parveen nestled into their handmade world. The joy they felt was beyond words. Because the grave was a mystery, holding no memories, it became a fanciful thing. As the years went by, they invented sto-ries for Margaret. The stories of Princess Jenny became a bedtime ritual. Parveen drew charcoal sketches to bring the fantasies to life. Princess Jenny was a unicorn ridden by a fairy, a ferocious black panther with golden eyes who was the protector of a golden queen. Princess Jenny was the favorite companion of princes and kings and queens and paupers and blacksmiths because Derek and Parveen knew that in real life she had in fact been someone's beloved companion. She lived in the time of miracles, when dragons breathed fire and covetous gods gazed down from castles in the clouds. Margaret would take her dolls and her mother's sketches and play beside the grave for hours, a handy spot for Parveen to keep a watchful eye on her from the picture window.

It was July and muggy when a silver Cadillac Escalade pulled into the Lane Farm, as it came to be known. A distinguished-looking elderly man stepped out. Parveen was working in her garden and came toward him, toweling her hands as she came. It was no one she knew. She guessed that he just needed directions. She noticed that on such a hot day he was wearing a winter suit of rust-colored corduroy and a wide, dated tie. He looked like the gamekeeper of an English estate. He was tall, pale, and clearly uncomfortable. His white hair was long and slicked down. His moist blue eyes were kindly and faintly apologetic.

"Good afternoon, young lady," he said. "My name is Lyle Collins and I'm here for Princess Jenny."

Parveen dropped her towel. She stared at the strange old man who, with one sentence, had penetrated her intimate world, a world no one knew about except her immediate family.

"Do you know Princess Jenny?" Collins asked. "Have you found her grave?"

Parveen nodded, mute.

"I can see I've startled you," he said. "I'm sorry. I know this seems bizarre. Please hear me out. I lived here many, many years ago. I was not a well man. I was what they now call bipolar, although no one really knows what that means. I was a young professor at Notre Dame when I descended into illness. For a time I was homeless. I moved into this farm because it was deserted and no one cared about it. It was my home for almost two years. Early the first winter, a little dog came to the door." Collins took a white handkerchief from the pocket of his jacket and dabbed at his eyes.

"She was a brown-and-white cocker spaniel. I named her Princess Jenny and she became my only friend. We lived here together."

He turned from Parveen, his eyes wandering over the spacious grounds, the lovely white farmhouse with green shutters and trim. "Of course, it was nothing like this. Did you do all this?"

"Yes, my husband and I," she said proudly. "When we bought it, it was quite a mess."

"You've done wonders with the place. It's beautiful."

"Thank you," Parveen said.

"Of course, I was able to move in unnoticed because it was for-gotten and abandoned," Collins continued. "Without running water. Without electricity. Heat from wood I put in the cast-iron cookstove. In winter we lived mostly in the kitchen near the stove. Sometimes Princess and I shared dog food. I could not be friends with people. In my illness I did not understand people and they did not understand me. But Princess Jenny and I understood each other and she was my friend." He paused, loosening his tie and unbuttoning the top button of his wrinkled white shirt. "I thought if I wore a coat and tie you might think me less weird," he said with a small, embarrassed smile.

"It's all right," Parveen managed. "I'm beginning to understand. You thought about Princess Jenny a lot while you were . . . away?"

"Every day," Collins said quietly. "Every day. At that time it was important to me that she immediately liked me and stayed with me. She didn't have to. She could have left me at any time, run off."

"What happened?" Parveen asked.

"One afternoon we were out for a walk in the woods when Princess stepped into a trap. I don't know, something for a fox or muskrat, perhaps. It slammed shut, almost severing her left front leg. By the time I got the trap open and carried her back to the house, she was gone. I stayed . . . stable . . . just long enough to bury her and make the marker. Then I became unable to function and was committed to the mental hospital near Gary. Eddystone. That was fifteen years ago." He looked intently at Parveen. "Medi-cation, therapy, and time have made me well. I was released several weeks ago and plan to return to my family's home in Wisconsin. They will have me now that I am well. I want to take Jenny there so that she can always be near me."

"I understand," Parveen said. "I understand how important she must be to you. You will probably be surprised to know that she has also become important to us. Come with me."

Parveen took him to the grave. Lyle Collins knelt down. Tears filled his eyes. "It's just wonderful the way you've made her part of your family," he murmured. "It's time now for us to be together again after all these lost years. I took great pains to bury her in a protected way." He looked up at Parveen. She was deeply moved. She held out her hand to help him up.

"Can you come back tomorrow at noon?" she asked. "I will talk with my husband tonight."

"Of course," Lyle Collins said.

Predawn, like going out on night patrol. Howard parked his green Jeep wagon in the northeast corner of the empty parking lot of the old church. It was the corner nearest the woods. He put the POLICE sign on his dashboard. The weeds growing in the gravel lot were knee-high, waving slightly in the dimness. He wondered how many years it had been since a service had been held here.

The skyline was tinted with gray light. It was already warm, the air thick with dew and slim strands of fog. Howard smeared himself with insect repellent and smudged his face with camo grease. He had his binos, water, and a sandwich. His cell was working. His Colt Trooper was loaded. He let his eyes adjust to the darkness, checked his compass, and stepped into the thick, tangled hardwoods. He didn't really need a compass, but it might save him a few minutes. It would be an up-and-down hike through thick woods, skirting just one farmhouse and one bog. He felt confident. Too bad Charlie Post wouldn't be here to see it.

When Collins returned the next day, the Lanes were waiting. Derek had come home straight from the office and planned to go back. He was wearing a dark tailored suit with a solid navy tie, a very formal contrast to his wife's bright yellow sundress. Collins wore the same dated corduroy suit he had worn the previous day.

Derek had a shovel and a wheelbarrow. He would spare the old man the digging. He shook hands with Collins and began digging. He removed the sod in squares so that it could be put back in place and shoveled the dirt into the wheelbarrow to keep the gravesite looking as undisturbed as possible. They had decided not to tell Margaret, who was now almost five. Someday they would explain, but not now. About 2 feet down, Derek struck something. Lyle Collins got down and with a trowel Derek gave him began gently scraping and digging around the object. After a few minutes he removed a military-issue waterproof PVC bag about the size of a car tire. Derek rinsed the olive-drab bag with the hose and Collins toweled it dry with a rag they gave him. Lyle Collins shook their hands and said he would never forget their kindness.

They did not see the shape at first. It arose by the far bench near their property line, moved down the small hollow and then up toward them. They heard the movement and turned and saw it at the same instant. It took them several beats to realize a big man was striding up toward them. As he neared they could see he was covered in woodland camouflage with black and green paint on his sweating face and a large blue revolver hanging from his right hand. Black binoculars were slung around his neck. He looked like he had stepped out of jungle combat in Quang Tri Province, Republic of Vietnam, in 1968.

He came up the slope extending his ID with his left hand. As they took a collective step back he swung his Colt Trooper in an arc, the long barrel glancing off the cheek of Lyle Collins. Collins dropped in a motionless heap. The man shoved the revolver into his green web belt, went down on both knees, jerked Collins's hands behind his back, and cuffed him. Collins was dazed, but recognition and fear were evident in his twisted face. The man got back up.

He held his identification closer for the Lanes to inspect. In their shock, they struggled to focus in on the gold badge and photo. "My name is Jim Howard, Northern Indiana Investigations Division. This man, Lyle Collins, is my prisoner." Howard stepped away, flipped his cell open, and called in. He gave the address and some codes.

"What'd you hit him for?" Derek asked angrily. "He wasn't doing anything."

"Can't be too careful," Howard said.

"For God's sake, call an ambulance or I will," Derek ordered, looking down at Collins's still form and bleeding cheek.

"He doesn't need an ambulance," Howard said. "I'm a paramedic." He kicked Lyle Collins hard in the stomach, and Collins groaned. "His vital signs are good."

The Lanes were staring at Howard in disbelief, trying to make sense of the last few bizarre, explosive moments. Howard tried to imagine how he must look to them and how little they knew about what was going on. "Look," he said, "this guy's a killer. He killed several people years ago, but we could never make the case stick. Smart bastard, slippery and crazy as hell. He's been locked away in a psych hospital for years. They just released him. God knows why."

"Are you telling us there's a body in that bag?" Derek asked, his skepticism apparent in his face and voice. The bag was obviously too small for that.

"No," Howard said. "He told you he was coming back for . . . what? Some precious pet? I've been tailing him, scoped his visit yesterday, saw your wife bring him back here. When I came on your place last night and saw the marker, I figured it out."

"You were creeping around our place last night?" Derek asked.

"Not creeping. Investigating," Howard said mildly, with a slight smile. "Lyle here is the guy who creeps around."

"I think there's a long-dead cocker spaniel in that bag and that you just struck a harmless old man," Derek said heatedly.

"Collins would just as soon barbecue a cocker spaniel as give it a pat on the head," Howard said.

"You're going to have a lot of explaining to do when I get through with you," Derek said threateningly, taking a step toward Howard. "You're way the hell out of line, and I'm just the guy who can make you pay for it. I'm an attorney and a county commissioner. Bill Phelps is a personal friend of mine."

Howard nodded, studying Lane, who suddenly looked like real trouble. He looked at the carefully positioned fieldstones around the grave and the orange and yellow flowers. He looked at the restored farmhouse. He looked at Trudy and Smoky, asleep together in the shade. Lovely couple living in Shangri-la, he thought. And a lawyer to boot.

"Okay," he said quietly, pulling latex-free gloves from a pocket of his fatigues. The green bag was curled several times at the top and clip-locked. He detached the clip and unfolded the top. He pulled out a tan hard-shell, carry-on-sized suitcase. It looked like it had just come off the shelf. He set it on the ground and tried to open it. It was locked. He dug through Collins's pockets, found his wallet, and dug through that, producing a key. He unlocked the suitcase and gently opened it. He stood up.

"Look but don't touch." The Lanes knelt down. A mild rotten aroma rose up. Panties caked with blood. There was a ripped nightgown. A wallet and a man's gold wristwatch. There was a loose assortment of photographs, some yellowed along the edges, revealing faces misshapen with terror and pain, faces in the last moments of life. There were photographs of entire bodies positioned just so, like artists' models. The lips of a blond-headed man had been made clown huge by smeared lipstick. His ears were gone. There was jewelry and a flattened Chicago Cubs baseball cap. There were two cased videotapes.

"Trophies," Howard said. "Maniac porn.

"Collins lived in South Bend. He hunted around here and also in Ann Arbor and Bloomington. Liked college towns. After all those years in the hospital, he needed a fix fast. I guess he wasn't ready to kill yet, so his trophies were the next best thing. Safer. This stuff would have kept him occupied for months.

"He's nuts, but he's bright," Howard continued, the Lanes looking up from the nightmare in the open suitcase to Howard's face, which was calm and reassuring. "Hiding this stuff here this way is pretty damn smart. Predators are very good at predicting what nice, normal people will do. They learn through observation, because they don't have such feelings themselves. One thing nice, normal people won't do is desecrate the grave of some little pet.

"The grave was here when you bought the place, wasn't it?"

"Yes, it was an old deserted farm," Parveen said. She reached out to touch something in the briefcase. Howard gently blocked her hand with the toe of his boot.

"Told you a good story, did he?"

"Yes," Parveen said. "It was perfectly plausible. I felt sorry for him. You know, we made up fairy tales about this grave for our Margaret. What will we ever tell her?"

"If I knew the answer to that I might have kids of my own," Howard said. He squatted on his haunches and snapped the suitcase shut. Parveen tried to stand. Her legs failed her. Howard took her weight against him and guided her to the bench. She sat hunched over with her hands between her knees, her face pinched.

"I can't tell you how many times Margaret has played next to that grave," Parveen said. "I would ask her to stay there, where I could keep an eye on her. Endless hour after endless hour. With something so hideous just beneath her." She looked at Derek.

"When we moved in," she whispered. "When we moved in, there was a big red smear on the basement floor."

Derek put his arm around her and pulled her tight. "I tiled the basement floor," he said. "Tiled right over it. Didn't try to remove it."

"Show us where it is, but I doubt if it's anything," Howard said. "I don't think Collins was ever in this place. He wouldn't have hid his trophies at a murder scene. He knew we'd be searching all along his tracks, so he had to come up with something creative, something without a trail. He made the marker somewhere else and was probably here only long enough to dig the hole."

"Even if it's red paint, it will always be blood to me," Parveen said. "Why didn't you tell us what you were doing after you saw him come here?"

"Would have changed your behavior. Couldn't risk that. Collins might have noticed. He's a student of normal people."

"The epitaph he carved," Derek said after a while. "Beautifully poetic. Terrible thing to have such words inside an animal like that."

Howard shrugged. "Words will do somersaults for anybody."

"What will happen now?" Parveen asked.

"Oh, we have him now," Howard said with satisfaction. "The suitcase is the mother of all connect-the-dots, a goddamn brass ring. With my testimony and yours, he'll probably get two or three first-degree-murder convictions. Worst-case scenario, recommitted to a hospital for life. Either way, he's off the streets for good."

Siren off, a black-and-white prowler pulled into the driveway, followed closely by two unmarked cars.

Howard touched Derek Lane's arm. "Look, counselor, you're right, I was a little over the top with Collins. I'd appreciate a pass, though. I clipped him for a friend of mine who died last Tuesday. Name of Charlie Post. Stayed on Collins for years. His daughter's boyfriend, kid named Billy Ferguson, was one of Collins's victims. He went missing and we damn well knew it was Collins. I mean, you stir things up, it won't bother me much. I know how to finesse a charge of excessive force. But it could screw up our case. Give some lawyer a foot in the door. We sure as hell don't want that."

"There was a scuffle," Parveen said quickly. "We really didn't see anything." Derek gave her a sideways glance.

"That works," Howard said. He looked at Derek. "Okay, counselor?"

Derek Lane looked thoughtfully at Howard. "Was my family ever in danger?"

Howard's eyes widened. He looked away for a moment. He looked back at Lane. "Just so we're clear, counselor, are you asking me if your family was ever in danger from a homicidal maniac who kills randomly and who has buried his trophy case next to your house?"

Derek Lane flushed. "There was a scuffle. We didn't see anything."

"Good. Thanks. I'll take it from there if anything comes up."

Derek looked over at the Escalade. "Nice ride. He must have money."

"Loaded," Howard said. "Furniture family up in the Wisconsin Dells. Had enough for dream-team doctors and lawyers. They took our cases apart. They were all circumstantial, no bodies. Sometimes there was blood, signs of a struggle, that's about it. The only real pattern, the only thread, was location and this joker here. He was always around and he was memorable because he acted so weird. He was finally put away not because he was a murdering son of a bitch but because he was nuts."

Howard went over to the approaching group of uniformed and plainclothes officers and spoke to them briefly. Two uniforms helped Collins up, put him in the back seat of the prowler, and drove off. Howard returned to the Lanes.

"Look, for all practical purposes your house and this whole area are going to be ours for a while. Crime-scene tape, CSI teams, holes dug, the whole nine yards. Maybe you and your daughter could take a vacation or something." The Lanes stared at him. "Yeah, well, just a thought. I really don't know what to tell you except that I'm sorry for all this." He shook their hands.

The Lanes watched as Howard went through the wooden gate Derek had made and began walking down the side of the gravel road back to where his Jeep was parked at the church some 2 miles away. Someone gave a shout: Did he want a ride? He waved them off.

Howard shoved his hands in his pockets and hunched his shoulders, movements he made when he was thinking. It made him look smaller. It was ninety degrees and he was sweating hard, camo fatigues soaked black. After so many long years of half-assed monitoring, it had been a very near thing with Collins. What if he hadn't been there to take the handoff from Charlie Post? What if Charlie Post had died before Collins was released? Would his contact have sought out anyone else? If Collins had left Indiana and set up shop in Wisconsin, hell, he'd have died of old age before he was caught. Officially there wasn't enough on him to make him a person of interest. The interest in him lived in the memories of guys like Charlie Post and his contact at Eddystone.

Howard liked the crunch of gravel under his Airborne boots. Made him feel military again. He thought maybe he should have stayed in the Marines, where buddies are around you all the time and teams were really teams and the order of battle always started out clear. It never stayed clear, but at least it always started out that way, and you didn't have to worry about brilliant defense attorneys and genius doctors and goofy judges and rose-colored cloistered couples from la-la land. "Was my family ever in danger?"

He stopped and looked back. Derek and Parveen were talking with two plainclothes, but both were still looking down the road at him, as if he was carrying off something that they wanted back. He wasn't. The something they wanted back was gone forever. They just hadn't realized it yet. From this day forward, spilled red paint would never be just spilled red paint. He figured the Lanes would move away within the year.

He began walking again. He had not told the Lanes about Princess Anne. What was the point? He could not remember her epitaph, but he remembered she had one. She was buried about 150 miles away on the back lawn of a dilapidated factory on the outskirts of Ann Arbor. Back in the day, his tracking of Collins had taken him through and around the idle manufacturing buildings. When he noticed the grave, he thought what the Lanes had thought about Princess Jenny. Final resting place of a beloved pet. In this instance, the cherished company mascot. He remembered that the company name, whatever it was, was in the epitaph. He remembered something about Princess Anne being a companion to each and every worker on each and every shift. Collins would have buried his collection that was Princess Anne long after the gates were chained and all those jobs were long gone to China. Hide in plain sight. Howard shook his head wonderingly. It was becoming almost a "normal" thing—ordinary people leading ordinary lives randomly cut down by some nut job playing Angel of Death.

His chin sank lower into his chest. He stared at the gravel just a foot or two ahead of his next step. Princess Anne had not been anyone's happy fantasy. Her grave had not been embraced by a loving couple and a sweet little girl. This grave was what it really was: a solitary obscenity. When moonlight shone upon the grave of Princess Anne, it was moonlight devoid of dreams. The chilly wind did not rustle over a bedtime story. It rustled over remnants of murdered lives. *It will always be blood to me,* Parveen had said. It was like that for Howard. Every day. In the morning he would call the Ann Arbor police and give them directions.

Snuff

FROM *One Story*

THERE WAS A GROUP of guys I knew from school gathered in a garage out back of Billy's house, and Billy had hung a bed sheet up on the wall and propped the projector on a milk crate stacked on a folding chair. He told us he'd gotten the movie from somebody's brother's best friend's cousin, and we all stood there and watched the film from start to finish, no credits, no title, no names, no sound. When the last jumpy frames of 8mm finally spun through the reels, everybody started talking at once, and Mike Toth said, *No fucking way,* and Lenny Richter leaned into me and whispered, *Nothing but corn syrup and food coloring.*

I was sweating even though the sun was long set, and I couldn't seem to get my mouth around anything to say, so I checked my watch and saw that I was close enough to curfew and decided it was best to leave. Without a word, I slipped out to the main road to chance hitching home. I lasted fifteen minutes walking with my thumb out on the empty asphalt before I bent and broke and went to the pay phone at a two-pump gas station, the only lit building as far as I could see in either direction, and I called home, hoping my sister Charlotte would pick up fast. She answered on the first ring.

Charlotte was seventeen and had always been pretty, but not beautiful. That summer she had discovered Fleetwood Mac and changed. My dad started making rules, more rules than ever before, asking things like *Where have you been?* Everything was a privilege, and bedroom doors had to be left open, phone calls were monitored, and, as Charlotte liked to say, *Privacy was part of the old regime.* I sensed there was a battle brewing and it was going to get ugly fast. My dad may have had more power than Charlotte, but she was smart and quiet as a sniper, and sneaking out had become her specialty.

"Why the hell are you way out there in the country?" she said on the phone. "Can't you get into trouble closer to home?"

I cradled the receiver between my shoulder and ear and dug my hands deeper into my pockets. "It's not that far," I said. When I left Billy's, talk had been loud, and there had been a lot of clapping and shouts, and by the time I started walking down the driveway the decision had been made by everyone else to watch the film again. I had seen all kinds of trouble that night, and for once I hadn't been the one in it, but I didn't say that to Charlotte.

I was six months away from a driver's license, and had a whole lot of nothing going on ever since I'd quit football. My dad said I had to have a job if I thought I was going to get a car, but jobs were hard to get, so I was mostly bored and looking for something to do. When we'd hitched out to Billy's together earlier that night, Lenny had said this was going to be the best kind of something.

"I can't get a ride, Charlotte. Please."

"Dad's home," she said. "But he's been talking with Johnnie," and I knew she meant Walker, but she didn't need to say it; it was our code for drunk.

I relaxed the phone into my ear and felt its warmth and could see my dad in his armchair, the footrest kicked up, the TV on, the glass empty. Around me the wind took less than a minute to become more than a gust, and I felt the edge under it and knew the August night was false, and even though the summer had mauled us, it was now packing to go. "I'll pay you," I said. "Twenty bucks."

"Stay where you are," she said. "I'm coming."

The girl in the movie had dirty blond hair, and she was thin and was standing and bent forward onto the bed. I could see her spine rising up, bony and knobbed, and her skin was pulled tight, her head away from the camera, with just her shoulder blades looking out like hollow eyes. I had stared at her back, at the blankness of her skin, and it was so smooth that it looked fake, except for the raised red marks that could have been a handprint, and I flexed my own fingers and wondered if they were big enough to fill that space.

In the parking lot the only other sound besides the wind was the bugs beating themselves blind against the single overhead fluorescent. It was a sickly sodium light, too bright and artificial, and the cloud of insects swarming made strange shadows on the cracked cement below. I could smell wet grass, irrigation, farmland, and creosote seeping from the railroad ties that served as the borders between asphalt, fields, and road. In the distance a dog barked and barked, over and over again, a tired and monotonous sound, and there was no shout to *quiet down,* no hassled owner opening up a door and forcing the animal to come in, and I wondered what purpose a dog like that served if there was nobody to pay attention. There could have been a thousand things to bark at and nobody to teach it about real threats. Above me a bat circled, clumsy and big, and I watched until its path took it out of the arc of light. I tied my shoelaces, retied them, sat on the curb and chucked rocks, counted moths, listened for a car to come from the distance, and finally it did. The first and only car to come down the road, my father's Dodge Royal Monaco two-door hardtop that I recognized from the engine whine when my sister drove, the 400 Lean Burn V8 held in full restraint under the hood, and the left hideaway headlight door stuttering like the engine to open up.

Charlotte had the heater on and the music loud, and I wondered how she had crept the car out of the driveway, but the very fact that she was there confirmed she had gotten away with it, and I was happy to slide in and pull the door shut and fold myself toward the warm vents in the dash.

"Stab and steer," I said.

Charlotte looked at me without blinking. "What?" she said.

"You never get anything. Just punch it and drive. I'm cold."

There were no cars on the road, no headlights in either direction, just house lights, and they were scattered few and far between, set back in the distance, as sparse and dim as city stars absorbed by the night. Charlotte signaled as she left the parking lot, though there wasn't reason to, and then we were swallowed by the fields on both sides of the road, the staggered fence posts. Even though I had been walking in the dark, I did not realize the immensity of it until it had become a throat hold around us, and the broken yellow line was lost beyond the one good headlight.

After the accident I would wonder if I had seen it coming, the shift in shadows, the sudden definition of a shape, a thickening in the air like a premonition, because when something goes terribly wrong there is always a before and always an after, but the moment itself is vague and hard to gather, and time jumps like a skip in a record, and so I tried to remember the before, tried to trace what happened during, but in the end it all came down to after and we were spun hood up into a dry drainage ditch, the broken headlight suddenly finding its too little too late and pointing straight and strong at nothing more than wide-open sky, the windshield shattered and fracturing the night into a thousand webbed pieces, and Charlotte bleeding from her nose and me with my mouth open to say something, but instead everything just hung quiet and still.

"What did we hit?" Charlotte asked, and she rubbed the back of her hand under her nose and the blood smeared across it, and in the weak light the blood was more black than red. I thought about what Lenny Richter had said, *nothing but corn syrup and food coloring.*

"We didn't hit anything," I said. "Did we?"

"I saw it," she said. "I just couldn't stop."

The engine was still on, the radio picking up the end of Kiss doing "Christine Sixteen," and I turned around in my seat and looked out the back window at the rise of ditch behind us, tall grass and weeds pressed against the bumper. I realized the car was still in drive, and Charlotte's foot was on the brake, because the slope of ground was lit bright and red.

"Turn off the car," I said.

It took her a moment to cut the engine, and then there was a different quiet, with only the headlights telling us nothing except that we were off the road and looking at the stars. I opened my door and I could smell the grass torn up where the back end had swung around when we spun, and there was the sharp burn of fresh rubber on asphalt hanging in the air, but I could not remember Charlotte hitting the brakes at all. The wind had died down, or we were far enough in the ditch to be out of the gust, and I could hear crickets, a million of them in all directions around us, and the sound of something on the road just over the soft shoulder above where I stood, something ticking out of sync with the noise of the engine cooling, something struggling to get its legs under it, something trying hard to get up and walk.

I heard Charlotte's door open, and the angle of the ditch forced her to put her weight into it so she could swing it wide enough to get free, and then she was walking up the short incline toward the road, and I stood there watching her, listening to the crickets, and trying to make sense out of the sound.

"Son of a bitch," she said. And there was a sadness in her voice that made me want to get back into the car and shut my door and slide onto the floor, let Charlotte deal with it and wait it out, because Charlotte was older and had always been the one to take the brunt, but I wouldn't do that this time. I was the one who had called her out here. She came for me.

My eyes adjusted to the dark, which had settled and thinned on the road. Even the smallest detail was defined and clear—the broken asphalt where shoulder met road, the yellow center line, the metal fence posts set back on both sides, leaning and loose with rusted wires marking acres. Behind me the wide, shallow ditch ran along the roadside, full of nothing more than dense grass gone to seed, trash, and my father's Dodge Royal Monaco, nose up and cooling quietly with both lights shining into the air. The bugs had already come, gnats and moths in greedy clusters, so that the beams held their movement like dust.

There was a body in the road—Charlotte had been right about hitting something—and it was bigger than something as simple as a raccoon or a cat. As I got closer, the shape took definition, and I could see that it was just a deer lying in the center of the road, one back leg still kicking out for grip, and Charlotte was standing over it, hands squeezed tightly in front of her, watching the struggle. I stopped walking, and from where I stood I saw its head rise up from the pavement, watched the panicked white of its eye roll around and see nothing, and then the deer dropped its head and the back leg tucked in. All of it went still.

Charlotte crouched down and reached out and touched the deer, and part of me wanted to stop her, tell her not to, yank her back to her feet and down to the car, but I knew if I had been closer, I would have done the same thing, reached out and touched it too. I watched her run her hand over it, ribs to thigh, and I watched the way her hand lifted over the slope of its side, the stomach distended and pulled tightly back from the ribs.

"I can feel it," Charlotte said.

"Feel what?" I asked. Everything around us had gone quiet; even the crickets had slunk back into the thicker grass and the night was still and the air felt warmer than it had before, the breeze now barely strong enough to bend and ripple the fields. I looked at the sky above us and there were a million stars. All of them seemed as if they were arranged in patterns I was supposed to understand, but I couldn't recognize anything except that they were brighter and closer than I had ever remembered them to be.

"There's a baby," she said. "I can feel the baby inside." I walked up next to her, careful to keep my footsteps quiet, and then I realized that the deer was maybe dead and there was nothing left to startle. I squatted down next to Charlotte and reached out my hand. I wanted to touch it, let myself feel the hair, stiff and coarse, and I knew I would be surprised by how warm the deer would feel, her skin radiating heat, and I would rest my hand against her rough side and hold it there, waiting for something to happen. But I could not touch the deer. I just stood there with my hand holding air.

"Is she dead?" I asked. I stood up and pushed at the deer with my foot, hooked the toe of my tennis shoe under her ribs and tipped her side up and off the asphalt. Charlotte grabbed my leg and pushed me backward, hard, so that I lost my balance and fell onto the warm road.

"What's wrong with you?" she said.

"I was seeing if she was dead."

"She's dead," Charlotte whispered. From where I sat, I could see around Charlotte to the deer's head resting on the ground, one eye open and fixed and staring up at nothing and her jaw slack, widened just enough so that her tongue lolled out and over the darkness of her lips. There was blood on the road underneath her, spreading around her shoulders and neck.

"The baby's still alive," Charlotte said, and she started rubbing the deer's side in small, tight circles. "I think we can save it."

The asphalt was comforting and warm, and I was surprised at the way it held the heat from the day despite the wind and the dark. I could feel small rocks biting into the palms of my hands and I reached forward and rubbed them clean on my jeans. I looked over the deer and down the road, looked in the direction that we had been going before we found ourselves spun into the ditch, and I looked for a pair of lights that would signal the approach of a car, the intervention of someone else to help us pull the Dodge out, move the deer, and get us back on track toward town, someone to interrupt the things that my sister was saying and gently tell her that what she wanted was an impossibility that should not even be thought about, let alone said out loud. But there was nothing around us in any direction, not even the promise of lights, no cars, no more barking dog in the distance, no houses with porches cast in a soft yellow glow, no gravel driveways, no mailboxes marking homes.

"We have to go," I said. "I want to be in my room before Dad wakes up." I didn't really want to be there, but I didn't know of anywhere else we could go, and Charlotte had Dad's car and we'd have to go back eventually.

At the mention of our father, Charlotte stood up and walked to the edge of the road and down the incline to the driver's side of the car, and I thought for a minute she might just get in, start it up, and leave me stretched out on the ground, but she pulled the keys from the ignition and kept walking and I could hear them rattling, knocking back and forth on the ring, and then the trunk lid popped up and there was light from the small bulb inside and I could hear her moving things around.

"Dad's tools are in here," she called to me, and I stood up and went down to watch her.

In the light from the trunk I could see the blood drying on Charlotte's face, a cracked thin smear across her upper lip and over one cheek, but there was no fresh blood and she looked all right to me. Our dad was pretty organized and not one to carry anything he didn't need, but the contents of the trunk had been tossed around and nothing appeared useful. There seemed to be too much and too many of everything, screwdrivers and wrenches, spilled nails, bolts, and washers, drill bits and sockets, some flannel shirts, a water jug, and a half-empty bottle of Jim Beam.

"Perfect," I said, and I pulled the bottle out, unscrewed the lid, and took a long drink, and it felt good. I realized I was thirsty and my mouth was dry and I swallowed all I could before my throat closed up against it.

Charlotte was picking up tools, holding them up for inspection under the trunk-lid light, and setting them back down again. "What about this?" she asked. It was a 12-inch flat-head screwdriver, and I thought about her bent over the deer, cutting it open with a screwdriver, and how much effort it would take to punch through and saw into the skin, and then I remembered the movie at Billy's, and how they had started with box cutters, the two men who tied the girl to the bed, and how she had been facedown and struggling, but not really, and maybe it wasn't real, or maybe she didn't actually know what was going to happen to her, didn't possibly think it was going to get as bad as it eventually did when they started with the box cutters and they were not kidding around.

"I have a knife," I said. It was a little 3-inch Smith & Wesson single combo-edge blade, smooth and serrated, a gift from our dad on my thirteenth birthday. He made me promise not to hurt myself or use it on anything that I wasn't supposed to, and since then I had used it to carve my name into picnic tables at the park and once to gut a bluegill that Lenny Richter and I accidentally caught on an empty hook out at his grandpa's pond.

"Give it to me," she said. She reached out her hand and I dug it out and handed it over to her, the black handle scratched and worn down over the past couple of years, and she took the knife and shoved it into the back pocket of her jeans and held her hand out toward me again, waiting, and then I gave her the bottle and she smiled for the first time since she had pulled into the parking lot to pick me up. In the dim light the shadows made her cheekbones dark and defined, and her lips were full and red, and with her straight blond hair tucked behind her ears and her face holding colors in a way that I had not seen before, I knew why our father worried.

"Are you going to help me?" she asked. She took a drink from the bottle, and I noticed its level was dropping fast and I wished there was more.

"This is crazy," I said. "You do know that?"

Charlotte picked up a flannel shirt from the trunk and used it to wipe her nose off. "I'm going to be in advanced biology next year," she said. "People do this all the time. Emergency C-sections. It's not that hard."

Above us, on the road, I thought I could hear a car coming in the distance, the drone and shift of an engine rounding a bend. I walked back up to the top of the ditch and looked in both directions, but the road was open and clear and dark as far as I could see.

"There's no cars out here," Charlotte said. "I learned to drive on this road at night. I was out here for hours and never saw anybody else. It's weird," she said.

"I didn't know Dad took you out here." I tried to think of our dad doing anything after the sun went down, anything that didn't involve the TV and his chair, or the tool bench in the garage, and a drink half full named after somebody else.

"I wasn't with Dad," she said.

I walked back toward the deer and looked down at it. From that angle it was harder to see how pregnant she was, if her sides were actually wide enough for her to be carrying something more than herself.

"Come here and help me," Charlotte said, and I went back to the trunk of the car, where she loaded me down with the flannel shirts and a dirty blue tarp, and she carried the bottle and a flash-light, and we went back to the deer and she lined everything up like a doctor would.

"What are you going to do?"

She spread the tarp out onto the road and tucked it under the side of the deer. I didn't like the sound it made when she moved it on the asphalt, a stiff and artificial scraping noise that made the hair on the back of my neck stand up.

"We're going to deliver the baby," she said. "We have a chance to save it. We killed its mother, but maybe we can still give it a chance to live." She took my knife out of her back pocket, opened the blade, held it up toward what little light hung in the air from the headlights that neither of us had thought to turn off, poured some Jim Beam on the blade, and wiped it clean on one of our dad's flannel shirts.

"I don't think you have to sterilize it," I said.

Charlotte looked up at me. "It's not for the mother," she said. "It's for the baby. Just in case I go too deep."

"Charlotte, what are we going to do with it?" I felt warm inside, maybe a little bit drunk, and the air felt good against my skin, and I could hear plants rustling, settling back and forth together in their even rows in the fields. When the wind died, nothing moved around us, nothing shifted, nothing bent or made noise, and I could feel the stillness like something I could touch.

She laid the knife down near her on the tarp and started rip-ping the shirts, first one and then another, into long neat strips like rags, and the last one she spread open and wide beside her. The crickets had scattered and were suddenly loud and distant, and the only sound that was clear and close was the noise of Charlotte moving around on the tarp.

"Dad can build a pen in the garage," she said. "I can raise it and feed it from a bottle. I can take care of it just like its mother."

A bird suddenly called from somewhere across the road, somewhere deep in a field, and it sounded big and close but I could not see it.

"Nothing works out like that," I said. "You can't just cut a baby deer out of its mother and take it home and call it your own." Our dad had never even allowed us to have a dog, because he hated pets. He said he hated the noise and the smell and the responsibility of looking after something else in the house, and even when we begged and promised we would do all the work, he said it was impossible, that he had been young once too, and he knew that kids failed, and it would become his dog and he didn't want one.

Charlotte tucked her hair behind her ears, sat back on her heels, and looked up at me standing over her. "You know Dad hates me," she said.

I thought about the way he yelled, the way he put his hand on her arm when she walked in the door sometimes, the way he yanked her around in the kitchen. *Where have you been?*

"That's just Dad," I said. "You know how he gets. He worries." I felt like a liar, making excuses. People were always doing that.

When I saw the girl in the film for the first time, I thought the men would be younger, that they would be in high school, that for some reason they would be boys, and I hadn't thought about them being anything else, but they had been men our father's age, or maybe even older, and they had tied the girl to the bed and her spine had stood out in a rail of bones, and I had seen the shadows of the men first, saw their shapes moving across her white skin like clouds, and she hadn't seemed scared at all, and I had flinched for her, felt something familiar in my stomach curl up and pull tight.

"He loves you," I said. "He's just weird about showing it."

"He hates me. He wishes I would just move away and never come back so he could say that he just has a son."

The headlights behind us had become so much of a presence I had almost forgotten about them and then the left one sputtered and the hideaway window folded it in with a soft pneumatic sound, a hush like an automatic door closing, and we were cut down to one weak beam staring up at nothing and the darkness filled in. I could hear Charlotte breathing through her nose, and the sound was heavy and thick.

"You know he caught me in June," she said. "Right after school got out. He caught me making out in front of the house. It was late and we were parked on the street and I thought everybody was asleep—the house was dark—and I didn't want to come in. You probably don't understand what I'm talking about, I don't know, but maybe you do. I can't really explain it and it doesn't make any sense, but I just couldn't stop, even though I knew I needed to go in. I just didn't."

I wanted to tell Charlotte that I knew all about what it felt like to feel something and not be able to stop, but instead I tried to imagine who Charlotte had been with and I couldn't. I had never seen her sit with anybody other than girls at school, had never heard her talk to a boy on the phone, had never heard her mention a name, or act strange, or get nervous. I had never known Charlotte to pay attention to anybody except for her best friend, Macy.

"It wasn't Pete Holbrook, was it?" I asked. He was the only one I could think of Charlotte liking and that was only based on the fact that I knew he had liked her the year before, had followed her around at lunch all the time—I had seen him in the cafeteria, trying to get next to her in line, sit by her and Macy at a table—and I knew he had asked her to a dance once but she said no.

Charlotte laughed. "Pete? God no," she said. "Not even close." She moved onto her knees, and I could hear the tarp shift underneath her, and I could hear her take a deep breath and hold it and then exhale. "Hold the flashlight, okay?" She clicked it on and handed it up, and the unexpected heaviness spun the light backward, blinding me for a second.

I pointed the beam down at the side of the deer, and I thought I was still seeing spots from the light, but then I realized they were ticks, standing out like blood-filled moles, and I wanted to look away, but Charlotte was pushing on the deer's stomach with her hand, running her fingertips over the brown skin, pulling the back leg so that she could see the entirety of the white belly underneath. I was shaking badly and I tried to hold the light steady, but it kept jumping around and landing everywhere except where Charlotte was pointing the knife.

"On the count of three?" she asked, and I nodded but said nothing, and she looked up at me, waiting for an answer.

"Okay," I said.

We both took a breath and started counting in unison, "One, two, three," and then Charlotte stuck the knife in, center of the stomach, buried to the handle, and there was blood, a darkening around where the blade went in, and I could hear Charlotte inhale hard through her nose, and she pulled the knife out and there was more blood and it flowed freely, thick and red.

I shifted the flashlight and caught the knife in the beam, and the blade was red and there were white and brown hairs stuck to it, and I realized that Charlotte's hand was shaking worse than mine and together we couldn't hold anything in focus for more than a second. She wiped the knife clean on a piece of flannel shirt and sat back from the deer, pulled her knees to her chest and hugged her arms around them.

"What time do you think it is?" she asked.

I looked down at my watch and could see the two tiny glowing hands beneath the glass. "It's after two," I said.

"Dad was asleep when I left," she said.

I imagined how it would be when we pulled into the driveway, our dad not knowing Charlotte had gone, his windshield smashed, the tires caked with dirt, bumpers full of weeds, and us carrying a newborn deer wrapped in one of his old shirts from the trunk. Part of me hoped everything would happen like something on TV and we would make breakfast even though the sun had not begun to rise, and we would be inspected for injury, turned this way and that under the kitchen light, and our dad would take the fawn and come up with a way to feed it, make it a bed in a box, and he would look at the car and shake his head and be happy both of us were fine, and we would tell the story of how Charlotte had delivered the baby on the road from the deer we had hit and our dad would be so impressed that he would put his arm around her shoulders and say, *That's my girl!* and he would repeat the story to his friends, too proud to keep from telling it over and over again for the rest of the week. But really I knew it would be nothing like that; it would be something that my mind did not want to imagine, and there were no pictures stored inside my head to give any kind of meaning to how it really would be, and I think that Charlotte knew it too, but maybe she believed in her own TV version a lot more than I did, or she had more hope, or more need, and maybe those were the things that made her put the knife into the deer again while I stood there, and make another narrow gash next to the first.

"You can't just keep stabbing at it," I said. "You have to keep the knife in and cut."

"I know what I'm doing."

When the men in the film had the box cutters in their hands, I didn't think they would really do it, that they would put them against the girl and carve into her back, so that narrow lines of darkness rose to the surface of her skin in shapes almost like words, and Lenny Richter had been standing beside me, and he had put his hand over his mouth, and I thought for a second he was trying to stop himself from getting sick, and then I realized that he was laughing. He had his hand over his mouth and he was bent forward and he was laughing. I had felt all the spit dry in my mouth, and my tongue had gone thick so that even if I had wanted to laugh and pretend I was not sweating through my T-shirt, I could not. All I could do was watch and not move.

Charlotte had the knife in a tight grip, and I could tell she wanted to drag it sideways, tear through the thin wall of skin that divided the second cut from the first, turn the 1-inch slit to 2 inches, but just when I thought she might do it, go ahead and run the knife the distance of the belly and make a line big enough for her to open the stomach and reach in, find the baby inside, and pull it out onto the tarp, she took her hand off the handle and sat back on her heels and left the knife stuck in the skin. She wiped her hands on the thighs of her jeans and stood up. She turned away from me and started walking back toward the car.

"I need to think for a minute," she said.

I stood there with the flashlight still pointed down at the deer, the beam suddenly steady, the knife just a small interruption in the slight curve of belly that was divided now by a thick line of color. The deer didn't look as swollen as I had thought she was in the dark. She was just a deer, caught in the open between one field and the next, dead on the road. I clicked the switch and cut the light and turned around and followed Charlotte over the embankment.

Charlotte was sitting in the Dodge, drinking, and I wished she had the keys back in the ignition so we could listen to the radio, but they were still hanging from the lock in the trunk. She passed me the bottle and I noticed with the door shut the car was too quiet and too still.

"Would you miss me if I left town?" Charlotte asked. She pushed the knob on the headlights and the single swath that had cut into the darkness went out and the gathered bugs scattered in confusion, and there were only prismed stars above us through the shattered windshield and the slope of the ditch rising around us outside the windows.

"I would miss you," I said. "But I don't think you'll go."

"I might," she said. "I might surprise you." She had a piece of flannel shirt in her hands and she was rubbing at her palm, trying to get it clean.

"Who did Dad catch you making out with in the car?"

I took another small drink and turned my head toward her so I could see her face. She was staring straight ahead, staring out the broken windshield and into the darkness.

"It doesn't matter anymore," she said. She stopped rubbing her hand and wadded the shirt into a ball on the seat beside her. "Do you think we can get out of this ditch on our own? I don't want to wait until the sun comes up for someone to drive by."

I looked over my shoulder at the angle of the car in the ditch, the way the back end hadn't slid so far that it was wedged into the slope, and if Charlotte cranked the wheel hard enough and put it in reverse, she could ease us down into the bottom of the gully and we would have a chance at punching our way up and over the incline if she was willing to wind the engine tight and hit the gas hard.

"You could do it," I said.

She took the bottle from me and emptied it in one long swallow. "Help me gather everything, okay?"

We collected the things from around the deer, rolled up the tarp, folded it all together with the torn shirts, put them back in the trunk, and went back to the road. We both stood looking at the deer, and Charlotte crouched down and put her hand on the doe's side and petted her.

"She's cold," Charlotte said.

The air around us was getting thinner, and I didn't have to look at my watch to know that somewhere over the horizon line the sun was on its approach and the darkness would begin to soften and give way to light before too long. There were more birds making noise, but they were still too far out to see, and the crickets had almost given up, and I realized I was tired and ready to be home.

"I'm sorry," Charlotte said. For a second I thought she was talking to me, but she had said it to the deer, and her voice was quiet and I knew that she was crying even though I could not see her face. "I tried," she said. She kept running her hand over and over the side of the deer, and then she reached forward and slowly pulled out my knife and handed it to me, bloody, and thick with matted hair, the handle sticky, the blade too stiff to fold.

I rubbed the knife against the hem of my shirt and was finally able to get it to close, and after I shoved it back into my pocket, Charlotte pointed me toward the front of the deer and she stayed at the back and we each grabbed a pair of legs and pulled. The deer had settled into the asphalt so that it was hard to free her, and it took us ten minutes to get her across the opposite lane. We dragged her to the side of the road and pushed her down toward the bottom of the other drainage ditch, away from the car. Her legs did not bend and she didn't make it very far down the ditch, but she was out of the way and off the road and nobody else was in danger of hitting her. We both stood on the blacktop shoulder, sweating and breathing heavily, looking at her dark body lying in the grass like nothing more than shadow.

"Why did you stop?" I asked.

Charlotte bowed her head and said nothing for a second, and then she wiped both her eyes and turned back toward the car. "It wouldn't have lived," she said. "It wouldn't have been natural to force it like that. It wasn't meant to be born yet." Behind her, in the thin light, I could see the narrow stain in the road.

She did just what I told her to do—eased the Dodge into reverse and turned the wheel so the entire car slipped back into the very bottom of the ditch, and we were only at a slight angle with the driver's side high-centered on the incline. I told her to put the car into drive and floor it, get enough forward momentum to push the car up the side and out of the ditch, and to keep a tight grip on the wheel and not let the car slide out from under her in the grass and the dirt, and she did those things too, and we hit the top of the ditch so hard we caught air and crossed to the other side of the road, and Charlotte had to guide us into our lane without overcorrecting, and she did that, and there was a little bit of fish-tailing and the sound of tires breaking loose, and then we were on our side of the road, with one good headlight pointing out the direction.

In the movie the girl had been almost naked; Lenny had said she would be, but it had taken a while. They had tied her across the bed and she had been shirtless without a bra, her back nothing but blank skin and bone, and she had been wearing panties, white and thin, and when she twisted around on the bed, rolling up off her hips, trying to loosen her hands from where they were knotted above her head, I saw the panties were the kind like my sister had for a while, the ones she used to hang out back on the line to dry, the kind with the days of the week on them, and the girl had been wearing a pair that said *Tuesday*. I was suddenly embarrassed for her, in the same way I was embarrassed when my sister did our laundry and hung everything out in the yard for the neighbors to see — all of our private things exposed.

I rolled down my window so the air would keep me awake and I could lean out to help guide Charlotte down the road. Everything smelled wet and sharp and alive and I watched it all fall behind us as we passed. We were finally leaving the country, the fields, and the fence lines, and I wasn't sorry to watch them go. Outside my window was the sound of metal on metal and tire rub as the car tried to shake broken pieces loose.

The knife was shoved deep in my pocket, like a warm spot against my thigh, and when I looked at it again in the daylight, unfolded the blade, there would still be blood on it, and strands of light-colored hair. Charlotte had her hands gripped tightly around the steering wheel, and I wanted to ask her what it had felt like to cut into the deer. If it had been me who had held the knife, I wanted to think that things would be different now. Maybe I couldn't have gone as far as Charlotte did. Or maybe I wouldn't have stopped.

Former Marine

FROM *A Permanent Member of the Family*

AFTER LYING IN BED awake for an hour, Connie finally pushes back the blankets and gets up. It's still dark. He's barefoot and shivering in his boxers and T-shirt and a little hungover from one beer too many at 20 Main last night. He snaps the bedside lamp on and resets the thermostat from 55 to 65. The burner makes a huffing sound and the fan kicks in, and the smell of kerosene drifts through the trailer. He pats his new hearing aids into place and peers out the bedroom window. Snow is falling across a pale splash of lamplight on the lawn. It's a week into April and it ought to be rain, but Connie is glad it's snow. He removes his .45-caliber Colt service pistol from the drawer of the bedside table, checks to be sure it's loaded, and lays it on the dresser.

By the time he has shaved and dressed and driven to town in his pickup, three and a half inches of heavy wet snow have accumulated. The town plows and salt trucks are already out. The plate-glass windows of the M & M Diner are fogged over, and from the street you can't see the half-dozen men and two women inside eating breakfast and making low-voiced, sporadic conversation with one another.

By choice, Connie sits alone at the back of the room, reading the sports section of the Plattsburgh *Press-Republican*. He has known everyone in the place personally for most of their lives. They are all on their way to work. He, however, is not. He calls himself the Retiree, even though he never officially retired from anything and nobody else calls him the Retiree. Eight months ago he was let go by Ray Piaggi at Ray's Auction House. Let go. Like he was a helium-filled balloon on a string, he tells people. He sometimes adds that you know the economy is in trouble when even auctioneers start cutting back, indicating that it's not his fault he's unemployed, using food stamps, on Medicaid, scraping by on social security and unemployment benefits that are about to run out. It's the economy's fault. And the fault of whoever the hell's in charge of it.

Connie has already ordered his usual breakfast—scrambled eggs, sausage patty, toasted English muffin, and coffee—when his eldest son, Jack, comes through the door. Jack nods and smiles hello to the other diners like a man running for office and pats the waitress, Vivian, on the shoulder. He shucks his heavy gray bomber jacket and pulls off his winter trooper hat, hangs them on a wall hook next to his dad's Carhartt and forest-green fleece balaclava, and takes the seat facing the door, opposite his dad.

"I was starting to think it was time to pack that stuff away," Jack says.

Connie says, "One of my goddamn hearing aids just told me, 'Battery low.' Like I can't tell when it's dead and that's why I'm getting no reception. Man my age, his batteries are always low, for chrissake. I don't need no hearing aid to tell me."

"Your hearing aids talk to you?"

"It's a way to get me to buy new batteries before I really need them. I'll probably buy fifty extra batteries a year, one a week, just to get my goddamn hearing aids to stop telling me my battery's low."

"Seriously, Dad, your hearing aids talk to you? You hearing voices?"

"Yeah, I'm a regular schizo. No, it's these new computerized units Medicaid won't subsidize. Over six grand! I shouldn't have listened to that goddamn audiologist and bought the subsidized cheapos instead. With these, there's a little lady inside whispers that your battery's low. Also tells you what channel you're on. I got five channels with these units—for listening to music, for quiet time, reverse focus, and what they call master. Master's the human conversational channel. And there's also one for phone. I can't tell the difference between any of 'em, except phone, which when you're not actually talking on the phone is like a goddamn echo chamber. It does help me hear with a cell phone, though."

Vivian sets Connie's platter of food and coffee in front of him. "That gonna be it, Conrad?"

"Please, Viv, for chrissake, don't call me Conrad. Only my ex-wife called me Conrad, and thankfully I haven't heard it from her in nearly thirty years."

"I'm kidding," she says without looking at him. "Connie," she adds. She takes Jack's order, oatmeal with milk and a cup of coffee, and heads back to the kitchen.

For a few seconds, while his father digs into his breakfast, Jack studies the man. Jack's been a state trooper for twelve years and studies people's behavior, even his seventy-year-old father's, with a learned, calm detachment. "You seem sort of agitated this morning, Dad. Everything okay?"

"Yeah, sure. I was just teasing Viv about that Conrad business. But it is true, y'know, only your mother called me that. She used it to give me orders or criticize me. Like she was afraid I'd take advantage of her somehow if she got friendly enough to call me Connie."

"You probably would've."

"Yeah, well, your mother took off before I really had a chance to take advantage of her. Smart gal. She quit before I could fire her."

"That's one way to look at it."

"You have to let it go, Jack. She didn't want the job, and I did. In the end, everybody, including you boys, got what they needed."

"You're right, Dad. You're right." They've had this exchange a hundred times.

Vivian sets Jack's coffee and oatmeal in front of him and scoots away as if a little scared of Connie, mocking him. Jack smiles agreeably after her and shakes out the front section of the newspaper and scans the headlines while he eats. Connie goes back to the sports page.

Jack says, "Looks like we got through March without another bank robbery. Maybe our boy has headed south, like Butch Cassidy and the Sundance Kid." He flips the front page over and goes on to national news.

After a few minutes, without looking up, Connie says, "You talk to Buzz and Chip recently?"

Jack looks over at his father as if expecting more, then says, "No, not in the last few days."

"Everything the same with them these days?"

"More or less. Far as I know."

"Wives and kids?"

"Yep, the same, far as I know. All is well. No news is good news, Dad."

"I wouldn't mind any kind of news, actually."

"They're busy, Dad. It's easier for me, I don't have a wife and kids. Plus Buzz has that long drive every day up to Dannemora and back, and Chip's taking criminal justice courses nights at North Country Community College down in Ticonderoga. And they both live way the hell over in Keeseville. Don't take it personally, Dad."

"I don't," Connie says, and goes back to reading the sports page.

Jack finishes his oatmeal, shoves his bowl to one side, and cups his mug of coffee in his large red hands, warming them. He's thinking. He suddenly asks, "You ever consider it a little weird that all three of us went into law enforcement? I sometimes wonder about it. I mean, it isn't like you were a police officer. Like me and Chip. Or a prison guard like Buzz. I mean, you ran auctions."

"Yeah, but don't forget, I'm a former Marine. And you're never an ex-Marine, Jack. So that was the standard you boys were raised by, the United States Marine Corps standard, especially after your mother took off. If my father had been a former Marine, I probably would have gone into law enforcement too. I always kind of regretted none of you boys were Marines."

"Dad, you can't regret something someone else did or didn't do. Only what you yourself did or didn't do."

Connie smiles and says, "See, that's exactly the sort of thing a former Marine would say!"

Jack smiles back. The old man amuses him. But he worries him too. The old man's in denial about his finances, Jack thinks. He's got to be worse than broke. Jack gets up from the table, walks to the counter, and tries to pay Vivian for both their breakfasts, but Connie sees what he's up to. He jumps from his seat and slides between his son and the waitress, waving a twenty-dollar bill in her face, insisting on paying for both his and Jack's meals.

Vivian shrugs and takes Connie's twenty, just to get it out of her face.

She hands him his change, and father and son walk back to the table, where both men pull their coats and hats on. "You take care of the tip," Connie says. "Make it big enough so you and I come out even and Vivian ends up forgiving me for being an asshole."

"Dad, you sure you're okay? I mean, financially? It's got to be a little rough these days."

Connie doesn't answer, except to make a pulled-down face designed to tell his son he sounds ridiculous. Absurd. Of course he's okay financially. He's the father. Still the man of the house. A former Marine.

It's a thirty-mile drive from Au Sable Forks to Lake Placid, forty-five minutes in good weather, twice that today. The roads are plowed and passable but slick all the way over—slowing to a creep through Wilmington Notch, where the altitude is more than 2000 feet and the falling snow is nearing whiteout.

It's a quarter to ten when Connie pulls his white, two-wheel-drive Ford Ranger into Cold Brook Plaza. He's filled the bed of the truck with a quarter ton of bagged gravel to give the vehicle traction in weather like this. The truck is seven years old, with a rust belt under the doors and along the seams of the bed. He parks it off to the windowless side of the Lake Placid branch of the Adirondack Bank, a low pop-up building not much larger than a double-wide. There are no other vehicles in the parking area. Nobody's using the drive-through or the ATM. He notices in the employees' lot behind the building a new Subaru Outback and one of those humpbacked Pontiac SUVs he hates looking at because they're so ugly.

The windshield wipers bump across runnels of ice forming on the glass, and he knows he should get out there with a scraper and clear the ice, but decides to let the defroster heat the glass from inside and melt it. He can't linger. Too easy to run into someone he knows, even this far from home. He sets the emergency brake, grabs the green gym bag off the floor beside him, and steps from the truck, leaving the motor running and the defroster and heater on high. He walks around the truck, making sure that both license plates are covered in hardened road-slush. When he gets to the bank entrance, he turns away for a second and yanks down his fleece balaclava, transforming it into a ski mask, a not unusual sight on a snowy day in a ski town like Lake Placid. Then he pulls open the heavy glass door and enters the bank.

There are two slender young tellers behind the chest-high counter, girls in their early twenties who appear to be counting money back there, and a middle-aged bank officer standing at the open door of her glassed-in cubicle. All three offer him a welcoming gaze when he comes through the door—the first customer of the day. The bank officer holds a notary stamp press in her hands as if it's a precious gift. She's a redheaded, round-faced woman wearing a two-piece green wool suit and tangerine-colored blouse. To Connie she looks like a social worker, the kind who interviewed him for Medicaid and food stamps. That humpbacked Pontiac is probably hers. The tellers are dressed more casually, in matching gray pleated skirts, black tights, long-sleeved button-down shirts, and fleece vests. They both have mud-colored shoulder-length hair and rosy cheeks. Connie thinks they must be twins and dress alike on purpose. Buzz and Chip, who are twins, used to do that in high school. Just to confuse people, he remembers. These girls are a little old for that.

He leans back against the counter and says to the bank officer, "Would you look at this, please?" He puts his left hand deep into his jacket pocket and holds out the gym bag with his right. She comes up to him, and he hands her the open bag.

She furrows her brow, puzzled, wary, but places the notary stamp press on the counter anyhow, takes the bag, and peers into it. It's empty, except for five words hand-printed in capital letters with a black Magic Marker on a white sheet of paper: FILL WITH CASH. OWNER ARMED.

"Oh, dear," she says. She takes the gym bag and, avoiding his eyes, passes through the low gate and goes behind the counter where the confused tellers stand and watch.

Connie says to the tellers, "You girls just step back a few feet from the counter there and don't touch anything. Keep your hands where I can see them. This'll all be over in a minute." To the white-faced bank officer he says, "Less than a minute, actually. Thirty seconds. I'm counting," he says and commences to count backward from thirty. By the time he reaches twelve, she has emptied the contents of the cash drawers into the gym bag. She zips the bag closed and passes it to him.

It's nice and heavy, about three pounds of money, he guesses. He thanks her with a nod and, still counting out loud, backs quickly away from the counter toward the door, right hand holding the gym bag, left hand deep in his jacket pocket clasping the grip of his reliable old Colt M1911 service pistol. At five he is outside the bank, and at one he's in his truck, then releasing the hand brake, and he has backed the truck up and turned, unseen, and is headed west out of town on Old Military Road.

In the falling snow traffic is light and slow-moving. A mile beyond the city limits, where the road enters the hamlet of Ray Brook, a pair of state police cruisers, their lights flashing, speeds toward him, and he pulls slightly off to the right to let them zoom past. A minute later he passes the Ray Brook state police headquarters, where until a year ago his son Jack was stationed. If Jack were headquartered there today, he'd likely be driving one of those cruisers that just blew by, and he might have recognized his dad's white, rusted-out Ford Ranger and wondered what he was doing way over here. But Jack's stationed in Au Sable Forks now, not Ray Brook, and that's why, after robbing four branches of three different banks in Essex and Franklin Counties in the last seven months, Connie has waited until now to rob the Lake Placid branch of the Adirondack Bank and why afterward he drove west, away from Au Sable Forks and home. He doesn't want his sons to ask him any questions that he can't answer truthfully.

He drives through the town of Saranac Lake, looping via Route 3 gradually north toward Plattsburgh, where he spends the rest of the morning into the afternoon hanging out at the Champlain Centre mall like a bored teenager. With the gym bag locked in the pickup in the parking lot and the money uncounted, un-examined—for all he knows it could be three pounds of one-dollar bills, although more likely it's tens, twenties, fifties, and hundreds, like the others—he roams through the tool department at Sears and drifts on to the food court, where he eats Chinese food, and then goes to a 2 p.m. screening of *Lincoln,* which he likes in spite of being surprised that Abraham Lincoln had such a high, squeaky voice. While he's watching the movie, the temperature outside rises into the mid-thirties and the falling snow dwindles and finally stops. It's almost 5 p.m. when he comes blinking out of the multiplex and decides it's safe now to drive back to Au Sable Forks.

The six-lane Northway is puddled with salted snowmelt and slush. In Keeseville, still 10 miles from home, he exits from the turnpike on the wide, sweeping off-ramp to Route 9N. Keeseville is where his two younger sons and their families live and is not so damned far from Au Sable Forks that they couldn't drop by to visit once a month if they wanted to, he thinks, and in order to power the truck through the curve, Connie guns it. The quarter ton of bagged gravel in the truck bed has shifted the weight of the vehicle from the front tires to the rear, and the centrifugal pull of the turn causes the rear tires to lose their grip on the pavement and slip sideways to the left. Connie automatically flips the steering wheel to the left, the direction of the slide, but the rear end whipsaws back to the right, putting the truck into a slow 180-degree spin, back to front, until he's facing the way he's come and the truck is sliding sideways and downhill toward the off-ramp guardrail at about 40 miles an hour.

It's only a concussion and a busted collarbone, Jack explains to his father. But the collarbone broke in two places and as a result is in three separate pieces. "They called in one of the sports docs from Lake Placid, guy who works on ski accidents all the time. He operated and put pins in it, but given your age and bone loss, he doesn't think the pins'll hold if you get hit in that area again. He said you'll have to protect your right side like it's made of glass."

"How long was I out?" Connie asks. He's just realized that Chip and Buzz are in the room, standing somewhere behind Jack. He's woozy and confused about where he is exactly, although he can tell it's a hospital room. He's in a bed with an IV stuck in his arm and an empty bed next to his and a chair in the corner and a window with the curtain pulled back. It's dark outside.

"You were out when I got to the truck, which was no more than ten minutes after the accident, I'd guess. A citizen with a cell phone in a car right behind you saw the truck go over and called 911. I happened to be driving north on 87 just below the exit. You came to in the ambulance, but they knocked you out when you went in for surgery. You don't remember the ambulance and all that?"

"Last thing I remember is the truck going into a slide. Hello, boys," he says to Chip and Buzz. "Sorry to bring you out like this." They look worried, brows furrowed, unsmiling, both in uniform, Buzz in his Dannemora prison guard's uniform and Chip in his Plattsburgh police officer blues. All three of his sons wear uniforms well. He likes that. "Hope you didn't have to leave work for this."

Chip says that he was on duty, but since that had him here in Plattsburgh, it was no big deal to come right over to the hospital, and Buzz says that he was just getting home when Jack called, so it was no big deal for him, either, to drive back to Plattsburgh. "Edie sends her love," Buzz adds.

"Yeah, Joan sends love too, Dad," Chip says.

Connie asks about his truck. He has just remembered the gym bag.

Jack says, "Totaled. Northway Sunoco came over and towed it out. You really put it all the way off the ramp and into the woods. Thicket of small birches stopped you. Good thing it wasn't a full-grown tree or you'd have gone through the windshield. You weren't wearing a seat belt. Where were you coming from?"

"Plattsburgh. The movies at Champlain mall. I wanted to see that movie about Abraham Lincoln everybody's talking about."

All four men are silent for a moment, as if each is lost in his own thoughts. Finally Chip says, "Dad, we've got to ask you a couple of tough questions." Jack and Buzz nod in agreement.

Connie's heart is racing. He knows what's coming.

Chip says, "It's about the money in the bag."

"What bag?"

Jack says, "The EMT guys gave me the bag, Dad, the gym bag, when they pulled you out of the truck. I didn't open it till after you were in surgery. I wasn't prying. I opened it in case there was a bottle in it that might've broke or something. Although I don't think you were drinking," he adds.

"No, I wasn't! Not a drop all day! It was the snow and ice on the road that did it."

Chip says, "We need to know where you got the money, Dad. There's a lot of it. Thousands of dollars."

Buzz says, "And we need to know why you were carrying your forty-five."

"It's not illegal," Connie says to him. "Not yet, anyhow."

Jack says, "But the gun and the money, they're connected, aren't they, Dad? I've been putting two and two together, you know. Connecting the dots, like they say. For instance, wondering where you got the money for those hearing aids that Medicaid wouldn't pay for."

"I'm doing okay money-wise. I had some savings, you know."

Buzz says, "I know what goes on inside prison, Dad. It's worse than anything you can imagine. I don't want you there. But you're looking at hard time. Armed robbery. You'll be there the rest of your goddamn life. What the Christ were you thinking?"

Of the three, Buzz is the only one who looks sad. Jack's face and Chip's show no emotion, not even curiosity, but that's because they're trained police officers. Connie says, "I don't know what you guys are talking about."

Buzz says, "Dad, what the hell do you want us to do? What do you think we should do? What's the right thing here, Dad?"

"You don't have to do anything. As an American citizen I can carry my service pistol if I want, and I can carry my money around in cash in a goddamn gym bag if I want. Who can trust the goddamn banks these days anyhow?"

Jack says, "It's not your money! It belongs to the Adirondack Bank branch in Lake Placid that was robbed this morning. Robbed by a guy in a ski mask and a Carhartt jacket with a gym bag that had a note in it that said, 'Fill with cash, owner armed.' The note's still in the bottom of the bag, Dad. Under the money. I checked."

"You checked? So you were snooping? Invading my privacy?"

Buzz says, "Jesus Christ, Dad, make sense! There's two of us standing here who can arrest you! Is that what you want? To be arrested by your own sons? And make the third your prison guard?"

Connie looks across the room at the window and through the glass into the darkness beyond. He wonders if it's late at night or very early in the morning. He says, "Sounds funny when you put it that way. Like I wanted it to happen."

But it's not what he wanted to happen. When his sons were little boys and their mother abandoned them all so she could go off to live with an artist in a hippie commune in New Mexico, Connie held it together with discipline and devotion to duty. All by himself, he held the fort and took perfect fatherly care of his sons. And after they graduated from high school he paid for Jack to go to college at Paul Smith's and for Buzz at Plattsburgh State for those two years when he wanted to be a radiologist. He paid for Chip's Hawaiian honeymoon with Joan. He even took care of them when they were in their early thirties by taking out a second mortgage and home equity loan, borrowing against his trailer and the land in Elizabethtown he inherited from his father, so his sons could buy their first houses. He wanted to take impeccable care of his sons, and he did. And after the boys grew up and no longer needed him to take care of them, he planned on continuing to hold the family together by being able to take impeccable care of himself. That was the long-range plan. They would still be a fam-

ily, the four of them, and he would still be the father, the head of
the household, because you're never an ex-father, any more than
you're an ex-Marine.

But the way things turned out, he can't take care of himself.
How can he explain this to his sons without them thinking he's
pathetic and weak and stupid? First the real estate market tanked,
and neither the trailer nor the land his father left him was worth
as much as he owed on them, so even if he wanted to, he couldn't
sell the properties for enough to pay off the loans and move into a
government-subsidized room or studio apartment in town. Who'd
buy his trailer and land anyhow? He'd still owe the banks tens of
thousands of dollars and would have to go on making the monthly
payments. Then he lost his job at Ray's Auction House. Without
it he could no longer make the payments to the banks, and when
he missed two consecutive months, the banks' lawyers threatened
to seize his trailer and the land. He was about to become an ex-
father.

"How late is it?" he asks.

Jack says, "Late. Quarter of three."

"What do you want us to do, Dad?" Buzz says again.

Connie asks them what they've done with the money, and Jack
says it's still in the gym bag, which he put on the shelf in the closet
of the hospital room, where they hung his clothes and coat.

"What about my service pistol? Where's it at?" A man's gun is
not to be disturbed, especially when the man is your father and a
former Marine.

"It's in the bag with the money," Buzz says.

"So nobody else knows about this yet, except for you three?"

Jack says, "That's right."

Connie says, "Then nobody has to do anything about this tonight, right? It's late. You boys go get some sleep, and tomorrow
the three of you sit down together and decide what you want to do.
It's your decision, not mine. I know that whatever you do, boys, it'll
be the right thing. It's what I raised you to do."

They seem relieved and exhale almost in unison, as if all three
have been holding their breath. Buzz reaches down and tousles
the old man's thin, sandy gray hair, as if ruffling the fur of a favorite dog. He says, "Okay. Sounds like a plan, Dad."

"Yeah," Chip says. "Sounds like a plan."

Jack nods agreement. He's the first out the door, and the others quickly follow. They catch up to him in the hallway, and the three walk side by side in silence to the elevator. They remain silent in the elevator and down two floors and all the way out to the parking lot. They stop beside Jack's cruiser for a second and look back and up at the large square window of their father's room. A nurse draws the blind closed, and the light in the room goes out.

Jack opens the door on the driver's side and gets in. "You want to meet for breakfast and figure out what's next?"

"Where?" Chip asks. "I've got the noon-to-nine shift, so breakfast is good."

"M & M in Au Sable Forks at eight? The old man's favorite breakfast joint."

"I can make it okay," Buzz says, "but I have to be on the road to Dannemora by nine."

Chip says, "I guess we already know what's next, don't we?"

Buzz says, "His pistol, is it loaded?"

"I didn't check," Jack says, getting out of the car. Buzz is already walking very fast back toward the hospital entrance, and Chip is running to catch up, when from their father's room on the second floor they hear the gunshot.

JAMES LEE BURKE

Going Across Jordan

FROM *The Southern Review*

WHO WOULD BELIEVE somebody could drive a car across the bottom of an ancient glacial lake at night, the high beams tunneling in electrified shafts of yellow smoke under the surface, but I stood on the bank and saw it, my head still throbbing from a couple of licks I took when I was on the ground and couldn't protect myself. The sky was bursting with stars, the fir trees shaggy and full of shadows on the hillsides, the cherry trees down by the lake thrashing in the wind. Most of the people we picked cherries for lived in stone houses on the lakeshore, and after sunset you could see their lights come on and reflect on the water, but tonight the houses were dark and the only light on the lake was the glow of the high beams spearing across the lake bottom, the ginks that had chased us through the timber with chains afraid of what their eyes told them.

Flathead Lake was a magical place back in those days, all 28 miles of it, the largest freshwater lake west of the Mississippi, so beautiful that when you stood on the shore at sunrise it was like day one of creation and you thought you might see a mastodon with big tusks coming down out of the high country, snow caked and steaming on its hide.

We called ourselves people on the drift, not migrants. Migrants have a destination. Buddy Elgin wasn't going anywhere except to a location in his head, call it a dream if you like. He was the noun and I was the adverb. We never filed an income tax form, and our only ID was a city library card. Like Cisco Houston used to say, we rode free on that old SP. Tell me there's anything better than the sound of the wheels clicking on the tracks and a boxcar rocking back and forth under you while you sleep. Buddy was like a big brother to me. Even though he was a water-walker and took big risks, he always looked out for his pals.

We worked beets in northern Colorado and bucked bales in the Big Horns during the haying season. I can still see Buddy picking up the bale by the twine and flinging it up on the flatbed, the bale as light as air in his hands, the muscles of his upper arms swollen like cantaloupes, a big Swedish girl in the baler not able to take her eyes off him. Buddy was on the square with women and never spoke crudely in front of them or about them, so any trouble we got into was political and never had female origins. Not until we got mixed up with a hoochie-coochie girl who could rag-pop your boots and leave you with a shine and a male condition that made it hard for you to climb down from the chair, pardon me if I'm too frank.

I loved the life we led and would not have changed it if you hit me upside the head with an iron skillet. I told this to Buddy while we were gazing out the open door of a flat-wheeler, the Big Horns slipping behind us under a turquoise sky and a slice of moon that was as hard and cold as a scythe blade.

He wore a gray flop hat that had darkened with sweat high above the band, one knee pulled up in front of him, the neck of his Stella twelve-string guitar propped against it. The locomotive was slowing on a long curve that wound through hills that were round and smooth and reddish brown against the sun and made me think of women's breasts.

"What are you studying on?" he asked.

"I was wondering why most men get in trouble over a reasonable issue like money or women or cards or alcohol, not because they cain't keep their mouths shut."

Buddy tried to roll a cigarette out of a ten-cent bag of Bull Durham, but a flat-wheeler doesn't have springs and makes for a rough ride and the tobacco kept spilling out of the cigarette paper cupped in a tube between his fingers. "It was a free country when I woke up this morning," he said.

"You don't hold political meetings in a bunkhouse. The people listening to you think Karl Marx has a brother named Harpo."

He worked on his cigarette until he finally got it rolled and licked down and twisted on both ends. He lit it with a paper match and flicked the blackened match out the door and watched the country go by. I wanted to push him out the door.

"What do those hills put you in mind of?" he asked.

"Big piles of dirt and rock and dry grass that I wish would catch on fire."

"It's beautiful. Except there's something out here that wants to kill you."

"Like what?"

"It."

"What's *it*?"

"Everything," he said. He picked up his guitar and formed an E chord and drew his thumb across the strings. "Sheridan coming up. Listen to that whistle blow."

We got hired with a bunch of Mexican wets on a street corner not far from the old cattle pens north of town and went to work for a feed grower and horse breeder who was also a cowboy actor out in Hollywood and went by the name of Clint Wakefield. Except Wakefield didn't really run the ranch. The straw boss did; he was a southerner like us by the name of Tyler Keats. He'd been a bull rider on the circuit, until he got overly ambitious one night and tied himself down with a suicide wrap and got all his sticks broken. You could hear Tyler creak when he walked, which is not to say he was lacking in smarts. It took special talents to be a straw boss in those days; the straw boss had to make a bunch of misfits who hated authority do what he said without turning them into enemies with lots of ways of getting even. Think of an open gate and dry lightning at nightfall and three hundred head of Herefords highballing for Dixie through somebody's wheat field.

Our third week on the job the hay baler starting clanking like a Coca-Cola bottle in a garbage disposal unit. Without anybody telling him, Buddy hung his hat and shirt on a cottonwood branch and climbed under the baler with a monkey wrench and went to work.

Ten minutes later Buddy crawled back out, a big grin on his face, the baler as good as new. Tyler kept studying Buddy the way a cautious man does when somebody smarter than he is shows up in the workplace. Buddy was putting his shirt back on, his skin as tan and smooth as river clay. Tyler was looking at the scar that ran from Buddy's armpit to his kidney, like a long strip of welted rubber. "Was you in Korea?" Tyler said.

"This scar? Got it up at Calgary, one second from the buzzer and seven seconds after being fool enough to climb on a cross-wired bull by the name of Red Whisky."

"You got bull-hooked?"

"Hooked, sunfished till I was split up the middle, stirrup-drug, stove-in, flung into the boards, and kicked twice in the head when I fell down in the chute."

"Mr. Wakefield needs six colts green broke. They've never been on a lunge line. You'll have to start from scratch."

"I like bucking bales just fine," Buddy said.

Tyler took a folded circular from his back pocket and fitted on his spectacles and tilted it away from the sunlight's glare. "You two boys walk with me into the shade. I cain't hardly read out here in the bright," he said.

I could feel my stomach churning. We followed him to the dry creek bed where two big cottonwoods were growing out of the bank, lint blowing off the limbs like dandelions powdering. The breeze was warm, the kind that made you want to go to sleep and not think about all the trouble that was always waiting for you over the horizon. The circular was ruffling in Tyler's hand. "This come in the mail yesterday," he said. "There's a drawing of a man named Robert James Elgin on here. The drawing looks a whole lot like you."

"I go by 'Buddy,' and I don't think that's my likeness at all."

"Glad you told me that, because this circular says 'Buddy' is the alias of this fellow Robert James Elgin. His traveling companion is named R. B. Ruger. It says here these two fellows are organizers for a Communist union."

"I cain't necessarily say I was ever a Communist, Tyler, but I can say without equivocation that I have always been in the red," Buddy said.

Tyler glanced up at the cottonwood leaves fluttering against the sky, his eyelids jittering. "Equivocation, huh? That's a mouthful. Here's what's *not* on the circular. I don't care if you guys are from Mars as long as y'all do your job. Right now your job is green breaking them horses. Is your friend any good at it?"

"I'm real good at it," I said.

"Nobody asked you," Tyler said.

I always said I never had to seek humility; it always found me.

"What's in it for us?" Buddy asked.

"Two dollars more a day than what y'all are making now. You can have your own room up at the barn. You don't smoke in or near the building and you don't come back drunk from town. You muck the stalls and sweep the floor every day and you eat in the bunkhouse."

Buddy waited on me to say something, but I didn't. I liked Wyoming and figured Tyler was more bark than bite and not a bad guy to work for; also, a two-dollar daily wage increase in those days wasn't something you were casual about. But I didn't like what was on that circular. I wasn't a Communist and neither was Buddy. "What are you going to do if we turn you down?" I said.

"Not a thing. But I ain't Mr. Wakefield. Communists are the stink on shit in Hollywood, in case you haven't heard."

Buddy picked a leaf off the cottonwood and bit a piece out of it and spat it off the tip of his tongue. "We'll move in this evening," he said. "Because I didn't get this scar in Korea doesn't mean I wasn't there. The only Communists I ever knew were shooting at me. You can tell that to Mr. Wakefield or anybody else who wants to know."

But Tyler had already gotten what he wanted and wasn't listening. "One other thing: the trainer I just run off brought a woman back from town," he said. "The only man who gets to bump uglies on this ranch is Mr. Wakefield."

"Wish I could be a Hollywood cowboy," Buddy said.

"I was at Kasserine Pass, son," Tyler said. "Don't smart-mouth me."

We moved into the room at the end of the stalls in the barn. Tucked into the corner of the mirror above the sink was a business card with Clint Wakefield's name on it. Buddy looked at it and stuck it in his shirt pocket.

"What'd you do that for?" I asked.

"I never had a souvenir from a famous person."

I didn't know why, but I thought it was a bad omen.

By midsummer the first shaft of morning sunlight in West Texas can be like a wet switch whipped across your skin. A sunrise in Wyoming was never like that. The light was soft and filtered inside the barn where we slept, the air cool and smelling of sage and wood smoke and bacon frying in the cookhouse. You could get lost in the great blue immensity of the dawn and forget there was any such thing as evil or that someplace down the road you had to die. I'd skim the dust and bits of hay off the horse tank and unhook the chain on the windmill and step back when the blades rattled to life and water gushed out of the pipe as cold as melt off a glacier. There was a string of pink mesas in the east, and sometimes above them I could see electricity forking out of a thunderhead and striking the earth, like tiny gold wires, and I'd wonder if Indian spirits still lived out there on the edge of the white man's world.

I didn't want to ever leave the ranch owned by the cowboy actor. But whenever I got a feeling like that about a place or a situation or the people around me, I'd get scared, because every time I loved something I knew I was fixing to lose it. I saw my dog snatched up by the tail of a tornado. I was in dust storms that sounded like locomotive engines grinding across the hardpan; I saw the sky turn black at noon while people all over town nailed wet burlap over their windows. I saw baptized Christians burn colored people out of a town in Oklahoma for no reason.

I saw a kid take off from a road gang outside Sugar Land Pen and run barefoot along the train track and catch a flatcar on the fly and hang on the rods all the way to Beaumont, the tracks and gravel and stink of creosote whizzing by 18 inches from his face.

I pretended to Buddy I didn't know what "it" was, and I guess that made me a hypocrite. The truth was, people like us didn't belong anywhere, and "it" was out there waiting for us.

On a July evening in Sheridan the sky could be as green as the ocean, the saloon windows lit with Grain Belt neon signs, the voice of Kitty Wells singing from the Wurlitzer "It Wasn't God Who Made Honky Tonk Angels."

The War Bonnet was in the middle of the block, right by the town square, and had a long footrailed bar and a dance floor and card tables and an elevated bandstand and Christmas decorations that never came down. There was also a steak-and-spuds café in front where a mulatto girl worked a two-chair shoeshine stand by herself and never lacked for customers. She called herself Bernadine, and if you asked her what her last name was, she'd reply, "Who says I got one?"

She was light-colored and had hair that was jet black and gold on the tips and she wore it in a big Afro that seemed to sparkle when she went to work on your feet. She wore big hoop earrings and oversized Levi's and Roman sandals and snap-button shirts printed with flowers, and when she got busy she was a flat-out pleasure to watch. I wanted to tell her how beautiful she was and how much I admired the way she carried herself; I wanted to tell her I understood what it was like to be different and on your own and clinging to the ragged edges of just getting by. Saying those kinds of things to a beautiful girl was not my strong suit.

Our second Saturday night in Sheridan I got up my courage and said, "What time you get off, Miss Bernadine?"

"Late," she said.

She touched my boot to tell me she was finished.

"That's Clint Wakefield at the bar. I break horses for him," I said.

She gazed through the swinging doors that gave onto the saloon. In the background Bob Wills's orchestra was playing "Faded Love" on the jukebox.

"I can introduce you if you want," I said.

"He's gonna put me in the movies?"

"Yeah, that could happen. You'd have to ask him, though. He doesn't confide in me about everything."

"Watch yourself getting down, cowboy," she said.

I not only felt my cheeks flaming, I felt ashamed all the way through the bottoms of my feet. The truth was I'd hardly exchanged five words with Clint Wakefield. I wasn't even sure he knew I existed. Most of the time he had one expression, a big grin. Actors train themselves never to blink. Their eyelids are stitched to their foreheads so they can stare into your face until you swallow and look away and feel like spit on the sidewalk. If you put those lidless blue eyes together with a big grin, you've pretty much got Clint Wakefield. He was leaning against the bar, wearing a white silk shirt embroidered with roses, his striped Western-cut britches hitched way up on his hips, his gold curls hanging from under a felt hat that was as white as Christmas snow. His wife was sitting at a table by herself. She was stone deaf and always had a startled look on her face. A couple of the guys in the bunkhouse said the ranch belonged to her and that Mr. Wakefield married her before his career took off. They also said he told dirty jokes in front of her, and the ranch hands had to choose between laughing and being disrespectful to her or offending him.

"Make any headway out there?" he asked.

"Sir?" I said.

"If I needed to change my luck, she's the one I'd do it with."

I could feel my throat drying up, a vein tightening in my temple. I looked through the window at the greenness of the sky and wanted to be out on the elevated sidewalk, the breeze on my face, the lighthearted noises of the street in my ears. "I'm not rightly sure what you mean."

"That's my restored 1946 Ford woody out there. Here's the keys. Take the shoeshine gal for a spin. Bring her out to the ranch if you like."

"Tyler said no female visitors."

"Tyler's a good man but a prude at heart. Your last name is Ruger? Like the gun?"

I tried to look back into his eyes without blinking, but I couldn't. "I didn't realize you knew my name."

"You carry your gun with you?"

"I'm just a guy who bucks bales and stays broke most of the time, Mr. Clint."

"I was watching you in the corral yesterday. You were working a filly on the lunge line. You never used the whip."

"You do it right, you don't need one."

He dropped the car keys in my shirt pocket. "I can always tell a pro," he said. "Bring your girlfriend on out and pay Tyler no mind. I think he pissed most of his brains in the toilet a long time ago."

I wished I'd given Mr. Wakefield back his keys and caught a ride to the ranch with the Mexicans, like Buddy did. At 2 a.m. I was drinking coffee at the counter in the café and watching Bernadine put away her rags and shoe polish and brushes and lock the drawers on her stand.

"Mr. Wakefield let me borrow his car. I think he used it in a movie," I said. "It's got a Merc engine in it that's all chrome."

"You're saying you want to take me home?"

"Maybe we could go out on the Powder River. The Indians say there's fish under the banks that don't have eyes."

"I can't wait to see that."

"Mr. Wakefield said we could go out to the ranch if you like."

"Is this your pick-up line?"

I scratched the side of my face. "I thought we'd get some bread and throw it along the edge of the current to see if the story about those blind fish is true. Fish have a strong sense of smell. Even if they're blind."

"Has anyone ever told you you're a mess?"

"Actually, quite a few people have."

She arched her neck and massaged a muscle, her eyes closed, her hair glistening as bright as dew on blackberries. "What part of the South you from, hon?"

"Who says that's where I'm from?"

"I thought that peckerwood accent might be a clue."

"The West and the South are not the same thing. I happen to be from Dalhart, Texas. That's where wind was invented."

Her eyes smiled at me. The owner had just turned off the beer signs in the windows and you could see Mr. Wakefield's station wagon parked at the curb, the wood panels gleaming, the maroon paint job on the fenders and the boot for the spare tire hand-waxed and rippling with light under the streetlamp. "How fast can it go?" she said.

"We can find out."

"You weren't lying, were you?"

"About what?"

"The man you work for being a movie star. About him asking me out to his ranch."

I looked at her blankly, disappointed in the way you are when people you respect let you down. "Yeah, he's big stuff," I said. "Maybe he'll give you an autograph."

"No, thanks. He's been in here before. He says mean things about his wife," she replied. "I just wondered who he was."

Outside, I opened the car door for her and held her arm while she got inside. The interior was done in rolled white leather, the dashboard made of polished oak. She looked up at me, uncertain.

"Anything wrong?" I asked.

"I don't know if I should do this."

"Why not?"

"Because this isn't my car. Because I don't like the man who owns it."

"You're accepting a ride from me, not from Mr. Wakefield. What's the harm?"

She gazed at the empty street and the trees on the courthouse square and the shadows moving on the grass when the wind blew. "Would you buy me a hamburger and a cherry milk shake?" she said. "I can't tell you how much I'd like that."

A half-hour later we were sitting in a booth by the window at the truck stop when four drunks came in and sat down at the counter, like a bunch of bikers coming into church with muddy boots on in the middle of a church meeting. One of them leaned over to the others and said something that caused them to glance sideways at us and laugh. Then I heard the word *nigger*. Bernadine looked out the window as though she didn't hear it. I stared at my plate, my ears starting to ping with a sound that was like being underwater too long. The steak bone on the plate had pieces of torn pink meat along the edges; it lay with my steak knife in grease that was black and streaked with blood, and it made me remember things I had taught myself not to think about, things I never wanted to see again. I stared at my plate for a long time. When I raised my eyes, two or three of the men at the counter were still watching us, like we were zoo creatures that shouldn't have any expectation of privacy or respect.

I stood up and lowered my hand down by my plate, still holding my napkin. "I'll be back in a minute," I said.

"Where you going?" Bernadine said.

I picked up my coffee cup. "Refill," I said.

"Those guys don't bother me. Leave them alone."

"That's a good attitude. There are people in this world who aren't worth spitting on. You're absolutely correct."

The drunks weren't expecting me. Their faces were bloodless in the artificial light, like white balloons that had started to go soft, the alcohol they had probably been drinking all night fouling their hearts and making their eyes go out of focus. "Hi," I said. There was a windup clock by the serving window and you could hear it clicking in the silence. "Can y'all tell me the best way to Billings?"

They wanted to look me straight in the face, but they couldn't keep their attention off my right hand and the napkin that covered the oblong object I held in my palm. I turned my gaze on the man who had made the others laugh. He had a double chin and was wiping at his nose with a paper napkin, like he had a head cold and an excuse for being gutless. He pointed at the window. "The highway is right there. It goes north to Billings and south to Cheyenne," he said.

"My vision isn't good. Can a couple of you go outside and point to it? My friend and me don't want to get lost and have to come back in here. Just walk outside and stand in the light and point, then we'll get in our car and drive away."

"What are you talking about?" the fat man said. He was breathing through his nose and there was a shine on his upper lip.

I moved my right hand onto the counter, the napkin making a tent over my knuckles. "I'm just asking two of y'all to point out the road to Crow Agency and Billings. All four of you don't have to go outside, just two of you. Y'all decide who goes out and who stays. It would be a big favor to us."

"We were telling a joke, but it wasn't about you," another man said.

"You're sure?" I said.

"Yeah. I mean yes, sir."

"I'm glad to learn that. But I still need you to show me the way to Billings, because darned if I can figure it out on my own."

The fat man walked to the window and pointed. "There's the goddamn highway. Is that good enough?"

"No, not really." I raised my hand from the counter, the napkin still draped across my knuckles.

"All right, you win," another man said. "Come on, Bill. Give the man what he wants. We were out of line. If it'll make him happy, let's go outside and put an end to this."

"I appreciate that," I said. "Tell you what, I've changed my mind. We're going to stay here and have a piece of pie." I turned toward the waitress and pulled the napkin off my hand. "This spoon has water stains on it, ma'am. Could I have a clean one?"

We went down on the Powder River, where those blind fish live way back under the cuts in the bank. The air was cold and damp and smoky from a stump fire, the sky black and sprinkled with stars. We went into a shack that had no door and no glass in the windows among a grove of cottonwoods, and lay down on some gunnysacks and listened to the trout night feed in a long riffle that came right down the center of the stream, as shiny as a ribbon of oil under the moon.

She had hardly spoken since we left the truck stop. I took her hand in mine and said her fingernails made me think of tiny seashells. "Are you a mermaid?" I said.

"You could have gotten both of us hurt back there," she said.

"I don't read it that way."

"Then you don't know very much about Wyoming."

"A man who abuses a woman is a moral and physical coward. That kind of man cuts bait as soon as you stand up to him. Truth is, I didn't feel very good about what I did back there." But I could tell that was not what was really on her mind.

"At the War Bonnet you split a paper match with your thumbnail," she said.

"Yeah, I do that sometimes." I lay back on the gunnysacks and watched a flock of birds lift out of the cottonwoods and fly low across the water, their wings drumming like they were made of leather. No, they were drumming as fast and loud as my heart. It's funny how your past always trails after you, no matter where you go.

"Where were you in prison?" she said.

"A P-farm down in Texas. I wrote a bad check for thirty-seven dollars. The gunbull sent me to get the water can off the truck and I took off through a swamp and never looked back. The mud pulled my shoes right off my feet. I rode under a freight car plumb to Beaumont."

She propped herself up on one elbow and looked me in the face. "Are you telling me the truth?"

"Who makes up lies about being an escaped convict?"

She put her fingers on my throat to feel my pulse and looked straight into my eyes. I could still smell the cherry milk shake on her breath. "You're no criminal," she said.

"I don't think so either."

She laid her head on my chest. I put my hand under her jacket and spread my fingers across her back. I thought I could feel her heart beating against my palm.

"Buddy Elgin and me are going to get us some land up in Montana," I said. "We've got a spot picked out near a place called Swan Lake. The lake was scooped out of the land by a big glacier, right at the foot of this mountain called Swan Peak. The trout in the lake are big as your arm. It's country that's still new, where you can be anything you want."

She felt the tips of my fingers, then felt between them and around the edges of the joints. "Did you ever pick cotton?"

"From cain't-see to cain't-see. Till my fingers bled on the boll and then some," I replied.

"My father cropped on shares and preached on the side. He called me a hoochie-coochie girl once and I got mad at him. He explained a hoochie-coochie girl had music inside her. He used to preach out of what he called the Book of Ezra. He said before the Flood, people ate the flowers from the fields, just like animals grazing. He said the wind blew through the grass and made music like a harp does."

"I heard about people digging up dinosaurs that had flowers in their stomachs. Maybe that's what your father was talking about. It was an article in *National Geographic*."

I heard her laugh. She curled against me and kissed the top of my hand and folded it against her breast. That's when I saw headlight beams bouncing through the trees and heard a diesel truck grinding down the dirt track, a car with a blown muffler following 30 yards behind. There was a man in a fedora on the running board of the truck; he was waving to the car to close up the gap, like they'd found what they were looking for.

I know the differences between kinds of people. The drunks back at the truck stop worked at jobs that anyone could do and went to church on Sunday with wives who had been a hundred pounds thinner in high school, and woke up every morning wondering who they really were. The man in the fedora and the two men getting out of the diesel and the three getting out of the car were guys who avoided victimhood by becoming victimizers. Hollywood actors could stare down people till they blinked. These guys could make people wet their pants.

The man who was obviously in charge was at least six-foot-five and wore a heavy cotton shirt and a yellow wool vest buttoned to his throat and a tall-crown Stetson hat of the kind that Tom Mix wore. A badge holder with a gold badge in it was hung over his belt. "You two get your asses out here," he said.

I went out first, in front of Bernadine. I heard the muted sounds of moss-covered rocks knocking together under the surface of the river, like the earth wasn't hung together proper and was starting to come apart. The windshields of both vehicles were clear of dust where the wipers had scraped back and forth across the glass. Inside the car, sitting in the passenger seat, I could see Buddy Elgin staring back at me, one eye puffed shut, swollen as tight as a duck's egg.

The man in the Stetson pulled the keys from the ignition of the woody. He looked at Bernadine and stuck his finger through the key ring. "You know what grand auto can cost you in this state?" he said.

"Mr. Wakefield let me use it," I said.

"He says you took off with it."

"That's not true. You can ask at the War Bonnet. The bartender saw him give me the keys."

"That's Mr. Wakefield setting up there in his Cadillac on the highway. You want to walk up there and call him a liar to his face?"

I knew how it was going to go. I'd been there before. I wondered how bad they had hurt Buddy. The man in the fedora opened the passenger door of the car and pulled Buddy onto the ground. Buddy's hands were cuffed behind him and his shirt was unbuttoned on his chest. He wasn't wearing his boots and in the moonlight the toes of his white socks were soggy with blood.

"We were invited to Mr. Wakefield's ranch," Bernadine said. "He probably thought we stole his car because we didn't go straight there. Ask him."

The man with the badge hooked me up, crimping the steel tongues tight in the locks, bunching the skin and veins on my wrists. He turned toward Bernadine. "If I was you, I'd go with the flow, girl," he said.

He shoved me headlong into the back seat of the car, then picked up Buddy by his hair and the back of his shirt and did the same thing with him. I saw Bernadine's face slide by the window as we drove away.

They didn't take us to a regular jail. It was a basement under a brick warehouse, with windows like gun slits that had bars high up on the wall, and a toilet without a door in one corner. The man in the fedora gave Buddy back his boots, but his toes had been stomped so bad he could hardly walk after he got them back on. At noon a man in a filling station uniform with greased hair that was combed straight back and a face like a hatchet brought us a quart jar of water and a hamburger each. He refused to speak no matter how many times we asked him what we were being charged with. "What did y'all do with Bernadine?" I said.

"*We* didn't do anything," he said. "You'd better not be saying we did, either."

He went up a set of wood steps and locked the metal door behind him. Buddy was sitting in the corner, his knees drawn up in front of him. He drank from the water jar but didn't touch his hamburger. "They're studying on it," he said.

"Studying on what?"

"What they're going to do with us."

I unwrapped the paper from my hamburger and started to eat, but I couldn't swallow. "Mr. Wakefield set me up, didn't he?"

"His wife flew out late last night to visit her mother in Denver. He thought you were going to bring the girl out to the ranch. I heard him yelling at Tyler. He was mad as hell."

"About what?"

"He wanted his way with her. What do you think?"

I couldn't believe I'd been so dumb. I'd been on the drift since I was fifteen. You learn a lot of lessons if you're young and on the drift. If you're thumbing, you find out your first day that only blue-collar people and people of color will pick you up. A rich man never picks you up, and I mean *never*, unless he's drunk or on the make. That's just the way they are. I'd gone and forgotten the first human lesson I'd ever learned.

Suppertime came and went, but nobody brought us any more food or water; if we wanted a drink, we had to dip it out of the toilet tank with the jar. The sun was a red ember inside a rain cloud when we heard somebody unlock the metal door and come down the steps, one booted foot at a time. I hoped it was Mr. Wakefield. I wanted to tell him what I thought of him, and expose him for the cheap Hollywood fraud he was. But that was not all I was thinking. I was drowning in all the memories that traveled with me everywhere I went. At age fifteen I was sent to Gatesville Training School for Boys. Nobody knows the kind of place Gatesville was. People would run from the stories I could tell. That's why even today there are nights I keep myself awake because I don't want to give my dreams power over me.

Our visitor was not Mr. Wakefield. It was the man in the Stetson; under the overhead light his hat darkened his face and seemed to give him a permanent scowl. He was dressed in an unpressed brown suit and was wearing a spur on one boot, and I could see tiny wisps of hair on the rowel. There was no sign of his gold badge.

"You," he said, pointing at Buddy. "Upstairs."

"What for?" Buddy said.

"Because you look like you have more than three brain cells."

"Anything I do includes R.B."

"Your window of opportunity is shrinking by the second, boy. Don't misjudge the gravity of your situation."

Buddy followed the man in the Stetson up the steps, trying not to flinch each time his weight came down inside his boot.

"What about Bernadine? What about *her*? Did y'all leave her out there on the river? What'd y'all do?" I said.

I got no answer. The man in the Stetson clicked off the light and the room dropped into darkness. An hour later the man in the filling station uniform came and took me upstairs and through the back door into an alley where a pickup truck was idling. Buddy was sitting in the bed, his shoulders hunched over, one eye still swollen shut. His guitar and duffel bag were next to him, and so was my old cardboard suitcase, a rope holding the broken latch together. Tyler was talking to the man in the Stetson by the side door of the building. Tyler was smoking a cigarette and listening and not saying anything, his face pointed down at the walkway. The man in the filling station uniform told me to get in the back of the truck. "Where we going?" I said.

"It's okay, R.B.," Buddy said.

"The heck it is. Where's Bernadine?" I said.

He didn't answer. Tyler dropped his cigarette on the walkway and stepped on it and approached the truck, looking right through Buddy and me.

"Buddy, you've got to tell me what's going on," I said.

"We're leaving town," he said. "If that doesn't suit you, go back to that damn ranch and see what happens."

I hadn't believed Buddy would ever speak to me like that. I thought someone else had stepped inside his skin. The Buddy I knew was never afraid. He had been with the First Marine Division at the Frozen Chosin; he'd never let a friend down and never let himself be undone by finks and ginks and company pinks. If you were his bud, he'd stay at your side, guns blazing, the decks awash, till the ship went down.

I climbed onto the truck bed and pulled up the tailgate and snapped it into place. "Is she hurt?" I said.

When he looked up at me, I knew they had busted him up inside, probably in the ribs and kidneys, maybe with a phone book or a rolled-up Sunday newspaper or a sock full of sand. "The guy in the Stetson?" I said.

"He's an amateur. They all are," Buddy said.

"Are you going to tell me what happened to Bernadine?"

"Use your imagination."

I tried to make him look into my face, but he wouldn't.

Tyler got in the passenger seat of the pickup and the man in the Stetson clanked the transmission into gear and drove us out to the train yards, both men silhouetting in the cab when lightning leaped through the clouds. I suspected rain was swirling across the hills and mesas in the east, washing the sage clean and sweeping through the outcroppings of rock layered above the canyons, threading in rivulets down to streambeds that were braided with sand the color of cinnamon. But for me the land was stricken, the air stained with the stench of desiccated manure blowing out of the feeder lots and the offal and animal hair burning in the furnaces at the rendering plant.

Tyler and the man in the Stetson watched us while we threw our gear inside a boxcar and climbed in after it. "I'm sorry about this, boys," Tyler said.

"Like hell you are, old man," I said.

Buddy sat against the far wall, away from the door, staring into space with his eye that wasn't swollen shut.

"You made a deal with them?" I said.

"They've got an antisedition law in Wyoming," he said. "I'm not going to jail because I don't know when to get out of town."

"We're Judases," I said.

"Call it what you want. I'm not the one who went off with a girl in the boss man's car and brought a shitstorm down on our heads, plus—"

"Plus what?"

"Why do you think Clint Wakefield took his Caddy down to the river? He wanted to try out a colored girl without having any social complications. You gave him total power over both us and her, so you stop trying to rub my nose in it."

My face felt as though it had been stung with bumblebees. I couldn't wait for the boxcars to shake and jostle together and begin moving out of the yard, carrying us into the darkness of the countryside, away from the electrified ugliness of the cattle pens and loading chutes and rusty tanker cars and brick warehouses and gravel and railroad ties streaked with feces that for me had come to define Sheridan, Wyoming.

We crossed into Montana and went through a long valley backdropped by sawtooth mountains that were purple against the dawn, and you could see the grass in the valley flattening as green as wheat in the wind. The wheels of the boxcar were clicking louder and louder as the locomotive gained speed, and I thought about Bernadine and her father and the story she had told me about the wind blowing through a field that was like a grass harp and I wondered if I would ever see her again.

The train followed the Yellowstone River and by midmorning we were climbing the Continental Divide, over 6000 feet high, the hillsides littered with giant broken chunks of yellow rock and spiked with ponderosa pine and Douglas fir trees, the wheels of the boxcar screeching and sparking on the rails as we slid down the west side of the divide into Butte. We caught a hotshot straight into Missoula and thumbed a ride up to Flathead Lake, where you could make twelve to fifteen dollars a day picking cherries on a ladder in orchards that fanned up from the lake onto the hillsides and gave you a fine view of water so green and clear you could count the pebbles on the bottom.

I tried to forgive Buddy and forgive myself for what had happened in Wyoming, but unfortunately the conscience doesn't work like that. We'd bailed on Bernadine. But how could I make it right? If we went back there, Buddy could end up in prison as a syndicalist, a man who had the Silver Star and a Purple Heart. Then something hit me, the way it does sometimes when you least expect your thoughts to clear. Buddy and I were standing on ladders, deep inside the boughs of a cherry tree, the lake winking at us from down the slope, the sun spangling through the leaves, and I blinked once, then once again, and realized I'd been taken over the hurdles. "How'd those guys know you were a union organizer?" I said.

"I guess they have their ways."

"No, they don't. They're dumb. The only one who knew was Tyler Keats. I didn't make Tyler for a fink."

"Search me. I'm done thinking about it," he said. His eyes were fixed on his work, his fingers picking the cherry stems clean of the branch, which was the only way cherries can go to market.

"They told you they were going to send you to the pen as a Communist agitator, but you never asked where they got their information?" I said.

"I don't rightly recall, R.B. How about giving it a rest?"

"It wasn't you they were going to send up the road. It was me."

"What difference does it make? They were holding all the cards."

"Somebody called down to Texas and found out I'm an escapee."

He climbed back down his ladder, his canvas bucket brimming with cherries, his shoulders as wide and stiff as an ax handle. "Clint Wakefield raped Bernadine," he said. "They got us out of town so we couldn't give evidence against him. The real issue is Wakefield's reputation. The guy is a western hero. He knows guys like us cain't send him to the pen, but we *could* smear his name, so he got us out of sight and out of mind."

"Where is she?"

"Probably at work. What is she going to do? Stop living? Quit fretting on what you cain't change."

"Why didn't you trust me enough to tell me the truth?"

"Because you're a hardhead. Because you would have stayed in Sheridan for no purpose and ended up in a joint like Huntsville Pen."

I stepped down from my ladder and followed him to the water can the labor contractor kept on the tailgate of his truck. The wind was cool in the sunshine, the lines of sweat drying on Buddy's face. He filled two paper cups with water from the can and handed one to me, his gaze never meeting mine. I could tell there was something he hadn't told me.

"Wakefield is right on the other side of the mountain, over on Swan Lake. He's got a cottage there," he said. "They're shooting a western at the foot of Swan Peak."

"You're making this up," I said.

"Here's the rest of it. I talked to Bernadine. I mailed her some money for a bus ticket. She'll be here tomorrow. I thought you might like that."

I didn't know what to say to her when she got off the bus, and I didn't try. I think Bernadine was one of those people who didn't expect a lot from the world. It was Saturday and there was a dance and cookout up by the motel where a lot of the pickers stayed during cherry season. We drank wine out of fruit jars and ate potato salad and barbecue pork and pinto beans and homemade ice cream a church group brought. The moon came up big and yellow over the mountains and you could see fireflies lighting in the aspens and birch trees down by the water. Buddy got his old Stella twelve-string from the motel and sat in with the country band, and started playing one Woody Guthrie and Cisco Houston song after another. I guess I should have known what he was thinking about. Buddy came out of the coalfields of eastern Kentucky and would be a radical and labor agitator till somebody put pennies on his eyes. No matter what the circumstances, there was always a vinyl record playing in Buddy's head, over and over again, and the lyrics weren't written by Hank Williams or Lefty Frizzell.

About 9:30, when the summer light at the top of the sky began to fade into the density and color of a bruise, I picked up Bernadine's hand under the picnic table and curled my fingers in hers. "I'm sorry for leaving you behind in Sheridan," I said.

"You couldn't have changed anything. Nobody there is going to stand up to Clint Wakefield."

In my mind I kept seeing the things he had probably done to her. But I couldn't bring myself to ask how bad she had been hurt, or how, or where, or if she was suffering now. "Did you talk to any cops?" I said.

"His lawyer called me a liar. When I left the sheriff's department, I looked back through the window and saw the deputies I'd talked to. Clint Wakefield was with them. The three of them were laughing."

"I'm going to make him pay for what he did."

She took her hand from mine. "Not on my account you won't."

"In Gatesville Training School I saw boys killed for a whole lot less. I know where there are unmarked graves. Things happened there that I don't ever talk about. If Clint Wakefield was a boy, he wouldn't last a week in Gatesville."

I saw the fatigue in her face, and realized I was making her re-
live not only the assault on her body but the theft of her soul. The
air had turned cold, and the candles burning in the jelly jars were
flickering and about to go out. I took off my denim jacket and
draped it over her shoulders. "We got you your own room at the
motel," I said. "It's a dollar and a half a day, but it's right nice."

"What's that song Buddy's singing?"

"'Union Maid.'"

"Songs like that get people in trouble," she said.

"You bet they do."

"Why does he sing them?"

I shook my head as though I didn't know. But that wasn't the
case. I *knew*. Buddy was going to spit in the soup for all of us. And
he wasn't through with Clint Wakefield by a long shot.

A week later we had moved to the orchards higher up on the lake,
close to Bigfork. The cherries were so red they were almost black,
and our crew picked truckloads of them from first light until shadows covered the trees and made it hard to pick the cherry and the
stem cleanly from the limb. Bernadine and Buddy and I worked
as a team, and would talk to each other inside the leafy thickness
of the tree, like kids playing on a summer day rather than adults
working at a job. I couldn't help noticing that Bernadine paid a
lot of attention when Buddy talked, even though the subject matter seemed to roam all over creation, from the Garden of Eden to
Jesus and Joe Hill and ancient highways in Montana he said primitive people had used even before the Indians showed up.

"There're two or three roads under the lake," he said. "If you
look carefully along the banks, you can see the worn places in the
rocks where people rode over them with carts that had wooden
wheels. They were probably going to the glaciers, right across the
lake, where all those buttercups are."

"How do you know all this?" Bernadine asked.

"You trust what your eye tells you and then you have to believe
in things you cain't see," he said.

"Believe what?" she said.

"That all these things happened and are still happening. We
just cain't see them. Maybe those ancient people are still living out
their lives all around us."

There was no question about the expression on Bernadine's

face. She was looking at Buddy in a way she had never looked at me. I wanted to climb down my ladder and dump my bucket in one of the boxes on the flatbed and keep walking all the way back to the motel, or maybe just head on up the road to British Columbia.

"You're kind of quiet, R.B.," he said.

"The conversation is obviously over my head. Excuse me. I got a crick in my neck," I said.

When I walked to the truck, the pair of them were buried from the waist up in the cherry tree, talking like they already knew what the other one was going to say, like they could talk on and on now that they didn't have to stop and explain themselves to a third party. I felt a spasm in my innards that made my eyes cross.

There was nothing unusual about Buddy organizing farm workers, but it was unusual for him to try it with the cherry pickers, particularly in the orchards along Flathead Lake in a remote area like northwestern Montana. The cherry harvest was a one-shot deal that offered at best only a few weeks' employment, and the people who did it were a strange mix—drifters like us, wetbacks, college kids, Romanian Gypsies, and white families from Oklahoma and Arkansas who weren't interested in politics or unions.

The most successful attempts at union organizing always took place within shouting distance of a metropolitan area. Union people organized in the San Joaquin Valley, but they operated out of San Francisco or sometimes Fresno or Bakersfield. The fort was never far away. Did you ever hear of anybody organizing cotton pickers in Mississippi? Why didn't they? There was no fort. The labor organizers' life expectancy would have been about five minutes.

Buddy started by distributing leaflets in a bar where a lot of the pickers hung out. The bartender told him to lose the leaflets or hit the bricks. "No problem. Give me a shot and a Grain Belt back, will you?" Buddy said. "Did you know Clint Wakefield was making a movie over on Swan Lake?"

The bartender didn't reply. He had cavernous eyes and the hands of a man who had pulled the green chain or boomed down fat ponderosa logs on a semi or dug postholes in twenty-below weather. His eyes seemed to smoke when he stared back into Buddy's face.

"It's a fact," Buddy said. "I know Mr. Wakefield personally. He's looking for a saloon to shoot a couple of scenes in."

"Wonder why he didn't mention it when he was in here," the bartender said. His eyes drifted to the front window. "That's him, across the street, signing autographs. Why don't you say hello?"

Buddy and I walked outside into the evening shadows and the coolness of the wind blowing off Flathead Lake. The mountains that loomed over the water had turned dark against the sun and looked edged with fire on the peaks. Clint Wakefield was standing by his 1946 woody, wearing a white western-cut suit and hand-tooled boots and a black vaquero hat that had small white balls hanging from the edges of the brim. I was glad Bernadine was down at the drugstore and in all probability had not seen him. I could only imagine what she would feel looking at the man who had raped her. My own feelings were such that I could barely deal with them. It was like looking at somebody you saw in your dreams but who disappeared at daylight and was not quite real. But here he was, flesh and blood, standing on the same street, breathing the same air we did, people gathering around him like flowers around a toadstool. His trousers were hitched up so you could see the thickness of his penis against his leg. He signed autographs with a grin at the corner of his mouth but glanced at his watch like he had to get on the road in the next few seconds. Even in the gloaming of the day, his eyes were blue orbs that had the brilliance of silk when they settled on a young girl's face. I had to clear my mouth and spit.

I began to see things that I thought I had left at Gatesville, things I believed were not a part of my life anymore and that were not me and that had been imposed by mistake on my boyhood. I saw myself walking into a concrete latrine in my skivvies, a shoe-polish handle outfitted with a sharpened nail file gripped tightly in my palm, the sound of a flushing toilet as loud as Niagara Falls.

"You got any ideas?" I said.

"I think I'll get in line," Buddy said. "I've never gotten the autograph of a famous person."

I couldn't move. I kept staring at Clint Wakefield, who was no more than 30 feet away from me, my pulse jumping in my throat like a crippled moth. I thought he recognized me, then realized he was squinting into the last rays of the sun and probably couldn't see past the glare. When it was Buddy's turn to get an autograph, I stepped forward so Wakefield would see us both at the same time. I heard Buddy say, "Would you write 'To my pal Bobby James,' please, sir? Actually the full name is Bobby James Elgin of Pikeville, Kentucky."

The grin never left the corner of Wakefield's mouth when he wrote on the back of the leaflet Buddy had given him. He didn't speak when he handed it back to Buddy, either. Maybe his eyes lingered two seconds on Buddy and then on me, but that was it. Who or what we were and the damage he had done to us either didn't register on him or wasn't worth remembering.

I put my hands in my pockets and followed Buddy back across the street and stepped up on the high sidewalk in front of the saloon. Down the street I could see Bernadine coming out of the drugstore. "Let's get her out of here," Buddy said. "Did you hear me? Stop looking at Wakefield."

I wanted to say, *I aim to fix him proper.* I wanted to show people what it's like to carry a stone bruise in your soul. I wanted to give him a little piece of Gatesville, Texas.

I felt Buddy's fingers bite into my upper arm. "You get rid of those thoughts, R.B.," he said. "You're my bud, right? We don't let others take power away from us."

Bernadine was walking toward us, her dress swirling around her knees in the wind, proud of the new silver belt she had notched tight around her waist.

No, we just take away our best friend's girl, I thought.

"*What* did you say?" he asked.

"Not a dadburn thing," I replied.

That night Buddy did something that I thought was deeply weird, even for him. He sat down at the small table in our motel room and studied the inscription Wakefield had written on the back of Buddy's leaflet, then took out his wallet and removed the business card he had found tucked into the mirror above the lavatory in Wakefield's barn. He started writing on the back of the business card, then realized I was watching him. "You're standing in my light," he said.

Two days later we started seeing new pickers on the job. All of them were white and looked like hard cases; a Gypsy said they

were from the stockade down in Sanders County, working off
their sentences at a dollar and a half a day. That night we saw a
new '53 Ford parked across the two-lane from our motel. Dried
mud was splattered on the fenders and tags, and two guys in
suits and fedoras were sitting in the front seat, smoking cigarettes. Buddy came away from the window and turned out the
light.

"Goons?" I said.

"No, feds."

"How do you know?"

"County cops don't have vehicles like that. Climb out the
back window and get Bernadine and stay gone for a while. I'll
handle it."

"We'll handle it together."

"You're an interstate fugitive. Maybe these guys have already
found your jacket. They can put you on a train to Huntsville."

I tried to hide my fear by clearing my throat, but I felt like somebody had just dipped his hand in my chest and squeezed my heart
into a ball of red gelatin. "Well, what's stopping them, then?" I
said. "Let them do whatever they damn want."

"Your thinking powers are questionable, R.B., but nobody can
say you're not stand-up. Before those guys knock on the door, I
want to know what's been eating you. I thought you'd be happy
when Bernadine arrived."

"She likes you more than she likes me."

"That's not my perception."

"You see things out there in the world other people don't. So
does she. Y'all are a natural fit. It's just kind of hard for me to accept that."

"I don't have any idea what you're talking about."

"She believes in stuff about primitive people eating flowers
instead of killing animals and the wind singing in the grass and
something called the Book of Ezra, whatever the hell that is."

"That sounds like you talking instead of her."

"I just repeat the kind of stuff you and other crazy people talk
about. Mastodons and sea monsters and cave people throwing
rocks at each other and such. You ought to listen to yourself. You
put me in mind of somebody living in a comic book."

"Bernadine didn't tell me any of this, R.B. She told it to you.
You sure she's right in the head?"

I didn't know what to say.

The knock on the door shook the wall.

The agent who entered the room didn't bother to remove his hat or give his name; he smiled instead, as though that was enough. He was so tall he had to stoop under the frame. He had long fingers and knobby wrists and small teeth and no color in his lips, unless you wanted to call gray a color. He opened the flap on a government ID and closed it quickly and returned it to his coat pocket.

"Could I see that again?" Buddy said.

"No," the agent said. "You must be Elgin."

"That's me," Buddy said. "Why's the other guy standing outside?"

"He's got a fresh-air fetish. He doesn't like places that smell like a locker room. You know what the McCarran Act is?"

"Something a senator down in Nevada put together to keep working people in their place?" Buddy said.

"No, more like a law that requires representatives of the Communist Party to register as such."

"Then I guess I'm not your huckleberry. Sorry you had to drive out here for nothing."

"Who are *you*?" the agent said to me.

"R. B. Ruger."

"Wait outside."

"This is my room."

"It *was* your room. It's mine now." He smiled again.

I sat down on the side of the bed. "If you don't mind, I think I'll stay."

The agent opened the bathroom door and looked inside, then looked in the closet.

"When did you start rousting guys like us?" Buddy asked.

"You're like a bad penny, Mr. Elgin. Your name keeps going across my desk. We don't have labor problems here. I think you'd like Seattle or Portland this time of year. Or even Salt Lake City. Or did something happen in Salt Lake City?"

"Yeah, Joe Hill got shot by a firing squad," I said.

I glanced through the front window. The other agent was gone. I could hear my blood start to pound in my ears.

"Is there a problem, Mr. Ruger?"

I stood up from the bed, my ears ringing, the backs of my legs shaking. I wasn't good at going up against guys who wore suits and badges. My words were clotting in my throat.

"You worried about your shine?" the agent said.

"What?" I said.

"You heard me."

I wanted to believe he had said something about a shoeshine girl, but I knew better. "She doesn't have anything to do with unionizing people," I said.

Buddy took his billfold from his back pocket and thumbed open the pouch where he kept his paper money. "Did you know we have friends in high places?" he said.

"Dwight Eisenhower, somebody like that?"

"No, better than that. A famous Hollywood actor. You don't believe me? He's one of us, not just up there on the screen but down here in the trenches." Buddy took Clint Wakefield's business card from his wallet and handed it to the agent. "Check it out. See what happens if you try to push Clint around."

The agent held the card in the flat of his hand and stared at the words written on the back. I leaned forward just long enough to read them too:

Dear Buddy,
      Keep up the good work. Call me if the feds come around. I'll have them transferred to Anchorage.
      One big union,
      Clint

"Keep it," Buddy said. "See if that's not his handwriting. He's over on Swan Lake. Go talk to him. Get in his face and see what happens, Mack."

"I might do that. By the way, we talked with your boss about you guys. You might get a cigar box to go with your guitar."

"We were looking for a job when we found this one," I said.

The agent laughed to himself as he left. I went down to Bernadine's room. When she opened the door, the side of her face was filled with creases from the pillow. "I'm sorry I woke you up," I said.

"I was having a bad dream," she said. "Land crabs were trying to tear us apart."

The neon VACANCY sign in front of the motel lit up in orange letters. Maybe it was coincidence. Or maybe I was losing my mind. "I killed a kid when I was fifteen. It's haunted me all these years," I said.

I went inside her room and told her all of it: the boys who wrapped a horse blanket around my head and arms and dragged me into a stall and stuffed my shirt in my mouth and spread-eagled me face-down over a saddle; the staff member who gave them permission because I sassed him, and smoked a cigar outside while they did it; the boys who spit in my food and put chewing gum in my hair when I was asleep and shoved me down in the shower and called me Anybody's Pork Chop; the ringleader nicknamed Frank the Blank because he had only one expression and it could make you wish you hadn't been born.

Frank's upper lip wedged into an inverted *V* when he smiled, exposing his teeth. His face was as white as a frog's belly and sprinkled with purple acne, his eyes like wide-set green marbles. When I found him in the concrete latrine, he was sitting on the commode, his jeans and Jockey underwear bunched around his ankles. He looked at what I was carrying in my right hand and couldn't have cared less. He stood up and tucked in his shirt and buckled his jeans. "Go into the shower and wait for me," he said.

I didn't know what he meant. That's how dumb I was. No, that's how scared I was.

"This is your big night. It's just you and me," he said. "You can fold one of those rubber mats under your knees."

Then I saw myself going outside of my skin, just like I had left half of me behind to be a spectator while another me attacked Frank and did things to him he thought would never happen. I saw the surprise and shock in his face when the first blow hit him; I saw the meanness go out of his eyes and I saw the helplessness in his mouth when he realized something had gone wrong in his voice box and that his cry for help had become a gurgling sound he couldn't stop. I broke off the shank inside him and pulled the cover off a shower drain and dropped it down the pipe.

I told Bernadine all these things while she sat on the side of her bed and trembled with her hands between her knees. "Don't say any more," she said.

"I'm not the guy you think I am," I said. "I feel ashamed because I left you behind in Sheridan. I feel ashamed of what I did in Gatesville."

"If you hadn't left, they would have killed you. Lie down next to me."

"I see Frank the Blank in my dreams sometimes. He still has that surprised look on his face, like he'd gone backward in time and was a little boy again and couldn't believe what was being done to him."

"You're a sweet boy, R.B. Now lie down and go to sleep," she said.

And that's what both of us did, side by side on top of the covers, while a rain shower swept across the lake and tinked on the windows and the cherry trees, and the orange VACANCY sign blinked on and off inside the fog.

Buddy and I got fired from the orchards and went to work for a man who made log houses and shipped them as kits all over the country. I got a driver's license and we cut and hauled and planed trees north of Swan Lake, up in the timber and cattle country where he and I had always hoped to buy land and start up our own ranch. But Buddy wasn't going to let go of his vendetta against Clint Wakefield. He made telephone calls to two or three newspaper reporters, who blew him off, then wrote a letter to a gossip columnist in Los Angeles and told her Wakefield was under investigation by the FBI for possible Communist activity.

I thought he was spitting into the wind. What kind of credibility did a pair like us have?

One month later big piles of monkey shit hit the fan for Clint Wakefield. The gossip columnist used professional snoops to look into his past. One of his ex-girlfriends was on the Hollywood blacklist; another said Wakefield's mother was from Russia and had a picture of Joseph Stalin in her home. A male prostitute said Wakefield had invited him to a western movie set in San Bernardino, on a Sunday, for private riding lessons.

The Polson chapter of the American Legion flushed a Labor Day speech he was supposed to make. A reporter at the local newspaper called up Wakefield's press agent and asked where he'd served during the war years. The press agent said Westfield had been deferred as the sole supporter of his family but had dedicated himself to doing volunteer work with the USO. Not in the South Pacific or even London. In Los Angeles.

On a Saturday afternoon in the last week of August, the boss paid us our salary and as an afterthought told us to deliver a truck-load of fence posts and rails to a cherry grower on Flathead Lake. We picked up Bernadine at the motel and dropped off the fence materials and decided to take a ride down to Swan Lake and have dinner at a roadhouse where Bugsy Siegel and his girlfriend Virginia Hill used to hang out. The shadows of the ponderosas and fir trees were long across the two-lane highway, the lake glimmering like thousands of bronze razor blades in the sunset, the tips of Swan Peak at the south end of the lake white with fresh snow. It was a grand way to end the summer, with a case of longneck beer on the floor of the truck, chopped-up chunks of ice jiggling between the bottles, and Buddy snapping off the caps with an opener he'd tied on a string around his neck.

Up ahead, on a slope where a group of asbestos cottages were nestled in a grove of beech trees, we saw Wakefield's movie cast and film crew eating their dinner at picnic tables. There were Indians in feathered bonnets and buckskin clothes, and cowboys in costumes no cowboy would wear, and women dressed like cowgirls with ribbons in their hair, and platters of fried chicken and dark bottles of wine on the tables. They made me think of carnival people, in the best way; there was even something lovely about them, like they had created something out of a West that had never existed. I suspected they were at the end of filming and were having a party to celebrate. We saw no sign of Wakefield.

"Keep going," Bernadine said. She was sitting between us, a warm beer balanced on her knee.

Buddy drained his beer bottle and set it on the floor. "Pull over," he said. "I want to talk to these guys."

"Why borrow grief?" I said.

He opened the glove box and took out a sheaf of the same pamphlets that had gotten us fired from the orchards, and I knew Buddy was going up on that knoll and fix it so the whole house came down on all of us.

"If you're not up to it, bag it down the road, R.B.," he said. "I'm staying."

"It's a bad idea," I replied.

"One big union," he said.

After I slowed the truck to a stop, he got out and walked into the beech trees, his body bent forward, like he was leaning into a wind.

"I have to go with him," Bernadine said.

"I don't want to hear that."

"He's your friend."

"That's what I mean. My friendship with him keeps getting us in trouble."

"Then why do you stay with him?"

"Because he's the best guy I ever knew."

That was the history of my life: trapped one way or another. I got out of the truck and slammed the door. Then I went around to the other side of the cab and helped Bernadine down.

"Most of these are union workers, aren't they?" she said.

"Of course not. Film companies make movies in Canada or out in the sticks so they can use scab labor."

"I didn't know that."

"Am I the only sane person here?"

Like it or not, we followed Buddy into the trees. I had heard his speech before. The reactions were always the same: curiosity, amusement, sometimes a thumbs-up, and sometimes the kind of anger you don't want to mess with. People don't like to be told they're selling out their principles by going to work at the only job that's available to them. It's not like what you'd call a mild yoke to drop on somebody. You got screwed by the bosses when you tried to feed your family, then a nutcase shows up and tells you you're a traitor to the working class. That's not what Buddy said, but I suspect that's what they heard.

"Ginks" is the name union organizers gave heavies back in those days. They came out of the shade like flies on pig flop. I saw Clint Wakefield emerge from a cottage and stand on the porch and watch it all, his hands on his hips, the shoulders of his white satin cowboy costume embroidered with stars on a field of dark blue. I knocked a guy down with a rock and almost tore his ear loose, but that didn't help us. They knocked me down and kicked me in the head and shoved Bernadine and me back onto the road and slapped me silly against the truck. They grabbed Buddy by his arms and stretched him across a picnic table and smashed the backs of his hands with wine bottles. They broke the windows in the truck and pushed me behind the steering wheel, then picked Bernadine up in the air and threw her in the passenger seat.

I could see Buddy struggling up the knoll, his T-shirt torn off his back. There was nothing I could do to help him. I got the truck started and into gear and gave it the gas, the frame lurching over some large rocks, the lake glittering with thousands of tiny metallic lights through the fractured windshield. There was spittle on Bernadine's face and in her hair. Her eyes had a darkness in them that was like water at the bottom of a stone well.

One mile down the road, the needle on the oil pressure gauge dropped to zero and smoke poured from under the hood and streamed through the firewall into the cab. I had ripped out the oil pan on the rocks. We were both choking when we got out on the asphalt, our knees weak, the truck useless, all our means of escape taken from us. The sun had disappeared behind the mountain on the far side of the lake, and the wind was cold and cutting long lines across the water and smelled like fish roe, as though winter had descended unfairly upon us.

Then I saw Wakefield's 1946 woody come down an embankment, skidding through saplings onto the asphalt, almost going into Swan Lake. The woody fishtailed, the rear tires burning rubber on the road surface, and came straight at us. I thought Wakefield had gone on a kamikaze mission and was about to take us out in a head-on collision and a blaze of gasoline. I should have known better. Wakefield was a survivor, not a self-destructive avenger. The woody skidded to a stop and Buddy leaned out the window, a lopsided grin on his face. "I boosted his car. Grab a few beers and pile in," he said. "These guys are in a nasty mood."

Nasty mood?

We roared northward, toward the top of the lake, the Merc engine humming like a sewing machine, the twin Hollywood mufflers rumbling on the asphalt. The sky had turned dark by the time we crossed the bridge over the Swan River and reached the highway that bordered the eastern rim of Flathead Lake. We could have turned right and kept going to the Canadian border, but somehow I knew Buddy would choose otherwise. Maybe for some people the book is already written and a person becomes more a spectator in his life than a participant. I'm not qualified to say. But we'd signed on with Buddy Elgin and I figured however it played out, we'd be together one way or another.

The ginks blocked the road halfway down the lake. We turned off on a gravel lane and headed toward the water. "What the hell are you doing?" I said.

He stopped the car and cut the lights but left the engine run-

ning. I could see small waves sliding up on a beach at the end of
the lane. "You guys jump out," he said. "Head back through the
cherry trees and keep going north. They'll be chasing me."

"What are you doing, Buddy?"

"Watch."

"Don't leave us."

"You don't need me anymore. Take care of each other. Stomp
ass and take names, R.B."

"Listen to him," Bernadine said, pulling on my arm.

And that's the way he left us, powering down the lane, full throt-
tle, the woody in second gear, the windows up, the high beams
back on. When he dipped into the water the woody went straight
down the incline, the exhaust pipes bubbling, the sediment from
the lake bottom rising in a gray-green cloud.

We moved off into the trees and continued to watch as the ginks
ran to the water's edge and stared in disbelief at the headlights
crossing the lake bottom. But what Bernice and I saw next was not
the same thing the ginks saw, or at least what they later claimed
they saw. They said the woody never made it to the other side of
the lake, that it was dredged out of the water the next morning by
a wrecker, full of mud and weeds. They said Buddy had drowned
and that his body was still at the bottom, probably near Wild Horse
Island. I saw the woody come out on the far shore, the high beams
still on, water spilling out of the exhaust pipes. Buddy had said
there were ancient highways under the lake, and I knew that's how
he had crossed over and that one day he'd show up just as sure as
the sun comes over the mountain.

That's why Bernadine and I live way up here in Alberta, where
the golden poppies grow on Lake Louise, and the wind and the
animals drift through the grass, just like they would in a dream. We
didn't cross Jordan, but at least we made it to Canada.

PATRICIA ENGEL

Aida

FROM *The Harvard Review*

THE DETECTIVE WANTED to know if Aida was the sort of girl
who would run away from home. He'd asked to talk to me alone
in the living room. My parents stood around the kitchen with the
lady cop and the other detective, an old man who looked to be on
his last days of the job. They were telling my parents Aida would
walk through that front door any minute now. She probably just
got distracted, wandered off with some friends. Our mother wasn't
crying yet but she was close. I sat in the middle of the sofa, my
thighs parting the cushions. The detective sat on the armchair
our mother recently had reupholstered with a fleur-de-lis print because the cat had clawed through the previous paisley.

He looked young to be a detective. He wore jeans with a flannel
shirt under a tweed blazer even though it was August. He wanted
to know if Aida ever talked about leaving, as if she had plans beyond this place, something else waiting for her somewhere.

I shook my head. I didn't tell him that since we were eleven,
Aida and I had kept a shoebox in the back of our closet that we
called our Runaway Fund. The first year or two we added every extra dollar we came across, and when our piles of bills became thick
and messy we took them to the bank and traded them for twenties.
We planned to run away and join a group of travelers, sleep under
bridges beside other refugee kids and form orphan families like
you see in movies and Friday night TV specials. Those were the
days before we understood how much our parents needed us. Aida
insisted on taking the cat with us. Andromeda was fat but could fit
in her backpack. Aida had lied to our parents and said she found

the cat alone one day by the river behind the soccer field, but she'd really bought her at the pet shop with some of our runaway savings. I didn't mind. The cat always loved her more than me, though.

"Does she have a boyfriend? Somebody special?"

She didn't. Neither did I. Our parents told us boys were a big waste of time and we kept busy with other things. School. Sports. Jobs. Painting classes for Aida and piano lessons for me. Our parents said just because we were girls who lived in a small town didn't mean we had to be *small-town girls*.

"Did she have any secrets?"

"Not from me."

"Even twins have secrets from each other."

He made me tell him all over again what happened, even though I'd gone through it several times in the kitchen while the old man detective took notes and the lady cop leaned against the refrigerator, arms folded across her blockish breasts. The young detective said he'd keep whatever I told him in the strictest confidence. "If there's something you left out because your parents were around, now is the time to tell me, Salma."

"There's nothing," I said, and repeated all I'd already told them. How Aida was coming off her summer job as a gift-wrapper at the children's department store at the bottom end of Elm Avenue, while I was sweeping and cleaning the counters before closing at the coffee shop on the top end, where I worked the pastry case. We had this routine: whoever finished their shift first would call to say they were on their way to the other. Or we'd meet halfway at our designated third bench on the sidewalk in front of Memorial Park and we'd walk home together. That night, a little after seven, Aida had called and said, "Sal, I'll come to you." When she didn't show up, I took my purse and walked across the intersection to the park. I sat on our bench for a few minutes before walking the periphery of the park to see if maybe she'd run into some kids from school. Aida was friendly with everyone. Even the dropouts most everyone in town avoided, though they hung around the bus station and liquor store and you couldn't walk through the park without getting a whiff of their weed. Aida had a smile for everyone. People liked her. Sometimes I got the impression they just tolerated me because we were a package deal.

I called her phone but she didn't answer, then I tried our parents to see if they'd heard from her. It started from there. The calling around. Probably for the first time ever, the town employed that emergency phone chain where each person is assigned five others to call, to see if anyone had seen Aida. Around here, you can't get a haircut without it being blasted over the gossip wires, but nobody knew where she was. This is a town where nothing terrible ever happens. There are perverts and creeps like anywhere else but never an abduction or a murder. The worst violent crime this town ever saw beyond an occasional housewife wandering the supermarket with a broken nose or split lip was back in 1979, when one sophomore girl stabbed another with a pencil in the high school cafeteria.

The old man detective reminded us we had the good fortune of living in one of the safest towns on the East Coast. "This isn't some third-world country," he told our mother. "The likelihood that your daughter was kidnapped is extremely remote." He told our parents it was common for teenagers to test boundaries. If he only had a dollar for every time a parent called looking for a kid who it turned out had just taken off to a rock concert at the Meadowlands or hopped in a car with some friends and headed down the shore. And it'd only been four hours, he emphasized. Aida couldn't have gotten very far. Our mother argued that four hours could take her to Boston, to Washington, D.C., so far into Pennsylvania that she might as well be in another country. Four hours was enough to disappear into nearby New York City, her dark pretty face bleeding into millions of others. But the old detective insisted, "Four hours is nothing, ma'am. You'll see. You'll see."

Our mother and father arrived late to parenthood. Our mother was a spoiled Colombian diplomat's daughter who spent her childhood in Egypt, India, Japan, and Italy. She never went to university but was a dinner party scholar, a favorite guest, and indulged her international friendships for two decades of prolonged escapades in Buenos Aires, Los Angeles, London, Marrakesh, and Barcelona. She had many boyfriends, was engaged three or four times but never married. She was a painter for a while, then a photographer and an antique dealer. She sometimes worked in boutiques or found a man to support her, though she never wanted to be tied down. She was thirty-eight when she met our father in a Heathrow airport bar. He was a shy history professor from Marseille who'd written three books on the Marranos of the sixteenth century. She thought he was boring and lonely yet stable, tender, and adulating—everything she needed at that particular moment in her life. They married and tried to have a baby immediately, but our mother had several disappointments until she received the good news of twin girls at the age of forty-four. We were born during our father's sabbatical year in Córdoba. Our mother said those prior broken seeds had been Aida and me but neither of us was ready for our debut.

"You were waiting for each other," she told us. "You insisted on being born together."

Our father never liked when she talked that way. He said she was going to make us think we had no identity outside our little pair. Our mother insisted this was the beautiful part of twinship. We were bound to each other. We were more than sisters. We could feel each other's pain and longing, and this meant we'd never be alone in our suffering. When Aida was sick, I'd become sick soon after. Our father blamed it on practical things like the fact that Aida and I shared a bedroom, a bathroom, and ate every meal together. Of course we'd pass our germs around, be each other's great infector. But our mother said it was because we were one body split in two. We'd once shared flesh and blood. Our hearts were once one meaty pulp. Our father would scold our mother for her mystical nonsense and our mother would shoot back that he was always dismissing her; just because she didn't have fancy degrees like he did didn't make her an idiot. She'd cry and it would turn into the song of the night, with our mother locking herself in the bathroom and our father calling through the door, "Pilar, don't be like that. I just want them to know that if anything should ever happen, they can live without each other."

He wanted us to be individuals while our mother fought for our bond. We knew we held a privileged intimacy as twins, but Aida and I were never exclusive. We had other friends and interests away from each other, yet it only made our attachment stronger, and we'd run into each other's arms at the end of each day, reporting every detail of our hours apart.

Ours was a brown Tudor house on a slight hill of a quiet block lined with oaks. Aida and I lived in what used to be the attic. It was a full-floor room with slanted ceilings and strange pockets of walls so we each had niches for our beds, desks, bookshelves, and dress-

ers, with a small beanbag area in the center. There was an empty
guest room downstairs that either of us could have moved into,
but we didn't want to be separated, even as Aida's heavy metal
posters took over her half of the walls and she started to make fun
of my babyish animal ones. We liked living up there even though
it was hot in summer and cold in the winter. We couldn't hear our
parents' late-night fights once we turned our stereo on. Every now
and then we'd lower the volume just to check in, see how far into
it they were so we could gauge how long before we'd have to go
downstairs to help them make up.

Aida and I considered ourselves their marriage counselors. It
was like each of our parents had an only child; I was my father's
daughter and Aida belonged to our mother. When the fights became so bad we weren't sure they could make it back to each other
on their own, Aida and I would assume our roles. I'd find our
father alone in his study, hunched over his desk or slumped in
the leather reading chair staring out the window at nothing. Aida
would go to their room, where our mother was always on the bed
lying fetal in her nightgown. Aida would tell me that our mother
would often ask her who she loved best, and Aida would declare
her devotion to our mother and say that if our parents ever split,
Aida and our mother would run off together to Paris or Hong
Kong. Aida would always tell me this part laughing, because we
both knew she would never leave me and I would never leave our
father. That was our trick. That's how we kept our family together.

Fliers of Aida's face went up on every telephone pole and shop
window in town. Though the detectives briefly tried the idea that
she'd run away, it was a missing persons case. The police searched
the town. The detectives made rounds of the homes of all Aida's
friends. They focused on the boys, especially the ones with cars.
But Aida wouldn't have gotten into a car with someone she didn't
know. Our mother was mugged in Munich in the seventies and
sexually assaulted behind a bar in Majorca in the eighties. She
raised us on terror stories of vulnerable wandering women being jumped by aggressive, predatory men. We were each other's
bodyguards, but when alone, which was hardly ever, we were both
cautious and sensible, even in this stale suburban oasis. If held at
gunpoint, Aida would have run. She had long muscular legs, not at
all knock-kneed like me, and the track coach was always trying to

get her to join the team. Aida was a brave girl. Much braver than me. She would have screamed. She would have put up a fight. She would not have simply vanished.

A group of local volunteers quickly formed to comb the grass of Memorial Park, hunt for witnesses, go to every apartment and storefront with a view of the avenue and back alleys. The story made it to the evening news and morning papers, and a tip line was set up for people to phone in. Our parents didn't leave the kitchen. Our mother waited, an eye on the front door, for Aida to show up in yesterday's clothes. Several people called and said they'd seen her the night before just as the summer sky began to darken. She was in cut-off shorts, brown leather boots, and a white peasant blouse that had belonged to our mother. They'd seen her at the bottom of Elm and someone else had seen her further up, approaching the park. She was alone. But someone else saw her talking to two young guys. Someone saw her later on. A girl in cut-off shorts and brown boots walking along the far side of the park across from the Protestant church. But she was in a blue shirt, not a white one. That girl, however, was me.

Aida and I hadn't dressed alike since we were little girls and our mother got her fix buying identical dresses to solicit the compliments of strangers. But the day she disappeared we'd both put on our cutoffs, though every time we wore them our mother warned we'd grown so much they were pushing obscene. We'd also both put on our brown gaucho boots, sent to us from one of our mother's friends from her bohemian days in Argentina. We were both running late for work that day and that's why neither of us decided to go back upstairs to change.

One of the volunteers found Aida's purse by the Vietnam veterans' monument in the middle of the park. Her wallet was inside, though emptied, along with her phone, the battery removed. Our mother wanted to take the bag home, but the police needed it for their investigation. The only other things they found were her lip gloss and a pack of cigarettes, which was strange because Aida didn't smoke. Chesterfields, our father's brand, probably swiped from the carton he kept on top of the fridge. The box was almost empty. I would have known if she'd been smoking, and our parents wouldn't have particularly minded. They were liberal about those sorts of things—the benefit of having older parents. They served us wine at dinner and spoke to us like colleagues most of the time, asking our opinions on books or art or world events. They'd trained us to be bored by kids our own age and to prefer their company over that of anyone else. We had no idea how sheltered we really were.

In the days that followed, there were more sightings of Aida. Somebody saw her cashing a check at the bank. Somebody saw her cutting through the woods along the train tracks. Somebody saw her by the river behind the soccer field. Her long dark hair. Her tan bare legs in those same frayed shorts, though this time she was wearing sandals. And each time our parents would have to tell them it wasn't Aida they'd seen. It was her twin.

Three different people called to say they'd seen her, the girl whose photo they recognized from TV and the papers, hitchhiking on a service road off the turnpike near the New York State border. Someone else had seen her at a rest stop a few miles down. A woman had even said she'd talked to Aida at a gas station in Ringwood and only realized it was her after she caught the news later that night. She'd asked Aida where she was headed and Aida had said north, to Buffalo.

Aida didn't know anybody in Buffalo and she'd never take off. Not like that. She worried about everybody else too much. When we were little she would say goodnight to every stuffed animal in our room before falling asleep, without skipping a single one so she wouldn't hurt anyone's feelings. She wouldn't leave the house without letting everyone know where she was going. I'd joke that she had separation anxiety and she'd say, "No, that's just love, you moron." Even so, after I heard the bit about Buffalo I went up to our room and knelt on the closet floor until I found our old shoebox under the dusty pile of plush animals. It was empty, but I knew she couldn't have taken our money with her. Two years earlier we'd used the savings to buy our parents an anniversary gift of a sterling silver frame for their wedding picture. We'd depleted the funds but started adding money to the box again. Not much. Just dollars whenever we had some to spare. We didn't think of it as our Runaway Fund anymore but as our petty cash. Maybe she'd used it for something and had forgotten to replenish it.

In Aida's absence, Andromeda howled around the house the way she had before she got spayed. She slept in Aida's bed next to her pillow, as if Aida were still there, nestled under the covers.

She purred against my knee and I ran my hand over her back, but she stiffened and looked up at me, hissing and showing her teeth before running off, and I knew she too had mistaken me for my sister.

Aida and I turned sixteen a month before she disappeared. The other girls in town had lavish sweet-sixteen parties in hotel ball-rooms or in rented backyard tents. Aida and I didn't like those sorts of parties. We went when invited and sometimes danced, though Aida always got asked more than me. We were identical, with our father's bony nose and our mother's black eyes and wavy hair—tall, dark, and Sephardic all over, as our parents called us —but people rarely confused us. Aida was the prettier one. Maybe it had to do with her easy way. Her trusting smile. I've always been the skeptical one. Aida said this made me come off as guarded, aloof. It made boys afraid to get near.

We were both virgins but she was ahead of me by her first kiss. She'd had it right there in our house during a party our parents hosted when our mother's jewelry collection got picked up by a fancy department store in the city. She could call herself a real designer now, not just a suburban hobbyist, selling her chokers and cuffs at craft bazaars. One of her friends brought her stepson, who'd just failed out of his first semester of college. Our father was trying to talk some wisdom into the kid, whose name was Marlon, and inspire him to go back. Later Aida arrived at Marlon's side with a tray of crudités. For a virgin, I'd teased her, she had her moves. She brought him up to our attic cave and he'd gotten past her lips to her bra before our mother noticed she was gone from the party and found the two of them unzipped on our beanbags. A minor scandal ensued. Our mother called him a degenerate ped-ophile in front of the whole party, and his stepmother said Aida was too loose for her own good. After all the guests had left, our mother sat us down at the kitchen table and warned Aida and me that the world was full of losers like Marlon who'd come along and steal our potential if we weren't careful, while our father just looked on from the doorway, eyes watery for reasons I will never know.

Neither of us was ever interested in the boys at school, though. Sometimes we'd have innocuous crushes, like Aida's on the gas sta-tion attendant up on Hawthorne Avenue or mine on the head lifeguard at the town pool, boys who were just out of reach. But our parents had always told us we were better than the local boys, suburban slugs who would peak in their varsity years and come back to this town to be coaches or commuters. We, on the other hand, were sophisticated gypsies, elegant immigrants, international transplants who spoke many languages. We had our mother's inherited Spanish, Italian, and quasi-British private school inflections and our father's French and even a bit of his father's Turkish. The fact that we'd settled here was incidental, temporary, even though Aida and I had been here all our lives.

"You're not like them," our mother would say every time we were tempted to compare ourselves to the local crowd.

For our sixteenth birthday our parents took us to the Mostly Mozart Festival at Lincoln Center. It was a warm July night. During the intermission we went out to the fountain so our father could smoke a cigarette and Aida and our mother drifted up toward the opera to look at the hanging Chagalls. I stayed with our father. I asked him to let me have a smoke too, like I always did, because it gave him a laugh, though he never gave in. But that night, even though we were supposed to be celebrating, he was somber.

"I don't want you to pick up any of my bad habits, Salma."

Sometimes our father put things out there, like he wanted me to push him to say more, but I wasn't in the mood.

I'd always been his confidant, like Aida was our mother's. For a while now, he and our mother had been doing well, hardly any fights. Aida said the Angry Years were behind us. The crying, the oversensitivity, the accusations, the hysteria. Aida said our mother was too romantic for our father. He didn't appreciate her capricious moods and found them unnecessary. Aida said that it had nothing to do with our father's affair but something deeper between them and that our mother was too progressive to get hung up on infidelity. She'd found out the usual way when the girl, one of our father's students, called our house and told her she was in love with her husband and that he wanted to leave her.

I'd had my suspicions since the day our father was promoted to chair of his department and our mother decided this was our father's way of undermining her intelligence yet again. She'd locked herself in their bedroom, but instead of pleading to her through the door, our father went out to the backyard to smoke, and when

I arrived at his side he looked at me and said, "Can I tell you some-thing, baby?"

He only called *me* baby. Never Aida, whom he called darling.

"I don't love your mother anymore."

"Yes, you do."

He shook his head. "No, I don't."

I never told Aida. She thought she had our parents all figured out. When we later discovered love notes in his briefcase from his college girl, Aida said it was probably just a crush gone wrong. It would pass, she said; our parents were too old to leave each other and start new lives. They'd eventually accept that this marriage was the best they could do. I let her have her theory. But I knew my father truly loved that college girl, even if just for a moment, and even if it had nothing to do with who she was but with who she wasn't.

It was the end of the summer. Another week until I started eleventh grade and our father was due to go back to the university for the fall semester. Our mother said I didn't have to go to school anymore. I could be homeschooled, work with tutors, and spend my days in the house with her. Watching. Waiting. She hardly ate. She drank sometimes. Just a bit to wash down her Valium, which she hadn't taken in over a decade, but one of her Manhattan friends showed up with a vintage vial for the rough nights. Our father didn't try to stop her. He was drinking and smoking more than usual too, as if with Aida gone we'd become short-circuited versions of ourselves.

I wasn't sleeping so much as entering a semiconscious space where I'd talk to my sister. Our mother believed someone was keeping Aida prisoner. In a shed. A garage. A basement. In a wooden box under a bed. I tried to picture her in her darkness. I knew wherever she was she'd be able to hear me speak to her in my mind. Our mother used to buy us books on telepathy. She said it was one of our special twin gifts. We'd play *Read My Thoughts* games in our bedroom every night. We learned to speak to each other silently from across a room and know what the other was thinking. In seventh grade, when Aida fell off her bike, I knew it before the neighbor from across the street spotted her hitting the curb. I'd felt her fainting, her fall, the impact of the sidewalk hit-ting her cheek, the sting of broken skin and warm fresh blood.

I waited for the pain. Something to tell me what was happening to Aida. I tried to feel her. I wanted to make our bodies one again. Remember that her veins were once my veins and her heart was my heart and her brain was my brain and her pain was mine. I waited for the sensations. I wanted them to hit me and within them I'd be able to know the story of her disappearance. I'd know who stole her. What they were doing to her. How they were punishing her.

I knew she was alive. Otherwise something in me would have signaled her death. If she'd been hurt or tortured or even killed, my body would have turned on itself. One of my limbs would have blackened. My fingers and toes would have contorted or my skin would have bubbled up in boils and cysts. I didn't dare consider the possibility that I could be like the starfish, a self-healing amputee capable of regeneration.

I heard the phone ring downstairs. Aida and I had our own line in our room, but it hardly ever rang. The family line never quit until night, when the calls cooled and our house fell into a cemetery silence. I heard footsteps and knew it was our father. Our mother hadn't been up to our room since the day Aida went missing, when she searched her drawers for a diary, photographs, or letters. I think our mother was hoping Aida wasn't as good as we all thought she was. She searched for evidence, anything that would give her a suspicion, a place to look. I watched her rummage through Aida's drawers and even accuse me of hiding things, but I told her, just like I'd told the detective, Aida didn't have a secret life beyond the one we had together under those lopsided attic walls.

Our father pushed the door open. I never bothered closing it all the way. His eyes avoided Aida's half of the room, and he settled onto the edge of my bed. I was lying above the covers with my day clothes on even though it was close to midnight. I thought he was just coming in to check on me, since I hadn't bothered saying goodnight. He wouldn't look at me, his chin trembling.

"They found her shirt." He folded over and cried into his hands.

I sat up and put my arms around his shoulders as he choked on his breath.

Later I'd learn that her shirt was ripped almost in half and was found stuffed into a bush behind the high school parking lot. I, however, took this as a good sign. A sign that Aida was real again, not the lost girl in danger of becoming a legend, the girl people were starting to get tired of hearing about because it made them scared and nobody likes to feel scared. A ripped shirt meant she'd resisted. But it also meant she was up against someone brutal. The high school parking lot meant she'd been close to us that first night. So close we might have even passed by her when I went out with our father in his car to retrace her steps and mine to every familiar place. The school grounds were empty that night. I'd stood out by the bleachers and called her name. I'd felt a lurch inside my chest, but around me there was only silence, wet grass, a low moon. On the ride home our father had driven extra slow while I stuck my head out the open window hoping to see her walking on the sidewalk or under the streetlights, making her way home.

"We moved out here because we thought it would be safer for you girls," our father had said as if to both of us, as if Aida were curled up in the back seat.

We took a long time to get out of the car after we pulled into the driveway. Our father turned off the headlights and kept his fingers tight around the wheel. I wanted to tell my father it would be okay. We'd walk into the house and find Aida sprawled across the sofa just like last night when we sat around together watching dumb sitcoms. I wanted to tell him Aida had probably gone off with other friends. I didn't mind that she'd forgotten about me. My feelings weren't hurt. I wanted to tell him we shouldn't be mad at her for making us all worry like this. I wanted to tell him nothing had changed, everything was just as it had been the day before, Aida, guiding our family like the skipper of a ship through choppy waters, reminding us all to hold on to each other.

I didn't go back to school right away and never went back to my job at the coffee shop. Our friends came by less and less, and I understood it was because there was no news. Our father went to work but I spent the days in the house with our mother. I followed the home school program and did my assignments with more attention than I'd ever given my studies before. Aida was always the better student. It took some of the pressure off. When I wasn't studying, our mother and I orbited each other with few interactions. Sometimes I'd suggest we do something together. Go to a midday movie or watch a program on TV. Sometimes I'd bring up a book I knew she'd read just to give her the chance to talk about anything other than Aida, but she never took me up on any of it. She spent most afternoons in a haze, drifting from bed to kitchen to sofa to bed, taking long baths in the evenings when I thought she might drown herself accidentally or on purpose. The people in town were still holding candlelight vigils at the Memorial Park every Friday night in Aida's honor, but our mother never went. I went twice with our father, but we agreed that turning Aida into a saint wasn't going to bring her home any faster.

The vigils continued, though, and the volunteers kept searching the wooded areas around town, the shrubbery along the highway, the vacant buildings and abandoned lots next to the railroad tracks. The reporters kept the story in the news, and when they found her shirt the TV stations wanted a statement from our parents, but they were too broken down to talk, so our next-door neighbor, whose dog once tried to eat Andromeda, spoke on their behalf. The police wouldn't let me do it because they didn't want whoever had Aida to see me and know there were two of us out there.

Sometimes people brought us food. Casseroles, lasagnas, hero sandwiches. The church ladies dropped mass cards for Aida in our mailbox. The department store where she worked set up a fund in Aida's name to help send some kid to art school, and there was a community initiative to raise money to contribute to the reward my parents had already publicly offered for Aida's safe return or information about her disappearance. Our father said we should be grateful to live in such a supportive and generous town, but our mother resented it. She hated that she was the one, the mother who'd lost the daughter. She hated that her life, which she'd curated so meticulously, had become something else. Her Aida was no longer her Aida but a story that belonged to all of them now. But our father didn't want us to come off as unappreciative, so he took me aside and told me I was in charge of writing thank-you notes, and on every note I was to sign our mother's name.

Aida and I had a plan. After high school, we'd go to college in Manhattan. I'd go to one of the universities and study history and she'd go to one of the art schools. We'd share an apartment and get jobs near each other so we could see each other for lunch or meet after work like we did here in town. We'd make extra money by signing up for twin research studies like we always wanted to do, though our father never let us. We'd never live apart. We'd have to meet and marry men who could get along like brothers and tolerate our bond with good humor. If not, we'd be happy to live as a twosome forever. We'd move back in with our parents and look after them in their old age. It wouldn't be so bad.

Our mother liked to think she raised us to live in a bigger world, but Aida and I only wanted a world together. Our father tried to undo this attachment early on by sending us to separate summer camps, but Aida and I protested until they finally let us go to one in New Hampshire together. It didn't become a trend, though. Aida and I quickly figured out that our absence had led our parents to the brink of divorce. When we returned, our father was sleeping in the guest room. I urged him to offer endless bargain apologies—for what, I had no idea—and Aida encouraged our mother to forgive, and after she was done forgiving to forgive some more.

I often wondered how our parents survived six years alone together before our birth when they had so little in common. "It's just love," Aida would say, as if that explained everything. She always had more answers than I did about why things were the way they were, so one day I asked her if she would love me this much if I wasn't her twin, and she didn't hesitate before telling me, "It's *only* because you're my twin that I love you this way."

The night our mother caught her on our beanbag with Marlon, Aida told me that being kissed for the first time was like being shot in the chest. I said, *That doesn't sound very nice,* but she assured me it was—the feeling of being ripped apart followed by a beautiful hot internal gush. In the early days of her disappearance, our mother's suspicions had gone straight to Marlon. His father and stepmother lived a few towns over and he hadn't yet gone back to school. The police looked into it. Marlon admitted that after their encounter he and Aida had called each other a few times, which I never knew, but he insisted they'd never seen each other again. He had a solid alibi for the night Aida disappeared in his stepmother, who said he'd been home watching television with her. As the months passed, our mother became obsessed with him, regularly phoning his stepmother to call her a liar and Marlon a monster, until the lady filed a complaint and the police told our mother she had to stop harassing them or else.

Every now and then we'd get word of another sighting. Someone saw Aida in Texas the same day she was also seen in Seattle. There was a spotting in the next town over, down the shore, up in the Ramapo Mountains, and down by the reservoir. The police followed these leads but they all led to nothing. Even as the reward money increased, there was no solid theory for what might have happened to her. The locals started worrying maybe there was a serial killer on the loose, but that would suggest Aida was murdered and there was no body. The reporters liked to say that for the missing girl's family the worst part was not knowing, but our mother always said that not knowing preserved hope that Aida would soon come home, and hope is never the worst thing. Our mother warned the police and detectives not to use words like *homicide* in our house. Aida was alive. She might be half dead, broken apart, mutilated, and of course she would never be the same, but Aida was alive, and unless the police could present her cadaver as proof, we were not allowed to think otherwise.

At dinner our mother pushed her food around her plate. We didn't bother nagging her to eat anymore. Her hunger strike was for Aida, who she was sure was being starved in some psychopath's home dungeon. Sometimes she had visions. She saw Aida chained to a radiator crying out for help. She saw her bound and gagged in the back of a van, being driven down some interstate far from us. She saw Aida drugged, captive in a dingy den, man after man forcing himself on her.

Our mother never left home in case Aida returned after escaping her captor, running to our house, where she'd find the door unlocked, our mother waiting with arms open. Even at night our mother insisted on keeping the door ajar. Our father told her it was dangerous, but she said she feared nothing now. Everything she loved had already been taken from her.

A few days into December we got the call that a hiker up in Greenwood Lake found Aida's boots. They were ruined from months of rain and snow, but the police took them for analysis. Just like with her purse, there were no discernible fingerprints, but Aida's blood

was found in trace amounts. It could have been from before. A
cut. A picked-over bug bite that left a smudge of blood on the
leather. After all, our mother offered, Aida had that terrible habit
of scratching an itch until it became an open sore. Or the blood
could have come after.

I slept with my identical pair of boots for weeks after that. I held
them to my chest and closed my eyes, waiting for images to burn
across my mind, but they never came. I spent hours in bed staring
at Aida's half of the room, still afraid to cry because I told myself
you only cry for the dead.

That Christmas passed like any other day. The year before, Aida
and I had helped our mother with the cooking while our father
fumbled with the fireplace and played old French records, but this
year there was no music and the three of us ate reheated food delivered by the townspeople. Our parents floated around the house
avoiding each other while I divided my time between them, then
alone upstairs in our room with Andromeda. Days earlier, a documentary-style crime show called, asking if they could do a one-
hour special on Aida's disappearance with family interviews and
all. They assured us it wouldn't be tacky or macabre and said that
in a few cases their shows had helped witnesses to come forward
with information about the disappeared. Our father had agreed,
but when he told our mother I could hear all the way in the attic
as she cried out, "What do they want from me? There's nothing
left for them to take."

Our father thought publicity would be good for Aida's case.
The campaign to bring her home, like some POW, was down to
its final embers, and the detectives had recently come by to warn
our parents with weak, well-meaning smiles that there was a good
chance we might never know what happened to her. They encouraged us to join a support group and gave us a list of all sorts of net-
works for families of missing people. But our mother insisted that
because Aida was alive, that kind of publicity would force whoever
had her to cause her more harm or finish her off out of fear of
being caught. She didn't trust the media, believing their stories on
Aida were meant to sell papers rather than find her. She regularly
accused the detectives of incompetence, calling them small-town
sleuths who never investigated more than a stolen bicycle and who

secretly wanted to abandon Aida's case because it tarnished the town's "safe" image. She considered all the neighbors suspects. Every man who'd ever met Aida was a potential kidnapper or rapist, and every woman a jealous sadist. It was a community conspiracy. It was because we were outsiders. It was because Aida was so perfect that people wanted to hurt her. It was because we never belonged here that they wanted to hurt us. Our father didn't disagree with her anymore. I wondered if it was because he'd given up trying to reason or if it was because he was starting to believe her.

I celebrated our seventeenth birthday twice. Our mother was finally willing to leave the house for hours at a time, so she took me to dinner at an Indian restaurant in town. For dessert the waiter brought me a mango mousse with a candle jammed into its gooey surface. I smiled at our mother. I knew she was making an effort. She held my hand as I blew out the candle. It was strange to see her thin finger free of her wedding band.

When we walked back to the car a group of kids driving fast down Elm shouted, "Hi, Aida!" They did this sometimes when they saw me around; whether it was a sincere error in recognition or just to torment us, I never knew. Our mother pretended not to hear them. She was getting stronger about these things.

That weekend I celebrated again with our father. He took me to Mostly Mozart again, and this time he offered me a cigarette by the fountain. He'd moved out two months earlier. He swore to our mother it wasn't for another woman but because he just needed to be on his own, to discover who he really was. Our mother turned to him with a stare that was somehow vacant while containing the sum of her life.

"If you don't know who you are by now, my love, not even God can help you."

He rented a small, dark studio near the university. It had an interior view, a Murphy bed, and a kitchen with no stove. It was all he could afford as long as he was still paying the mortgage on our house in the suburbs, and there was no way, as long as Aida remained unfound, that our mother would let him sell it.

He admitted to me that he'd been planning to leave our home since long before we lost Aida. He loved us, he said, but he always felt wrong among us, out of place, as if he'd made a wrong turn somewhere. He said there was a time when he thought he and our mother would grow closer from the pain of Aida being gone, but he was tired of trying and tired of hoping.

"You understand, baby," he said, and I was embarrassed to tell him I didn't.

"You're all grown up now. Only another year and you'll be off to college. There will be new beginnings for all of us."

We still didn't know how to talk about Aida. I asked him, because I knew he would tell me the truth, if he thought we'd ever find her, or at least know what happened to her.

"No. I don't."

Just like our mother couldn't go on without Aida, I knew the only way our father could hold on to her was by letting go.

Later that summer some teenagers getting high up on Bear Mountain came across what they thought was a deer carcass and started poking around until they spotted a human skull. When the forensics results came back conclusive, the newspapers decided, as if they were the judges of such things, that our family could get closure now, find some peace in knowing the search was over, and Aida's broken, abandoned body could finally be laid to rest. The community held a big public memorial at the same spot in the park where they'd held all their vigils, but our mother insisted that Aida's funeral service be kept private. And so we sat on a single pew before the altar, watching a priest who never knew her bless my sister's pine casket, the four of us together in an otherwise empty church for the first time since our tandem baptism, though our family was far from religious and, if anything, Aida and I were raised to believe in only what is seen.

A few days before Aida's remains were found, I walked slowly through the park on my way home from school the way I often did in a sort of meditation, whispering her name with each footstep, wondering what would become of us, what would become of me, all those empty years spread out ahead in which we were supposed to go on living without her. Across the brick path I saw a pair of kids chasing pigeons and I thought of my sister, the way she would have walked over to them and explained with her boundless patience that it was wrong to scare helpless animals, they belonged to nature just as much as two-legged wingless folk did and had the right to live without fear of unreasonable human violence. And then I heard her call my name, loud, with laughter just beneath it, the way she would call to me when we'd meet each other halfway after work, her airy voice rushing through the mosaic of dried leaves on the wilting grass, shaking the naked branches overhead, then departing just as quickly as it came, leaving the park and every breath of life within it entombed in stillness. Anybody else would have called it the wind, but me, I knew it was something else.

ERNEST FINNEY

The Wrecker

FROM *The Sewanee Review*

I'M SITTING AT THE BAR in the semigloom of the Silver Dollar, as far away as I can get from the loud music. A babe comes through the door. It's still before nine; too early for anyone else to be eyeing the sign taped to the bar mirror: NOBODY'S UGLY AT 2 A.M. I watch her in the mirror. She looks around—a dozen or so patrons, the usual crowd. The Dollar is still a workingman's bar, no video games, no retro pinball machines, no happy hours, no grill. The clientele comes from the big Basque bakery next door and what's left of the failed industrial park down the road where I live. About a fourth of the customers are women: after eight hours of unloading ovens in 110-degree heat, they're here to replace body fluids, and they're not romantically inclined, but that's weekdays. Fridays—paydays—like tonight, and Saturday nights are different.

This woman is dressed mostly in white. Blond, probably in her late twenties, shapely. Stunning. If we're looking her over, she's looking us over too, unhurried, calm, unaware of the effect she's having, or maybe just used to it. Her eyes are adjusting to the low fluorescent lights and the kind of alcohol-induced boredom that takes the place these days of outlawed cigarette smoke. The woman walks over and sits down beside me.

I look what I am: a forty-three-year-old tow-truck owner and operator. Tall, like my mother's brother. I went through the windshield of a Camaro when I was a kid and the scars crisscross both sides of my face. I briefly thought I was tough, and got my nose broken twice while I was in the army. I stay in shape because I'm crawling around wrecked cars night and day. My hair is thinning on top, which I don't notice too often. Even in my driver's license photo, I look normal.

I'm still in uniform, my dark blue coveralls with *Dwight* over the pocket and the name AAACE TOWING stitched across my shoulders. I don't stutter; I can spell; it's AAACE so my ad in the yellow pages will be first, stand out. Trust me, it makes a difference. I'm in a competitive business.

I'm thinking this woman might be part of the fallout from the book about the Silver Dollar written eight years ago by a sociology professor at one of the local colleges. We called him Doc; he liked that. He'd bring his seminar class in on Saturday nights. Cellophane-wrapped young women and men, untouched, who turned everyone's head, as if we'd all got a magic wish: twenty years off our ages, young enough to act foolish again. We learned words like *ambience* and *acculturation*. When the book came out, *Closing Time at the Silver Dollar*, you couldn't get in the place; it was jammed with gawkers. Local TV kept doing segments, and the newspapers never passed up a chance to mention the place. City officials, politicians, famous athletes—you name it, they were there. Everyone knows the rest of the world wants to come to California, but not necessarily to the capital. A tour bus full of people from Warsaw, Poland, stopped here once. Our part of Sacramento had never seen anything like it. Larry had to hire two more bartenders. We locals from the neighborhood were left outside. It didn't last; a year, eighteen months. It was like a blackout: the electricity goes, you're left in the dark, the lights come on, it's over; and you go back to where you were. A brief interruption. Doc still comes around—misses the camaraderie of the Dollar, he says—and shares his opinions and keeps track of things. He's the one who taped the other sign on the bar mirror: NEVER GO TO BED WITH ANYONE WHO'S GOT MORE PROBLEMS THAN YOU. SIGMUND FREUD. Sex and money are his usual topics.

I'm perplexed. Good-looking babes don't usually sit next to me or hit on me. If I'm surprised, Larry, the owner and bartender, is in shock. He moves toward us like he's afraid to come too close. "Give me what he's having, and hit Dwight again," she says. She puts down a fifty-dollar bill. The jukebox is still playing, but it's quiet now, like we're waiting for someone. I have to look in the bar mirror at our reflection. She speaks to my image in the mirror. "Do you remember me?"

Nowhere in my memory bank do I have this woman. It's like there are four of us in the conversation, the two in the mirror and the two of us sitting on the stools. I'm confused, and I shake my head.

"You came out when I was rear-ended by those drunks in April. On 99 by the Fruitridge exit."

I remember. I'd heard the CHP call on the scanner and raced out there to beat out the other tow trucks. Five belligerent drunks, too many for the CHP patrolman. Backup was on the way. The drunks were blaming the woman for being in their way. The cop had cuffed one, but another had jumped on his back, and a third had him around the legs. The two other drunks were chasing the woman. Normally I don't participate in crashes. I don't stop the bleeding or console the bereaved. And I never ever subdue the unruly. What I do is tow your car and sweep up the broken glass, an added service for the state. Cops like that. But this time I say to the drunks chasing the woman, "Hey, slow down; you're just making it worse for yourselves." The big one pauses to spit a stream of tobacco juice in my face. I lose control and head-butt him. My forehead smashes his nose, and he goes down. The other one lets go of the woman and tries to punch me, and I kick him in the nuts. I'm too pissed off to stop there. I pull the guy off the CHP's back and punch and kick him into silence. The CHP clubs the other drunk. Quiet. It's three o'clock in the morning—no traffic, no gawkers slowing down to stare. Between the red glare from the road flares and the smoke, it's like the blacktop is burning. I back up my wrecker and tow the drunks' car away. End of story. How could I forget this woman?

"I want to thank you, Dwight. I didn't get a chance that night."

"That's okay." Smooth as always. She's sipping the beer but knocks back the shot of bar whiskey and pushes the shot glass toward Larry, who nearly kills himself rushing over to refill her glass. "Give us a bag of chips," she says, and when she opens the bag she slides it toward me so we can both partake. We take turns, chip for chip. I wish I could think of something to say, but I can't. But the silence isn't awkward; its like we've known each other a long time and talk isn't necessary anymore. I don't know what I'm expecting, but I turn my pager off.

"From now on, Dwight, I want you to call me Jamie."

She's waiting for a reply. I speak to her image in the mirror. "All right, Jamie."

Licking her fingers, she whispers, "I know who you really are."

I'm not taken aback by the statement. I catch on now. She thinks I'm part of the Petrov family. We exchange looks in the mirror. I nod. A couple of years back the Petrovs ran supreme in the tow-truck business on 99 from Stockton to Redding. They were from somewhere in the former Soviet Union, and there must have been at least 120 in the extended family; there was even a seventy-eight-year-old grandmother who got indicted. You get the picture. I got hired just before the ring got busted, started working for Nick Petrov in the storage yard about half a mile from here. This was after the army had given me a medical discharge but denied me any benefits—I had problems from the Gulf War, which should have been a 65 percent disability. Anyway, I was a trained diesel mechanic, and I did maintenance on the Petrov trucks for eleven months, until the place was raided.

It turned out the Petrov family wasn't just towing wrecks or disabled cars. They had extended their business by towing expensive cars out of driveways and parking lots and taking them to their storage yards. The owners, assuming their cars were stolen, reported their loss to the cops and insurance companies. After an appropriate wait, the Petrovs sent the owners a bill for storage fees at a hundred dollars a day, and took the owners to small claims court if they protested the fees. If it got messy and an owner tried to fight back, his car disappeared into one of the chop shops to be sold for parts. It had been going on for twenty years.

About thirty-five of the Petrovs got indicted and sentenced. Mr. Petrov got twenty-three years; the grandmother, who I'd met once, fourteen years. When the state was ready to sell some of the Petrovs' properties, I was ready to buy the yard I'd worked at. It was going cheap: the light-industry park by then was mostly vacant buildings with fading FOR LEASE signs. I'd received three years back medical payments from the VA, enough for a down payment on the half-acre storage yard with shop, office, and apartment. All I had to do was change the name to AAACE TOWING.

When Jamie stands up, and says, "Let's get out of here," I'm not the only one who's surprised when we walk out of the place together. She clicks the doors open on a black Mercedes convertible parked in front. I still can't think of anything to say, but it doesn't matter as we glide under the streetlights. I don't come much to this part of Sacramento where we're driving, but I remember that Ronald Reagan lived around here when he was governor.

I'm too unsettled to see much of the living room because I'm sitting on a white sofa with my greasy boots on her white rug. The place is just too big to take in. She's standing in front of me, hands on hips, looking down at me. She is so perfect. It's the only word I can come up with. She is beyond anything I can imagine. "I want you to do something for me, Dwight." I wait for more. "I have two brothers who are cheating me. I want you to beat the shit out of them for me." The words don't convey any real message to me. "When the time comes I'll give you more particulars." I'm still waiting for a sentence I can grasp. It isn't the drink. I'm not hammered. "I know I can find you at the Silver Dollar."

She pauses. "Go home now, Dwight. I'll call a cab." And that's what she does, walks me to the street, gives the driver some money, and says goodnight. I have the cab let me out at the Dollar. When I step through the front door there is a spontaneous burst of clapping and someone says, "That a boy." I give them a low bow in return.

When I was a kid I stayed one whole summer with my mother's aunt, Carmen, who ran a bar, the Dog House. Some guy owned it, but he was too old to put up with all the aggravation that comes with the business. It was situated near the old Governors' Mansion, and there were stories that the first Governor Brown used to cross the street in his bathrobe to use the swimming pool at one of the motels opposite the mansion. The Dog House was about a half-mile away from where the Silver Dollar is now. We lived upstairs over the place, and I could hear the music from the jukebox as I fell asleep. I had little jobs, separating the empties into their own beer boxes, sweeping, swamping the place out, taking the trash to the Dumpster. This was in the eighties. I begged my mother to let me stay with Carmen.

Once she opened, I wasn't allowed in the bar. In the daytime we'd go to eat at what Carmen called greasy spoons, restaurants in the neighborhood, anything from Chinese to the Pronto Pup Palace. Carmen didn't cook or drive. We walked everywhere. She had been everything—from a waitress on roller skates at a drive-in to a welder in the shipyards during the war. At night, after she opened, I'd climb up on the roof of the place once it got dark and watch through the skylight, through smoke so thick it was like looking down through the clouds. I'd hear the jumble of conversations above the music, and I would speculate about the people down there. Who was the drunkest. The best-looking woman. I couldn't wait to join this crowd; it all seemed so exciting. I didn't understand that nightlife is artificial—this whole business of looking for a good time, real or imagined, such a small part of what matters.

I stick around for another beer, but I leave early. I'm pretty sure I'll see Jamie again. It's just a matter of time. I usually check in at the Dollar a couple of nights a week, working my way through the smokers gathered outside the entrance, most of them looking through the glass door as if they're missing something. There's a butt can outside and a bench, and also a fine spray of mist to cool the smokers off. It gets hot in Sacramento in the summer, and humid.

I don't see Jamie until Saturday. She comes in like last time and sits down next to me. I'm wearing better clothes this time, ones I bought for my mother's funeral. Larry is attentive, wiping the bar top in front of us with a clean towel. Everyone is cool, not staring too openly. Jamie will never belong here.

"How have you been, Dwight?"

"Pretty good." I'm cool. We knock back our shots. We sip our beer, crackle a few chips. I'm waiting for her to start up, give me the next installment.

"My family owns one of the largest vineyards in the Sacramento Valley, twenty-three thousand acres. Our grapes are made into jug wine. We're not some cute Napa Valley boutique winery making vintage wines. We make the bulk wine winos drink. We sell our grapes to small wineries who pretend they're the ones who grew the vines. No one gives us gold medals at the state fair.

"When my father died, he left me and my two older brothers each a third of the business. They sent me to school to get me out of the way. I'm the one with a degree in viniculture and the MBA from USC, and they want me to run the tasting rooms, jolly the tourists into buying cases of our three-dollar wine."

I've heard a lot of grievances in bars: spouses vs. spouses, sib-lings, whole families battling over houses and jewelry and pet dogs. There is a certain similarity in the stories. I listen. She only pauses to sip her beer. She's not ordering any more whiskey. She's all business now. I'm realizing she's like everyone else, except for the amount of money her family plays with.

I've been so worked up about the chance she might show up tonight, I've forgotten supper. When she pauses, I ask, "Are you hungry?" The Greek place a street over delivers, so we order pizza and eat it at the bar. She's hungry too. "Sometimes I'm so pissed off at my brothers I forget to eat," she tells me.

We stop chewing eventually, and she wipes her mouth with a napkin. "Let's go to your place, and I'll fuck your brains out." I agree to that, although I've heard the line before.

I've partaken in the closer-relationship thing before. It always starts out with such enthusiasm on the part of both persons—a letting go, a release. You think this one will last forever. Jamie and I do all the things you do with someone new: laugh a lot, shower together, drink more, eat more, screw like we just invented it. We tell each other our life stories, the less important parts, as if we are rushing to get through the first week before the newness rubs off. And I almost stop wondering why she's really here with me. The apartment built onto the cinderblock office has 8-foot ceilings and only a couple of windows; it's dark and dank. The yard is dirt with patches of pea gravel; the wind blows the dust up in waves; fourteen cars left over from the Petrov era are parked to one side. The 6-foot Cyclone fence surrounding the whole property has con-certina wire coiled along the top. But she doesn't mind the place, stays over sometimes. Spending a few evenings at the Dollar, walk-ing back to the yard hand in hand after the place closes, we're a couple now. An item. The talk of the neighborhood.

Towing is a waiting game; you have to be patient till someone runs out of gas or breaks down, has an accident, locks himself out of the car. But in the meantime I have an arrangement with a loan company that uses me to repossess cars. Jamie insists on coming along. "It can get messy," I tell her. She gives me her grin of happi-ness. We drive to an apartment complex with overflowing Dump-sters and a tangle of abandoned shopping carts by the driveway. The vehicle I'm looking for is parked on the street, a 2009 Dodge

Ram pickup. In about forty seconds I have my slim jim down the inside of the window, the car door open, the brake off, and the front end up hanging from the hook on my wrecker. I'm home free until the owner comes out carrying a baseball bat, yelling what he's going to do to me. When I took Doc with me a couple of times, he gave me some long theory on how when you repossess a man's car you're not only taking his transportation, possibly his livelihood, but his whole identity, his self-image, his manhood even. *It's because we're a car culture,* he said. I'm calm: it's a no-sweat situation. I've done this so many times I know there's only a couple of possible outcomes.

The guy takes a swing when he's close enough, and I duck back out of the way of the bat. And before he can recover I kick him in the kneecap with my steel-toed boot. From the ground he decides he's had enough. I tell Jamie as we're driving away how I used to try and reason with people. I'd ring the bell and explain I had to take their car. I'd tell them, *I'm just doing my job.* That never made any difference. They'd still call me a bloodsucker and a scab, and I would still say, *Why didn't you make your payments?* and they'd always have good reasons. Now I take the car any way I can, as long as it's fast.

Jamie asks me to pull onto a dirt road, and we brush through some willows to the river. Sex is sex. But this time with Jamie on the front seat, with the guy's Ram pickup hanging from the hook on the wrecker, it's spectacular. In Technicolor. It's like rainbow lightning is striking the wrecker. Again and again . . .

We are hanging out full-time together. She's living with me in the yard. Jamie doesn't come with me anymore for calls out on Highway 5, where everyone is going at least 80 miles an hour. Not after the first time, which was a pickup with a camper sideswiped by an eighteen-wheeler. The camper had fifteen people inside, fruit pickers on their way to Butte County. Its aluminum side was split open like the lid on a can of beets; 25 yards of blood and flesh was spread out 3 inches thick against the blacktop. Five cars got rear-ended trying to avoid the bodies. The tanker caught on fire. Ambulances, cops, Caltrans workers, and fire trucks; the highway was closed; cars backed up for 5 miles. I tried to warn her. Even with airbags it can get messy.

Jamie takes on some of my paperwork; there is a lot of it in this business. She gets a couple more filing cabinets and paints the cement-block office walls light green, which makes the room a little less dark. She's not one of those people who can just sit there and answer the phone. She has too much energy, too many ideas. She talks me into buying two flatbed trucks. The front end of most new cars is all plastic; you can't hook them; the best way is to winch them up onto a flatbed. I hire two guys: one lives in Roseville and the other in Elk Grove. They take the flatbeds home with them.

There is no money in scrap metal, and the pick-a-part places don't need any more old cars, so Jamie phones Sister Meredith's soup kitchen and donates all the leftover Petrov cars in the storage yard. They come right over and drag the cars away. The yard is looking good, empty, and I have a couple of dump-truck loads of pea gravel spread over where the dirt is showing. Jamie plants flowers in the new flowerboxes in front of the office. Gets business cards made and thumbtacks them in every 7-Eleven, bar, and liquor store in the neighborhood.

I've always been reluctant to get bigger, maybe because of what happened to the Petrov family, and I don't store disabled cars for that reason. But with Jamie handling all the paperwork, it doesn't seem too big a step. The money is rolling in. We only go to the Dollar on Friday and Saturday nights; we're too busy. Doc would call us domesticated now. Jamie likes to cook. She plants some parsley out back.

She wants to take me to a friend's Labor Day picnic. Somehow she thinks I think she's ashamed of me. My job. My mother was a waitress. Et cetera. "What's wrong with you?" she says. "Why can't I introduce you to some of my friends?" I decline to answer. She wouldn't understand. I believe there's a shelf life to a romance like ours, though maybe if you can get past the use-by date you might be on to something. Doc used to go into that a lot. He'd been married four times. We're not very close to the shelf date, but I'm counting. She likes telling me I'm the best thing that ever happened to her. I buy it and I don't buy it. I have no release mechanism that allows me to reciprocate. For her it's like the clichés are true: love, soulmate. For me they're still clichés. I'm wary.

Jamie surprises me on Saturday night by bringing two couples into the Dollar. Her friends. Nice people. I'm wearing my coveralls so I drive a wrecker for the night. I don't ask what they do, and they don't volunteer anything. We sit in a booth and chat. Everyone is polite. Doc says American society is egalitarian.

When the grape-picking season starts in September, Jamie moves over to her vineyards in Yolo County. She's still battling with her brothers but has not mentioned anything more about roughing them up. She's trying to wrest control of her third of the family property. I really miss her. She phones me every night, and there's always plenty to talk about. She gets away one Saturday night and meets me at the Dollar. I am so glad to see her. We can't keep our hands off each other. "I've been thinking," she says, "why people buy into the whole package—marriage, kids. It's like taking the next step." I listen, surprised. Noncommittal.

Doc happens to come in that night, and I introduce him to Jamie. He's impressed. She's read my copy of his book on the Dollar and has a lot of questions for him. Jamie can't be anything but what she is: smart, educated, rich, and beautiful. I go to piss, and Doc comes in after. He says to me, taking the big brother tone, "Dwight, do you know what you're doing?" I know what he's talking about, but I'm stumped for a comeback. "She may be out of your league." I still can't think of anything to say, until I realize he's jealous. "Go fuck yourself, Doc," I tell him.

I try to relax around Jamie, not always jump to the wrong conclusions. I can see her making an almost visible effort to slow to my pace. She throws me off: she's always so happy to see me. She wakes up in the morning bursting with energy, like those commercials on TV with athletes smashing through some paper wall to get onto the playing field. Early one morning she takes me to the country club, and we wait on the road by the first hole of the golf course. We're in her convertible. She hands me her binoculars. "See those two with the plaid shorts? Those are my brothers. I've been thinking, it'd be better if we killed them instead of just beating the crap out of them. It would be easier. I don't mean you—I mean get someone in your family to off them. I'll pay a hundred thousand dollars. Each. Is that the going rate?"

Is this a test? I'm not ready for this. I know this could be the end of us, too. Why would she stick around if I say no? But I want to be explicit. We are not going to be conspirators. "Listen to me, Jamie. I have no association with the Petrov family. I don't want to rough up or do anything else to your brothers. Do you understand that? If that is why you're with me, just forget it. I'm not going to do your dirty work. You shouldn't ask me that."

She doesn't answer me. We drive back to the yard, but she doesn't pull in through the gates. Lets me off at the entrance. Won't answer when I ask, "What about tonight?" Is this the last I'll ever see of Jamie? I'm full of regrets.

What no one knows is that I am in touch with Mr. Petrov. His trial lasted three months. I was the only one working for him who wasn't indicted. The only money coming into the company legally was from what I was bringing in with my wrecker. That's what I thought. Until he phoned me from his lawyer's office and told me to look carefully in the tire rack for a 16-inch 650 Michelin on a chrome rim. The tire was full of hundred-dollar bills. He must have known he was going down and felt he had to trust me. Over the last five years I've paid people, maybe half a million dollars: family, when they get out of jail. I get a phone call, probably one of his lawyers, saying, *My good friend So-and-so will come by,* and then the amount I'm to pay out. I'm Mr. Petrov's bagman. I owe the man. To tell the truth, it was some of his money I used for the down payment on the yard.

I don't see Jamie for a week. Then two. But I don't want it to be over. I think a lot about ways we could get together. But then there would always be that unspoken deal between us. I go to the Dollar early on Saturday night. Doc is there. Always generous, he buys me a drink. That means I have to buy him one back, so we're on our way. I'm just getting comfortable when two uniformed cops come into the Dollar. This is not unusual. The place quiets down except for the two customers playing liar's dice at the bar, banging the leather boxes hard against the top of the bar. But this time they come for me. One cop reads me my rights. Doc asks, "What's he supposed to have done?"

Attempted murder. I know the rest of the story before they go on. The brothers have been shot up but are still alive. Doc yells, "Don't say another word. I'll call my brother-in-law; he'll meet you at the station." One of the cops knows me from service calls; his wife is always running out of gas. Whispers, "You dumbbell, you dropped one of your business cards at the scene."

When we get to the station, Doc's lawyer brother-in-law is there. "Dwight, have you been shooting a firearm in the last few days?"

When I say no, he demands that the cops give me some test to see if I have any residue from firing a weapon. It turns out there are no witnesses; the brothers, sedated now, never saw their assailants. As I'm being fingerprinted I can hear Doc's brother-in-law yelling, "If you found my card, would you arrest me too?"

They don't set bail. I'm put in the drunk tank for the night. Waiting is not easy when your mind is full of things that won't let you alone. I don't want to think that Jamie had anything to do with me sitting here on a hard bench with half a dozen other guys. I did a couple things when I was younger. Once you get in the system, it's like a card game you can't win. You may have a full house, but they always have four aces. It's better never to sit down at the game. Worry and despair enter the big cell like it's being filled with water.

I'm surprised: I'm out by noon. I have an alibi. The cops on their own checked their accident reports and found out I was on the scene of a fender bender on I-5 during the time of the shooting. There's a CHP report. No one is waiting for me, so I take the bus back to the yard. I feel relief; I can't say how much. I strip my clothes off and hop in the shower. Thinking it all over, I speculate that one of the Petrov family must have got out of jail and come by the office without the usual phone call, and Jamie made a deal. Whose idea was it to drop my card? After a lot of thought, I decide it was too obvious a move for Jamie. I like to think she would have known better.

I follow the story in the *Sacramento Bee*. The brothers recover enough to buy their sister out. Jamie relocates to Chile and buys one of the largest vineyards in the region. I could get her address, if I want it. Sometimes I think of taking a trip to South America.

Doc never tires of telling me I'm a lucky fuck. "You got in over your head." And sometimes he adds, "What did you learn from that?" Always the teacher. I stay in character: I'm someone who drives a wrecker. After taking my time to think it over, I say, "Nothing."

I Will Follow You

FROM *West Branch*

MY SISTER DECIDED we had to go see her estranged husband in Reno. When she told me, I was in a mood. I said, "What does that have to do with me?"

Carolina married when she was nineteen. Darryl, her husband, was a decade older, but he had a full head of hair and she thought that meant something. They lived with us for the first year. My mom called it *getting on their feet*, but they spent most of their time in bed so I assumed *getting on their feet* was a euphemism for sex. When they finally moved out, Carolina and Darryl lived in a crappy apartment with pea-green wallpaper and a balcony where the railing was loose like a rotting tooth. I'd visit them after my classes at the local university. Carolina usually wasn't home from her volunteer job yet, so I'd wait for her and watch television and drink warm beer while Darryl, who couldn't seem to find work, stared at me, telling me I was a pretty girl. When I told my sister, she laughed and shook her head. She said, "There's not much you can do with men, but he won't mess with you, I promise." She was right.

Darryl decided to move to Nevada—better prospects, he said —and told Carolina she was his wife and had to go with him. He didn't need to work being married to my sister, but he was inconsistently old-fashioned about the strangest things. Carolina doesn't like to be told what to do and she wasn't going to leave me. I didn't want to go to Nevada, so she stayed and they remained married but lived completely apart.

I was asleep, my boyfriend Spencer's arm heavy and hot across my chest, when Carolina knocked. My relationship with Spencer left a lot to be desired for many reasons, not the least of which is that he only spoke in movie lines. He shook me but I groaned and rolled away. When we didn't answer, Carolina let herself in, barged into our bedroom, and crawled in next to me. Her skin was damp and cool, like she had been running. She smelled like hairspray and perfume.

Carolina kissed the back of my neck. "It's time to go, Savvie," she whispered.

"I really do not want to go."

Spencer covered his face with a pillow and mumbled something we couldn't understand.

"Don't make me go alone," Carolina said, her voice breaking. "Don't make me stay here, not again."

An hour later we were on the interstate, heading east. I curled into the door, pressing my cheek against the glass. As we crossed the California border, I sat up and said, "I really hate you," but I held on to her arm too.

The Blue Desert Inn looked abandoned, forgotten. Mold patterns covered the stucco walls in dark green and black formations. The neon VAC NY sign crackled as it struggled to stay illuminated. There were only a few cars in the parking lot.

"This is exactly where I expected your husband to end up," I said as we pulled into the parking lot. "If you sleep with him here, I will be so disappointed."

Darryl answered the door in a loose pair of boxers and a T-shirt from our high school. His hair fell in his eyes and his lips were chapped.

He scratched his chin. "I always knew you'd come back to me."

Carolina rubbed her thumb against the stubble. "Be nice."

She pushed past him and I followed, slowly. His room was small but cleaner than I expected. The queen-sized bed in the middle of the room sagged. Next to the bed were a small table and two chairs. Across from the bed, an oak dresser covered with used Styrofoam coffee cups, one bearing a lipstick stain.

I pointed to the large tube television. "I didn't know they still made those."

Darryl's upper lip curled. He nodded toward the door leading to the next room. "You should see if the room next door is available." He patted the bed and threw himself at the mattress, which groaned softly when he landed. "Me and your sister are going to be busy."

In the office, an older man with a large gut and thick head of red hair leaned against the counter, tapping a map of the hotel, explaining the merits of each of the available rooms. I pointed to the room adjacent to Darryl's.

"Tell me about this room."

The motel clerk scratched his stomach, then cracked his knuckles. "That there is a fine room. There's a bit of a leak in the bathroom ceiling, but if you're in the shower, you're already getting wet."

I swallowed. "I'll take it."

He looked me up and down. "Will you be needing two keys or will you be needing company?"

I slid three twenties across the counter. "Neither."

"Suit yourself," the clerk said. "Suit yourself."

The air in my room was thick and dank. The bed carried a familiar sag, as if the same person had gone from room to room, leaving the weight of their memory behind. After a thorough inspection, I pressed my ear to the door separating my room from Darryl's. Carolina and her husband were surprisingly quiet. I closed my eyes. My breathing slowed. I don't know how long I stood there, but a loud knock startled me.

"I know you're listening, Savvie."

I pulled my door open and glared at my sister, standing in the doorway, hands on her hips. Darryl lay on his bed, still dressed, his ankles crossed. He nodded and grinned widely.

"Looking good, little sis."

Before I could say anything, Carolina covered my mouth. "Darryl's taking us out to dinner, at a casino even."

I looked down at my outfit—faded jeans with a frayed hole where the left knee used to be and a white wifebeater. "I'm not changing."

The Paradise Deluxe was loud in every way—the carpets were an unfortunate explosion of red and orange and green and purple, classic rock blared from speakers in the ceiling. The casino floor was littered with bright slot machines, each emitting a high-pitched series of sounds that in no way resembled a discernible tune, and at most of the machines drunk people loudly brayed as they pushed the Spin Reels button over and over. As we walked through the casino, single file—Darryl, Carolina, me—Darryl nodded every few steps like he owned the place.

The restaurant was dark and empty. Our waiter, a tall skinny kid whose hair hung greasily in his face, handed us menus encased in dirty plastic and ignored us for the next twenty minutes.

Darryl leaned back, stretching his arms, wrapping one around Carolina's shoulders. "This," he said, "is paradise. They serve the best steak in Reno here—meat so tender and juicy a knife cuts through it like butter."

I pretended to be deeply absorbed in the menu and its array of cheap meats and fried food.

Darryl kicked me beneath the table.

I set my menu down. "Must you?"

He slapped the table. "The gang's together again."

While we waited, Carolina idly rubbed her hand along Darryl's thigh. He did weird things with his face and started smoking, ashing his cigarette on the table.

"I don't think you're allowed to do that," I said.

Darryl shrugged. "I've got pull here. They're not gonna say anything."

I stared at the small mound of ashes he was creating. "We are going to eat at this table."

He exhaled a perfect stream of smoke.

Carolina touched my elbow lightly and looked across the table. "Leave her alone," she said.

Darryl and my sister had married at the justice of the peace. I stood by her side, wearing my best dress—yellow, sleeveless, empire waist—and pink Converse high-tops. His brother, Dennis, stood up for him. Dennis couldn't even bother to wear pants—he hovered next to Darryl and my sister in a pair of khaki shorts. While the justice droned about loving and obeying, I stared at Dennis's pale knees, how they bulged. Our parents and brothers stood in a stiff line next to Darryl's mother, who chewed gum loudly. She always needed a cigarette in her mouth. After ten minutes without one, she was hurting real bad.

After they exchanged vows, we stepped into the busy hall filled with people going to traffic court and renewing their driver's licenses and seeking justice. We had been in the courthouse three years earlier seeking something, but we didn't speak of it that day.

We pretended we had every reason to celebrate. Dennis reached into a backpack and pulled out two warm beers. He and Darryl cracked them open right there. Carolina laughed. A cop whose gut hung over his pants watched them through half-lidded eyes, then looked down at his shoes. Everyone started slowly shuffling toward the parking lot, but Carolina and I stayed behind.

She pressed her forehead against mine.

Something wet and heavy caught in my throat. "Why him?"

"I'd be no good to a really good man, and Darryl isn't really a bad man."

I knew exactly what she meant.

Darryl worked nights managing a small airfield on the edge of town. It was a mystery how he had fallen into the job. He knew little about managing, aviation, or work. He invited us to join him like he was afraid if he let Carolina out of his sight she might disappear. A friend of his, Cooper, was going to bring beer and some weed. As we drove to the airfield, I sat in the back seat, staring at the freckles on Darryl's neck pointing toward his spine from his hairline in a wide *V*. When Carolina leaned into him like they had never separated, I looked away.

"Don't you have actual work to do?"

He turned around and grinned at me. "Not as much with you ladies here to help me."

"You could just take me back to the motel."

Carolina turned around. "If you go back, I go back," she said sharply. "You know the deal."

"Are you two still joined like those freaky twins, those what you call 'em, you know, like the cats?"

I picked at a hole in the back of the driver's seat. "Siamese?"

Darryl slapped the steering wheel and hooted. "Siamese, yeah, that's it."

I nodded and Carolina turned back around. "We're something like that."

We were young once.

Where Carolina went, I followed. We are only a year apart, no time at all. Our parents moved out of Los Angeles after I was born. With four children—Carolina and I nestled in the middle —it seemed more appropriate to live somewhere quieter, safer. We ended up near Carmel in a development of large Spanish casitas surrounded by tall oaks.

I was ten and Carolina was eleven. We were in the small parking lot adjacent to the park near our neighborhood. There was a van, with a night sky painted on the side—brilliant blues filled with perfect dots of white light, so pretty. I wanted to touch the bright stars stretched from the front of the van all the way to the back. Carolina's friend Jessie Schachter walked up to us, and they started talking. The van was warm against the palm of my hand, so warm. I had always imagined stars were cold. The stars started moving and the door was flung open. A man, older like my father, crouched in the opening, staring, a strange smile hanging from his thin lips.

He grabbed me by the straps of my overalls and pulled me into the van. I tried to scream but he covered my mouth. His hand was sweaty, tasted like motor oil. Carolina heard how I tried to swallow the air around me. Instead of running away, she ran right toward the van, threw her little body in beside us, her face screwed with concentration. The man's name was Mr. Peter. He quickly closed the door and bound our wrists and ankles.

"Don't you make a sound," he said, "or I will kill your parents and every friend you've ever had." His finger punctuated every word.

Mr. Peter left us at a hospital near home six weeks later. We stood near the emergency room entrance and watched as he drove away, the shiny stars of his van disappearing. I clutched Carolina's hand as we walked to a counter with a sign that said REGISTRATION. We were barely tall enough to see over it. I was silent, would be for a long time. Carolina quietly told the lady our names. She knew who we were, even showed us a flier with our pictures and our names and the color of our eyes and hair, what we were wearing when we were last seen. I swayed dizzily and threw up all over the counter. Carolina pulled me closer. "We need medical attention," she said.

Later our parents ran into the emergency room, calling our names frantically. They tried to hold us and we refused. They said we looked so thin. They sat between our hospital beds so they were near both of us. Our parents asked Carolina why she jumped into the van instead of running for help. She said, "I couldn't leave my sister alone."

Weeks later, when we were released, detectives took us to a

room with little tables, little chairs, coloring books, and crayons, as if we needed children's things.

On the first day back to school, three months had passed. I sat in homeroom and waited until Mrs. Sewell took attendance. When she was done, I walked out of the classroom, Mrs. Sewell calling after me. I went to Carolina's classroom and sat on the floor next to her desk, resting my head against her thigh. Her teacher paused for a moment, then kept talking. No matter what anyone said or did, I went to Carolina's classes with her. The teachers didn't know what to do, so eventually the school let me skip ahead. My sister was the only place that made any sense.

At the airfield we followed Darryl into the tiny terminal. A long window looked onto the tarmac. He pointed to a small seating area—three benches in a *U* shape. "That's the VIP area," he said, laughing. He showed us a cramped office filled with dusty paper, bright orange traffic cones, some kind of headset, and a pile of junk I couldn't make sense of. Carolina and I sat in the seating area while Darryl did who knows what. A few minutes later he said, "Go to the window. I'm going to show you something." As we stood, I leaned forward. Suddenly the entire airfield was illuminated in long rows of blue lights. I gasped. It was nice to be surrounded by such unexpected beauty.

Darryl crept up behind us and pulled us into a hug. "Ain't this a beautiful sight, ladies?"

A while later, a heavy-duty truck pulled up in front of the window. Darryl started jumping up and down, flapping his arms. "My buddy Cooper's here. Now we're going to party." He ran out to greet his friend. They hugged, pounding each other's backs in the violent way men show affection. They jumped onto the hood of the truck and cracked open beers.

I turned to my sister. "What the hell are we doing here, Carolina?"

She traced Darryl's animated outline against the glass. "I know who he is. I know exactly who he is. I need to be around someone I understand completely." She pulled her hair out of her face.

Carolina was lying, but she wasn't going to tell me the truth until she was ready.

She ran to the truck, and the guys slid apart so she could sit between them. I watched as she opened a beer and it foamed in her face. She tossed her head back and laughed. I envied her. I didn't understand a single thing about Spencer, not even after nearly two years.

I wanted to know how he felt about that, as I called him on my cell. He answered on the first ring.

"I don't understand you," I said. "I need to be with a man I understand."

Spencer cleared his throat. "Pay strict attention to what I say, because I choose my words carefully and I never repeat myself. I've told you my name: that's the who."

"You know what, Spencer? Goodbye."

I hung up before I had to listen to him say another stupid thing.

I joined my sister and Darryl and his friend on the tarmac. Carolina grinned and threw me a beer. "How's the video clerk?"

"We're through."

Carolina threw her arms over her head and crowed. Then she was crawling up the windshield and standing on top of the cab and shouting for me to join her. Cooper reached into the truck and turned up the volume on the radio. We drank and danced on the top of that truck while the boys passed a joint back and forth below us. The night grew darker, but we didn't stop dancing. Eventually we grew tired and crawled into the truck bed. We stared up at the stars, the night still warm. I wanted to cry.

Carolina turned toward me. "Don't cry," she said.

"We're not going home, are we?"

She held my face in her hands.

I woke up and blinked. My eyes were dry and my mouth was dry. My face was dry, the skin stretched tightly. The desert was all in me. I sat up slowly and looked around. I was back in my motel room. The dank smell was unbearable. I grabbed my chest. I was still dressed. The door to Darryl's room was open and Darryl was asleep, sprawled on his stomach, one of his long arms hanging over the edge of the bed. Carolina was sitting against the headboard, doing a crossword, her glasses perched on the tip of her nose.

"You didn't sleep long."

"How long have we been here?"

She looked at the clock on the nightstand. "A couple hours." Carolina set her crossword down and led me back to my room.

She helped me out of my jeans and pulled a clean T-shirt over my head. She washed my face with a cool washcloth and crawled into bed with me.

I turned to face her. "You should sleep."

She nodded, and I pulled the comforter up around us. "You keep watch," she whispered.

My chest tightened. "Hush," I said. "Hush."

I stared at the ceiling, brown with age and water damage. Carolina started to snore softly. When I grew bored, I turned on the television and listened to a documentary about manatees off the coast of Florida, how they were on average 9 feet long and how most manatee deaths were human-related. When the scientist said this, the interviewer paused.

"Man always gets in the way," he said.

We were young once and then we weren't.

Mr. Peter drove for a long time. We were so little and so scared. That was enough to keep us quiet. When we stopped, we weren't anywhere we recognized. He didn't say very much, his hands clamping our necks as he steered us from the van into a house. He took us to a bedroom with two twin beds. The wallpaper was covered with little bears wearing blue bowties and it had a bright blue border. There were no windows. There was nothing in that room but the beds and the walls, our bodies and our fear. He left us for a minute, locking the door. Carolina and I sat on the edge of the bed farthest from the door. We were silent, our skinny legs touching, shaking. When Mr. Peter returned, he threw a length of rope at me.

"Tie her up," he said. I hesitated, and he squeezed my shoulder, hard. "Don't make me wait."

"I'm sorry," I whispered, as I looped the rope around Carolina's wrists, loosely.

Mr. Peter nudged me with his foot. "Tighter."

Carolina started babbling as I pulled the rope tighter. She begged him to take her. He refused. When I was done, he tugged on the rope. Satisfied, he pulled on my shirt. Carolina stood and held my hands. Her fingertips were bright red, knuckles white. As Mr. Peter dragged me out of the room, Carolina tightened her grip until he finally shoved her away. My eyes widened as the door closed. My sister went crazy. She yelled and threw her body against the door over and over.

Mr. Peter took me into another bedroom with a bed as big as my parents'. There was a dresser, bare, no pictures, nothing. Carolina was still yelling and hitting the door, sound from a faraway place.

"We can be friends or we can be enemies," Mr. Peter said.

I didn't understand, but I did: there was the way he looked at me, how he licked his lips over and over.

"Are you going to hurt my sister?"

He smiled. "Not if we're friends."

He pulled me toward him, rubbing his thumb across my lips. I wanted to look away. His eyes weren't normal, didn't look like eyes. I did not look away. He forced his thumb into my mouth. I thought about biting down. I thought about screaming. I thought about my sister, alone in a faraway room, her wrists bound, and what he would do to her, to me, to us. I did not understand why his finger was in my mouth. My jaw trembled. I did not bite down.

Mr. Peter arched an eyebrow. "Friends," he said. He pulled me to him. My body became nothing.

Later he took me back to the other room. Carolina was slumped against the far wall. When she saw us, she rushed at him, barreling into his knees.

He laughed and kicked her away. "Don't make trouble. Me and your sister are going to be good friends."

"Like hell," Carolina said, rushing at him again.

He swatted her away and tossed a box of fruit roll-ups on the floor and left us alone. After we heard him walk away, Carolina told me to untie her. I stood in the corner, wanted to wrap the walls around us.

My sister studied at me for a long time. "What did he do?"

I looked at my shoes.

"Oh no," she said. "Oh no."

We fell into a routine—we'd explore Reno during the day and go to the airfield at night with Darryl. Sometimes he let us play with equipment we had no business touching. As planes landed, we stood on the edge of the runway, arms high in the air like we were trying to grab the wings. After planes touched down, we chased after them like we could catch their wind.

Spencer never called, made no grand gesture to win me back. I didn't care. Our parents were long accustomed to Carolina and me chasing after each other. Once they were assured we were safe, they sent us text messages every few days to remind us they loved us, to call if we needed anything. They didn't understand. They did not know the girls who came home after Mr. Peter.

One morning I couldn't sleep and found Darryl in bed, watching over Carolina, who was asleep. I crawled in next to her and he looked at me over my sister's narrow frame.

It's like he knew exactly what I was thinking. "I'm not that guy anymore," he said. He kissed her shoulder. I nodded and closed my eyes.

Every day Mr. Peter came and made me tie up my sister. He took me to the other room. He took what he wanted from my body. Carolina went mad, always trying to reach me, always trying to make me tell her what happened. I couldn't. It was worse for her until Mr. Peter made her tie me up. I screamed until my throat bled. I spit blood at his feet. "We were supposed to be friends," I said. "You promised."

He laughed. "Your sister is going to be my friend too, little girl."

While she was gone, I threw myself against the door, bruising my body with rage, calling out her name. I knew too much. When he brought her back, she limped over to me and untied my wrists. We sat on the floor. She said, "It's better this way, more fair."

After that, Mr. Peter came for us every day, sometimes more than once a day. Sometimes there were other men. Sometimes we lay next to each other on his big bed and stared at each other and we would never look away, no matter what they did to us. We'd move our lips and say things only we could hear. He bathed us in a little bathroom with a sea-green tub where we sat facing each other, our knees pulled to our chests. He wouldn't even leave us alone to clean ourselves. He made our whole world the windowless rooms in his house, always filled by him.

The smell of the Blue Desert Inn was driving me crazy. The air was moldy and too thick. It covered my skin and my clothes and my teeth. One morning I saw a cockroach lazily ambling across the television screen and snapped. I stomped into Darryl's room and found my sister curled up in his arms while he smoothed her hair. I looked away, my face growing warm. I hadn't considered that such intimacy was possible between them.

"I am not staying here for one more day."

Carolina sat up. "I don't want to go home." The edge in her voice made my heart contract.

I was ready to argue, but she looked so tired. "We can stay somewhere nicer." I waved around the room. "But we're not going to live like this."

She poked Darryl's chest. "What about him?"

"Aren't you guys playing house right now?"

Carolina grinned. Darryl gave me a thumbs-up.

As we pulled out of the parking lot of the Blue Desert Inn, the sign read VAC Y.

The police caught Mr. Peter when we were fifteen and sixteen. His name was Peter James Iversen. His wife and two sons lived in the house behind the house where he kept us. The authorities found videotapes. We didn't know. Two detectives came to our house. Carolina and I sat on the couch. The detectives talked. We did not blink. They told us about the tapes; they had watched. I leaned forward, my forehead against my knees. Carolina put her hand in the small of my back. Our parents stood to the side, slowly shaking their heads. When I sat up, I couldn't hear anything. The detectives kept talking, but all I could think was *People have seen videotapes*. I stood and walked out of the room. I walked out of the house. Carolina followed. I stopped at the end of the driveway. We watched the traffic.

"Well," she finally said. "This sucks."

A convertible sped by. There was a woman in the passenger seat and her red hair filled the air around her face. She was smiling, all white teeth.

"That bastard," I said.

We went back into the house and said we wanted to see the tapes. At first the detectives and our parents protested, but eventually we got our way. A few days later my sister and I sat next to each other in a small windowless room with a TV and VCR on a cart. Concerned adults hovered over us—a detective, some kind of social worker, a lawyer.

"Our parents can never see these," Carolina said. "Not ever."

The detective nodded.

We watched hours of black-and-white videos of the girls we used to be and what we were turned into. I held my hand over my mouth to keep any sound from escaping. After a particularly disturbing scene, the detective said, "I think that's enough." Carolina said, "Being there was worse." When we were done, I asked if the tapes could be destroyed. That was the one thing we wanted. No one would look us in the eye. *Evidence,* they said. As we walked out of the police station, my legs threatened to give out. Carolina did not let me fall.

The criminal trial went quickly. There was too much *evidence.* Mr. Peter was sentenced to life in prison. There was a civil trial, because he had money and our parents decided his money should be ours. We both testified. I went first. I tried not to look at him, sitting next to his lawyer, the two of them in their blue suits and neat haircuts. My words rotted on my tongue. Carolina testified. Between the two of us, we told as much of the story as we were ever going to tell. When she finished she looked at me, her eyes flashing worriedly. She stared at her hands, fidgeted. The courtroom was quiet, only the occasional shuffling of paper or a body shifting in the gallery. The judge excused her, but Carolina wouldn't move from the stand. She shook her head and gripped the rail in front of her. Her lower lip trembled and I stood. The judge leaned toward my sister, looked down, then coughed and cleared the courtroom. I went to my sister. I smelled something sharp, her fear, something more. I looked down, saw a wet pattern on her skirt, stretching along her thigh. She had wet herself. She was shaking.

I took her hand, squeezed. "This is not a problem. We can fix this."

"Come with me," the judge said. We froze. I stood in front of my sister and she buried her face in my back, her trembling arms wrapped around my waist. I did not let her fall. The judge's face flushed. "Not like that," he stammered. "There's a bathroom in my chambers."

We followed, warily. In the bathroom Carolina wouldn't move, wouldn't speak. I helped her out of her skirt and her underwear. I washed her clean as best I could with dispenser soap and paper towels.

A while later, a knock, our mother, whispering. "Girls," she said. "I've brought a change of clothes."

I opened the door, just a crack. My mother stood in her Sunday suit, a strand of pearls encircling her neck. I reached for the plastic bag, and as she handed it to me, she grabbed my wrist gently.

"Can I help?"

I shook my head and pulled away. I closed the door. I dressed my sister. I washed her face. Our foreheads met and I whispered the soft words I give her when she locks up.

On the drive home, we sat in the back seat. Our parents looked straight ahead. As we turned onto our street, our father cleared his throat and tried to sound happy. "At least this is over."

An ugly sound came out of Carolina's mouth.

My father gripped the steering wheel tighter.

The new hotel was much nicer. There was room service and daily maid service and many *amenities*. While Darryl strutted around their room, Carolina and I sat on my bed, poring over a thick leather portfolio detailing the benefits of the hotel. There was a pool, Jacuzzi, and sauna.

While we studied the room service menu, I bumped Carolina's arm gently. "What's really going on here? No more bullshit."

"I just woke up one day and realized we never left that town, and for what?"

"They have French toast." I pointed to a bright picture of thick French toast, covered with powdered sugar.

Carolina reached for her purse and pulled out an envelope, the words DEPARTMENT OF CORRECTIONS in the upper left corner. She smoothed the letter out.

"No," I said, but it sounded like three words.

Her hands shook until she closed her fingers into tight fists. I started reading and then I grabbed the letter and jumped off the bed, kept reading, turned the letter over.

"Don't freak out," Carolina said.

I kicked the air. I set the letter on the nightstand and started banging my head against the wall until a dull throb shot through the bone of my skull.

Carolina closed the distance between us and grabbed my shoulders. "Look at me."

I bit my lip.

She shook me, hard. "Look at me."

I finally lifted my chin. I have spent the best and worst moments of my life looking my sister in the eye. "You brought us here to hide," I said. "You should have told me the truth."

Carolina leaned down and dried my tears with her hair. She sat next to me and I saw her at eleven years old, throwing herself into the mouth of something terrible so I would not be alone. "This is the truth: he knows my address and he sent this letter and that means he can find us. I don't want to ever go back there," she whispered. "I don't ever want him to find us again."

The jury awarded us a lot of money, so much money we would never have to work or want. For a long time we refused to spend it. Every night I went online and checked my account balances and thought, *This is what my life was worth.*

My sister and I went to work with Darryl. We sat in the back seat as he drove.

"You girls are awful quiet," he said as we pulled up to the airfield.

I held his gaze in the rearview mirror. I wanted to say something, but my voice locked. Carolina handed him the letter from Mr. Peter. As he read it, Darryl muttered under his breath.

When he was done, he turned to look at us. "I may not seem like much of a man, but that SOB isn't gonna hurt you here, and he won't find you either."

He carefully folded the letter and handed it back to Carolina. Right then I knew why she found her way back to him.

While he worked, my sister and I lay on the runway between two parallel lines of flashing blue lights. The pavement was still warm and the ground held us steady. Our bodies practically glowed.

Mr. Peter was up for parole because California prisons were overcrowded. Mr. Peter was a changed man. Mr. Peter needed to prove it, and to prove it Mr. Peter needed our help. Mr. Peter found God. Mr. Peter wanted our forgiveness. Mr. Peter needed our forgiveness so he could get parole. Mr. Peter was sorry for every terrible thing he did to us. Mr. Peter couldn't resist two beautiful little girls. Mr. Peter wanted us so bad he couldn't help himself. Mr. Peter was an old man now, could never hurt another little girl. Mr. Peter begged for our forgiveness.

We were young once.

I was ten and Carolina was eleven. We begged Mr. Peter for everything—food, fresh air, a moment alone with hot water. We begged him for mercy, to give our bodies a break before they were broken completely. He ignored us. We learned to stop begging. He would too.

Carolina pulled the letter out of her pocket and held the corner to an open flame before tossing the burning letter into the air. The flame burned white. The ashes slowly fell to the ground, drifting onto our clothes, our faces, our deaf ears, our silent tongues.

MICHELLE BUTLER HALLETT

Bush-Hammer Finish

FROM *The Fiddlehead*

St. John's, July 2013

THE TROUBLE with Paulette, Nish Flannigan decided, reaching for his cufflink: she overreacted. The cufflink had fallen beside the wedding photo of Paulette that Nish kept on his dresser. He studied it: Paulette, filling out a sleeveless beige dress, standing on a wharf between wooden lobster traps, and holding not a bouquet in front of her belly but a red buoy, scarred and beaten. Her red hair tumbled over her freckled shoulders, and her beige high heels stood before her, almost hiding her polished toenails. She'd tucked her chin down and looked up at the photographer, mouth in a smirk, eyes glinting. *Mischievous,* Nish had called her, *wicked.*

A thread dangled from his cuff. Nish turned around, arm stuck out before him, about to call for Paulette's help. Instead he strode to the adjoining bathroom and hauled open medicine cabinet, cupboards, and drawers, scowling as nail scissors refused to appear. He found them in Paulette's drawer, hiding beneath a stray panty liner and three bobby pins with long red hairs caught in them. The tiny scissors slipped off Nish's broad fingers, and he kept missing the thread. He threw the nail scissors at the toilet. They bounced off the raised seat and fell to the floor. The thread, he tore.

Checking his bow tie in the mirror, he wished he'd not gone bald, not gotten fat, not become so damn vain. He slapped the light switches down and walked to the kitchen, where he poured some malt whisky and raised a cheer to his gala invitation, pinned to the fridge with a magnet. *To The Rooms, Alice, to The Rooms.*

Trying not to loom, Nish smiled at the arts reporter. —It's always an honor to be nominated for these things. The victory's in the nomination.

The arts reporter gazed up, and Nish recalled signing a book for her and suggesting she join one of his workshops, once he got them back on the go. She looked ten years younger than Paulette, midthirties maybe, and dyed blond. She finished asking a question Nish had been expecting.

He smiled again. —Yes, well, that two former protégés of mine are also nominated only sweetens the evening.

His two former protégés stood at the far end of the room. About the same size and height, they looked quite comfortable with each other, talking and laughing, looking up at the same moment.

The reporter cleared her throat and stepped back into Nish's line of sight. —The Torngat is the Atlantic region's most prestigious award for writing, and this year the gala's not only being held in St. John's, but all three nominees are Newfoundlanders: yourself, of course, Patrick O'Mara, and Paulette Tiller. Do you think—

—Last time we hosted the Torngat, there wasn't a single Newfoundlander on the goddamned *long*list. So I think it's about time.

Her polite laugh failed. She'd transferred from Halifax, a city she considered the cultural center of Atlantic Canada, and she found people in St. John's arrogant: sure, we'll talk to ya, but don't think you can get too close. —You're sixty-two this year, and it's been eight years since your last book. Is this novel your swan song?

—God, I hope not.

—Return of the phoenix?

Nish waved this idea away.

—You've won a few big awards in your time, the Giller, the GG, and you even came close to the Impac, but you've never gotten a Torngat. This is your third nomination. Any thoughts on how this evening might play out?

The Ceeb exiled you here to punish your incompetence, didn't they?
—No. All I can do is write the best book I can.

—Thank you, Mr Flannigan.

—Nish, please.

She smiled. *Friendly Newfoundlanders, my ass.*

Nish watched her navigate the crowd to reach Patrick and Paulette. The reporter's look and tone as she'd thanked him reminded Nish of the librarian at the Centre for Newfoundland Studies. She'd squinted but kept her face straight when Nish asked to see his own papers and notebooks, donated ten years before. *They're still mine,* Nish had explained. *I have every right to see them.* That had been two years ago, around the time he'd argued with Paulette about her wanting to publish as Paul Tiller. *Jesus, Paulette, what are you tryin to prove? This is St. John's. Everyone knows who you are.* She'd done it, though, Paul Tiller, all long hair and lipstick in the author photo.

She wore a short and sleeveless black dress tonight, showing off her arms and legs. Nish knew the dress, and those ugly flat boots. The expensive clutch beneath her right arm had been a gift from him, but those fancy patterned tights were new. Her hair, pinned up in a chignon, salon-fresh and red to the roots, shone.

Jesus, Paulette.

He needed a drink.

Patrick sipped his ginger ale, and his dark hair fell into his eyes. —No one?

—Foster care, right? When I was in a home, it was me and half a dozen other kids, most of them already in trouble with the law, and only the one adult home most of the day. Then I lived in a hotel, me and a social worker, so really, who had time to read to me?

—Spose, girl.

Paulette smiled, looked at the floor. —I think it's sweet, a sign you really want to look after someone, if you read aloud to them.

—My grandfather read me a story every night, guaranteed.

Paulette glanced at the crowd. —Arts reporter, three o'clock.

—Where ya goin? You're nominated for this too.

—She wants to talk to *you.*

—Patrick O'Mara? Hi, I'm from the CBC.

Paulette smirked into her drink. Patrick's bad-boy charms were mellowing as he approached forty, but his dark eyes still flashed, and his snug jeans fit well. Many women, and more than a few men, got a bit gooey about the brain when talking with him. This evening, in character, he'd not rented the expected tuxedo. Instead he wore his biker boots, dark jeans, a white silk shirt, and a velvet jacket, black and blue, that made Paulette think of Elizabethan portraits.

A delicate flush spread over the reporter's upper chest as she asked Patrick about his stonework: was it just a hobby, or was it serious competition for his writing? Patrick laughed. He then answered what Paulette considered a particularly stunned question about ideas and inspiration by saying he didn't know what *roman à clef* meant.

Frowning at this, the reporter shoved her mic at Paulette's mouth. —Paulette Tiller—or Paul, I guess—you're nominated for your first book. Wow. You got your start under Nish Flannigan?

Swallowing, Paulette tried to avoid memory: Nish on top, insistent, artless. *Heave away, me jollies.* —I suppose.

Patrick gestured to Paulette that he'd get them both fresh drinks.

The reporter's eyes followed Patrick's reflection in the glass behind Paulette. —People are calling you a female Patrick O'Mara.

—*What?*

—Shouldn't you be flattered?

—For the love of God!

Paulette strode off. The reporter glared after her.

Nish, leaning against the bar, half hearing a drunk poet who only ever discussed "The Love Song of J. Alfred Prufrock," watched Paulette leave the reporter and watched Patrick smile and accept congratulations from woman after woman. Wondering what Paulette might be overreacting to this time, Nish ordered two drinks and waited.

—Young fellah Paddy.

—Nish, how are ya?

—Here, you take this.

Patrick accepted the drink, held it up: some fruity cocktail, finished with a maraschino cherry impaled on a little plastic sword, a straw, and a paper umbrella. He said nothing.

—Balls-out and fuck-black-tie in that fancy jacket, aren't ya? I read your novel. I recognized the bit where your adolescent protag entraps the pedophile teacher. I think that was the first thing you ever brought to one of my workshops. God, time flies. Remember askin me to blurb your first book?

Patrick studied Nish's drink: malt whiskey, neat.

—I spent the whole night on your manuscript, Paddy. I never told you that. It was like sittin up with a sick child.

—At least my new one here tonight doesn't read like I devoured my old notebooks, all my used-up ideas, and then puked up the mess. Be awful if that happened.

Nish took a good swallow. —You know what your trouble is? You can't decide. Are you a writer or a rock-breaker? Man up, my son, and figure it out.

—Yeah, really fuckin dreadful, havin more than one talent. Dunno how I bear it, some days.

Nish said nothing as he walked away. Patrick knocked back the girly drink—out of spite, he told himself.

Two men in their fifties, famous Atlantic Canadian writers who'd made the Torngat longlist, jumped in fright at the urinals as Paulette banged the men's room door off the wall. Staggering, she helped Patrick to a stall. He made it, falling to his knees. Paulette dampened some paper towel and tried to ignore the man on her right as he turned red.

The man on her left snorted. —O'Mara can't handle his liquor?

Paulette nodded at the man's open fly. —Isn't that awfully small to be out by itself?

Hearing the phrase *Bitter cunt*, Patrick retched.

Not long after, Paulette helped Patrick get into a cab. He'd slurred when calling for it, then gone quiet. On a summer night like this, west wind stirring the trees and beating off the fog, he'd walk home. Right now, however, he felt quite separate and in some danger, as if he'd been tucked in a glass box and placed on the edge of a deep hole. Despite all his gifts with language, he could not explain this.

He dug his credit card out of his wallet and handed it to the driver, who told him to put it away for now, because they hadn't even left yet.

Paulette touched Patrick on the shoulder. —What is the *matter* with you?

Patrick struggled to get the card in his jacket pocket. —You're —wait—

—Shove over.

Back inside The Rooms, at the upper windows, the arts reporter stood near Nish. Angry with Paulette still, and spying the departure, she'd made sure to bump into Nish and, in her stumble, draw his attention to the scene outside.

Nish took a sharp breath.

—Wait.

Patrick rolled off his bed, got to his feet. Stonework glittered in lamplight, hurting his eyes. He did not remember leaving his lamp on. Nor did he remember placing that big bowl near the bed. Sweaty, not sure if he'd vomit or urinate first, he got to the bathroom.

Seat's down. Did I—

He looked down: fully dressed, boots and all.

He washed his hands, checked his phone, swished mouthwash to chase off a shocking foulness, and shuffled to the living room. Turned away from him, dozing on the futon, red hair down: Paulette, curled in a tight fetal position, fists near her face. She also wore her clothes from last night. Patrick lifted the blanket on the rocking chair and draped it over Paulette.

—Jesus! Patrick! I thought you were Nish.

—Oh, thank you very much.

She'd rolled over and thrown off the blanket. Perched on the edge of the futon, she took some deep breaths. —What time is it?

—Just gone six. You know, normally when I bring a beautiful woman home, I expect to find her in the bed *with* me.

She rubbed her bare arms. —You're lucky you fuckin *got* home. What the hell happened to you last night?

—I remember you gettin in the cab. Here, you're frozen.

Patrick took off his jacket and passed it to her. She tugged it on, relishing warmth and scent. Patrick, picking the blanket up off the floor, muttered about a virus or maybe a migraine, but his head felt fine, which made no sense, because the scattered times he got a migraine . . . He peered at her. —Wait, who won?

—I did.

—*You* did? That's excellent. That's—ah, Jesus, everyone's gonna think I left because I got pissed off it wasn't me. And Nish would have said—I'm sorry—I mean—I only had the one drink.

—You look ghastly. You want to go see a doctor?

—I'm fine. Let me make you some tea. I could do some eggs too.

She nodded.

Once in the kitchen and out of Paulette's sight, Patrick scowled. He felt like his blood had gone gelatinous. —You did the right thing, leavin Nish. It's none of my business. I'm just glad you didn't hang around for months on end, like some women do. At least he wasn't beatin ya.

—What did the police say about your break-in?

Patrick thought about what he'd just said; he thought about the blanket. —I never went to the police after.

Buttoning the jacket, Paulette walked into the kitchen. —For the love of God, Patrick, someone broke in and stole your gear!

—So I lost a bush hammer and some stone out of it. Thief's a wannabe mason, I spose. He left the upstairs alone, though. I figured he knew no one's livin there. Drugs, girl, guaranteed.

—And you don't think the Constab should know that maybe some arsehole drug dealer's got a spiked hammer?

—Cops won't listen to the likes of me.

She rolled her eyes. —The likes of you?

—That little punk who ambushes the pedo in my novel, beats the livin shit outta him: scattered bit autobiographical.

She accepted a mug of tea. —I figured that.

—Young offender's record out of it.

—Patrick, think it through. That record's sealed, and you're almost forty.

—This is Newfoundland, Paulette: the only secrets we got are the ones everybody knows. Besides, I'm after tellin the story, now, aren't I?

—Paranoid much?

He dropped sugar in his tea. —Pragmatic.

Maybe an hour later, head down to avoid the drizzle and fog, Paulette left the old house where Patrick rented his basement apartment. She noticed the flimsiness of his door, a late addition to the house obscured by a concrete stairwell: an easy break-in.

Parked around the corner, at the far end of a private lane between houses, Nish watched her. —Walk of shame, right down to the goddamned jacket.

He let her go a good two blocks before driving to catch up.

Rain started; Paulette groaned. *The jacket.* A pickup truck pulled over.

Nish's truck.

The passenger-side window descended, and Nish leaned over, smiling his peaceful smile. The dark circles beneath his eyes crinkled. —You're gonna get soaked. You want to come back to the house and call a cab from there? Just to the porch?

A rainy Sunday morning, empty streets, drawn curtains: the entire neighborhood bore down on Paulette, like the presence of someone hungover, someone whom she feared to disturb. She patted her dress, knowing even as she did so that she'd left her damn phone in that damn clutch back at The Rooms—putting it down when she saw Patrick stagger—left it on the cushioned bench under the painting of the eighteenth-century soldier whose red coat frayed into a hundred threads.

A half-hour walk. I say no, he can follow me, find out where I'm living.

She'd slept so badly, thrilled about the award, angry about not being able to celebrate, worried about Patrick.

—All right.

Nish said nothing as they drove, and Paulette just looked out her window.

At the house, Nish held the door for her and then hurried to the kitchen, as if not wanting to eavesdrop. He didn't know she didn't have her phone, and she almost called out to him. *I don't need his damn permission to use the phone. This was my house too.* She zipped off her boots—Nish hated dirt on the carpets—and tiptoed to the living room.

For the love of God, Nish.

He'd piled a month's worth of mail, newspapers, and magazines around the sofa. She caught an odor she'd not known since living in the crowded foster home: old piles of dirty laundry. She looked for the phone book, unable to recall a single taxi company's number as other memories plagued her: Nish buying her roses on their first date when she said she'd never gotten flowers; Nish praising her writing in a workshop; Nish carrying her into the bedroom; Nish proposing to her the night he won the Giller; Nish telling her off for leaving his side at a party; Nish punching her belly and dragging her to the living room floor, where he kicked her and—

Not rape. Bad as it got, she couldn't call it rape. The kicks had been more or less by accident too; she'd been rolling on the floor, snotting and begging. The punching? A problem, yes, but then she'd pissed him off somehow.

Tea things clinked. Nish bore a tray. —Could we talk? I just want to talk.

Neck stiff and kinked, eyes raw and swollen: she'd been crying, and her face slid on her own tears and sweat, on plastic. She wanted to vomit. *Patrick must have picked up a virus, and*—

Clammy plastic stuck to her bare legs, her upper chest, her face. Pain: breasts, shoulders, wrists, ankles, labia, vagina. The weight of her hands bore down on the small of her back.

Paulette, you stupid cunt!

She'd feared a little setup like this for months, telling herself she was overreacting, because no matter how he looked at her, spoke to her, or even how he struck her, Nish would never try to *keep* her. The futon down in his study, his finished office in the basement, his precious little windowless sound-insulated room all cut off from the world so he might create in peace, handy bathroom nearby—had to be the futon, had to be the study. Nish sometimes explained things to Paulette in the study. She did not enjoy her visits. Hands behind, ankles together: whatever he'd tied her with felt sharp and hard. She rolled onto her side, pressing her strained shoulder. She rolled back, trying to look around. Nish had removed his desk. He'd sealed the futon in plastic and tacked some more plastic sheeting on the walls, leaving the sound foam bare. Words uttered in Nish's study became sterile and solitary; the sound foam sucked the room dry of echo. Paulette groaned. Then she shouted the only word that mattered.

—Nish!

Tightening a cable tie around the wires of his computer, desk now set up near the bathroom, Nish smirked. His knees cracked as he walked to the study door and unlocked it.

Breathing hard, Paulette looked at Nish's feet. She needed to hear his voice, gauge his mood, before daring to meet his eye.

He wore dark socks, perhaps from last night. He seemed to be waiting for something.

Finally he spoke. —I might hit two thousand words today.

Paulette knew the tone well: reasonably calm but delicate— volatile. The wrong word, just the wrong intonation, would anger him. —That's great.

—Of course, the trick is to make it two thousand *good* words.

—Always. Nish, honey, I wonder if you could let me up.

—In a little while. I've done some renovatin, keepin busy.

—I noticed. Could you get me a glass of water?

—Sure.

Outside, he keyed the lock shut.

She listened to his tread on the stairs. Up in the kitchen he ran water, then cracked the old-fashioned ice tray, the one with the aluminum handle. Beneath his weight the ceiling creaked, reminding Paulette of a frightening day in the foster home. The older boys had invited her to play hide-and-seek with them in the basement, beneath the kitchen, while their foster mother made supper. That ceiling had creaked so loudly that Paulette feared the entire house would collapse. The boys had laughed first, but then they agreed, taunting her. Any moment now the ceiling would give out, and it would all come tumbling down and bury them. Maybe an arm would stick out of the rubble, maybe a head. Any moment.

Nish returned, carrying ice water and a box cutter. He put the glass on the floor, sat next to Paulette, and sawed through the plastic ties. As he dragged her up to her feet and escorted her to the bathroom, she felt pain in her right ankle. *When did I twist that?* She thought about Nish's eyes and the spray bottle of tile cleaner beneath the sink. She thought about the bruises, old and new, on her thighs. She thought about the keeping of secrets. *Pants and long sleeves for the next few weeks, girl. Today is going to leave marks.*

Paulette stumbled. Nish caught her. Arm around her waist, he guided her back to the futon. —Better?

She nodded.

He kissed the top of her head, and sighed. —Why?

—I'm sorry. I can see I hurt you. I'm so sorry.

—You're sleepin with him, aren't ya?

—Nish—no, honey, no.

—No? Whose house were you comin out of this mornin? Whose goddamned fancy jacket were you wearin, hey, and with whose goddamned credit card in it?

First-person, girl, first-person, don't make him think you're blaming him. —I know, I know, it looks bad, but I just wanted to make sure he got home okay. But I'm here now, so you can just give him back his stuff, okay? Can you do that for me, Nish? Please?

—Here, you're thirsty.

She gulped water. The glass slipped from her numb hands; Nish managed to catch it.

—Oh my God, Nish, I'm sorry, I'm sorry.

—It's okay. You want help with the rest of it?

—No, no. I'm fine.

—So it really doesn't leave any taste? I was gonna give it to you last night and bring you home then, but young fellah Paddy got in the way. As usual.

Paulette closed her eyes. Havoc—cable ties, locked doors, some drug or another, but something else, quite strong all by itself: dread.

Nish took another cable tie from his pocket and wrenched it around her wrists.

—You're hurting me.

—Jesus, Paulette—you're overreactin.

—You're tying my hands!

—In front this time. What, you need me to remind you what *hurt* means?

—Nish—

—Because it sounds like you've forgotten.

—No! No, I haven't forgotten.

He eased her onto her back. —Then settle down.

Damp from a shower, bathrobe on, Nish crossed his arms and nearly filled the front doorway. —O'Mara. What the fuck do you want?

—Have you seen Paulette?

—Paulette no longer lives here, but I think you knew that.

Patrick winced. —Yeah, that's none of my business.

—Goddamned right, it's not. So again: what the fuck do you want?

—I think Paulette's got my credit card by mistake. I want to check with her before I go through the hassle of reportin it stolen. I've been tryna reach her for hours, but her cell must be turned off. Her landlady hasn't seen her since yesterday, and you weren't answerin *your* phone—

Landlady. You know where she's livin. —Couldn't you satisfy her?

—Well, I didn't expect her to stoop to a mercy fuck, but you are lookin pretty smug there. Hey, if that's all you can get—

—Looks like you paid her with your plastic. Used to that, are ya?

—Flannigan—ya fuckin drama queen. Do you know where she is?

Nish slammed the door.

Constabulary headquarters, designed in the architectural shadow of brutalism, felt like a dark brick bunker. Inside, bright and copious lights gave people a sickly cast. On this quiet Sunday afternoon, the lights shone on a duty sergeant and a nervous visitor, a man slipping his hands in and out of his pockets.

The sergeant rubbed his bloodshot eyes with the pads of his fingers. —You want to contact your bank about a stolen credit card, Mr. O'Mara.

—It's not stolen. It's missin. And I'm afraid the woman who's got it might be too.

The sergeant flipped his notepad to a fresh page. —Hang on. I'm getting over a stomach flu. Bastard of a bug on the go.

Patrick nodded. —Had it yesterday.

—Her name is Paulette Tiller, and she was over to your apartment last night? And she left this morning?

—Walked home.

—But just this morning?

—I know, I know, but she always takes my calls. This—this is gettin complicated—her husband—

—What's his name?

—Nish Flannigan.

The sergeant added "domestic" next to the names. —Nish from Ignatius. I had an uncle called Nish.

Patrick wanted to leap across the desk and shake him.

The sergeant pretended to give Patrick another lazy glance, noting his features and body language, his anxiety, his voice. —Is there a history here?

—I dunno what to be thinkin. She's frightened to death of him, but I never noticed it till this mornin. If she's that scared, why didn't she just leave earlier?

—It's never as simple as just leaving, Mr. O'Mara.

—Yes, it is! You just walk out the door.

—Do it.

—Wha?

The sergeant pointed to the main entrance. —Walk out.

—I can't. We're in the middle of a conversation, and besides, you'd come after me. You're a cop.

—Yet you're perfectly free to just leave.

Slouching in his chair, Patrick tried to figure it out.

—How long ago did Ms. Tiller separate from Mr. Flannigan?

—Maybe a month ago.

—Dangerous time.

Patrick nodded, though he didn't understand. He also didn't expect the hard look and the question he got next.

—Mr. O'Mara, why is this complicated?

Nish squinted at the Constabulary officer on his doorstep.

—Don't you wait forty-eight hours or somethin? Who's after reportin her missin? Paddy O'Mara, I suppose.

—Mr. Flannigan?

Nish sighed. —She left me, all right? Four weeks and three days ago.

—I'm sorry to hear that. When did you see her last?

—Last night. Socially, at the Torngat party, but we didn't speak. She spent most of the night talkin to O'Mara. They even left together. He was over here earlier, throwin that in my face. You know that little shagger's been up on assault charges, right?

Considering possible conflicts between words and meanings, the officer passed Nish a card. —Call me at this number if you hear from her.

Think it through, Nish.

He tugged medical gloves onto his sweaty hands, thinking it through quite clearly, thank you. He'd have to risk a drive to the bog, that patch up the shore Paulette liked so much, because his carpentry just wasn't up to building anything like a false wall. Nor was he about to dig up the backyard, not with his creaking knees. *Know your weaknesses,* he'd always told his students, *and work around them.* He wrenched open the bedroom closet door and dug beneath a pile of laundry, some of it clean, most of it not. His fingers brushed the smooth handle, the spiked head, of Patrick O'Mara's bush hammer. Nish had quite enjoyed burgling Patrick's apartment—*in broad fuckin daylight, no less, easy as droppin by for a cup of tea*—easy and thrilling, like writing fiction used to be. Nish even liked saying the silly verb aloud, conjugating it: I burgle, you burgle, he she it burgles. Wearing medical gloves that afternoon too, Nish had examined several of the stoneworking tools, recalling Patrick's explanations. *The bush hammer—yeah, I know, I always laugh too—the bush hammer's got these spike things in the head, so when you beat metal or stone with it, you get this distressed look. Right beautiful, sometimes. The stone pick, though, that's the one that scares people, all curved and long and comin to a point: right vicious-lookin. Wicked.*

Wicked. Like Paulette, holding the buoy.

Nish imagined discussing this scenario in a workshop. *So your protag's made up his mind. What does he choose? Not the pick. It's too easy.* He swung the bush hammer, finding its range, testing its weight. Then he noticed a particularly sweet detail, good for the bog: a name etched in the handle, letters burned black.

O'MARA.

He laughed.

He dropped the hammer on his foot.

Paulette jerked awake. Nish was yelling—in another room, good, but yelling. Her sweat cooled quickly, and her swollen hands throbbed. How many more lessons before this little stunt ended? So much weight, splitting her open—*Come on, Nish, give your balls a chance to fill up*—because he would own her. Break her too. Sure. You were free to break what you owned. Paulette understood that.

Nish unlocked the door and limped into the study. Paulette recognized Patrick's bush hammer. She recognized many things in that moment, as fight-or-flight bowed to dread. Big conversation in a little room: she'd not get to say much. She'd not get to finish the next book. She'd not get to apologize to Patrick about the jacket. She'd not have to worry about long sleeves and pants.

Nish studied her, curled up on the futon, tied fists protecting her face. Speech rapid and pressed, she bargained: never talk to Patrick again, break her lease, move back in, never so much as look at another man—

She took the first blow on her shoulder. Screamed. The second blow, skull, finished it.

Shut her up, at least.

Nish pried the hammer free of Paulette's head: much less blood than he'd expected. He started rolling up the plastic.

Jesus, Paulette, either you're gettin heavy or I'm gettin old.

*

I feel like the proper fuckin stalker here.

By sunset Patrick had called Paulette's cell eight more times. The Constab had contacted him again, a different officer, this one hinting through wayward questions about violent pasts. Would Mr. O'Mara feel angry, hypothetically, if Ms. Tiller returned to her husband, angry enough to do something about it? Patrick had killed that conversation with a request that anything else the police wished to say to him beyond *We found her, Mr. O'Mara, thank you for your help* could be said in front of a goddamned lawyer.

He stared up through his kitchen window; trees darkened as the light failed.

He set out shortly after nine.

Nish and Paulette's neighborhood smelled of barbecued suppers, and Patrick, suddenly hungry, had no trouble sneaking around the back of their house. Or was it just Nish's house now? *How the hell does that work, her leavin, her payin rent while he stays put?*

Mature trees and a stone wall kept the yard dark.

Nish's pickup was backed in, just below the deck. *A townie's truck*, Patrick had called it, *always so goddamned clean, neither sign of work stainin it.* Cautious of creaks, Patrick walked up the steps. On the deck he glanced back at the pickup: empty lined cab. He sidestepped shovels and the old charcoal barbecue; he peered in the kitchen window.

Nothing.

Fuckin foolishness. Go home out of it.

Turning away, he caught movement inside. The door leading to the basement opened; Nish seemed to be hauling some burden.

Patrick squinted.

Nish flicked on a light.

A racket of snow shovels clanging against the barbecue, of a body thudding the deck, of clothespins spilling: Nish cried out. He hit the outside lights, took a good look, and laughed, opening the window. —Jesus, Paddy, ya got no gift for subtlety.

Blushing, Patrick wrenched himself free of the barbecue.

—Door to the deck's not workin right. Come round the front. We'll have a drink.

Nish kept Patrick waiting a few minutes, but he was smiling when he unlocked the door. Patrick asked to wash his hands.

—You've been here dozens of times. You know where everythin is.

Patrick disliked visiting the bathroom on the upper floor, because he had to pass through the master bedroom. *Gives me a chance to look around, though.* The sight of the bed, rumpled on one side, neat on the other, made Patrick wince. The bathroom: nothing strange. Nail scissors on the floor, plenty of dust, a few sour facecloths, one toothbrush.

Paranoid much?

Patrick dried his hands on his jeans.

In the living room, he sat on the sofa. Nish gave him one of two glasses of malt whiskey, a three-finger measure.

Might be a long chat.

It was a long chat, and mostly in Nish's voice: writing, women, writing, Paulette. —I'm not—I'm not complete, without her. It's that simple. And Paddy, I really owe you an apology. Last night—I couldn't help thinkin—y'all right, or what?

—I'm after pickin up a stomach flu.

Patrick stood, wobbled, fell back on the sofa.

Nish shook his head. —Man up, my son: that's twice. No, put that fancy phone of yours on the coffee table.

Patrick did this, feeling agreeable. So obedient: his will and good sense screamed at him, but the noise seemed small, and far away, confined.

—Lie on your front.

—I gotta—

Patrick vomited on a pile of newspapers.

Nish sighed. —Whenever you're ready.

—Flannigan, ya fuckin drama queen. Whadja use?

—God knows, but it's easier to buy than weed.

Patrick's nausea burrowed. He knew quite well that Nish Flannigan, award-winning novelist and former mentor, had just drugged his drink and now tied him hand and foot with bright little plastic collars he'd purchased at an office supply store, likely getting a few pens and ink for the printer while he was at it. Patrick knew all this, but he hardly cared. He no longer had the will to care. He needed the room to stop spinning, so he could remember how he'd gotten there. *One goddamned crisis at a time.*

Nish shouted from the kitchen. —What's your through line here, Paddy? Are you tryin to rescue the girl, or are you just tryin to piss me off? Because you've definitely pissed me off. I had a trip to a bog all planned out. Revise-revise-revise, is it?

—Wait!

Patrick rolled off the sofa, ramming his shoulder into the floor. He got himself on his back, and he stretched his neck, trying to see into the kitchen. His own weight crushed his hands; his tears sharpened his vision. Nish booted something that rolled into Patrick's line of sight, something wrapped in plastic. Roll of carpet, maybe. Except his velvet jacket was tangled up with it. So was Paulette's red hair.

Nish returned to the living room, carrying the bush hammer. He dangled it over Patrick's face, letting it swing back and forth like a pendulum. Long red hairs, stuck to the hammer with blood, tickled Patrick's lips. Nish dropped the hammer on Patrick's chest. Patrick's next vision: a large can of charcoal lighter fluid and a long tube of matches, the tube decorated with pastel-colored Christmas trees. Patrick wanted to tell Nish that charcoal lighter fluid probably wouldn't do it, and had he thought it through? Nish arranged mail and newspapers around himself and Patrick. Hands shaking, Nish cursed the lightness of the can. He sprinkled paper and flesh. Patrick, gasping, tried to understand.

Nish lit a match.

Arms tight to his chest, Patrick shuffled out of the burn unit. Patients and visitors waiting for the elevator tried not to stare at his face. He tried not to notice. The hospital, and his injuries, still felt like another country. Queasy, latest dose of hydromorphone kicking in, he took the stairs.

Nodding at the nurses, he sat in the chair beside the bed. Unresponsive, a doctor had told him, injured more by the blow to her head and the smoke inhalation than the burns. Her limbs twitched, and her heart monitor beeped too fast, signs of agitation, or pain. Her nurse frowned. From the bedside table, Patrick picked up a book, a fat novel he'd read many times. He knew it well, yet he had trouble recognizing it. Narcotics blocked him, blocked him and changed him, but other forces worked him too: pain, and, despite death, dread.

The hydromorphone gave him vivid dreams. He dreamt of Nish's voice and flashing red lights.

Understanding nothing, Patrick read aloud to Paulette.

Her heart rate slowed; her twitching calmed.

CHARLAINE HARRIS

Small Kingdoms

FROM *Ellery Queen's Mystery Magazine*

ON THIS PARTICULAR spring Tuesday, Anne DeWitt was thrown off her regular schedule. Between brushing her teeth and putting on her foundation, she had to kill a man.

Most mornings Anne was as accurate as a precision watch. Between the moment she rolled out of bed and the moment she got into her car, attractively groomed and dressed, Anne used a total of forty-five minutes. Following a fifteen-minute drive, during which she reviewed the day to come, Anne walked in the front doors of Travis High School at ten minutes before eight o'clock. Her secretary had better, by God, be sitting behind her own desk when Anne's heels clicked on the office floor.

But this Tuesday morning was not like most mornings, due to the short struggle and the longer effort of body disposal.

On the drive to work, she figured he'd scaled the roof while she was asleep, broken in a dormer window in the attic, and let down the attic steps while she was in the shower. (She'd noticed some specks on the carpet under the attic opening. Insulation?) Anne wasn't pleased that she hadn't foreseen this possibility, but she tried not to be too hard on herself either. A woman had to sleep. A shower made noise.

It was her fault, however, that she hadn't included the attic windows in her security system. She'd rectify that immediately.

It was Anne's good luck that she was looking in the mirror. If she hadn't been, she might have missed the flicker of movement as he came through the bathroom door, might not have realized the man was there until the wire cinched around her neck.

It was the would-be killer's bad luck that Anne was standing before the mirror naked, trimming a few errant hairs in her bangs, scissors in her hands. She pivoted instantly, her knees bent, and drove the sharp points upward into his throat, the two blades sinking in with a minimum of effort. Anne never bought inferior steel. Anne's hand came away, leaving the scissor blades in the double wound to minimize the inevitable leakage.

As a bonus, the dying man landed on the cotton bathmat with its no-slip rubber backing, which soaked up the trickles of blood.

Anne squatted by the body as the man died and looked at him intently. She was mildly surprised to discover she knew him: Bert Sawyer, her neighbor of two months, who'd moved in two doors west. He'd come over to borrow her jumper cables a week before. Anne spared a moment to think about that as she got the extra shower-curtain liner, still in its packaging, from the bathroom linen closet.

She assumed "Bert" had had backers. They'd taken time to set this up, time and money. If Bert had been acting on his own, his preparation was even more impressive. This had been a carefully thought-out plan. None of the kids at Travis High School would have recognized their principal as she smiled at the failure of this plan, at her victory.

But it had been a victory by too narrow a margin. Anne's smile faded as she called herself to task. She was alive only because Bert had made stupid choices.

Why hadn't he attacked while she was asleep? Why had he waited until daylight, until she was clearly up and about? She stared down at the body, tempted to give it a kick. She was pretty damn irritated about losing the scissors.

A glance at her wall clock told her she was already running five minutes late, and there was a small spot of blood on her left shoulder. Dammit! She stepped back in the shower and washed herself off in case there were specks she hadn't noticed, careful not to get her hair wet since she'd already styled it for the day. She didn't want to spend the extra time to repeat the process.

As the water beat down, she thought hard about her next step. She was tempted to leave the body where it was until she came home from work, but there was always the chance that they (if there was a "they") would call the police, concoct some story that might compel the police to check out the inside of her house. *Heard screams . . . saw smoke . . . think someone's broken in . . .* any of those might make a conscientious cop insist on checking out the interior.

Anne puffed out her cheeks in exasperation as she completed her makeup. No, she had to do a certain amount of cleanup. Now she would be late, no doubt about it, and her record at this job had been as perfect as her record at her previous employment. Son of a bitch.

Her jaw set in a grim line, Anne pulled on rubber gloves and removed the plastic liner from its packaging. Anyone might use rubber gloves to clean, just as anyone might keep an extra shower-curtain liner. Right? Hindered by the small floor space, Anne (who was very lean and athletic) managed to roll the body and the bath-mat onto the clear plastic sheet and began securing it from the feet up, using duct tape from a fresh roll.

She left the scissors in the man's throat with a pang of true regret. She'd looked at many pairs of scissors before she'd selected those, and she'd used them exclusively to trim hair. That was why they'd maintained their great edge.

Well, she thought, *it was worth it*. She'd wiped off the handles, of course. She was sure any tiny snips of her hair that might have adhered to the blades would be too degraded by the time the body was found to be of any use to criminalists. In time she'd acquire some more scissors for the rare self-trim job. Before she covered the dead man's face, she took another look.

Like Anne's, Bert Sawyer's hair was thick, though his was sable brown, several shades darker than hers. She wondered if Bert's hair was dyed, like hers; probably. She had another sudden thought, and pushed aside the would-be killer's hair in a couple of spots close to his ears. Huh. He'd had plastic surgery. She turned his face to the overhead light again, really concentrating on its contours, but there'd been so many faces in those ten years she'd run the school at her previous job.

And that had to be why he'd come here.

Anne deployed the duct tape until Bert Sawyer was encased and leak-proof. She cast a critical eye around the bathroom. There was no blood visible to the naked eye on the vanity or the mirror, but she ran a washrag over them nonetheless. All the while she puzzled over Bert Sawyer's true identity. But she dismissed her concerns after a glance at her watch; twenty minutes late, and the body to dispose of!

She called her secretary. "Christy, I'm running late today," she said. Anne's policy was never to apologize for things she couldn't have prevented.

"You are?" Christy, the doughy, fiftyish school secretary, couldn't hide her astonishment. "You're sick? Oh, I hope you haven't had an accident?"

Anne said, "My car wouldn't start. It's running now, but I'm behind."

"No problem," said Christy reassuringly.

Anne tried not to snarl at the phone. Of *course* the disruption of her routine was no problem for Christy; but it certainly was to Anne. "I'll be in as soon as I can. The Meachams aren't due for another forty-five minutes."

"Right," Christy said. "Oh, and Coach Halsey is in here. I'll tell him to come back."

The baseball coach had never come to her office for a one-on-one before. Anne almost asked what Holt Halsey wanted, but it was hardly Christy's job to find out, if the information hadn't been volunteered. "Do that," Anne said pleasantly and evenly.

She went into the bedroom to put on her underwear and went back to the bathroom to check her shoulder-length hair, stepping over the corpse on her way. Then Anne put on the outfit she'd laid out the night before: gray trouser suit, well cut, with a darker gray silk blouse. Garnet earrings and a necklace with a garnet pendant, small and tasteful. But then she put on sneakers, grabbing the black pumps she'd selected to go with the outfit.

Anne bounded down the stairs, passed through the gleaming kitchen with its block of sharp knives, and opened the door to the garage. After placing her high heels on the floorboard of the passenger-side front, Anne opened her trunk, spreading out another plastic sheet (just in case). There was a cheap yellow rain slicker, the kind you could buy in a hanging pouch from the rack of any dollar store, hanging on a hook by the back door. Anne pulled it on, carefully drawing the hood over her chestnut hair. She went back up the stairs to her bathroom to grab the ankles of the plastic-shrouded corpse. Tugging carefully, steadily, digging in her feet, Anne dragged the body down the stairs.

Bert Sawyer's head bumped against each wooden step. Anne, who'd heard much worse noises, ignored the sound.

Getting Bert into the trunk was tricky, but nothing Anne hadn't done before. When the body was completely inside, she pulled off the cheap slicker and stuffed it in with the body. She went into the house one final time to grab her purse and give her hair a once-over look in the mirror. Finally—finally!—she was on her way to work. She'd been thinking while she stuffed Bert in the trunk, and she'd thought of a good spot to dispose of him.

The winding roads and pleasantly rolling hills relaxed Anne, as always. The four-lane was moderately busy, but due to Anne's unwilling delay, there were fewer cars than usual. When she got close to the spot she'd chosen, she drove in the slow lane until the road was clear. Then she whipped right and went down a gravel road just wide enough for her car. Luckily it hadn't rained recently, or she would have had to make a different choice. But Bert would molder nicely out here. It would only get warmer and damper every week now that spring had arrived in North Carolina.

At the end of this service road was some sort of electrical relay tower, surrounded by a high gated fence liberally posted with warnings. The gate was heavily padlocked, which was fine with Anne, since she had no interest in gaining entrance. Her car was far enough into the woods to be invisible from the four-lane, and she maneuvered Bert's body out of the trunk with the facility of experience. As a bonus, the gravel road was slightly raised for drainage, so she was able to roll the plastic bundle into the forest and then drag it through the pines until it could not be seen from the gravel track. After leaving the body behind a copse, Anne grabbed a fallen branch. On her way back to the car, she swept away the swath the passage of the corpse had cut through the winter leaves and pine needles. She was glad the temperature this morning was in the high fifties; she didn't want to work up a sweat.

Good enough, Anne thought as she stood by her car brushing her jacket and her pants. She swung the car around on the apron before the fence, and when she returned to the four-lane she stayed back in the tree line until the road was clear.

It was less than 2 miles to Travis High School, where Anne had worked for four years—two as assistant principal, two as principal. After she'd parked in her designated parking space, she exchanged her sneakers for the high heels.

She looked up at the big wall clock as she entered the school lobby. She was now fifty minutes late. *Damn* Bert Sawyer, and whoever had recruited him. Anne shoved the anger aside. She would have to think seriously about Bert and his garrote later. No one had tried to kill her for three years.

For now her head should be in its proper place. This school was her kingdom; she was its ultimate ruler. She relaxed because she was within the walls of her domain.

She got her second surprise for the day when she opened the door to the outer office, Christy Strunk's domain. Coach Holt Halsey was still waiting for her. This surprise wasn't exactly either good or bad, but it was unprecedented. Her respect for the baseball coach, who'd come on board two years ago, was not only based on Halsey's winning record but also on the fact that Halsey seemed to solve his own problems in a rational way.

Christy looked at her with some apology, and Anne understood that she'd tried to get the coach to return later, with no success. Anne said, "Good morning, Christy."

A few brisk steps took her abreast of Halsey, who'd risen from his chair. It didn't bother Anne at all to look up at him. She was not intimidated by large men. But she hesitated before using his first name, since she'd never done so. "Holt, how long do you need? I have less than ten minutes, if that'll do the job."

The coach nodded. "I only need a few minutes," he said. She walked over to the inner door, the door to her office, with her name on it. She loved the sight of it, no matter how many times she passed it. That she'd been born neither Anne nor DeWitt made no difference to her pleasure.

"I'll hold your calls, Mrs. DeWitt," Christy said unnecessarily. That was SOP in this office.

"Come in," Anne said. Christy had been in to turn on the light and deposit her messages, but everything was as Anne had left it the evening before. She checked automatically as she moved behind the desk to put her purse in its drawer. She'd carefully arranged the office to make it seem as though she'd led a complete life. There were two pictures of her parents, one of her sister, and one of her deceased husband.

None of these people existed. Of course she had had parents, but she'd never met them. She'd never been married. To the best of her knowledge, she didn't have a sister. "Have a seat, Holt," Anne said, pulling out her own chair and sitting. There was a handful of call slips lined up beside her mouse pad. It had taken her two weeks to break Christy of the habit of telling her about each call as she entered the office. She allowed the fearful idea that she might have to leave, that there might be another attempt —who had the would-be assassin alerted when he'd tracked her down? With grim determination, she shoved this conjecture back to the corner of her mind.

Coach Halsey was sitting, elbows on knees, in one of the lightly padded chairs positioned in front of Anne's neat desk. Holt Halsey was a broad-shouldered man, a couple of inches over 6 feet, and he had a face that might have been chiseled out of granite. He wasn't unattractive in a rough-hewn way, but he didn't work that attraction, and he didn't show a lot of emotion. Anne liked both qualities.

"Clay Meacham is a problem," Holt Halsey said, without further ado.

"Odd you should bring him up. His parents are coming in right after I finish talking to you."

The coach's flinty face managed to convey his opinion of the Meachams in a precise, economical tightening of the lips.

Brandon and Elaine Meacham, the parents of Travis High's star pitcher, were active in the Baseball Boosters Club, and they spent a lot of time volunteering at other school activities. Clay was their only child. They didn't miss a single opportunity to support and promote the handsome junior.

If Clay had been as good a young man as he was talented, Anne would have thoroughly approved. Clay's academic and athletic glory was the school's (and therefore her) glory. But Clay was not a good young man, and his judgment was deeply flawed.

"What's he done?" she asked.

"He was messing with Hazel Reid."

Their eyes met while Anne absorbed the implications. She considered wasting time with things a normal woman would have said, like "How is she?" or "Should we call the police?" None of that was on the table: if it had been, Holt would have led with the worst news. Hazel Reid was mentally and emotionally handicapped. But she was also a physically mature sixteen. Anne said, "How far did it go?"

"He'd taken her shirt off," the coach said.

"Where?"

"In the woods in back of the school. If she hadn't been wearing bright pink, I wouldn't have spotted them."

"So, after school. But on school property."

"Yeah."

"Why wasn't she on her bus?" Hazel was supposed to catch the vehicle derisively called "the short bus" to her home.

"Her mom was here for teacher conferences. She'd parked Hazel on the bench outside to wait. Clay saw her when he was walking to his car after practice. I guess he was in a bad mood. Or maybe a good one."

"Does he know you know?" she asked.

"Not for sure. I called him on his cell phone, asked him if he'd seen Hazel in the parking lot, her mom was looking for her."

Anne checked the list of phone calls she'd gotten that morning, and Mrs. Reid wasn't on it. "Hazel didn't tell," Anne said.

"I don't think she minded," the coach said. "But she's not mentally capable to consent or refuse."

"Noted," Anne said. She thought for a moment, and Coach Halsey let her.

Her previous job had been far tougher than this one, and when she'd left it so abruptly, she'd sworn to herself she wouldn't ever get so invested again. But here she was, thinking of Travis High and its reputation.

Did Anne care about each individual student? No. But this was her turf, and she would protect it. She would make it as perfect as she could. When she looked up at the rugged, impenetrable face of her baseball coach, she surprised a look almost of . . . sympathy. And for a second . . .

"Do I know you?" she asked, with no premeditation.

He smiled. It was like watching rock move. "It's time for the Meachams to get here. I'll hear from you later." It wasn't quite a question.

"You will," she said, and stood up. They eyed each other for a moment. It was as though Holt Halsey was willing her to realize something. But then he turned to go, and she had to change gears to deal with Clay's parents.

The Meachams weren't anything special, in Anne's expert esti-mation. Brandon, handsome like his son but not as mean, might look at other women but he never touched. His wife, Elaine, a former pageant queen, made a creditable effort to conceal the fact that she didn't give a shit about anyone else's child but her own. She would clap for another child's achievement, she would tell the other moms how much she admired their progeny, but in truth she believed the sun shone out of Clay's ass.

All in all, Anne couldn't feel surprised that Clay had no sense of guilt in taking advantage of a handicapped girl. He was sure that everything he did was fine, simply because he, Clay, wanted to do it.

"Mrs. DeWitt," Elaine Meacham said, flashing her broad white smile. "Thanks for making the time to see us today."

"Of course. What do we need to talk about this morning?" Anne asked, trying to cut through the pleasantries. She gestured them to the chairs in front of her desk, took her own seat again.

"I saw you at the last game," Brandon said, to make sure she knew he appreciated her. "I know the kids think it's really cool that you go to all the sporting events."

"Of course I do," Anne said. *This is my school,* she thought. *I'm going to go to everything I physically can.* She adopted her fallback face: pleasant but not encouraging. Not only did she have to think about Coach Halsey's tale; the pile of paperwork in the in-basket wasn't going to take care of itself. She had two other meetings scheduled during the day too, one with a prospective temporary replacement for the enormously pregnant Spanish teacher and one with a vendor who wanted the school to switch to his software system in the chemistry lab. The vendor would ask her out for a drink after work: she would refuse him. She was going to have to be more forceful in her refusal this time.

Barely able to restrain some manifestation of her boredom and her itching desire to get to the work on her desk, Anne had to sit through a few more platitudes before Brandon got down to brass tacks.

"Principal DeWitt—Anne—we hope the school will help Clay achieve his goal," Brandon said very seriously.

"Which goal is that?" Anne worked to keep her voice neutral. She was thinking of how much she'd like to kick Clay Meacham's ass. The enormity of the boy's offense was sinking into her psyche.

She didn't even want to imagine the headlines, the disgrace of the school, the navel-gazing that would inevitably follow the exposure of Clay's little after-hours adventure with the hapless Hazel Reid. Anne found herself thinking wistfully of some of the more inventive punishments she'd employed at her previous job.

Instead of getting to the point, the Meachams began the litany of what Clay had meant to the school: class president, star athlete, honor roll, captain of the debate team. "And what goal would that be?" Anne prompted again, when she felt her impatience building to a dangerous level.

Cut off in midflow, Elaine looked comically surprised. "I'm sorry?" she said.

"I'm very well aware of Clay's position at Travis," Anne said evenly. "Can you tell me what you think Clay needs from this school?"

"Sure," Brandon said. "Sure. I'm sorry, we got kind of carried away, like parents tend to do." He smiled at Anne in what he surely felt was an ingratiating manner, though he couldn't suppress the snap of irritation in his voice.

She tried not to let her shoulders heave in a sigh of exasperation, but maybe the lines of her face conveyed her strong desire to extract some specifics.

"It's his senior film." Elaine again bathed Anne in the radiance of her brilliant smile.

"Clay isn't in the drama department's film class," Anne said. "I'm afraid I don't follow you."

"He needs a film to send to recruiters. Clay's such an outstanding pitcher, we want to be sure he's placed at the right college, with a good scholarship. So he needs a film to send out to athletic departments early next school year. We've got some examples." Elaine extracted some DVD cases from her purse and set them on the edge of Anne's desk.

"So you'll hire someone to film Clay's games?" Anne said, not reaching for the DVD cases.

"We were kind of hoping that we could use clips from the school's game films," Elaine explained. She kept the smile in place. "It seems like a shame to duplicate effort."

She meant it was a shame for the Meachams to spend their own money. Anne had wondered how Meacham Motors was doing in this recession. She thought she'd just learned the answer.

It was true that the school lined up an employee or some astute volunteer parent to film every baseball game—and all the other sports events too, of course. This was invaluable as a teaching tool, the coaches assured her.

The politically correct response would be that of course Clay's recruiting film could be composed of clips from the game recordings, and Coach Halsey would be happy to help with such an effort. But what if Clay's recent misdeed came to light? Wouldn't the school suffer, especially if it had offered this extra support to an athlete who'd proved to be a rotten, degraded egg? While Anne allowed herself a lot of moral leeway—she had no problem killing people who attacked her—she did deplore Clay's self-indulgence and poor judgment in attempting to seduce a girl who would never be an adult mentally or emotionally.

"I'll discuss it with Coach Halsey," Anne said briskly. "Who would you expect to do the work involved in editing the film, excerpting Clay's pitches? I'm assuming you'd also want the times he comes up to bat included in the recruiting film. I don't know what would be involved, but I'm assuming you two do?"

"Well," Brandon said, doing his best to look as if he weren't being pushy, "I think we were hoping that since Clay is the best pitcher Travis High's ever had, and him going to a good school to pitch would be a great feather for Coach Halsey's cap . . ."

"So you think Coach Halsey should do this work."

Elaine spread her hands. "Well, we were just hoping! Since he's fairly new here, still making his name . . ."

Anne knew how many hours Halsey put in on his job, for slim money. "It's baseball season now," she said, as if they needed to be reminded. "I don't know how much time the coach could devote to doing this for one player, no matter how gifted. Of course we all want to see Clay succeed, and we want him to play for the college of his choice. Has he told you where he'd like to go?" She put on a somewhat brighter smile and got up, signaling the end of the interview.

Somewhat bewildered, the Meachams rose too. "He was thinking of the University of Arkansas—they're in the top five. Or Louisiana. Maybe UCLA, though we don't want him that far from home."

Three top baseball programs. The Meachams were aiming very high. Was Clay really that good? She would ask Coach Halsey.

Anne finally got the Meachams out of the office with promises to "get back with them" after talking to Coach Halsey. Then she returned the calls on Christy's list. Then she dove into the paperwork. Before she knew it, the bell rang for first lunch, the sophomore seating.

Normally Anne would have brought a salad to eat at her desk, or even shared the students' meal choices in the cafeteria, though that was strictly an exercise in morale boosting. But today she went home for lunch, as she was careful to do at least once a week, though never on the same day. Her house, tidy and spruce with its fresh paint and neat yard, had an interior air of slight dishevelment, like a bed made crookedly. Her breakfast cereal bowl still sat by the sink, unrinsed. Upstairs, the bathroom looked curiously incomplete since the bathmat was missing. Her makeup was not aligned on its tray. Her pajamas were still lying across the bench at the foot of her bed. But Anne left these little signals of disruption. She'd take care of them after more pressing matters.

She took her gun with her when she let down the attic stairs and ascended them.

She didn't seriously believe there was another assailant in her attic. But then, she hadn't expected the first one either. That failure was bitter to Anne, whose job in the past had been to teach others to be masters of close fighting. Quicker, smarter, faster, tougher, able to take more stress and dodge more punishment than other human beings. And many people who'd passed through Anne's hands had become wonderful killers.

Standing in her own attic, seeing the evidence of last night's intrusion, Anne was bitterly aware she had failed. She'd been lulled by her artificial life into an equally artificial sense of security. In her own home, her lack of readiness had come very close to getting her killed.

There were three dormer windows in the attic, which was painted and floored. Its walls were lined with everything that belonged in a storage space. There was a modest box of Christmas decorations underneath a wreath hung on a wall hook. There was a box of old pictures in aged frames, which any casual visitor would assume were ancestors of Anne's.

Well, the long-dead faces belonged to someone's ancestors, but not hers, as far as she knew. She was proud of a trunk of fake memorabilia that had belonged to her fake dead husband. There was an antique quilt inside, among the report cards and trophies, a quilt that must have been stitched by someone's grandmother; it might as well have been "Brad's." There was an old rickety rocking chair by the trunk, just the kind of chair such a grandmother might have rocked in as she quilted. There was a crate packed with a very old set of china, and one full of the sort of scholarly books Anne DeWitt might have collected over the course of her academic progress: Jacobean poets, theories of education, the psychology of leadership. The attic was as carefully staged as the rest of the house.

Bert Sawyer had come in through the west dormer. The dormers faced the road, but in the wee hours of the morning there was not likely to be anyone up or about on this quiet residential cul-de-sac, one carved out of the woods. The house between Anne's and Sawyer's belonged to the Westhovens, and they had left for Florida the previous week. Maybe that was why Sawyer had chosen the previous night for his move on Anne.

The pane on the window had been cut out and removed, and cool spring air flooded the attic, carrying the pleasant scent of budding plants.

Obviously Bert had ascertained that the dormers weren't hooked up to the alarm system. He must have made a preliminary trip to her roof on some previous night. She'd have to figure out how he'd scaled it, because she didn't see a rope and there was no ladder leaning against the eaves, for God's sake. She thought about all these things as she noted the tiny signs of his presence in her attic; the dust on the trunk had been smudged, probably by his butt as he sat on it to wait for the sound of her shower running. There was a small ring in the dust too. Anne decided he'd had a tiny flashlight, and he'd used it to check out the story her attic was supposed to tell. It must have been in his pocket when she dumped him.

The woman she'd formerly been would have learned how to replace her own glass, but Anne DeWitt would not do such a thing. She decided to tell the repairman that a bird must have flown into the window, and she'd found it broken. Of course, Anne DeWitt would have cleaned the mess up immediately. Anne found the pane of glass, leaning carefully against a wall. She put it on the floor and stomped on it. Then she fetched a broom and dustpan from the kitchen and swept up the fragments. She called the handyman who helped her out with things Anne DeWitt couldn't do. He agreed to come the next afternoon at five.

Anne would wait a couple of days to call the alarm-system people.

After another, more thorough cleaning of the bathroom, Anne had only time to grab a granola bar to eat on the way back to school. Her stomach growled in protest, and she promised herself she'd have a good dinner.

On her way back to Travis High, she saw a pickup truck emerging from the gravel road to the electric tower, the spot where she'd dumped Bert Sawyer's body. Every nerve in her body went on the alert as she passed the road and the truck pulled out behind her.

She recognized it. It was Holt Halsey's.

He drove behind her all the way back to the school. She went to the administrative parking lot, and he went left to park by the gym complex.

There was nothing Anne could do about the coach that afternoon. He was a riddle, for sure, and one she'd better solve sooner rather than later. It was no coincidence that he'd gone down that obscure track; and she didn't believe it was a coincidence that he'd emerged from it just when she was approaching.

He'd found the body.

He hadn't told anyone.

After an hour had passed, she knew he wasn't going to.

The meeting with the salesman, her last of the day, was over by five o'clock. Christy was itching to leave, opening and closing drawers on her desk with annoying frequency, as Anne could see (and hear) through her open office door. When this salesman (she mentally called him the Jerk) visited, she always left her door open. She didn't want to have to break his arm, which she had been sorely tempted to do more than once.

The second she stood up to conduct the Jerk out, Christy was out of the door like a shot. The Jerk took the opportunity to put his hand on her arm. "Please reconsider. I'd love to take you to dinner at the lake," he said, smiling his most sincere smile.

Anne looked at him, thinking about pulling out his teeth one by one.

"Sorry," said Holt's deep voice from the doorway. "The principal and I have things to discuss this evening."

The Jerk covered his chagrin well—after all, he was a salesman

—and Holt and Anne regarded each other. There was so much texture and complexity to that look she could have worn it like a sweater. When the Jerk was gone and the school was quiet and empty around them, Holt said, "Well, you had a busy morning. No wonder you were late."

And Anne heard herself saying, "Who *are* you?"

This was a talk that had to be private, but Anne was not about to go to Holt's house, and she didn't want him in hers, not yet. They drove separately to a restaurant that was nearly empty at this time of day. They asked to be seated on the patio, which had just opened for the season. It was almost too cool to sit in the open air in the late afternoon, but Anne was willing to be a little chilly if it meant no one would be close to them.

After they'd ordered drinks and a plate of nachos, he said, "Holt isn't the name I was born with, but I expect to use it for some time. I know you're Twyla Burnside. My little brother was in your tenth class."

Anne considered all this while their drinks came. "So you know all about the event."

"The one that got you fired? Yes."

"Why are you here, at Travis?"

"I did the same training, but in a different location," he said. "The guy in charge was as tough as you can imagine. He was coming up a couple of years before you got your job. David Angola."

She nodded. David Angola had saved her ass at the secret hearing. "I lost one person in almost every class," she said. "Until the tenth class, they always considered it the price of doing business. It was my job to make sure the grads were the best my school could produce. They had to pass the tests I set. Of course the tests were rigorous. I would fail in my mandate if they weren't as challenging as I could possibly devise . . . to ensure the grads were completely prepared for extreme duress and with extraordinary survival skills. Until my tenth year as an instructor, one loss a year was acceptable." She shook her head. "And that year, the lost student was the one with connections."

Holt smiled, very slightly. "You have a huge reputation, even now. David himself said he was a pussy compared to you."

She smiled, a wry twist of the lips. "That's a huge compliment, coming from David. That woman's brain aneurysm could have gone at any time. You can't tell me it gave because of 'undue rigor' or 'borderline cruelty.' Her bad luck, and mine. Her dad had a lot of pull."

Holt's face held no judgment. "They give you the new identity when they fired you?"

"Complete with references."

"Me too."

She raised an interrogative eyebrow.

"Shot the wrong person," he said. "But it was a righteous mistake."

She absorbed that. "Okay," she said. "And you're here because?"

"David heard some people were coming after you. You got some enemies."

"No one's tried for three years."

"Right before I got to Travis, huh?"

"Yeah. This guy was waiting in my car after I chaperoned the senior prom."

"Garrote?"

"No, knife. The man this morning, he had a garrote."

Their nachos came then, and they ate with some appetite.

"David actually sent you here?" she asked, when she'd eaten all she could.

"When they cut me loose with a coach persona, David gave me a call. He thought this might be a good place for me to land."

"I've never felt like you were watching me. Are you that good?"

"I didn't need to watch you too closely. You're great with your cover. This morning, when you came in, I could tell you'd broken your routine because something had happened, and I got a little whiff of blood from your hair."

Anne was intensely angry at herself. She should have taken fifteen more minutes to rewash and restyle her hair.

"So you figured out . . ."

"If I assumed someone had gone for you, I knew where I would have dumped him. I figured I might as well check."

"You're cool with this."

"Sure," he said, surprised. "I had a look at him. Chuck Wallis. He was the brother of . . ."

The name triggered a switch. "Jeremy Wallis. He died in the fifth class. So. Now what?"

"Now we figure out what to do about that little shit Clay."

She smiled. It was not a pleasant smile. It was Twyla Burnside's smile, not Anne DeWitt's. She would have to rebury herself in her new character all over again, but it felt so good to let Twyla out. "I think we need to put the fear into him."

"The fear of God?"

"The fear of us. Oh, by the way, let me tell you why the Meachams came to my office this morning. It'll get you in the mood."

The next afternoon Coach Halsey kept Clay after practice. The kid was tired, because the practice had been extra tough, but he didn't complain. Clay knew that Coach Halsey hated whiners. After he finished the extra exercises the coach had outlined for him, he trudged out to his car. It was dark by now, and he called his mom to let her know he'd be late. He was thoughtful like that, no matter what people said.

At first Clay didn't know what was suddenly poking him in his head. Something hard and small. He felt the presence of someone behind him. "Hey, jerk," he said angrily, beginning to turn. "What the hell?"

"What the hell indeed," said a strange voice, a voice as metallic as the gun that tapped his cheek. "Keep a polite tongue in your mouth. If you want to keep your tongue."

Since nothing awful had ever happened to Clay Meacham, he didn't realize the genuine seriousness of this moment. "Listen, asshole, you don't know who you're messing with," he growled.

He was instantly slapped by something that felt soft but weighty. It stung. He staggered. "You're asking for it!" he yelled.

And then he couldn't yell anymore, because he was seized by two strong arms and gagged and blindfolded by two deft hands. As Clay's fear began to swell and explode in his brain, he was bundled into his own car, his keys were extracted from his pocket, and the two hooded figures drove him down country roads and dirt tracks, deep into the woods.

Once he was on his knees, the metallic voice said, "Clay. We need you to be the best you can be. If you're going to represent all of us when you're in college, you need to be bulletproof. If you're going to be bulletproof, you have to stop molesting women who aren't able to say yes or no. You have to stop being a taker. Because someday someone will call you on it. And then you'll let us down.

I can't tell you how much we don't want that to happen. So, Clay, you need to tell us now about what you've done before, things you're not going to do in the future."

Though his first confession had to be coaxed out of him, Clay found himself telling the two invisible presences everything. Everything he'd ever done to people, people smaller and weaker and less handsome than himself. And he'd done a lot.

After an hour, he was sorry for it all.

By the time Clay got home that night, he flinched whenever his parents asked him a question. He told them repeatedly he'd had a bad day and he only wanted to go to bed. When they demanded to know why his face was so reddened, he said a ball had hit him at practice. He went to his bedroom as though he were dragging a chain behind him, and Elaine and Brandon were too worried to remember to ask Clay if the coach had mentioned working on the recruiting film for him.

Clay only went to school because he was scared to be at home by himself after his parents had left for their jobs. At school he jumped when his friends slung their arms around him, punched him in the shoulder, and in general acted like kids on the cusp of becoming men. For the first time in his life, Clay knew what it was like to be weak. To be lesser.

When his best buddy strolled past Hazel Reid's table in the lunchroom, his fist raised to pound on the table to make Hazel jump (a trick that never grew old with Clay's friends), Clay caught that fist and said simply, "No. Not anymore."

"Awww, man," the friend said, but he'd heard the pronouncement of the most popular boy in school. Not anymore.

Clay turned to leave the lunchroom and saw Principal DeWitt standing, straight and lean as an arrow, about 2 yards away. He was seized by an almost uncontrollable impulse to rush to her and tell her what had happened to him. Everyone said DeWitt was a smart woman and a good principal. She would be able to figure out who'd kidnapped him.

Or maybe not. There were so many candidates.

There were a lot of sins Clay Meacham had never thought twice about committing, sins of which he was now painfully aware. His eyes had been opened last night, even though he'd been blindfolded.

Clay was only seventeen, and he wasn't clear on how he was supposed to attain perfection, but the guidelines he'd been given last night had been pretty clear.

He saw the principal again that day, when she came to watch the team practice. That wasn't an uncommon occurrence. While Clay was waiting to come up to bat, he saw Coach Halsey look at Mrs. DeWitt. It made Clay shiver. Clay'd been scared he'd pitch poorly that day, but now that he knew there'd be a price to pay if he failed, his focus was amazing.

After practice, Principal DeWitt drifted over to talk to Coach Halsey. After a second Coach beckoned Clay over. He trotted over to the two adults.

"I hear you need a recruitment film," Coach Halsey said.

"My parents say I need one to send out next year, yessir," Clay said.

"I'm willing to help you make it, but I won't do all the work," Coach said. "You'll have to put in some hours helping me do other things, so I'll have some free time."

The old Clay would have been sullen about giving up anything to get something that was his due. The new Clay said, "Yessir. Just say when." He turned and went into the locker room.

"I think he's been turned around," Anne said.

"At least for now." Coach Halsey looked down at her. "Want to get dinner Saturday night?"

"I think so," she said after a pause. "There are a few things we might want to talk about."

"Oh?"

"Sarah Toth's dad is hitting her."

"Well," Holt said. "We can't have that. She won't get the high test scores if she's being beaten at home."

"If she scores two points higher the next time she takes the SAT, it'll be a state record."

He smiled. No one else would have enjoyed that smile but Anne. "Then we'd better get cracking."

They both laughed, just a little. "By the way," Holt said. "What happened to the principal before you? You became assistant here the year before she killed herself, right?"

Anne nodded, her expression faintly regretful. "Mrs. Snyder was having sex in her office with a married teacher, Ted Cole.

Christy overheard a conversation between them and came to me with it."

"Then it would have been all over the school in short order." He smiled. "Good job. Proactive."

Anne smiled back before she glanced down at her watch. "I have to be at my house to let the handyman in," she murmured. But she lingered for a moment. "Snyder almost didn't hire me. She was not a fan, from the first interview until the last. But the school board liked me. And the minute I saw Travis High, I knew it was a place where I could make a difference. Now . . ." She looked up at him and away, almost shyly. "Now there's no limit."

"No limit," he agreed, and they stood silent in the lowering sun, their long shadows streaking across the practice field.

JOSEPH HELLER

Almost Like Christmas

FROM *The Strand Magazine*

THE COFFEE WAS GONE AGAIN. Mercer swore softly, tiredly, and carried the coffeepot to the basin. He moved slowly. His eyes were red and he ground them mercilessly with the heels of both hands while the percolator was filling. He needed a shave now, and the total relaxation of his heavy face gave him the hopeless, stupid, waxen look of a drunkard. Carter sat limply at the large pine table and watched him, scarcely seeing him in his own fatigue. It had been a long night, he was thinking, a fantastically wicked, confused, and diabolical night, and it was only just beginning.

He watched Mercer start back across the room and stop at the window to stare out glumly at the entrance to the hospital across the street. The chill fog outside had streaked the glass with drippings of mist that gleamed like cheap jewelry in the light from the naked yellow bulb in the room. The window was dirty, and each time that Carter's eyes fell on the coarse patterns of grime he was reminded of photographs of diseased tissue that he had seen a long time before in *Life* magazine. They had been drinking coffee for hours, and the warm odor was thick and stale in the air and made him nauseous.

"Is anybody out there?"

"A few men," Mercer replied, after a full minute had gone by. "Men from the railroad, probably."

He turned from the window and set the coffeepot on the electric burner. For several seconds there was a quiet fury of hissing and sputtering as the water on the outside of the can boiled off.

Only Henney was in the room with them now. Beeman and

Whitcombe had gone to the hospital to wait for news of the Wilson boy. There were no prisoners in the jail downstairs, and there was little for Henney to do. There never was any real need for a night porter, but Henney was Mercer's cousin, a consumptive, simple-minded man with very weak eyes who could not hold down a job anyplace else, and Mercer maintained the sinecure for him. Henney was reading the newspaper. He had been reading the same eight pages all night. Suddenly he began humming aloud, uncon-scious of the annoyance he was creating.

Mercer stood it as long as he could, and then said, "Henney, go down to the diner and get some chicken sandwiches. Don't let him put any butter on."

Henney came to his feet with a start and hurriedly folded the newspaper. "Sure, Jay, sure."

"Cigarettes," Carter said moodily.

Mercer gave his approval, and Henney walked out. The cof-fee was bubbling already, sending rapid puffs into the air. Mercer brought the pot to the table. Carter shook his head, but he filled both cups anyway and poured condensed milk into them from a can. There was no sugar. Carter stirred the brew and took a quick gulp. The coffee scalded his throat but left his body cold. Mercer sat down facing him.

"Why don't you go home, Carter?" he said slowly. "Get some sleep. Get up early and go away for a few days. Stay out of town awhile. They may get after you also."

Carter shook his head, although he knew Mercer was right. His eyes were stinging with rawness, and there was a stabbing ache in his temples, his jaws, and in the back of his neck. He had caught cold during the chilly vigil. His eyes were tearing, and he wiped them with his hand every few minutes. He needed sleep badly. He rested his head in his upright hands, massaging his face torpidly against his fingers. The contact brought a fleeting relief, but soon the points of his elbows were sore against the rough, unvarnished wood.

He had a busy schedule the next day. He had classes all through the morning and into the afternoon, the first one at eight, and after that the football team to coach until dusk. His puzzlement increased at the thought of the football team. If anyplace, it was there, with all the physical contact that the game required, that he would have expected an outbreak, but that had gone smoothly, better than even he had dared to hope, and then, just as he was beginning to relax, to triumph, abruptly, fiercely, irrevocably, everything that had been accomplished, everything for which he had toiled so long, with a suddenness that left him dazed, was rudely, cruelly, decisively, and insensately obliterated by the primordial brutality of an alley fracas.

His consciousness was throbbing now with the dim recognition of atavistic pressures that were emerging uncontrollably all about him. He could see but not understand them, and they were horrifying in their mute and immutable finality. All afternoon he had been watching the terrible recrudescence of savage animal passions, and he was tormented by the helpless despair of being unable to arrest it, of being unable, even, to try. His confusion rose suddenly, filling him with panic, and he dug his nails painfully into his forehead and shivered.

The sound of footsteps roused him to attention. His eyes went hopefully to the door, but it was only Henney returning with the sandwiches. He stepped into the room spryly, swinging the door closed behind him, and delivered a brown paper bag to Mercer. There was no stop on the door, and it slammed shut with a sharp, reverberating boom that rattled hollowly through the walls of the building and seemed to shake the foundations. Carter winced and Mercer frowned, and Henney, himself surprised by the report, shifted uneasily and smiled at Mercer with apology.

Mercer pushed a package of cigarettes to Carter and began tearing the bag along the seam, doing it slowly, with very deliberate caution. His thoughts were obviously elsewhere, but the intense preoccupation they gave his manner solemnized the act, and for a moment he seemed like a surgeon making a careful incision. There were four sandwiches inside, each wrapped sturdily in thick wax paper. Gazing at them, Mercer spoke to Henney. He said, "Did you see Beeman?"

Henney shook his head. "No, Jay. They said he was still in the hospital."

"Who said?"

"The men outside."

Mercer sighed with exhaustion and looked up at him.

"Henney, what's going on outside?"

"Nothin', Jay," Henney said quickly. "Just a few men waitin' around to see what happens."

Mercer regarded him steadily for a moment and then stared down at the table. He had large hands, Carter noticed, with strong, callused, fleshy fingers. There were spots of dirt on each of the big knuckles and in the folds of skin between them.

"I spoke to Whitcombe," Henney said suddenly. He glanced significantly at Carter, and then went on in an excited voice that kept rising gleefully with a shrill, whinnying, malicious hysteria. "He says we're goin' up tomorrow an' burn 'em all out. He says we're gonna get rid of 'em for good. He says it doesn' matter what happens to the Wilson boy. He says we're goin' up anyway an—"

He might have continued indefinitely had not Mercer interrupted.

"Did you let him put butter on these sandwiches?" he demanded.

The sudden inquiry caught Henney by surprise, and he blinked his eyes in confusion.

"What's 'at, Jay?" he stammered.

"Nothing, Henney," Mercer said, in a softer voice. "It's not important."

He pushed a sandwich to Carter. Carter pushed it back.

"You'd better eat something," said Mercer, with rough solicitude. "You look like hell."

"So do you," Carter replied sullenly.

He took the sandwich and bit into it. The gums on one side of his mouth were inflamed, and he moved the food over with his tongue and chewed it slowly. He drank some coffee and then took another bite and washed that down with more coffee and then, even while he was reminding himself that he had eaten nothing since lunch and was telling himself that the chicken tasted good, he laid the rest of the sandwich aside and forgot it.

"I tol' 'im no butter," Henney said defensively, finally understanding. "I didn' watch 'im, but I tol' 'im not to put any butter on."

Mercer was silent, and Henney picked up his newspaper and resumed reading.

Soon Beeman and Whitcombe returned. Whitcombe was a brash young man of twenty-six who wore his uniform with a careless insolence. Beeman was older, almost forty, and hard as nails. He had a pale, gaunt, angular face, with very thin lips, strong bones, and a small, round, wrinkled scar high up on one cheek, and he was the coldest and most efficient-looking man that Carter had ever seen. He wore black leather gloves, thin, black, tight leather gloves that gave him a menacing air of competence.

"He's going to die," Beeman said, when he had crossed the room and was standing by the window.

"Did he say anything?" asked Carter.

"He's in a coma."

"Did he say anything before that?"

"He don't have to," Whitcombe drawled placidly from the side. "There are witnesses."

"But did he say anything?" Carter implored vehemently.

"He said that Jess Calgary did it," Mercer said, without looking up.

"Is that all?"

"That's all."

Carter cursed silently. Beeman had poured out a cup of coffee, and he came to the table for the can of condensed milk and the wet spoon that lay at Carter's elbow.

"They know you up there, Carter," he said, in his dry, precise voice. "You could bring him in for us."

"I'm a schoolteacher," Carter said. "Not a policeman."

"Not for long," said Whitcombe. "I guess this puts you out of business."

Carter saw the wink he sent in Henney's direction and the unsuccessful effort Henney made to repress a chuckle. He was too weary to resent it.

"We'll pick him up in the morning," Mercer decided. "It's too late to do anything now."

"He may be hard to find," Carter argued.

"There'll be enough people helping us," Beeman replied.

"There sure will," echoed Whitcombe.

Henney, encouraged perhaps by Whitcombe's manner, took a bold step toward Carter.

"Yes," he exclaimed broadly, his pale eyes glinting with a vindictive light. "You're goddamn right there will. You an' your smart college ideas. Puttin' 'em all in the same school like that. We all knew this would happen, but you wouldn' listen. No, you were too smart. Well, it's all your fault, goddammit, an' it serves you right!"

Carter sat without looking at him, listening to his voice as if to some incomprehensible noise in the distance. When he finished, Mercer let out a long breath and spoke to Whitcombe.

"Find something for him to do downstairs."

Henney followed Whitcombe out docilely, glancing back at Carter with dogged emphasis. He was very careful with the door this time, too careful, and after he had gone it swung open with a creaking moan and wavered there slightly in the draft from the hall. Carter stared at it morosely. It distracted him terribly, like a crooked picture hanging on the wall, and he rose finally, swearing, and slammed it shut. Every bone in his back gripped him with pain, and when he sat down he could do nothing but curl forward over the table like some monstrous fetus.

"Go get him, Carter," Mercer said. "It'll be better that way."

"Will you take care of him if I do?"

"We'll do what we can."

"How much will that be?"

Mercer was honest. "You know how it is, Carter," he said regretfully. "We're all relatives here."

Carter laughed scornfully and shook his head.

"Be smart, Carter," said Beeman. "They're your friends, not ours. If we go, every car in town will go with us."

Carter gave no reply. The coffee was making him sick. He carried the cup to the basin and turned the faucet on to rinse it. The force of the water almost tore it from his hand. When he drank finally, the water was tepid and colored slightly with the faint shadow of rust and still tasted strongly of coffee.

"I'll think about it," he snapped irritably.

"Think fast, Carter," Beeman pursued remorselessly. "He has to be here by morning."

The inflexible logic of his reply and the cold and hostile persistency with which it had been delivered were more than Carter could stand.

"Let me alone!" he cried furiously.

He slammed the cup down with a bang, shattering it into a noisy spray of fragments, and stared angrily from the slumping reluctance of Mercer to Beeman's trim and rugged and clean-shaven rigidity, his eyes darting defiantly from one to the other and back again, and then to the faded, yellow squalor of the old walls with their loathsome clots of squashed mosquitoes and to the mute black wound of the window where the sparkling moisture and crusted patterns of soot distorted the amputated reflections on the glass, and finally he turned abruptly and strode from the room and down the stairs to the landing where Whitcombe and Henney stood in quiet conversation and past them swiftly without a glance and down the last flight of steps, stumbling over the bottom few, and through the door and out, finally, into the street.

The cold, fresh air brought him to a stop. He stood there, panting, and allowed himself to grow calm. It was still dark out, although the first sinister rays of green were already creeping into the sky. A number of men shifted slowly in a group across the street. In their shaded movements, they seemed like the amorphous images of a dream. The streetlamps had long since been extinguished, but the paved road was dimly visible in both directions, looking like shrouded marble in the paling darkness. It was a few minutes before Carter realized he was cold. He pulled his coat closer about him and walked down the street to the diner.

Three men were at the counter, a young mechanic from the filling station and two older men from the railroad.

"They've been sitting around all night," the mechanic was complaining insistently when Carter entered, "just like they expected him to walk in alone and lock himself in a cell."

They fell silent at Carter's appearance. Carter paused in the doorway, caught in the harsh spotlight of their belligerent curiosity. He swayed uncertainly a moment and then walked to the other end of the counter.

"Hear anything about the Wilson boy, Mr. Carter?" the mechanic called after him.

Carter shook his head and sat down directly in front of the cake stand. A solitary cut of coconut pie was before him. It was soggy and yellow, and grew after a minute to resemble some festering organ of the body. He shifted to another seat.

Freddie Hawkins approached slowly, flicking idly at crumbs with a clean white towel.

"I'm sorry, Mr. Carter," he said quietly.

"Thanks, Freddie. I'm glad someone is." Carter kept his own voice low. "Bring me some coffee, please."

"Strange thing, Mr. Carter," Freddie said, with an abstracted air of puzzlement, as he set the cup down, "that Calgary boy getting into trouble. He did some work for me when I enlarged the place.

Funny fellow. Anyway, Mr. Carter, here's what stumps me. He's
a big fellow, and that Wilson boy ain't no wider than a splinter.
Why'd he have to stab him?"

"I don't know, Freddie. I don't know anything anymore. Freddie, you've been listening to them. What's going to happen tomorrow?"

Freddie shook his head. "There's going to be trouble, Mr.
Carter. It's like a holiday, a real holiday, and they're going to have
it, no matter who pays for it. It's almost like Christmas the way everybody's walking around in a fever of excitement. Don't let their
anger fool you. It's a chance to feel important, and they're going
to use it."

"Why, Freddie? Why?"

"That's hard to say, Mr. Carter. Maybe they just want to be respectable. Everybody wants to be respectable, and joining a mob is
the easiest way."

Carter nodded, and after a few seconds said, "Freddie, what are
you going to do tomorrow?"

"Me, Mr. Carter?" Freddie said. "I get pretty tired by the time
I finish up here. I guess I'll just go home and sleep. There's not
much else I can do, is there?"

The door opened before Carter could reply, and Mercer entered, moving sluggishly with a ponderous fatigue. He stood motionless a moment, his eyes going through the oblong interior until they found Carter. The tough stubble on his face was black now
and very dense.

"Hey, Mercer!" one of the men from the railroad demanded.
"When the hell are you getting busy?"

Mercer ignored him. He walked slowly to Carter and sat down
beside him.

"You need a shave," Carter said.

"Go get him, Carter. It's the only thing that will keep the people
in town."

"Do you think it will?"

"It might," Mercer said. "We'll hold him as long as we can.
Maybe they'll be too tired for anything else."

"Turn him right over," Freddie suggested. "Don't give them a
chance to win anything. Maybe you can put some shame into them
that way."

"Who let you in?" Mercer said to him.

"I did," answered Carter.

"Bring me some coffee, Freddie."

"Some cold water," Carter added. "A glass of cold water."

Freddie moved off with a nod. Mercer watched Carter steadily, waiting for his reply. Carter shifted uncomfortably.

"Get me some gum," he said. "My throat is sore."

Mercer called to Freddie for chewing gum. Carter had forgotten the cigarettes. When Freddie returned, Mercer sent him for a pack. Carter began quickly on a slice of gum, but his back teeth started aching almost immediately, and when he turned irately to spit the gum out it stuck to his lip, and after he had plucked it off with his hand it adhered to his fingers and wouldn't shake off, and he was forced finally, cursing aloud by this time, to twist it off with a paper napkin.

"I'll go talk to him," Carter said. "I'll go hear what he has to say."

Mercer nodded and said nothing.

"That's all," Carter insisted. "That's all I'm going to do."

Mercer nodded again. Carter rose and walked outside. Dawn was coming with a rush, bold, brazen, and bright, and the blackness that had consolingly made the hours seem unreal was mixing already with a dull gray morning light that stirred like heavy dust in the air and gave the forbidding pallor of tombstones to the concrete sidewalks and the two imitation marble Corinthian columns in front of the bank and to the flat white facades of all the buildings that stood small and square on both sides of the quiet street. Mercer was beside him.

"It's too early," Carter said.

"They'll be getting up early."

"All right. I'll go now."

"Thanks, Carter."

"Don't thank me!" Carter said, with vicious feeling. "For Christ's sake, don't thank me!"

He turned from him and strode back past the police station to where he had parked his car in the afternoon. He had forgotten to put the top down, and the steering wheel and the two brown leather seats in front were coated with moisture. He had left the cigarettes behind again. The windshield was a solid blank of mist. He entered the car and drove slowly toward the river, gravely intrigued by the ground fog bunched up into thick white veils. It was going to be a nice day. The sun was full already, and the few clouds in the sky were puffed up like clean bedding and scattered remotely through the heavens. An empty shell of a moon hung in profile overhead. A raw chill was in the air.

He crossed the bridge and went faster as he moved into the hills where the small community of Negro farmers, whose begetters of a generation before had emigrated from the Deep South to purchase the land from the town on a plan dictated by the authorities, contended with the tough earthen slopes for substance.

Soon he passed Will Perkins alone in his field, a mule in traces and a bulky hand plow before him in silhouette, standing motionless as a monument as he watched Carter speed by. There was something odd about the scene, and when he had passed some more of their farms, each with a solitary sentinel staring somberly toward the road, he realized what it was. There was no smoke in the chimneys, no sign of a woman or child; the only motion came from the restless thrusts of a hound or the scratching flurry of chickens or from a fat sow swaying through the yard with a squealing litter at her heels. The families had been moved out overnight; the men had remained behind and were waiting. There was pathos in the landscape, in the utter lack of activity, in the grim, gray, ominous quiet, and Carter was reminded for a moment of Sudbury and Hales taking the sacrament in the tower with the knowledge that at that same moment their lives were being traded to the mob. The need for haste swept over him, and he drove faster still.

He had been to the Calgary place before, but he was not sure now that he remembered the way, and when he arrived at the dusty thoroughfare that marked the settlement, he left his car and hurried into the general store. About a dozen men stood inside. Carter scanned each of the men quickly.

"Where's Ira Calgary?"

There was no sound. He scowled impatiently and picked out a man whose name he remembered.

"Raymond, where's Ira Calgary?"

"Ah don' know, Mista' Cahta'," Raymond answered. "Ah 'spect he's at his place."

"Take me there."

Raymond moved forward soberly, a square, good-looking man with a face made for sport and virile merriment. A voice from the back intoned, "How's the Wilson boy, Mr. Carter?"

Carter came to an abrupt stop. There was a long moment of silence before he could reply.

"He's all right," he answered slowly, turning a bit to face them. "Yes, he's all right." He paused uncertainly in the doorway and then turned sharply and walked out.

They passed two homes to get to the Calgary place, each with a man in dark clothes gazing at them with lugubrious interest. Ira Calgary was waiting at the gate to his yard, a corroded feeding pail in his hands and a few brown hens clucking at his feet.

"You'd better give them something to eat," Carter said, trying to smile.

Calgary turned with obedient melancholy and chucked a handful of corn to the ground. He looked back at Carter and waited. He was a tall, thin man with a long face, heavy lips, and big teeth. His eyes were mottled with moist flecks of yellow and protruded slightly. There was a goitrous swelling on his neck.

"Too bad about that scrape yesterday." Carter paused, but Calgary remained silent, and he swallowed nervously and went on. "Good thing no one was hurt. The Wilson boy is all right. They want Jess in town to sign a paper. I'll drive him in and then take him on to school when he's finished."

Calgary regarded him suspiciously. "You say no one was hurt?"

"No. It was only a scratch. Where's Jess?"

Calgary looked dubiously at Raymond.

"Go get him, Ira," Raymond said.

"He says no one was hurt," Calgary argued.

"Go get him, Ira," Raymond repeated firmly.

Calgary turned and walked despondently into the house. Carter and Raymond waited without talking. Far below them the town rested like a somnolent white island, its anchored insularity intensified by the brief contact it made with the state highway that tapped it obliquely and then darted swiftly into infinity like a jagged cable. The dirt road he had traveled was clear and sharp. A heavy haze enriched the color, and it unrolled slantingly into town with the softness of a ceremonial carpet, the dark hues alternating in radiant planes of purple and deep red in the shifting daylight. A rooster sent an echoing question into space.

The door to the house opened and Ira Calgary reappeared. Jess was with him, walking in passive silence, tall and thin like his father, but not nearly as tall and a good deal wider. A bandage bound his head from front to back. One side of his face was badly smashed; the broken flesh was swollen and discolored. Carter turned cold when he saw him.

"You're hurt, Jess," he said softly.

"Yes, suh, Mr. Carter."

Carter gazed at him with morbid awe. He forced down a rising taste of nausea, burdened to his soul suddenly by that viscous paralysis that came to him always with the spectacle of illness, violence, or injury, and he balanced himself against a feeling of dizziness that awoke every nerve in his body to the pains and cruel pressures of all his tired and infected parts. He swallowed again and said, "They want to ask you some questions, Jess. I thought I'd drive you in and then take you to school when you're finished."

"He says no one was hurt."

"Yes," Carter said. "Will you come?"

Jess nodded. His gaunt air of submission was both meek and sullen. He lingered an instant and then moved forward regretfully and came listlessly through the gate and began walking steadily down the path, his eyes staring blankly at the ground, his arms dangling at his sides loosely.

"You bring him back, Mista' Cahta'," Calgary said. "Do you hear? You bring him back, now."

"Mista' Cahta'," said Raymond guardedly, "if the Wilson boy ain' hurt, then it's safe to send for the women, ain' it?"

"I don't know." Carter glanced about helplessly and wondered dismally what to say. "You'd better wait, Raymond. The Wilson boy is all right, but there's no telling what a few hotheads might try. Yes, Raymond, you'd better wait."

Raymond nodded and stepped back, and Carter turned and walked to where Jess had stopped to wait. They returned to the car in silence. A steady wind was blowing up from the river, pungent with the smell of burning leaves. A spotted mongrel joined them from the side. He sniffed at their heels for a few paces, was disappointed, and loped off ahead. The men were assembled outside the store to watch them go. Each of them seemed round-shouldered.

Carter held the door open for Jess and then came around the front and sat down behind the wheel. He did not look at him until they were on the road, and then his eyes were drawn up his face slowly to the edge of the bandage. An appalling sorrow went through him.

"That looks bad, Jess. You'd better have a doctor see it."

"I guess not, Mr. Carter," Jess decided. "I guess a doctor won't be much help."

No, Carter remembered, *I guess not.* He forced his eyes back to the road, but soon the full realization of what he was doing swept over him, and he gripped the wheel with all his strength, feeling that his limbs would go wild with panic were he to relax his arms even slightly.

"Why'd you have to stab him, Jess? Couldn't you whip him with your hands if you had to?"

"I guess not, Mr. Carter," Jess said, and went on resentfully. "There were three of them, Mr. Carter, three of them hitting me with a lead pipe." His fingers twitched nervously on his thighs. He had large, sinuous veins that spilled erratically over the backs of his hands. "I guess you didn't know that, did you?"

"No, I didn't. Simpson and Suggs said they found you fighting in the alley."

"They didn't find me," Jess said, with a low, mirthless laugh. "They were *there.*"

Carter said nothing. Jess gazed ahead for several moments and then turned abruptly.

"I don't carry a knife. Here, Mr. Carter. Here, look at this!"

And before Carter realized what he was doing he had torn his shirt free from his trousers and had clawed open the buttons to reveal a thick, wide calico strip girdling his bare waist just above the hips. A thick wadding of gauze had been stuffed underneath on one side, but the blood had soaked through anyway in three places, one dark blot and two very faint stains, and it was impossible to tell whether it had flowed from one wound or many. Carter was horrified.

"It wasn't my knife that cut him," he heard Jess say.

Carter stared down at him with amazement, letting his eyes dwell sickly on the awesome sight, growing sicker and sicker with what they saw until he thought he would vomit. It was right over the kidney.

"Doesn't it hurt?" was all he could say.

"Yes, suh, Mr. Carter. It hurts."

Carter let another minute pass and then made up his mind, and

he slammed the brakes on as hard as he could, hurling himself
forward and banging Jess up hard against the front. He whirled
immediately to speak, but the car had skidded through a dry patch
and the wind caught the harsh dust and rammed it fiercely into his
face, blinding and choking him, so that he was reduced to cough-
ing and clutching helplessly at his eyes.

"I've been lying to you, Jess," he gasped, when he could finally
speak. "You're in trouble and there isn't much time. Get out and
run, and for God's sake, hurry!"

Jess remained perfectly still. Carter shook him roughly.

"Do you understand, Jess? The Wilson boy is dying. They want
you for murder!"

Jess spoke very softly. "Yes, suh, Mr. Carter," he said, staring intently down into his lap. "I knew I hurt him pretty bad."

Carter gaped with astonishment. "Then what are you doing
here?" he cried frantically. "Why did you come?"

"I guess it's best this way," Jess continued, in a sad and steady
voice. "Maybe they'll leave the rest of us alone."

"Jess," Carter asked, with hoarse wonderment, "do you know
what will happen to you?"

"Yes, suh, Mr. Carter."

"And you still want to go?"

"Yes, suh, Mr. Carter."

"I can't take you," Carter decided, his confusion rising into a
muddled despair. "I told your father I'd bring you back. No, I can't
take you."

"He knew you didn't mean it," Jess said.

"He knew also?"

"Yes, suh, Mr. Carter. We all knew it was pretty bad. We had a
meeting last night and decided I was to give myself up if the police
came for me alone. I'm glad it was you, Mr. Carter. I don't like the
police."

"Oh, God," Carter realized, with an overpowering shame. "They
all knew I was lying."

"You did it for the best," Jess said.

"Shut up, Jess," Carter pleaded. "For Christ's sake, shut up!"

Jess looked down humbly.

"It's none of my business!" Carter exclaimed. He banged his
hand down on the steering wheel, hurting himself but not feeling
the pain until later. "I'm washing my hands of the whole thing. You

get out here and do what you want. I'm not having anything to do with it."

He waited, breathless and furiously distraught, until Jess reached for the door.

"Jess," he asked, almost whispering, "what are you going to do?"

"Walk into town, I guess."

Carter gazed at him and went limp with a sense of futility. The resistance drained out of him, leaving him hollow, cold, and numb.

"All right, Jess. I'll take you."

Jess sat back, and in silence they spiraled down through the hills toward the level ground. They passed Perkins, the solitary plowman watching them ride by, and soon came to the bridge. After the bridge the town was before them. Carter stared ahead tensely for a sign of motion on the road. It was empty. A few minutes out, he brought the car to a stop and put the top down. He rolled each of the windows up tight. A flock of crows went winging overhead.

"I'm sorry about the school, Mr. Carter," Jess said when they were driving again. "Pap and the other men, they didn't like it, but we liked it fine."

"It wasn't your fault," Carter said.

"I tried not to fight, Mr. Carter. I thought if I kept my hands down they'd stop hitting me, but they kept after me like they'd beat me to death. I had to do what I could. I had to try to save myself."

"Sure, Jess. Of course."

Carter turned off before he reached the first buildings and circled the outskirts so as to come up behind the police station. He entered town finally, driving slowly now, and as they rode past the comfortable white houses, all with their fine shade trees and spotless picket fences or stunted hedgerows, the bell in the church steeple began to sound. It tolled eight times. Jess smiled grimly.

"I guess we're both going to be late for school."

"There won't be any school today," Carter said.

In another minute they were there. An atmosphere of excitement filled the area. People had collected in small groups on both sides of the street. Others were streaming up. Mercer and Beeman stood together at the top of the steps. They came hurrying down as soon as Carter appeared. Mercer got into the car. He had shaved and washed, and he looked hard now and wide awake.

"Any trouble?"

Carter shook his head.

"You can decide," Mercer went on rapidly. "There's still time to take him out, but they'll sure as hell get after the whole bunch if we do."

"He wants to stay."

"Do you?"

Jess nodded. He was beginning to look frightened. Mercer gave him no time.

"Walk fast when we get out."

He took hold of his arm and pushed the door open. Beeman fell in on the other side, and they moved quickly across the sidewalk and into the building. The people near the door began crowding forward, and then Beeman stepped out to face them.

That was all Carter saw. He had put the car in gear and was rolling forward, and it all vanished behind him like the macrocosm of a turbulent dream. He crawled forward aimlessly for a few blocks, wondering dully where to go, and then turned at the crossroad and drove slowly toward his house. He was tired and sick, and there was nothing for him to do now but sleep.

DAVID H. INGRAM

The Covering Storm

FROM *Ellery Queen's Mystery Magazine*

AS THE TRAIN chugged across the Galveston Bay Bridge toward the Virginia Point station, Wendell Asquith made a show of touching the watch pocket of his vest, then patting his frock coat's other pockets. "Of all the deuced luck!"

His wife, Amelia, remained focused on her embroidery. "What is it, my dear?"

"In the rush to leave for the station, I forgot my pocket watch."

Amelia looked at him, surprised. "It's hard to imagine you ever being without that watch."

"Imaginable or not, it's happened."

"I'm sure you can secure a temporary replacement once we reach Fort Worth."

"That won't do. It's my lucky watch. My father sent it to me when I started my first business, engraved with his best wishes. I can't just leave it behind."

Amelia stuck her needle into the stretched linen and set down the embroidery hoop beside her on the bench seat. "What do you propose, Wendell?"

"I'll jump off at Virginia Point and take the next train back to Galveston. You continue on with the servants. I'll catch the afternoon train and meet you in Fort Worth tomorrow."

Amelia sat forward, her face troubled. "Must you? I fear there's a bad storm on its way." She glanced out the window and shuddered. "Those clouds."

Wendell remembered the bizarre clouds that had greeted the dawn on that second Saturday of September. Luminescent pink they were, though shards within the clouds caught all the colors of the rainbow. Soon enough they changed into the black-and-gray thunderheads that often traversed the sky above Galveston. While threatening, those clouds were reassuringly familiar.

"I have my umbrella, and should it worsen I'll put on a rain slicker at home. I'll be fine, Amelia."

"Rain's not the worst of it. The streets will flood again."

"I'll take a cab from the station. But really, anyone who can't take getting their feet wet shouldn't live in Galveston." The streets of the town were notorious for flooding, since the island Galveston occupied rose less than 9 feet above the sea. The city fathers had raised the sidewalks to 3 feet above the plank-paved roads to help keep people dry, but apparently they'd forgotten people had to *cross* the streets. Soggy shoes and socks were the rule whenever it rained.

"Why don't you have Arthur accompany you? I'd feel better, knowing you're not alone."

Wendell strangled a sharp retort. *There's no place in my plans for bringing along witnesses, especially my own butler.* Instead he smiled at his wife.

"I can certainly handle such a minor task by myself." He slid forward on his seat and took hold of Amelia's hand. "Besides, darling, I'll feel much better knowing Arthur's watching over you."

A blush blossomed on Amelia's cheeks, and once again he thanked the stars that this gorgeous woman had accepted his proposal. Even after ten years and giving birth to twin daughters, Amelia's beauty had not faded. If anything, the journey from twenty-year-old bride to thirty-year-old pillar of society had sanded away youthful immaturities and left a polished, poised woman.

She was *his* wife, and no blackguard would take her from him. He would see to that.

When the train halted at the station, Wendell stood and grabbed his hat, a slate-gray bowler that matched his frock coat. A quick glance in a mirror confirmed that his diamond stickpin was still centered in his ascot. After a tug on his maroon brocade vest, Wendell turned back to Amelia and again reached for her hand, this time bringing it to his lips.

"Don't fear, my dear. I'll see you tomorrow."

"Do say goodbye to the twins, dear. They'd be horribly distressed if they found you'd disappeared."

Wendell grabbed his leather toiletries case from the rack above him and secured his umbrella between the handles. As he slid open the compartment's door, he glanced back at Amelia, already engrossed in her embroidery again. *This is for you, my love, though you'll never know what I do this day*. With that benediction, Wendell left the compartment.

After hugs and reassurances to Isabel and Charlotte, his seven-year-old twin girls, that he'd meet them in Fort Worth, Wendell left them with their nanny and made his way to the end of the coach. Instead of stepping off onto the platform, he swung down from the Pullman on the side away from the station and moved along the final car in the train. The initials of the Gulf, Colorado and Santa Fe line were painted with gold highlights on the car's side. Wendell snorted briefly. As a member of the line's board, he knew the name was a fiction. The company was in fact fully owned by the Atchison, Topeka and Santa Fe, yet it was listed as a *subsidiary* of the larger line since Texas law dictated that the owner of a business had to reside in the state. The board was a sham, but it kept everyone happy. Wendell couldn't use such a deception himself, so he remained a resident of Galveston in spite of his far-flung business interests. On the plus side, the law meant that by that year, 1900, Galveston had as many millionaires residing within its boundaries as that northern enclave of wealth, Newport, Rhode Island.

Past the caboose, Wendell cut over to the far side of the right-of-way, close to the border of live oaks and brush. Moments later the train pulled away from the station in a cloud of steam while its whistle tooted.

As he walked briskly toward Galveston Bay, Wendell reached into his trouser pocket and withdrew his watch and chain: 10:32 a.m. The next inbound Galveston train was due around one. He needed to cross the channel and manage his mischief, then reach the terminal close to that train's arrival. He'd spin the same fiction for the station agent about his watch and arrange for a ticket outbound that afternoon. That would account for his time should the police make inquiries, though he doubted they would. His and Amelia's departure for Fort Worth had been announced in the *Galveston News*. In a town like Galveston, even the police read the society pages. But Wendell had become a millionaire by planning for every eventuality and analyzing every risk before pursuing an endeavor. He was cautious in planning, ruthless in execution.

The approaching storm was unforeseen, but Wendell realized it was a blessing. The rising wind and bursts of billowing rain beginning to fall would drive most people inside. He could dash anonymously along the sidewalks with the umbrella low over his head.

He slid the umbrella from between the handles and unfurled it. When he reached the bridge approach, Wendell shuffled down the loose stone incline to the beach. Ahead of him, a sailor was guiding a compact Bermuda-rigged sloop toward a dock. Running forward, he waved his bag back and forth to catch the man's attention.

The sailor stood up in the boat's cockpit. His face was deeply lined and most of his white hair had migrated from his crown to his chin, forming a luxuriant beard that flowed down to his chest while his head was left bald.

"Ho, there," Wendell called out. "I need to get back to the city immediately. Could you take me?"

"There's a blow a-comin'," the sailor shouted back. "Best gets away from the water."

"I'll pay you well, sir."

A wily look crossed the man's face. "*How* well?"

"Ten dollars?"

The sailor looked Wendell up and down. "Make it twenty, sir, and you's got yourself a boat."

Wendell was loath to waste time haggling. Setting his bag on the dock, he withdrew his wallet and selected two tens, holding them high for the sailor to see.

The sailor, Croft, was a retired steamboat captain who'd run the Caribbean Islands and the north coast of South America for forty years before retiring. "I still sail most days. The sea's a mistress I cain't give up, even though she's taken many a friend over the years." As they slipped beneath the railway trestle, Croft eyed the span. The mast barely cleared it. "Water's piling up in the sound. I'll be using the main channel whence I returns."

"Can you drop me near where Avenue O approaches Offatts Bay?" Wendell asked.

"Aye," Croft said. He was frowning.

"What's troubling you?"

"Those clouds are a-runnin' straight nor'west, but the wind's blowin' from the north. The channel's rising and I felt my ears a-poppin'. There's a cyclone headin' our way."

Wendell shook his head. "I checked the flagpole above the weather bureau this morning. They hadn't raised a storm warning. Besides, Dr. Stine of the bureau says all major hurricanes turn north by Havana at the latest. Any storm that breaks that pattern would be a minor one."

"I ain't got no fancy education like that feller, but I knows the sea and sky. And there ain't no such thing as a minor hurricane when you's in 'em. Been through a couple; thought they'd likely kill me."

"But you survived."

"Not from the storm's lack of tryin'." Croft's old eyes filled with compassion. "Don't stay on the island."

"Not to worry, Croft. I'm taking the afternoon train out of town."

Croft nodded, but still looked concerned.

"Godspeed, Croft," Wendell called out as the sailor headed back into the bay.

"And God's mercy on you, sir." Croft's voice was almost lost in the wind.

The waters of Offatts Bay had swamped the beach, so Croft had dropped Wendell near where the Avenue O sidewalk began. By now it was raining in earnest, the large drops lashing at Wendell as he walked briskly along the avenue. As Amelia feared, the streets had become torrents as the high sidewalks focused the runoff like a river canyon's walls. About the only ones out in the weather were the children playing in deep puddles, splashing each other as they chortled with delight, their clothes muddy disasters. *Yes, I'll take a cab home from the station,* Wendell decided. *Clean, dry clothes; that's the ticket. I'll have the driver wait while I change, to witness my movements.*

He glanced at his watch again: 11:12 a.m. When he came to Twenty-ninth Street, by the southwest corner of the Garten Verein, the social center and gardens for the city's German population, Wendell turned south. Just ahead he saw his destination, the home of Archibald Kenyon Tate.

The man had crossed the line of propriety and needed to be taught a lesson. Wendell was determined to tutor him personally.

Decades earlier, Wendell had come to Galveston with a stake from his wealthy father back in Philadelphia and an innate cunning for managing business deals. Now he ruled over a network of interests: cotton exports in the South, Kansas granaries, fruit farms in California, and Texas cattle stockyards and lumber mills. He'd even invested in docklands for Galveston's neighbor and rival, Houston. The two towns were fighting to be the financial and population center of the state, though the latest census figures showed Galveston pulling away, having grown 30 percent in the past ten years. Wendell didn't mind exploiting Houston for profit, even if he could never imagine living there. While Galveston could be beastly hot, it was a gleaming gem on the sea compared to dusty, unrefined Houston.

Tate's holdings and personal wealth mirrored Wendell's in size, but the men themselves were polar opposites. The gossip was that Tate had simply been Archie Kenyon when he emigrated from England and that he'd worked his way up from poverty through some shady land deals that involved quick exits from towns. Twelve years earlier, he'd arrived in Galveston with the Tate attached to his name and a small fortune that he soon parlayed into a large fortune. Back in Philadelphia, Tate's nouveau-riche background would have left him shunned by society, but Galveston was a uniquely accepting town. German, Jew, Irish—it was no hindrance. Even skin tone didn't preclude opportunities.

Tate's arrival coincided with Wendell's courting of Amelia Baumgartner. The daughter of one of the oldest Galveston families, Amelia had "come out" at a ball held at the Artillery Club, which was for men only but opened its doors to women on such special occasions. Wendell was immediately bewitched by her beauty. He managed to dance with her several times, and within days he'd gained her father's approval to squire her about town. Wendell took her to dances, concerts, and lectures, the main sources of entertainment.

During the two years Wendell courted Amelia, Archie Tate had presented himself as a possible rival. With his dark eyes, chestnut hair, and strong chin, Tate was a focus of attention for the ladies of Galveston. Yet he'd set his eye on Amelia, cutting in on Wendell at dances and always grabbing a chair close to her at the lectures. Then, on New Year's Day in 1890, Wendell proposed and Amelia swiftly accepted. After that, Tate left them alone. Wendell was grateful for Tate's sensitivity and eventually put the rivalry out of his mind.

Until Monday night.

Wendell was accompanied to the Artillery Club by Jamieson Maret and his son, Donald. Maret was an elder statesman of the business community who had helped Wendell when he was building his companies. Now Maret was grooming Donald to take over his investments. Wendell felt a kinship with Donald, who was only a decade younger than him. Besides their business dealings, Wendell and Amelia often socialized with Jamieson and his wife, Margaret, before she passed away the previous year.

"Donald has an idea you may want to invest in," Jamieson had told Wendell earlier in the day.

"I'm always open to a new idea. How about joining me for a drink, and I'll listen to Donald's proposal?"

"In vino veritas?" Jamieson said, chuckling.

"Hopefully," Wendell said, grinning himself.

He'd put in a full day in the office despite being alone, thanks to the federal holiday enacted six years earlier. As they settled in their seats, Maret said, "I still don't understand it. Giving people a holiday simply because they labor? I say an extra day of work would be more fitting."

"After that Pullman strike," Donald said, "Congress had to mend fences with the labor vote. Window dressing, that's what it is."

It was Jamieson who noticed Tate at the bar. "Archie's knocking back bourbons. Doesn't surprise me. I heard his slaughterhouse in Dallas burned to the ground last night."

Wendell felt sympathy for Tate. He'd faced his share of setbacks himself. But unlike Tate and most other businessmen, who maximized their profits by ignoring insurance, Wendell always fully covered his endeavors. He turned to Donald.

"You have a proposal for me?"

"Yes, sir. I have a vision for a chain of nickelodeons across the South—"

"Ah, my old friend Asquith," a slightly slurred voice said.

Wendell looked up. Tate was approaching his table.

"Tate," he said, acknowledging him with the briefest of nods.

"Had another wonderful day making money?" Tate pulled back the fourth chair at the table without invitation and slid into it. He plunked down his bourbon-filled glass, sloshing the liquor over the rim. Wendell stared at the offensive brown spot despoiling the expanse of white linen tablecloth.

"We're having a business meeting here, Tate."

"Why aren't you home with your honey, 'Dell? If I had Amelia at home, I'd find it hard to leave for work every morning." Tate took a sip of his drink. "My God, you don't know what a lucky bastard you are, 'Dell. Your greatest treasure warms your sheets at night."

Wendell's voice turned chilly as an arctic breath. "I think you've drunk enough tonight, Tate."

Tate was oblivious to the piano-string tightness of Wendell's words. "You'd best live a long life, 'Dell, 'cause I'll tell you what: If you weren't here anymore, I'd be calling on your widow the moment she could take off the black. I'd woo her and wed her like I should have a decade ago, then I'd take her to my bed—"

"You go too far, sir!" Wendell didn't realize he'd slammed his hand on the table as he spoke. Everyone in the room was staring at them.

"I should have gone farther. Fought for her." Tate's voice was filled with regret. He drank down the remaining liquor and rose to his feet. Before shuffling away, he repeated, "Yes, I should have gone farther."

Mortification poured over Wendell like lava. Jamieson and Donald had the sense to avert their eyes. Not that it mattered. Wendell knew the scene would spread throughout Galveston society like a spilled bottle of India ink. Jamieson's comment came back to him. There was truth in drink, and the truth was, Tate still harbored an obsession for Amelia—had for the past decade. It left Wendell stunned.

Wendell only half listened to Donald's proposal. Instead he turned over scenarios in his mind. His honor, as well as Amelia's, had to be restored. He dismissed Donald with a "Let me consider it" and had a second cognac after they left. Once a plan formed in his mind, he headed home.

"Amelia," Wendell announced at supper, "I think it's time we visited your cousins in Fort Worth."

The raindrops were now thick missiles flying almost parallel to the land as Wendell entered the alley behind Tate's house. Swirling in the flood were shingles stripped off roofs along with horse dung and sodden scraps of paper. Wendell opened the door and slipped inside Tate's stable. With its raised floor, the barn had only a few inches of water covering the cement floor. Tate's horses whinnied and circled nervously in their stalls. Wendell walked to the door that led to Tate's backyard and set his bag on a hay bale. After stripping the clothes from his upper body and hanging them on nearby nails, Wendell withdrew from his bag a rough cotton shirt and slipped it on. It was a worker's shirt, far different from the silk shirts men of Wendell's class wore. Setting a soft tweed cap on his damp, windblown hair, Wendell now looked like a laborer. The polluted flood and mud had robbed his trousers and shoes of their luster of wealth. No need to change them.

Lastly, Wendell knotted a large kerchief behind his neck and raised it to perch on his nose, covering his lower face.

There'd be gossip that he'd hired a thug to exact revenge for Tate's drunken display Monday night. Wendell, though, knew he had to do it himself, for honor's sake.

Wendell was familiar with Tate's habits. After working from 6 a.m. to 11 a.m. on Saturdays, Tate returned home for a nap on the chaise lounge in his front parlor, then lunch at the Tremont Hotel, since he gave his staff Saturdays off. The nap time in the house deserted of staff was the perfect moment to strike.

He dashed across the backyard and up the steps to slip inside the kitchen. With the roar of the wind and the rain exploding against the wooden house, stealth was unnecessary. He could have wandered the downstairs banging a bass drum and still gone unnoticed.

In the parlor Wendell found Tate slumbering. Grabbing the poker from the fireplace's tool stand, he approached Tate, raising the iron bar above his head.

At the last moment, Tate's eyes popped open. He managed to raise an arm to block the first blow. The poker connected with a satisfying, bone-shattering crack.

"You don't covet another man's wife," Wendell panted, punctuating his words with blows to Tate's chest.

It may have been his voice, or perhaps Tate saw something in his eyes, visible above the mask. Tate whispered one word, his tone filled with disbelief.

"Wendell?"

He's recognized me! He'll denounce me!

Fear gripped Wendell. The next blow struck Tate's forehead, cutting a bloody line in the flesh.

And then all of Wendell's pent-up rage exploded and he roared as he raised the poker. Another blow. Another. Another.

Wendell stared disbelievingly at the carnage. The gore-encrusted poker dripped blood onto the carpet, and scarlet ribbons had sprayed across the floor and onto the walls, his shirt, his face. Wendell stumbled backward, dropping the poker. *What have I done?*

Then a ghastly smile twisted his face.

I'm not here. I'm on the train.

His laughter nearly spiraled out of control, but then his ruthless discipline reasserted itself. He saw Tate's watch fob extending from his vest pocket. Careful to avoid the splattered blood, Wendell grabbed the shovel from the fireplace tools and brought it down hard on the pocket. There. The broken watch would set the time of the attack—a time that Wendell could establish he was not in town. *Now I must get to the train station and complete the charade.*

After wiping the blood from the shovel and replacing it in the stand, he retraced his path through the house.

In the stable he found a basin and fresh water. He washed himself before dressing again in his own clothes. Wendell dumped the basin into the deepening flood and watched the crimson-toned water twist in the flow before disappearing. He checked his watch: 12:14. Now to make his way to the station.

As he stepped outside into the alley, the wind lifted his bowler and sent it flying away. Wendell glanced down at the bloodstained shirt, kerchief, and cloth cap in his hand. He'd planned to dispose of them as he walked to the station, but instead he raised his arm. The wind ripped the clothing from his hand and sent it flying to join the anonymous debris of the storm.

The umbrella was now only a partial shield against the stinging rain. He headed for the station, slogging through the flood. An apothecary sign sailed past his head, soaring like a kite. North of the Garten Verein, the wind ripped the umbrella from his hands. Wendell raised his coat collar above his head and grasped it closed below his chin, like a shawl. He kept moving.

Wind battered him while the waters clawed at his legs. While the flood receded as he reached the highest point on the island, the wind and rain redoubled their attack. He had to bend low, shuffling sideways, fearing that at any moment he could be ripped from the earth and sent sailing like his hat. Past the crest, the waters rose, swamping the sidewalks, reaching his waist.

When the terminal appeared through the driving rain, the scene stunned him. Out to the west, the inbound train stood stalled on the tracks. Steam poured from the engine's swamped boiler. Lines were strung between the train and the station as men helped the women and children through chest-high waters to the terminal.

There would be no afternoon train, no escape from the island.

Wendell felt something bump against him.

It was the body of a young woman, floating facedown in the water.

The trip south to his mansion was an excursion through the nightmare landscapes of Hieronymus Bosch. Collapsed houses, a trolley abandoned on the street, dead animals, and in the midst of it all a plague of small toads, thousands of them, clinging to the debris in the water.

And more bodies.

He could no longer establish his alibi. But could anybody challenge it? He could say that when the train died, he left his compartment and headed directly home. He'd wait out the storm and catch the next train to Fort Worth.

Yet gnawing at his brain was the knowledge that he was a murderer. Tate was dead at his hand. He might insulate himself from charges, but he'd never escape that condemning knowledge.

He plowed through the water. Then he was dropping, lost in a crater scoured away by the waters, submerging him in the vile mixture. He fought for the surface, finally breaking into a twilight world, brightened only by lightning.

It was sweet relief when he trudged up the steps of his home. The waters outside had not yet reached within the house, thanks to the pilings it was built upon, like most of the houses in Galveston. Wendell found a lantern and lit it, using its light to climb to the second floor. He stripped to his skin in the upstairs bathroom, leaving his clothes in a sodden, stinking pile. They were ruined, fit only for burning. Only his pocket watch was salvageable.

After drying himself, Wendell went into his bedroom and dressed. He stretched out on his bed, meaning to rest for a minute. But after the trials of the day, Wendell was asleep when his head touched his pillow.

He looked up and saw Tate above him, his face smashed and bloody. Tate's eyes glowed a hellish yellow as they gazed down at Wendell. In Tate's hand was a poker. Wendell watched as it rose high above him, and then . . .

Wendell cried out, waving his arms to block the blow. His eyes popped open and Tate vanished.

Still, Wendell woke into a nightmare. The rain outside sounded like a million nails being driven into the walls. The room's windows had imploded, allowing a tornado of wind to roar inside. The walls groaned and twisted as Wendell watched.

Grabbing the lantern, he ran to the upstairs landing. He couldn't take in what he saw. The downstairs was submerged beneath black waters. Waves lapped at the top staircase steps.

Is this my fault? Is this storm mirroring my own loss of control? Then the floor rose beneath Wendell's feet, bucking him back into the bedroom. Again it heaved, and with a final shiver the house floated free of its pilings.

He fought his way through the lashing wind out of a window, grasping hold of the roof. The house jerked and twisted in the flood. Then his piece of roof ripped free of the house, swirling away in the waters. Looking back, Wendell saw his home crumple as if God's hands were wadding it up like a piece of paper.

The only light came from lightning flashes. What he saw confounded him. He could have been in the middle of a storm-tossed ocean, except for a few houses still standing, with their second floors and widow's walks rising above the waves.

"I've been a fool, Amelia," he shouted, hardly hearing himself above the wind. "Why did I leave you? Why did I lie? I'm sorry. So sorry. But I—"

He never saw the shingle whipping through the air. It simply appeared embedded in his chest. Blood whelmed up around it. He tasted blood in his mouth. *Can't breathe.* Then his body went limp and he fell backward off the raft.

So cold, he thought as the waters covered his fading eyes. *So dark.*

Amelia looked up at the knock on the parlor door of the house she'd rented in Fort Worth. Arthur entered, followed by Donald Maret, both wearing grim expressions. The butler held a letter along with a small box.

"The report has come, Mrs. Asquith. I summoned Mr. Maret from his hotel so he could hear the news as well."

She remembered when Arthur had told her on the train that "young Mr. Maret" was also a passenger, traveling on business to Fort Worth. Arthur had seen Donald in the dining car while getting a tray for Amelia. It seemed a lifetime had passed since that Saturday, yet it was only three weeks.

"Quite right, Arthur," she said, taking the letter and box from him.

The first reports they'd heard placed the death toll at five hundred—a horrendous number but still a small fraction of Galveston's population. But as time passed the number kept rising until it was unimaginable. Yesterday the paper said the final death toll would never be known but could be over ten thousand. With Arthur's help, Amelia had dispatched a private detective to search for Wendell and Jamieson in the ruins of Galveston.

Amelia opened the envelope and withdrew the report, unfolding it carefully. She read it aloud:

> Sept 25th, 1900
> Houston, Tex.
>
> My dear Mrs. Asquith,
> Per your request, I traveled to Galveston. Train service is still restricted since the trestles have collapsed, but I found a man here with a sailing boat. He said he was from Virginia Point and had made it to Houston just before the hurricane. When we sailed past, we saw that Virginia Point had been wiped away.
> Nothing remains of your home. Every structure south of Avenue N or east of 12th Street is gone. Destroyed buildings near the beach created a pile of debris. Pushed by the wind and waves, it plowed through everything in its path.

The authorities tried burying the victims at sea, but within two days the corpses washed back ashore. Instead they're burning them. The toll was so enormous that the pyres still burn, filling the air with ash and the stench of charred flesh.

Jewelry or other possessions are often the only way to identify the dead. Amongst the recovered remains I found the watch you described. Your husband, Wendell, is listed among the dead. The other man you requested information on, Jamieson Maret, was severely wounded. He expired in the makeshift hospital here three days after the storm.

Please accept my condolences . . .

Laying down the letter, Amelia wiped a tear from her eye. Donald still stood beside Arthur, his head bowed. While Arthur maintained his stoic control, Amelia could see his eyes were full.

She opened the box. There was Wendell's pocket watch, sitting on a bed of tissue paper. She stared at the dented cover; smelled the seawater in which it had been immersed.

Amelia stood up and held the box out to Arthur. "Please secure a graveyard plot and bury this watch there. Have them place a headstone above it with Wendell's name and years. Also, send Elizabeth to me. I shall need black outfits."

"Yes, ma'am," Arthur said.

"I could never believe something like this could have happened," Donald said as Arthur left the room, closing the door behind him.

Amelia looked at Donald. After a quick glance over his shoulder to confirm they were alone, Donald stepped toward her, smiling. Amelia fell forward against him, grateful at last to be enfolded in his loving embrace again.

ED KURTZ

A Good Marriage

FROM *Thuglit*

I

We were at the Allens' anniversary party, which I hated, and Hannah hated it too. It was not as though we didn't like the Allens—Joe Allen, anyway, a big, fat, affable bear of a man—it was all just so tacky. I was of the opinion that notifying other people of one's forthcoming birthday was vulgar enough (*Don't forget my gift!*), but an anniversary always seemed like a private thing, a husband/wife thing, nothing to do with me or my debit card. Joe could buy his wife lunar real estate for all I cared, just leave me out of it. As far as I knew, Hannah felt much the same way.

But Joe insisted, and his wife made sure to send us their wish list by e-mail, so with twin engine grumbling we went and presented them with the Waterford vase they wanted. She cooed hungrily over the damn thing and he nodded with appreciation. There were a lot of people there. The gifts were piling up in the corner by the fireplace. Finally, after the inimitable Mrs. Allen opened their (her) last gift, the assemblage was freed to drink, drink, and be drunk. A trio of hulky guys whose guts were threatening the structural integrity of their shirts swarmed the keg. Hannah and I opted for the crappy boxed wine.

"Jesus," she snarked in my ear, "what a disgrace."

I sucked at a mouthful of supermarket zinfandel and nodded. That's what husbands seemed to do best around here: nod. Even the troglodytes huddled around the keg were nodding like junkies while they took turns filling up red Solo cups.

"We've been married seven years," Hannah hissed. "Way I see it, these people all owe us back pay."

I laughed, felt some of the wine work its way up into my nasal cavity. Hannah *tsk*ed and went in search of a napkin as it dribbled from my nostrils. I felt a little stupid, and maybe more so when a woman in a powder-blue summer dress covered her mouth with her hand to stifle her giggles. Wiping my nose with the back of my hand, I smiled at her and shrugged. *What are you gonna do?*

The napkin flew to my face like a surface-to-air missile and Hannah, always the second mother to me, smeared it all over my face, her brow tightly knitting as though she were defusing a bomb. I took over from there, gently taking control of the napkin to prove that yes, I was wearing my big-boy pants today, but thanks for your assistance.

"What do you think?" she asked, her voice without a suggestion of tone.

"I think it's a miracle I didn't ruin this shirt."

"No, I mean *her*. What do you think of her?"

My head jerked up, mouth hanging open. Hannah gestured with her chin—a nice, subtle chin, I'd always thought—at the blonde in the summer dress. I tried not to look at her again, but it was automatic, like the old "Made you look!" game kids play. Now she looked discomfited, perhaps a bit distressed. She dropped her eyes and disappeared into the throng of partygoers.

"I don't know her," I said. "Never saw her before. Friend of Katherine's, I assume."

"You *know* that's not what I asked."

"You asked me what I think. I don't think anything, because I don't know anything about that woman."

That woman. Appropriately disparaging, I thought. Clinton-esque, as in *Oh, that woman.*

"You were looking at her. She tittered."

"Tittered?"

"Tittered."

"It's a party. People are having a good time, Hannah. Don't make such a—"

"Don't you dare," she growled low, her lacquered nails digging into my arm. I winced, held my breath. This was getting ugly fast. Spiraling out of control. "Is she pretty? Did you like her ass? You could practically see it through that dress, you know."

I knew, but I didn't say I knew. I just made a straight, clenched line of my mouth and felt my stomach make a fist.

"It's nothing," I said at some length. "Nothing to worry about. I promise you that."

Hannah's lips spread apart to show her perfect, picket-fence teeth.

"I think we both know what your promises are worth," she hissed at me.

That stung, but I kept silent. Because of course she was in the right. I had lied, and it only takes one to dissolve trust like a tab of Alka-Seltzer. Liars are like alcoholics: no matter how forthcoming and honest they are after the fact, they can never not be a liar again. It is a stigma, an ever-present black cloud that never gets burned up by the sun. The ex-drunks carry those chips around in their pockets, and I carried my guilt. Hannah never let me forget about that.

Joe came around then, a bottle of Mexican beer in his meaty hand and a toothy smile plastered across his face. Hannah immediately released my arm, assumed her role as the one everybody liked, the chipper optimist.

"Having a good time?" Joe barked.

"A *great* time, Joe," my wife said. "Thanks so much for inviting us."

"I don't even know half these people—Katherine's coworkers, 'the girls from the office,' you know."

"Invite one and you have to invite them all," she said pleasantly, cheerfully. "We move in packs."

She winked. Joe chuckled, squeezed my shoulder. I was covering my arm with my hand, concealing the broken skin, a cluster of red half-moons where Hannah clutched me with her talons. The music fell silent and the murmur of a dozen overlapping conversations rose up to fill the hole when Katherine came bouncing over, seized Hannah by the wrist, and bellowed, "Come on, help me pick some more songs!"

Joe's wife dragged mine across the room, Hannah's eyes big and helpless. Neither of us really cared much for Katherine, though we maintained that dirty little secret discreetly. I felt a pang for my wife, having to deal with her, but dismissed it when Joe pulled me into a crushing sideways hug, sloshing his beer all over the floor.

"You guys are so awesome together," he drawled, his tongue

thick with the buzz. "We're going to be like that, me and Kathy."

I tried to imagine Katherine drawing blood from Joe with her fingernails. The picture didn't fit.

"Hey, I'm gonna get another beer," Joe said. "You want anything?"

"No, I'll just mingle."

"Mingle," he chortled. "Yeah, you mingle."

With that he lumbered off in search of a new beer to spill all over his guests. A new tune came blaring from the Allens' surround-sound speakers: Top 40 stuff, all sugar and sound effects, definitely not Hannah's choice.

For once I was left on my own, so I didn't waste any time; I made a beeline for the tightly grouped revelers, following the blonde's path. After receiving a few accidental elbows to the ribs and stepping on some poor woman's toes, I spotted her through the sliding glass door on the back patio. She had both hands on her drink and swung her hips side to side with the music. A quick scan of the room revealed no Hannah within view, so I slipped outside among the mosquitoes and leaning tiki torches.

She wasn't talking to anyone, just swaying by herself, probably enjoying the hold the red drink in her hand was beginning to take. I slid up beside her and said, "Hey."

"Hey yourself," she said, the words syrupy.

She really was beautiful, objectively speaking. Dazzling blue eyes, like gems. Bee-stung lips. I swallowed dry and frowned.

"Listen, my wife . . ."

"I figured that's who that was. If looks could kill."

"Yeah, well . . ."

"Do you always try to pick up women when you go to parties with your wife?"

A faint grin played at her mouth, but it was the admonishing kind. *Tsk-tsk, young man. You ought to know better.*

"Pick up—? No, I'm not. I'm not." I shifted instantly into defense mode, which was my default gear. "That's not it at all. It's just —well, I think you should leave."

"Leave?" Her playful incredulity suddenly became a lot less playful.

"Yes. Right now, actually."

"You're serious."

She wasn't swaying anymore. The music shifted to a Leonard Cohen song. More Hannah's speed, which meant she was hopefully still occupied with Katherine.

"You have no idea how . . . possessive she gets. That little thing with the wine back there?"

"Terrible stuff, isn't it?"

"It's awful, but please—"

"I don't even know why I'm here, to tell the truth."

"Great, then really, you should *go*."

The blonde assumed a bemused expression, a matronly look of utter disappointment. I heard the back door slide squeakily open behind me and gave up.

"Is my husband bothering you?"

My eyes slid shut and a sigh whistled past my lips. Hannah's arm hooked mine and the blond woman laughed the way women do in awkward social situations. I'm an expert on that laugh.

"No, not at all," she said. Then, conspiratorially: "But I think he's a little drunk."

I wasn't, of course. Not even close. Hannah apologized for me anyway ("I'm so sorry, he never seems to know when enough is enough") and, with a courteous if formal goodbye, she ushered me around the side of the house to the car in the driveway. Not through the house, no "thanks for the party" to the Allens, but *around* the house. In the dark, like a couple of goddamn thieves.

Or not *like*, because when I slid into the passenger seat of my wife's Acura (she always drove, always insisted on unlocking and opening the door for me), she handed me her baggy purse to hold on to, whereupon I immediately took notice of its largest, most conspicuous occupant. The Waterford vase we'd given to the Allens no more than an hour before. An act of aggression, however mild; a subtle "fuck you" to the woman she loathed and my friend who always annoyed her with his loud voice and gregarious demeanor. Joe and Katherine would spend a while sifting through their gifts later on, frustrated with the absurdity of the lost vase. *It was right here! Where could it have gone?*

Tricky, slippery Hannah.

She stabbed the ignition with her key and cleared her throat in time with the rumbling of the engine. Home.

I could tell things were about to get bad again.

2

The mewling cries wafted up through the air-conditioning vents, from the basement to every room in the house. I hated it, that awful, pitiful sound, but I shut it out of my mind. Pretended as best I could that it wasn't really there at all. One of the secrets to a good marriage: put those things you just can't stand out of your head. Nobody's perfect.

I was in the spare room, once considered the future location of our first child's bedroom, since loaded up with towers of boxes, the minutiae of a shared life. The notion had occurred to me that it might make a decent home office. Upon expressing this thought to Hannah, her eyes went wide with delight—"No, no," she exclaimed, "a *crafts* room. Yes, that would be perfect."

So I was prepping the room for Hannah. Hannah and her crafts. And all the while the woman in our basement howled miserably: *No, why, why, why are you doing this to me.* A familiar line, a cliché. I was beginning to think that people based their words on oft-repeated lines we hear on television. The brain references the sundry crime programs they'd seen over the years, the dozen or so kidnapping scenarios, and it knows right off what the right words are. How often does it work on those shows? I wasn't sure.

I could take the doors off the closet, make it a nice little space for a sewing table. Soon Hannah would have two workrooms, this and the basement. She had so many hobbies.

In the late afternoon she emerged from the basement, shut the door, and locked it with her key. Her face was spotted with sweat and I thought maybe there was a small spattering of blood on her tank top. I wasn't looking too closely. I never did. She went right past me in the kitchen, hustled for the back of the house to take a shower. Just like she'd been working out. Which I guess she was. It wasn't easy, what she'd been up to.

Hannah chose a restaurant for dinner, didn't feel like cooking. I said I'd be happy to whip something up, but her mind was made up. She knotted a tie around my neck, still displeased with the way I did it, and we hopped into her Acura for a quick jaunt to a new Caribbean place she read about in the paper. She complained about Kathy Allen the whole way.

"Can you believe her? She asks what I want to hear, we're sitting together by the stereo and she *smells,* by the way, and she asks, 'What's your poison?' And then she just plays her own crap anyway."

I almost reminded her about the Leonard Cohen song, but I choked it down.

The place was called El Carib and it was full of tropical fish tanks and bustling waitresses. Televisions mounted in the corners of the ceiling played soap operas with the volume turned down. After we sat down I kept my eyes trained on the laminated menu. She asked me how the crafts room was coming along and I muttered something vaguely encouraging. I didn't look at the waitress when she came around to take our order. If she murdered somebody right then and there and the police asked me to describe the assailant, I couldn't have done it. I had blinders on. Sometimes I forgot, but not then.

Hannah pointed to something on her menu, asked if it had bananas in it. The waitress said she didn't think so and Hannah made her go back to the kitchen and make sure. When she came back positive that the dish—I don't remember what it was—was banana-free, my wife ordered it for both of us. I ate it like a prison meal, pausing occasionally to sip at my water and nod at Hannah while she talked about the thriller she was reading and our HOA and didn't the new mail carrier seem a great deal friendlier than the old one? Neither of us so much as alluded to the elephant in the basement.

Poor woman.

3

Monday I spent my lunch break with Patricia. I drove to the diner like a fugitive, taking odd turns, a circuitous route, terribly careful that I wasn't being followed. She was waiting for me in the last booth by the restrooms, a scarf on her head and enormous sunglasses disguising most of her face. I had to laugh. When I sat down across from her, I grumbled, "What's the password?"

"Swordfish" was her reply. She liked the Marx Brothers. I introduced her to them.

Patricia was an administrative assistant at my office for the better part of two years before she got married and resigned. We were friendly, but not friends. I didn't miss her when she left. Less than a year later she was divorced and came around for a lunch date with one of her old coworkers. She and I got to talking, and inside a month we were sweating in a tangle between musty sheets at her apartment. I had "gone home sick." I was never on guard at the office, not like I was at home.

She was sipping at a Bloody Mary and I ordered the same. I was so used to letting women make my decisions for me, I couldn't see why it should be any different with Pat. Still, she crooked her full red lips to one side and said, "You can get whatever you want."

"This is fine."

"You're tense."

"Hannah," I said. It was all that needed saying.

"Divorce her."

"Pat—"

"I know."

"I can't."

"I know."

I signaled the girl behind the counter for another one. Pat fired up a long, slim cigarette and exhaled like a femme fatale from some old noir movie. She certainly looked the part. Red hair, shoulder length, skin like alabaster. I didn't have a type, and even if I did, Patricia probably wouldn't be it. But still, we fit.

A couple of weeks earlier I had told her I loved her. Damnedest thing, didn't mean to say it, even if I was thinking it. Of course, just thinking didn't necessarily mean it was true. All the same, I said it, and she parroted it back to me. I loved her and she loved me. We were in love. And I was married to somebody else. What a bastard.

"I want you," Pat said, slipping off her sunglasses to gaze at the stream of blue-gray smoke spilling up from her cigarette's ember.

I checked my watch, said, "I'll have to get back."

"I mean *you*, all of you. No more 'swordfish.'"

It was a fun enough game, but she was getting tired of games. I guess I was too. I clenched my jaw and thought about the blonde from the party. My eyes watered, and Pat took that to mean I was reacting to our situation. She touched my hand and smiled sadly.

"What are we going to do?" she asked. *Make a decision for once in your life. Put your goddamn foot down.*

I said, "I don't know, Pat."

4

At night they were always quiet. The day wore them out, wore them down. The voice was whittled down to a scratchy whisper, the muscles didn't want to obey the commands to keep struggling, keep *trying*. Nevertheless, I never slept.

For the longest time I lay in bed, flat on my back with my arms crossed on top of the sheets, my eyes wide open. Listening to Hannah breathe. She never snored, but her sleep-breath was whistley, soft as cotton. When the digital clock hit two in the morning, it was as if I could hear it turn over, a sequence of heavy locks like the unleashing of a dam. Hannah whistled on. I got out of bed, twisted my shoulders, and pulled a T-shirt down over my torso.

My objective was a glass of water and a slice of toast. I stared at the toaster oven while the heating coil went lava red and the bread yellow, then brown. I slathered two slices with peanut butter and nibbled them at the kitchen table, swallowing water when it got too thick in my throat. Across the table from me was the basement door, as plain and unassuming as ever, apart from the steel lock keeping the status quo. Beyond it, down the uncarpeted steps, around the corner, and into the paneled 1970s room some previous owner used for his "man time," a blond woman waited for it all to start up again. I didn't even know her name.

I was willing to bet she knew mine.

Halfway through the second piece of toast I gave up on it and went for a glass of milk. The jug was hiding behind a metal bowl of ground beef mixed with onions and breadcrumbs, a taut layer of plastic wrap over the top. I pulled the milk out, my mind flexing hazily on the meat; tomorrow's supper, no doubt. Hannah was the house chef; she would never have dreamed of putting anything I prepared in her mouth.

I drank straight from the jug—what my wife didn't know wouldn't hurt her—and returned it to the fridge, careful to position it just like I found it. My gaze lingered on the ground beef a second longer before I closed the door.

An idea was percolating.

5

Patricia wasn't the first. Though now, in the fullness of time, I was coming to love Pat—actually *love* her—the first was what some people might call a fling. An error in judgment. A wild woman in a bar, flitting around me like a housefly, my subconscious screeching at me to get the hell out of there before I made a mess of things. I didn't listen. I made the mess.

Her name doesn't matter. I've tried to forget it, and for the most part I've convinced myself that I have. I am quite certain that it is engraved on her grave marker, that she probably had a sweet middle name like Rose or Eve, and that even now, all these years later, somebody still comes around with fresh flowers once a month. It's a nice thought. No consolation, but nice.

In the wake of my error, I learned quickly just how magnificent a detective Hannah was when she needed to be. Perhaps a lot of wives possess this particular set of skills, at least the betrayed ones. Men are what they are, and what they are often isn't very good. Some wives know that going in, I suppose. Hannah sure as shit did. So when she came home from her weekend in Little Rock (the old homestead), her bloodhound nose started to flare before the door squeaked shut behind her. Sex is like blood to a detective wife: no matter how hard you try to scrub it all away, you can never eliminate all the evidence. It remains in a twitch of the face, a dodged touch, a renewed vigor, a guilty confidence. My eyes could not connect, hold true and steady and meet her gaze head-on. There were lies behind my eyes, and to look into them was to see my crime as if through a glass, and not so darkly. She with her family, sipping iced tea on the porch as in the good old days, and me in room 325 of the Lonestar Motor Lodge, rutting between gray sheets like a hog searching out rotting corncobs in the mud. With *her*. Whatever her name was. Didn't matter—she was dead, and I might as well have killed her myself.

I could practically hear the screams clear across town, sitting in my cubicle, knowing how soon her lithe golden brown body would quit on her. Knowing that I had lured her into that web, asked her to meet me one more time.

Jackie was her name. I wished I didn't know it.

6

Pat lit a cigarette and blew the smoke straight up at the ceiling. She was unabashedly naked, lying on top of the comforter, and so was I. A small, dull-blue tattoo of a butterfly hovered at her left hip, a youthful indiscretion I hardly noticed anymore. Both of us had other lives, before and even now, that had nothing to do with what we had between us. That pervading sense that I was taking part in some manner of international espionage rarely settled in until I was on my way back to the office, or home. With Pat, I was strangely, stupidly calm.

My thoughts were not even invaded by the young woman in my basement. She had no place here, in Pat's bedroom, with me.

But something did, a vague notion tugging at my brain and ruining the afterglow. I swung my legs over the side of the bed and stepped into my trousers. Pat tamped her cigarette out in the jar lid on her nightstand and wrinkled her nose.

"There's still time," she said softly. "It's only a quarter till."

I was already buttoning my pants when I realized my drawers were bunched up on the carpet.

"Damn."

"This doesn't sound good."

"It's just something I have to do, before I have to get back."

"All right."

She turned on her side, watching me get my clothes situated like I'd never gotten dressed before. There was a dappling of sweat on her upper lip that made me stumble.

"It's nothing," I said. "An errand."

She whispered my name as I peered under the bed in search of my tie. It was lime green, a random gift from Hannah for no reason in particular. She sometimes did kind things like that. I favored that tie to remind myself of it.

"Maybe," she began, but her voice trailed off. She swallowed, pursed her lips.

I smoothed out my shirt, realized I was holding my breath. I let it out with a question: "What is it?"

"Maybe I can see you this weekend," she said, twisting her mouth up to one side like an awkward kid asking me out for the first time.

The answer, of course, was *I can't, you know I can't, it's impossible,* but instead I said, "I'll see what I can do."

For once, I wasn't lying.

7

The contraband was in my briefcase by the front door, and I could have sworn its odor filled the entire house. I wore my best poker face, a skill learned over time by liars who want to keep on lying, the peace of a man who did not in fact have a veritable ticking time bomb just a few yards away. My wife kissed me on the lips, a dry peck, and asked me how my day was. Practiced sitcom dialogue. Did everybody engage in charades like this at home, or only when the tension was so taut the backs of their necks tingled?

"Joe Allen called," she informed me, her voice singsongy, victorious. I could tell she'd been busy. "He and *Kathy* are doing a sort of potluck thing next Friday. Wanted to know if we were interested."

"What did you tell him?"

"I said I'd ask you."

I absently poked at a yellow onion on the kitchen counter. Next to it sat the metal bowl from the refrigerator, the plastic wrap taken away and the red-brown meat warming to room temperature.

"Let me think about it," I said, loosening my tie, which felt hot in my hands. Then, as if it only just occurred to me: "Damn, forgot to grab the mail on my way in. Be right back."

It wasn't Pat in my mind during the long walk up the driveway to the mailbox at the curb, nor even *her* (Jackie). They might as well have occupied my thoughts, because this—all of this, what I was doing—concerned them every bit as much, but *she* was gone and Pat was safe in the fiction that what we had was a regular, garden-variety extramarital affair. It was Joe and Kathy's friend (for Christ's sake, did they even know she was missing?) who, for all I knew, was already attracting flies in the basement or whatever landfill my beautiful bride had selected for her final resting place. A stranger to me, just some girl who laughed at a silly man's wine snafu and doomed herself in the process. Sorry, lady. I should have worn a sign around my neck: DON'T TALK TO ME ON PAIN OF DEATH.

Bills, a circular, a postcard from some plastic-faced car sales-man running for city council. Nothing more in the mailbox, apart from the black widow I invented to set my evening in motion. I dropped the mail on the ground and marched breathlessly back to the house. There was no stopping this now.

Naturally Hannah furrowed her brow upon hearing my breath-less explanation of the terror in the mailbox, that familiar *Are you kidding me?* expression. It was supposed to be the other way around. I was disappointing her again.

"I'll take care of it tomorrow" was what she said. No dice.

"I left the mail."

"It can *wait*."

"I'd really rather—"

She screamed my name: a shrill, up-from-the-soul scream that made my eyes water. There was a long minute that stretched by after that, her shriek still tearing through my ears, during which I watched her jaw tremble and eyes glow hatefully.

"I put up with a lot, you know," she said, each word a chore to pass through clenched teeth. "You— *hurt*—me, you know."

I couldn't determine if she meant it in the past tense or the present. Some verbs are funny that way.

"I don't mean—"

"Don't."

"It's just the spider, I—"

"Don't."

I breathed a sigh and fixed my eyes on the food spread out be-tween us, anything to keep from meeting her glare.

"It's like having a dog with a bladder problem," she went on, shaking her head. "So many messes, and nobody to clean them up but me. Sometimes I get tired of your messes, do you know that? Sometimes I wish you'd just quit *pissing on the goddamn floor.*"

I nodded, submissive and contrite. Hannah sucked a long, an-gry breath into her lungs and then stomped past me, disappeared into the little hall leading to the garage. She was going after the black widow. I had two minutes at most.

Two long strides returned me to my briefcase by the door, from which I extracted my weapon of choice: a single medium-sized ba-nana, overly ripe. Twelve years I'd known my wife, and if there was one thing that gave her chills the way I'd acted about my imaginary spider, it was her deep-seated terror of her one and only deadly allergy. Her throat, I recalled her telling me while I rapidly peeled the fruit and mashed it hard into the ground beef, would close shut in a matter of minutes, completely shutting off her air supply. Anaphylactic shock, I supposed; a death sentence if she wasn't administered an antihistamine or bronchodilator immediately. Easy-peasy, and lingering darkly at the back of my mind for years by then. My secret weapon. I kneaded the hell out of the banana-infused beef, until every trace of the fruit's color was absorbed. The peel I hurled out the kitchen window in the seconds before immersing my hands in hot water from the sink, scrubbing the offending material away with a wire brush. Finally, just as I caught sight of Hannah stomping back down the driveway, angrier than ever, I grabbed a can of air freshener from beneath the sink and sprayed it liberally to mask the scent of my crime. Vanilla bean, allegedly. It smelled awful.

"It was gone," she growled upon returning inside. "If it was ever there in the first place."

"It was there."

"Well, it's not there now."

I was sitting at the kitchen table, listening to the blood thumping in my ears. Hannah slammed the mail down in front of me and huffed for the counter when she stopped, midstep, and sniffed at the air like a dog.

"The hell did you spray that crap for?"

"I, uh . . ."

"Never mind. Jesus, you men."

She frowned and went back to work on supper. My work was done, thanks to an imaginary spider and now an imaginary fart. Twenty minutes later we were seated across from each other with tacos on our respective plates. Did I taste the banana in the beef? I imagined I did, but would I have recognized it if I hadn't known it was there?

Hannah didn't.

Killing one's wife is a tense business, as it happens. She sipped at her tea and picked at the lettuce and shredded cheese, like a bird. Normal people shoved the whole damn thing in their mouth and bit down. But Hannah wasn't normal people.

I was working on my second taco by the time she finally stopped picking and crunched into the shell, meat and all. Just then a whimper wafted up from the basement. Hannah's eyes widened, connected with mine. Up until that minute, I had no idea if the woman down there was still alive. Now I knew she was. I swallowed. Hannah did too.

And she made a face. Her eyebrows came together and she puckered her mouth. She glanced down at the stuffed taco shell in her hand, and then up at me. I tried to smile. I think it ended up looking like a grimace. Next thing I knew, she was knocking her chair back with the backs of her knees and clawing at her neck. Sweat beaded on her forehead and she started to wheeze. I gaped like an idiot, an idiot who had no idea what could possibly be the matter.

It was working. My plan to murder my wife was working.

I said, "Hannah? Hannah, what's wrong?"

She swept her arm out and knocked the Waterford vase off the counter. It shattered against the linoleum floor and she staggered away from it, into the living room. I followed, pawing at her, faux concerned.

"Talk to me, Hannah."

She collapsed onto the couch and undid the top few buttons of her blouse. Her face and neck had gone blotchy, her eyes leaked tears. It happened just as quickly as she'd told me, all those years ago. I wondered if she'd sussed out the why of it. I decided it didn't matter.

"I'm going to get you something," I lied. "Try to stay calm."

I bolted from the room, but I didn't head for the medicine cabinet. Instead I went straight for her purse, right by where I'd dropped my briefcase. Inside, I found her keys, and I quickly sorted through them for the one I needed. The one that unlocked the basement door.

8

She wasn't dead, but she was close to it. Gone was the attractive blond woman in the sheer summer dress from Joe and Kathy's party—replacing her was a sunken-faced woman in her underwear, spattered with dirt and blood and sweat, her wrists cuffed behind her back and connected by a length of steel cable to a ring bolted into the wall. The skin on her arms and shoulders was striped with deep lacerations, crusted over with new scabs. Some of her hair had been torn out in clumps, leaving pink spots of bald flesh all over her scalp. When she saw me, she gasped and scrambled backward until she was up against the paneled wall. The carpet was spotted with blood. I smelled her urine and didn't see anything resembling a chamber pot. Good old Hannah.

"I'm not going to hurt you," I said, because it seemed like the right thing to say. The woman only sobbed in reply.

I asked her what her name was, and she whispered, "Jennifer."

For a fraction of a second I thought she was going to say Jackie, the name I wished I did not know, and my stomach lurched. I reminded myself that it was all over now, all this madness, and that *Jennifer* was going to be all right.

"She's dead," I said as matter-of-factly as I could while flipping through the keys, so many damn keys, looking for the one that might unlock the handcuffs. "My wife, she's dead."

It felt good, saying it. I wasn't at all sure that it would—I was somehow afraid that it would hurt, that despite everything the vocalization of what I had done would undo me too. But it didn't. It felt terrific.

Jennifer's eyes were swollen and red, her face shiny with grime and tears. She muttered, "Help me."

"I'm sorry," I said.

It wasn't enough.

9

Jackie, not Jennifer, died on the fusty basement carpet in nothing but a filthy T-shirt several sizes too big for her. The shirt was mine: an old Arkansas Razorbacks championship T I used to mow the lawn in. It ended up at Jackie's apartment, where Hannah found it with my extramarital fling packaged snugly inside. I guessed it had some kind of significance for her, the other woman wearing her husband's treasured shirt, so Jackie got to die in it.

Jackie whose name I did not know. Jackie who bled to death on the floor, my name carved into the skin on her belly. Jackie who was plenty good enough to lay but apparently not good enough to save. Not when it was tantamount to destroying a good marriage.

10

I had Jennifer propped up against me, her left arm draped over my shoulders and my right one tightly gripping her waist. I'd yanked my shirt off and buttoned it up on her, a gesture of forced modesty nobody really cared about at this point. The parallel wasn't lost on me, but this time the girl was getting rescued in my shirt, not expiring in it. We made it to the top of the steps with a lot of stops along the way. I nudged the door all the way open with my knee and hefted her onto the linoleum floor.

Patricia gave a yelp and pivoted to face us, the kitchen phone gripped in her hand like a pistol. She babbled helplessly for a moment, then slammed her mouth shut and gawped at the girl in my arms. Caught by the other woman with another woman. I almost had to laugh, but the phone was alarming.

"Pat—who are you—?"

"Your—it's Hannah, I don't think she's breathing . . ."

"Oh," I said, and gingerly sat Jennifer down on one of the kitchen chairs. I strode over to Pat and slipped the phone from her hand, hung it up. "What are you doing here, sweetheart?"

"I'm not kidding, damn it—she's *blue* in there!"

"Allergic reaction," I explained. "Let me deal with it. You'd be a huge help if you'd just take Jennifer home."

"I think I need to go to the hospital," Jennifer put in. I shrugged.

"Or that."

"But *Hannah,* goddammit!" Pat hollered. I winced, tired of all the yelling. I had had enough of raised voices and shouting matches.

"Hannah's dead, Patricia."

"Jesus . . ."

"And Jennifer needs your help."

Jennifer's head bobbed. She looked even worse in the daylight than she had in the dimly lit basement. Her eyes were glassy and bloodshot and her innumerable cuts were already bleeding through my work shirt. I must have torn some of the scabs hauling her up the steps.

"But who is she?" Pat asked. "What the hell is going on here?"

"She's what turned my marriage bad," I said with a lopsided smile.

Neither of them seemed to get it.

But hell, *I* laughed.

MATTHEW NEILL NULL

Gauley Season

FROM *West Branch*

LABOR DAY. WE could hear the bellow and grind from the Route 19 overpass. Below, the river gleamed like a flaw in metal. Leaving the parking lot behind, we billy-goated down the fisherman's trail, one by one, the way all mountain people do. Loud clumps of bees clustered in the fireweed and boneset, and the trail crunched underfoot with cans, condom wrappers, worm containers. A half-buried coal bucket rose from the dirt with a galvanized grin. The laurel hell wove itself into a tunnel, hazy with gnats. There, a busted railroad spike. The smell of river water filled our noses.

Finally sun spilled through the trees, and we saw Pillow Rock rise as big as a church from the waters. A gaudy lichen of beach towels and bikini tops coated it over. Local women shouted our names. "Happy Labor Day!" When we set foot upon it, the granite seemed to curve to our bare soles, radiating an animal heat. Wolf spiders raced off. We made the top, where Pillow Rock flattened. The river nipped at its base. So much water. The Army Corps of Engineers had uncorked the dam below Summersville Lake. The water churned and gouged at the canyon walls. The Gauley had the reputation of a drowning river, even before the Army Corps wrestled it out of God's control and gave it power.

Upriver, scraps of neon: rafters. Dyes like that don't appear in nature. Their paddles flashed like pikes in the sun.

Rafting brings in millions of taxable dollars a year. The commissioner says it's the best thing to happen to Nicholas County since the coal severance tax. "Coal was king," he says. "Coal *was* king." Men in their twenties and thirties and forties shouldn't stand idle. We who'd lost our mining jobs would work in white-water, plow that wet furrow. Nice thoughts. Invigorating lies. For our bread, we worked filling stations, timber outfits, hospice care, county schools. The two big successes among us, Chet Mason and Reed Judy, started a welding outfit out of Reed's old echoing barn. The rafting operators—from Pennsylvania, Oregon, Croatia—brought their own people and did little hiring, until Kelly Bischoff started Class Five. He hired locals. The papers gushed over Kelly. He'd graduated from Panther Creek High School. One of us. Ex-miner. He looked rugged-good and dusky on a brochure, glossy and smiling, holding a paddle. His mother's from Gad.

On Pillow Rock, men and women spoke to one another, casual and cunning. Someone fiddled with a portable radio: white jags of static, the silver keen of a steel guitar. We pried open prescription bottles that carried names other than our own.

Too late for trout fishing, too early for squirrel season—time to sun ourselves like happy rattlesnakes and watch the frolic. Five weeks running in the fall, we did, every Saturday, every Sunday. Opening day was always best. Every few minutes another raft tumbled over Sweet's Falls and crashed in the shredding whirlpool. After a tense moment, the raft popped up like a cork in a sudsy bucket of beer. We cheered. Agonized faces glanced back, blooming with smiles. They loved us, or the sight of us. They held paddles aloft in pale white arms and their orange helmets shined. Some claim we don't care about those people, we just take their commerce. Not true. We wonder about their jobs, their towns, their faces, their names.

Kelly Bischoff swore he heard a cash register chime every time they tipped over the falls. *I love clientele,* he said. Kelly moved between the two worlds, sleek as an otter. He knew us. He knew the rafters. Their names, their faces. He had everything you could want.

"Look, that one's so scared he keeps paddling, not even hitting the water."

Laugher tumbled down the rock. "What a jackass."

"A happy jackass."

"Would you do that?" Chet Mason asked a woman. "Go over the falls?"

"I'd love to scream like that. I never scream like that."

"You hear that, Jason? Sounds like you're not taking care of your husbandly duties."

Reed Judy said, "You pay big money to holler like that. Old Kelly gets two hundred dollars a head. You got to come with a full raft too. He got *plenty* of rafts."

"How many heads is that?"

"One, two . . . six in that one, not counting the guide," Chet Mason said. "Slick as a hound's tooth, Kelly is. Course, fall's got to pay for winter, spring, and summer—that's awful heavy math. There he is. That's Class Five, that's Kelly's."

The forty-seventh raft that day. Class Five River-Runners had blue-and-yellow rafts, same colors as the Mountaineers' football team. We were proud of Kelly. After they sealed the Haymaker Mine, he took out a mortgage to start his outfit. Kelly punched out Mayor Cline last year at the festival. Wasn't even drunk.

"Hey, Kelly boy!" We cupped hands around our mouths. "Hey, Kelly!"

But he didn't wave back, riding closer on the careening swell. The raft hit at a bad angle. Rocks scraped the wet, blubbery rubber. As it made the lip of the falls—in our bellies, we felt a feathery sympathetic tickle—the raft toppled and shook out bodies.

Quiet. Then the screaming.

We bounded down to the water's jagged edge, we tried to tally them, keep the numbers right. Neon tumbling in that gullet of foam, and one frail arm. We reached and missed and cussed ourselves. Reed managed to hook a belt and flopped a man onto the rock.

One disappeared under a boulder for a few sickening moments and shot out the other side. His mouth a hard circle.

With a strong crawl, Kelly led some into a backwater that bristled with logjams and lost paddles. Their heads broke the surface. The current sucked them back.

Kelly and the girl reached up at the same time. Chet Mason was closest. He had one set of hands. He hesitated for a millisecond. He reached for Kelly. "Got you."

A sharp little yelp cut the noise. The girl's helmet disappeared downriver. She was gone.

Young boys slid off the rocks like seals. Tethered with rope, they felt for corpses with their feet; we fished for the dead and walked the living—Kelly and four rafters—up Pillow Rock.

Like nothing had happened, a raft came tippling over the falls. The rafters looked surprised when no one waved. Supplicants, we circled the rock with track cell phones raised in hand, trying for the best of reception. Soon an ambulance squalled onto the overpass.

The rescued were quiet now. Hard to believe they'd been wailing, keening, moaning. Flogged by the water, they looked haggard—pilgrims who'd been turned back from the country of the drowned. We sat them on beach towels and tried to give them sandwiches. They wore mere bruises and abrasions, but the paramedics nursed them just the same. One kept trying to slip a blood pressure cuff onto them. A blond woman with a tank top and a little too much sun wept and cussed in alternating jags. She did this while wringing water from her hair. She had a stiff shocked look, like a cat you just threw in a rain barrel.

The survivors sat a ways from Kelly Bischoff. He shivered under a towel, smoking a damp cigarette. He'd stripped off his life jacket and spread it in the sun to dry. His hair, gone gray in patches, had grown out like a hippie's. "Of all the goddamn things," he kept saying.

"How many times you been over the falls?" Reed Judy asked him.

"Three hundred and thirty-one."

"How many times you roll it over on you?"

"Three," he said, pulling on the cigarette. "This was the third. My line was right."

"Looked like you hit it funny."

"My line was right. They let out thirty-eight hundred cfs today. Too much river. That," Kelly said, "is God's honest truth." He pressed his ear against the warm granite to draw out the water. He was shaking.

Deputies arrived. They were locals, Hunter Sales and Austin Cogar, young, crew-cut, sweating from the hike. Austin stood by the survivors and jotted on a pad. "How old you say she was?"

"I don't know exactly," a rafter said. He was half of a whisper-thin couple who were holding hands on the rock. "She's my friend's daughter. She's in high school."

"Her name's Amanda," Kelly cried. It was sudden, like the fury of a wasp.

Everyone turned to him. Hunter took his arm and tried to lead him aside.

"I know all my clients," Kelly said. He liked calling them by their names. It set things in motion, the tumbling of keys in locks. It made us feel unprivileged.

Hunter asked, "How you doing, Kelly?"

"I been better."

"Turn a boat over, did you?"

"Looks like." Kelly flicked the cigarette into the waters.

"Got good insurance?"

"Damn good. The best."

Hunter told us to give them some room. He lowered his voice and began to question.

"I had one beer," Kelly said, more loudly than he should have. "Washed down my sandwich at lunch. Ask anybody."

The blond woman who'd been wringing her hair spoke up. "You drank three of them," she said, putting a nice little snap on her words. "You put them away fast." She turned to Austin. "He had at least two. Then he sneaked off at lunch with them and—"

Kelly said, "Christina, this is between me and the police. You'll get your turn."

We blushed at the mention of her name, like they'd admitted something sexual. Austin's pen quit scratching—it made you blush twice.

The blond woman walked over to Kelly. "I have something to say and it's my right."

"Aw shut up." Then he called her something that made us cringe, even the deputies.

"I'd like to speak to you in private," Austin told her. "All you people go. Come on, get."

She spoke in low tones, her hands fluttering in a crippled dove dance.

Slowly we folded our towels but didn't stray too far. Kelly sat off to the side like the condemned. Austin talked into a radio pinned on his shirt. "Blond teenager, female, fifteen years of age. Male, forty-three years of age, scar through his eyebrow."

The sun weakened. As the temperature fell, the air began to smell like rain. Deputies said go on home, they didn't need no more statements, though we'd have been proud to give them. The coolers pissed final streams of meltwater and we made our exodus, one by one. A drizzle fell. Kelly sat in the back of a Crown Vic cruiser on the overpass, head bowed against the seat in front of him. The drizzle turned to nickel-hard rain and we heard the blades whapping long before we saw. The helicopter dipped into view. Pterodactyl-ugly, it switched on a searchlight and circled many times. Then it swooped away, called back wherever it came from. The rain turned to roaring curtains. Faintly, the music of rescue disappeared over the ridge.

We found the dead girl wrapped around a bridge abutment at the mouth of Meadow Creek. Her skin was bleached canvas-white by the waters, her eyes pressed shut. For that we were thankful. This stretch of river the rafters aren't supposed to see. It's a world away from Pillow Rock. Here, Meadow Creek sloughed mine acid into the Gauley after any good rain. It streaked rocks orange and sent a cadmium ribbon of yellowboy unspooling downriver. No fish, no life. The sight of it could make you cry.

"You guys ought to pull on gloves."

We waved off the sheriff and waded in. Hadn't we been raised to treat our hands like tools, our tools like hands? Blue jeans drank up water and darkened.

We built a chain of ourselves, then pulled her from the shallows, her hair tangling like eelgrass around hands and arms, refusing to let go. On the green table of pasture we laid the dead girl's body: coltish, young, trim as a cliff diver's. An athlete. Her hair twisted into a wet question mark. One leg tucked under her at a funny angle. We pulled down her shirt where it had ridden over her small breasts. Leaves in her hair. "Walnut leaves," someone said.

She looked okay for someone who'd been traveling all night. We wrapped her in plastic and carried her to the road. Sheriff said, "Sure glad Kelly ain't here to see this."

Everyone nodded. It was a solemn occasion. It felt almost holy, to carry a visitor's body in the morning light. None of us had touched one before.

The dead girl's picture found its way into the newspaper, pixelated and gray. She was a high schooler from Bethesda, Maryland, her father a minor executive at the federal Department of Labor.

The mother an ex-wife. Her father was Greg Stallings. We never found his body. We learned the things we did not know. Amanda.

You couldn't have gotten all the leaves out of the dead girl's hair. Not even if you'd sheared it off.

With her death, life changed, a little. Insurance payments were made, rumor and accusation leveled, a dram of ink spilled in the papers. Kelly Bischoff sold his company to a fellow from Connellsville, Pennsylvania, who owned a northern operation on the Youghiogheny and the Cheat. Seventeen of Kelly's people went on unemployment and COBRA, drawing as long as they could. Connellsville had his own guys. No one made big lawsuit money off her death; rafters sign risk papers beforehand, absolving companies of blame. So earth turned, bears scouted their dens, the Army Corps eased their levers down. The river returned to its bed.

We have a tenth of the mining jobs our fathers had.

But Kelly had connections. He found work running a dozer at a strip mine—a fitting job, where he dumped blasted rock into the valley, stanching creeks and gullies with tons of shattered mountaintop. He crafted a featureless flatland where the governor promised malls, industrial parks, golf, chain restaurants. A new round of permits cleared the EPA.

It hurt to see Kelly out of the rafting game. And yes, maybe we're guilty of feeling something special for Kelly, of yoking our fortunes to his. We rooted for him. He showed what our kind could accomplish, if given the chance, in this sly new world. We could go toe-to-toe, guide with skill, make that money. We were just as good as outsiders, almost equals, we weren't just white mountain trash. The sting of the rafters' uneasy looks when we pumped their gas or offered directions—with a few more Kelly Bischoffs, why, all that would end. Now, nothing.

Then, December. Reed Judy was driving the overpass, making for the tavern at Clendenin Mill, the one that burned last year. A lone figure was washed in the spastic glow of headlights and sucked back into the darkness. Reed pulled over, grit and snow popping under his tires. The man walked up to meet him.

"Can I give you a lift?" Reed asked.

"No, bud. Just taking a look at the river."

Reed heard the Gauley muttering in its dumb winter tongue,

but the canyon was black, no river there. He could see the distant warning lights, like foundered stars, where the dam stood low in the sky. Where it divided river from lake. He asked, "You sure? It's blue-cold out."

"Oh, I'm parked down at the turnaround."

It was Kelly.

"Suit yourself," Reed said.

"You Steve's boy? The welder?"

"Yeah."

"You don't look like your mother." Kelly pinned him down with a stare. "Say—you were down there that day. You drug the river. I know you did. Down to Meadow Creek."

Reed panicked, lied. "No," he said. "Don't know what you're talking about."

"Yes, you do. You seen her. Amanda Stallings." Kelly winced. "Did she look okay? God, she was a good girl. She wasn't tore up too bad, was she?"

When Reed didn't answer, Kelly said, "I didn't mean to drown her."

"Course you didn't! Nobody said you did! You don't have to say that."

Kelly said mournfully, "I don't think you understand," and said no more.

Telling it around, Reed itched a particular place on the back of his hand. "Looks like he's aged twenty years, he does."

A month later Chet saw Kelly on the overpass, hands clamped on the rail. When Chet told the story, he fidgeted and blushed. The sight had shaken him. "I thought about hitting him with the truck and saving the poor crazy son of a bitch from . . . from . . . I don't know."

And this was something to say, because in a place with so few people, each life was held precious, everyone was necessary. We saw Kelly again and again that winter. State troopers made him walk the line. He was not drunk. "Kiss my red ass," he cried. "Public right-of-way."

We waited for him to jump.

Every night the dam drew Kelly there. To avoid Route 19, we looped far out of our way, over the crookedest mountain cuts. It hurt too much to see him. But others were vigilant. Every morning the dam operators of the Army Corps—three lonesome, demoted engineers—scanned the banks and the tailrace with binoculars. They had a pool going as to when Kelly's lifeless body would finally wash up. That sortie out of the powerhouse was the high point of their day. This, after all, was a backwater post.

Lyndon Johnson, a president we loved, dedicated Summersville Dam in 1966. Before cutting the ribbon, he made a joke about losing his pocketknife on the way and maybe having the Secret Service throw up a roadblock at the Nicholas County line to find whoever had pocketed his Schrade—too fine a thing to leave just laying around—since he reckoned all West Virginia boys come out of the womb knowing a good knife when they see one. We laughed and Lyndon took out a bandanna and swabbed at his brow, looking like any worried man.

Acres of virgin concrete. Smooth, vertical. The dam was tall as the face of God. There was nothing else to compare it to. Nothing of such stability, such mass.

The rising waters flooded the village of Gad, home to a store, a filling station, and three hundred people. Eminent domain moved them, even the dead from their graves. (When Kelly stood on the overpass, was he trying to see his mother's village through 90 feet of water? No. He was thinking only of the girl.) Quietly, later, Gauley Season was created in 1986 by an act of Congress. We had no idea how life would change.

Over unruly rivers and hogbacks, the rectangular Gauley River National Recreation Area was placed like a stencil. It's shaded aquamarine on the maps. Lord—maps and new maps. The rapids had names before the rafters came: Glenmorgan Crossing and Mink Shoals, Gooseneck, Mussellshell. They brought a new language: cubic feet per second, highside and chicken-line, hydraulic and haystack. They renamed the rapids: Insignificant, Pure Screaming Hell, Junkyard, the Devil's Asshole. Unwritten, our names flew away like thistledown on the wind. Except for Pillow Rock. Our fathers named the rock for the river drivers napping there in the sun after a punishing morning of busting jams and poling logs downriver. We snuck to the foot of the overpass and spray-painted in green neon, PILLOW ROCK AHEAD!!! The last thing a rafter sees before tipping over the falls. So the name remained.

True, the release goes against nature. Gauley Season scours the river, blasting fish from their lies, eyes agog, air bladders ruptured.

Even so, Gauley Season brings certain benefits. To atone for the fishery's death, the Department of Natural Resources grows California rainbow trout in hatcheries and drops ten thousand pounds into the canyon by helicopter. The fish have nubby snouts, open ulcers, and tattered fins from rubbing against the concrete raceways. Gray trout, we call them. They taste like they've been stamped out of cat food, but they're free. Come spring, we watch them rain and smack the waters. We cast hooks until every last one's caught and creeled. Sometimes the fish hit the rocks as the helicopter swoops away. Raccoons revel in the blood. They lick their wiry hands, fumbling them in an attitude just like prayer. They rejoice.

"There he is!" an engineer cried. "You win, Sully! He jumped! He finally jumped!"

The others ran out of the powerhouse. He adjusted the parallax of his binoculars in a gloved fist. "Shit. False alarm." What he thought was Kelly was a dead deer twisted—twisting—in sunken willows.

A year passed as they do, quickly, as if in a dream or a coma. We thought of the dead girl and her father less and less, or tried to.

Snow and thaw and rain. Hay was cut in the fields, sallies hatched off the river in lime-and-sulfur clouds, deer grew their velvet crowns. September gleaned a cool wind from the Alleghenies. Labor Day weekend, Pillow Rock gathered its people. We hollered as the Army Corps opened up the gates. Upriver, the beating of ten thousand hooves. We inhaled the water's breath of iron and cedar.

A standing wave broke over Sweet's Falls. The river augured and torqued, a muscular green. Shards of flotsam and jetsam: broken sycamores and garbage bags, bleached timber, a child's tricycle. A water-bloated calf wheeled downriver, eyes blue as heaven.

The air crackled with anticipation. Gas stations and hotels and campgrounds had pitched their banners early: RAFTERS WELCOME, COLD BEER HOT SHOWERS, ASK ABOUT OUR GROUP RATES. This would be a record-breaking season. The *Washington Post* had featured us in their Sunday magazine. The headline read "*Montani Semper Liberi*." "West Virginia's secret is out: the number-two river in America, number seven in the world. One question remains. Can the whitewater industry save this place?" With the glee of discoverers, they told of the spine-rattling third-world pike that is Route 19. That wasn't so bad—maybe the Department of Highways would be embarrassed and put in for federal money. What nettled most were the things they plucked out to describe: junk cars in the river, raggedy bearhounds jumping in their kennels, crosses at Carnifex Ferry that say GET RIGHT WITH GOD and THERE IS NO WATER IN HELL. All eye-battering, all to be laughed at. Didn't talk about the landing we poured, the oil-and-chip road we laid for their wobbling, overburdened shuttles. "Relax," Mayor Cline said. "Sometimes the fire that cooks your food burns your fingers—you can't bitch." It's dog Latin, the state slogan. We are, it says, always free.

Kelly Bischoff walked down the fisherman's trail in a ragged red backpack.

Pillow Rock went silent.

Work-blackened jeans, dirt in his hair. He peeled off his shirt, shook it of coal dust, and folded it with care. The words *Sweet* and *Sour* were inked in cursive blue over his nipples, with arrows offering up directions. A black panther climbed his bicep, claws drawing stylized blood. A Vietnam mark. He shucked his boots and tucked his cigarettes, wallet, and keys into them. Finally he pulled out a penknife and snagged off his workpants to the knee.

"You're back among the fold," Reed said to him.

Kelly smiled. "Good to see you all."

"You working that strip job?"

"Yes I am," Kelly said, looking side to side, daring anyone to say a word against it.

"Jesus Was Our Savior, Coal Was Our King. Say, you probably haven't watched from this angle."

Kelly said, "I seen them go over. Nineteen seventy-nine, it was. Fishing here. Seen Philadelphy Pete Dragan go over Sweet's, back in them too-big green army rafts. Said, *Hell, I can do that.*"

Kelly watched the falls, apart from the rest. What could he read there? The water herded yellow foam into the backwater, a rancid butterfat color, thick enough you could draw your name in it with a fish pole. Where we'd saved four lives last year. Five if we counted Kelly's. Hard to tell if we should or not. If Kelly longed for his old life, he did not say. He just watched the water's horseplay like he could augur it. Maybe he could.

Rafters! We waved and hollered as usual, but Kelly radiated a complex silence. So we grew quiet, not so joyful, and the day grew old. Shadows slithered on the rock. One hundred ninety-seven rafts. Not a one drowned. Clouds came and snuffed our shadows. The air had a little bite to it, so we pulled on sweaters and packed to leave. Slush tipped from coolers, the last orphan beer cracked and drained. Kelly just sat there.

"Them are your people," we said, waving at the last raft.

Kelly shrugged. We gave Reed Judy some hopeful looks, so he hunkered down next to our fallen idol. "You coming? We're going to Bud Shreve's, grill some food. Be fun."

"No, I'll set here awhile." Kelly rummaged around his backpack and found a gray surplus blanket. Was he too good for us?

"All right, bud. You hear about the blind kid up here got bit by the rattlesnake?"

"No, I didn't."

"Least he didn't see it coming."

Kelly smiled and looked at the ground. "That's a good one," he said. Didn't even flinch; there was hope for him yet. But then he whispered something that turned Reed pale and bloodless—and that Reed wouldn't tell about till years later. "You're the one lied about Meadow Creek," Kelly said. "Lied about finding her. Why would you do that to me?"

We left him there as the drawknife of dusk peeled back the world.

In heirloom fifteen-verse ballads, lovers of the drowned flung themselves in, so their bones could frolic and mingle. But Kelly never trucked in old ways. Instead he sat with us.

For the rest of the season, Kelly was the first on Pillow Rock and last to go. Word went round he'd slept there through the weekends, under a ragged tent of laurel. "But he looks to be shaving," someone said. Sure enough, he never missed a single raft. He perched there like an osprey. When the maples flared, he began telling stories of the dead girl.

It was hard not to listen. He'd sidle up if you broke away to piss or get another beer. She wanted to be an environmental lawyer, he said. She was an athlete. Once she ran a mile in five minutes and thirty-two seconds, a fluke—her average was six-fifteen. She stayed with her father weekends and summer. She loved dogs. "Oh, who doesn't?" Chet asked him.

On a coolish day in October, for the first and only time, he spoke to us as a group. Our numbers had trickled, as they do at season's end. Kelly chewed his fingernails, his thumbnail. Sucking the taste from them. Then he spoke.

In Bethesda, the dead girl's home was the size of . . . — he struggled for comparison — . . . of the county courthouse, the one with the statue of Nancy Hart, who seduced her jailer, shot him in his stupid mouth, and brought back a Confederate cavalry to burn the town. Why did our forefathers raise a statue to someone who destroyed them? Our people fought at Carnifex Ferry. Left the trees full of minié balls, as much lead as wood, so they grew hunched and buzzardy under their mineral burden. We sparred and set the boats on fire. They whirled like burning flags in the night and snuffed themselves hissing in the Gauley. Why not a statue to that?

"That's history," Kelly said. "Pull your head out your ass."

"Nothing happens no more. Day in, day out."

He said, "You have no idea."

"Idea of what?"

To prove us wrong, Kelly plucked up and spoke — confident now. He explained the last day of his rafting career.

When they broke for lunch in the canyon, Kelly offered to lead any stouthearted rafter up Barranshe Run to see the five falls, a stair-step of cataracts up the mountainside.

Hours from drowning, Greg Stallings asked, "Is it far?"

"Little bit. Just follow me, Greg. Anybody else?"

The group sat at a table made of the raft turned turtle. One stood up: the dead girl. Kelly kicked his accent up a notch. "A young thing. Great. You'll lead the pack, Amanda."

"I can take it," she said, with a measure of pluck.

Kelly looked the dead girl over: strong legs, sleek lines. "You can carry her up there on your back," he said, appraising her like a foreign coin. "She still your little girl, right?"

Greg smiled. The others waved them on, faces full of sandwiches and potato salad, bright in their water-sport clothes — chartreuse and pylon orange, same color as the Powerbait we sling to the government trout.

Ascent. The two of them did what Kelly did, clutching the same wet points of rock, the same dry patches of moss for footholds. The trail stitched itself in and out of the creek, where trout danced like Salome in the tannic water. Smell of rotting wood. Squelch and rasp of wet tennis shoes on rock. Kelly explained that Barranshe Run was named for a sow black bear that never whelped a single cub. "No one ran their dogs on her, ever, even when she was reelfoot and gray. Don't know why. We kill lots of bears here."

Greg said, "That sounds like a story to me."

"It's just what they say." Kelly knew the rafters were obsessed with fact. They paraded it at him again and again. "Would have been a mercy to kill her."

"That's so callous," the dead girl said.

"No. Animals aren't afraid to die. They just want to make another thing just like them. If they can't, they go someplace lonely and pine. Like here," he said, gesturing to the unraveling tapestry of rock, root, water, and vine. "Water?"

She unscrewed the cap and took a drink. She wiped her mouth, cocked her head at him.

The trail narrowed. She kept flicking him little looks.

Hands scrabbled for holds. Calves burned with acid. "One more bend," Kelly hollered. There, Great Swallow Falls, 30 foot tall. It sluiced over a mossy lip of stone and sent a misty perpetual rainbow into the air: a fisherman's cast net frozen midthrow. The world smelled of cold, rich limestone. Swallows nipped stoneflies. The colored hoop shimmered.

The dead girl showed Kelly how to work the switches on her camera. "Wait, show me again," he said, grinning. She slapped his arm. "Pay attention."

Kelly snapped a picture of father and daughter, perfect for the Internet. "Think that's nice, you ought to see the next one." Each falls more riveting than the last: deeper drop, darker hues, emerald, topaz, Prussian. The swallows piping like bone flutes.

Panting now, Greg said he couldn't go on. He sat on a log, nursing warm spots that promised to blister.

"But the last one's the best," Kelly said, pointing ahead. Now the trail ran vertical, just a thin trough of root and rubble through jagged stone. A deer couldn't run it. The ground called for a more agile animal, say a bobcat, a lean leaping ghost with splayed pads and tight haunches.

The dead girl wanted to try it. Kelly promised to bring her right back.

Greg hesitated. "It looks dangerous to me."

"We take people every day. Amanda be fine."

"Take your camera," her father called after.

Kelly led her around the bend. "You got to climb up this little rise to get there."

Her face went slack. "Are you serious?"

"Grab hold of that laurel, Amanda. That plant there. There you go. Give you a boost."

Kelly gave it — touching her! — and she pulled herself up. Over the rise, she saw the last waterfall. It was nothing more than a tiny gurgling delta. She began to laugh.

She turned around and found Kelly there. He had a dusky look, shards of coal dust embedded in his face. Nine years in the Haymaker Mine, riding the mantrip into the belly of the mountain. At night his skin leaked metal. He woke to blue slivers on the pillow. He kissed her open mouth. She felt his beard and its pleasant rasp on her skin. Swallows singing through the air, soft blue sickles. And the two worlds touch, in a way we always hoped could happen. Kelly jumped the wall. He became one of them.

"I turned that raft over. I turned it over on purpose." Kelly popped a finger into his mouth and began to chew at the nail.

"My God," said Reed, on the edge of hysteria, "them people fucking trusted you. My God, that's fucking awful, that's *terrible*."

Kelly stared at the river, the sculpted earth and water. He pulled the finger from his mouth. The air crackled with alarm.

"'Deed I did. Her dad was looking at us," Kelly said. "He come up behind and saw."

Reed went on mindlessly, "No, no, no."

"I know these falls. Think I'd make a mistake right here? These falls is my bread and butter. Been over better than three hundred times. Been over them blindfolded."

Everyone yelling, *What did he see? What was he gonna do?* Frenzied and shouting just anything that came to mind. No one could seem to ask him *Why?* but he answered anyhow. "I had to. I didn't mean to drown her," Kelly said. "Just her dad."

That settled in. Chet was saying, "Hold on! Kelly, listen to me . . . you did it because he seen you and her?"

"She wanted me to get rid of him."

"Wait —"

"She hated her dad. She didn't care if he saw us. He wasn't her kind. She was like us."

We took in his words.

"She told you that?"

"Listen," he said. "Listen to the water."

"What?"

"She told me yesterday," Kelly said and babbled on.

It started with cursing. You could taste anger in the air, taste it on your tongue. We'd been had. Kelly didn't have two worlds. He had one, ours, the lesser. "You evil liar," Chet Mason told him. Everyone howled at Kelly to stop.

"She told me today."

We shut him up the only way we could. He slid and danced under our hands. Reed had to take off his belt and hit him with the buckle. Grabbing hold of crazy arms and kicking legs, we flung Kelly into that blind sucking roar. He flopped in with a smack.

Raw white noise. Kelly was gone. Had we really done it? The Gauley took him under. We blinked wildly at one other. No one said a thing. Let it drag him to the ocean.

The river made a low shushing sound. We hadn't kept track of the days. Sweet's Falls trickled down to nothing. The Army Corps had lowered its levers. The water was placid. A carnival ride unplugged. Kelly floated to the surface, sputtering, blinking at the sky.

Gauley Season was over.

Kelly paddled to the riverbank and pulled himself ashore with fistfuls of cattail. Bloody, he managed a grin and gave us a thumbs-up.

Nothing's painful as embarrassment. Our credulousness stung like bedsores. Even now we nurse those wounds.

But outlandish as it was, Kelly's story nagged at you. There were three witnesses: two dead, the other lost in that white country of madness. Could it be true? Part of you wanted to believe Kelly flipped the raft on purpose. Kelly and the girl—rafters and locals, one people—a beautiful story. That is, a mawkish lie. And if Kelly Bischoff can't equal them—to know their names, brush their lips, be loved, respected—no one on Pillow Rock can. Once again the world let us know what we are. Swallows in flight. The rasp of shoes. Kelly built himself a legend on that. Maybe he'd come to cherish the girl out of a terrible guilt, which can midwife the strongest, most wretched kind of love into the world. Those cold nights on the Route 19 overpass, he believed. For a man like him, like us, one mistake—one botched run over the falls—could ruin him forever. It wasn't his entire fault. When they signed the papers, the rafters delivered their lives into Kelly's hand, they bought the thrill of giving yourself over to a stranger, and the bill came due. And we were the ones who chose Kelly, after all, one of ours. We let the girl die. When Chet Mason reached for Kelly's hand, we damned him to his own true life. A life with us. But Kelly couldn't let go of the dream. He couldn't join in our quiet decline.

Soured by it all, we gave Pillow Rock back to the rattlesnakes. Now we let them lie prone to soak up the heat like powerful conductors. And we gave it to Kelly.

We found ways to occupy our time: machining engines, welding catch-gates, jacklighting deer. The lesser waters no one coveted, so we dove off the cliffs at Summersville Lake till the state fenced it off. Then we cut the wire with bolt cutters—the "West Virginia credit card"—and dove at night, our jacklights trained on green water, attracting a fine mist of moths and mayflies.

But Gauley Season never ceased to be part of our year. The rafters buy potato chips and high-test, they flag us down for directions, but they don't miss us, our catcalls from the rock. They palm tips into knowing hands, book next season's trip, tighten luggage racks on foreign cars. As we do our chores, we imagine the shredding water, the cry of clients, the slur of rubber on stone. They slalom down Sweet's Falls with nothing but the growl of water in their ears. We hate them. We hate them with the fury that is the same as love.

The rafters notice a single man perched on the granite. Shirtless, Kelly Bischoff raises a hand or touches a hat brim. A wise, gray-bearded fisherman gone down to ply the waters. Hair lank, skin mottled like a Plott hound's. Bedraggled, harried by weather and briar, the river guide has earned this lonesome place by great effort, by true compass. Stalwart, wiry, keen of limb. A true mountaineer, rifle-true. But they know no better. The river guide has made good on his mortgage. With the yellow tusks of a bulldozer, he breaks the mountain. He draglines the coal.

Against the glossolalia of the water, the river guide cups his hands and calls to the rafters, but they can't hear, they tip over the falls and lose sight of him in a joyous crush. A plea is lost to history.

The nude crag of Pillow Rock, stripped of its people, scrawled

and scrimshawed in the shit of swallows. They don't know that we
—the true fishermen—will not return until season's end, rods
ready, faces hard, when the heavens part, the rotors of helicopters
mutter their staccato hymn, and we receive the silver benediction
of government fish.

ANNIE PROULX

Rough Deeds

FROM *The New Yorker*

IN NEW FRANCE, which people more and more called Canada, from the old Iroquois word *kanata*, Duquet was everywhere—examining, prying, measuring, observing, and calculating. Limbs and low-quality hardwood waste became high-quality firewood, and every autumn he packed twenty wagons full for the Kébec market and for Paris, when he could charter available ships with the promise of a good return cargo of tea or coffee or textiles, spices or china. Without the sure promise of a rich return cargo, he thought, let the Parisians freeze, for all he cared.

Leasing a Dutchman's ships was well enough, but he needed ships of his own. In 1712, a business acquaintance in Boston, an Englishman named Dred-Peacock, connected him to an English shipbuilder and a new but promising yard on the River Clyde, in Scotland, joined to England by the Act of Union, in '07. Duquet wanted a ship; the yard wanted wood.

"Regard the map, sir," Dred-Peacock said. "It's the closest point to the colonies—the briefest sailing time. There are signs of success on the Clyde, but they need good timbers. They will pay for them. It is an opportunity that cannot be neglected."

There were good precedents in New France for trading with the enemy, but arrangements with the English and the Scots were still secret, complex, expensive, even dangerous. Yet Duquet knew that there was profit in selling to the English, despite their colonial aims. Duquet took the plunge and Dred-Peacock took a goodly share of the profits, which increased year by year. Fifty acres of oak were needed to build one seventy-four-gun warship, and the hardwood stands along the rivers of New France began to fall to Duquet's ambitions. But he felt hampered by Kébec's distance from the money pots of the world and by the ice blockage of the Saint-Laurent River in winter.

"Duquet, it is past time for you to consider shifting your business operation to the colonies," Dred-Peacock told him as they sat over their papers and receipts in the Sign of the Red Bottle, near the wharves, the inn they favored in Boston. Never did Dred-Peacock present his ill-formed face to Duquet in Kébec; always Duquet made the trip south by schooner or by packet.

"Oh, I think on it," Duquet said, swirling the ale in his tankard until it slopped over the rim, as if that settled the question. "I think of it often. I am of half a mind to do so, sir."

"Damn, sir! It is quite time you acted. Finish with thinking and act. Every day those poxy whoresons of mill men push into the forests and gain control over the land. In Maine there are countless white-pine mast trees and lesser pines to be used for tar and pitch. You know there is a great market for these if you can get them on a ship bound for Scotland, England, or even Spain or Portugal."

Duquet nodded, but his face was sour. He knew that Dred-Peacock saw him as an ill-bred boor, a creature from the depths. True enough, he had escaped a cramped childhood spent pulling rabbit fur from half-rotten skins, pinching out guard hairs, plucking the soft fur for quilt stuffing. As a boy he had coughed incessantly, bringing up phlegm clotted with rabbit hair. The fine hairs had settled on every surface, matted on his family's heads and shoulders. Finally, in this clinging miasma of stinking hair and dust, his mother, choking blood, had lain on the floor as his father's black legs scissored away into the night, and Duquet began his struggle to get away from France, to become another person.

Dred-Peacock may have sensed Duquet's squalid beginnings, but his fantastic drive to make money was what interested the Englishman. Dred-Peacock went on, his voice vibrating, "Where there is a market, the businessman must act. And all this would be immeasurably easier if you operated from Boston rather than bloody *Kweebeck*. And with my help these affairs can be managed."

It was obvious and timely advice, and yet Duquet hesitated to commit to leaving New France. He had valuable connections there, and a lifetime dislike of the English language, with its vile obscenities, and those who spoke it.

Soon several ships belonging to Duquet but flying British flags ran the seas between Portsmouth and Boston harbors and the ever more numerous Clyde shipyards. It was like walking on a web of tightropes, but the money flew around Duquet like dandelion fluff in the wind. He had only to catch it in his net. And share it with Dred-Peacock.

During the next decade Duquet began to acquire tracts of wood-land in Maine. Dred-Peacock's genius in the legal procedure of ac-quiring remote "townships" was immeasurable, and an old acquain-tance from Duquet's first years in New France, Jacques Forgeron, scouted out the best timberland. Forgeron, a surveyor when he could get work, a voyageur when he could not, had joined forces with Duquet in his earliest days. Together they had entered the fur trade, had paddled, portaged, walked, and sung the rivers of New France. Forgeron was something of a Jonah, who attracted foul weather, but he had a curious regard for the wild forest and often told Duquet that it could be the source of great wealth. This man cherished his measuring chains and could use one as a weapon, swinging it around and around until it gained velocity and the free end leaped forward to maim. And if he had used it in this way in France, the old days counted for very little. Now he was a partner in Duquet et Fils, perhaps even a friend, if a business tie between two friendless men could be so described.

From time to time Duquet would join Forgeron in the Maine woods to explore his growing territory. One October afternoon they landed their canoe on a sandy Maine river shore fronting one of their new white-pine properties, twenty thousand acres at a cost of twelve cents an acre. There was a narrow hem of ice along the shaded shoreline.

"Frog ice," Forgeron said. In the rich autumn light, the decidu-ous trees stunned with xanthine orange and yellow. The men's swart shadows fell on the ground like toppled statues. Without speaking, they began to gather firewood. Forgeron held up his hand.

"Listen," he said quietly. They heard the sounds of chopping not too far off and began to move cautiously toward the source.

With an acid jolt of fury, Duquet saw unknown men in stiff, pitch-blackened trousers cutting his pines, other men limbing the fallen trees, and yet another scoring them. Two men worked with broadaxes to square the logs. Duquet was sure they had a pit saw-mill set up nearby. By their bulging pale eyes and doughy faces he knew them to be English colonists. Although Duquet et Fils had no hesitation in cutting big trees where they found them, it was intolerable when they were the victims of this poaching.

"Ho la! Who say you come my land, cut my tree?" Duquet shouted, forgetting his careful English. He was so furious that his voice strangled in his throat. Forgeron advanced beside him, lightly revolving a section of his 33-foot chain.

The startled woodsmen stared and then, still gripping their tools, they ran on an oblique course toward the river, where they likely had boats. But one with a dirty bandage on his right leg lagged behind.

Duquet did not pause. He drew his tomahawk from his belt and hurled it, striking the runner's left calf. He fell, crying to his com-rades for help in a high, childish voice. One of the escaping men turned around and stared at Duquet as he called something to the fallen one. The confrontation lasted only a few seconds but left Duquet with an unfading impression of a man swelling with hatred. Duquet would not forget the man's mottled slab of a face, encircled by ginger hair and beard, the yellow animal eyes fixed on him, the sudden turning away and violent dash for the river.

"They come from settlements along the coast," Forgeron said. "All Maine settlers are voracious thieves of fine timber. They are everywhere on the rivers."

They bound their wounded prisoner, a boy not older than four-teen, and dragged him to a pine, tied him up against it in a hollow between projecting tree roots.

"You, *garçon*, talk up or I cut first your fingers, then your balls. Who are you? What men you with? How you come here?"

The boy folded his lips in a tight crease, either in pain or in defiance. Duquet wrenched the boy's arm and spread his left hand against one of the great humped roots. With a quick slash of his ax, he took off a little finger and part of the next.

"Talk or I cut more. You die no head."

Duquet's bloody interrogation gave him the information that the thieves were in the employ of a mill owner named McBogle, an agent of the politico Elisha Cooke. He had been hearing of Cooke for years; all described him as a passionate opponent of Crown authority, especially that vested in the English surveyor-general, who struggled to enforce the dictate that all ship-mast pines were the property of the British Admiralty. But McBogle's name was new. Although Duquet's heart was pounding with anger, it occurred to him that Elisha Cooke and perhaps even McBogle might be useful men, and he fixed their names in his memory.

"Eh, no trees on Penobscot? Why you come here steal pine?" he said.

"We thought only to cut a few. Away from the surveyor's men." Duquet did not believe this.

"Show your wounds." When the boy held up his maimed hand, Duquet said angrily, "No, not that. Only scratch. Old wound." He could smell the stink of infection from a distance. With his good hand the boy unwrapped his right leg and exposed a deep and rotten gash in the thigh. A streak of red inflammation ran up toward the groin.

"How happen this?" Duquet demanded.

"Uncle Robert felled a big pine, and when it smote the ground it broke off a branch that bent double and then sprang to gouge my leg."

It was an evil mess. In contrast, the cut in the boy's calf inflicted by Duquet's 'hawk was clean, though it had nearly severed a tendon, and the chopped finger was a trifle. Nothing to be done.

They carried the youth about half a mile upstream to the interlopers' camp, which was strewn with abandoned clothing and cook pots, a deer carcass suspended in a tree, and laid him in the lean-to near the still-smoldering fire.

"We will stay here," Duquet said to Forgeron, "as the thieves have prepared a camp for us." He tried to speak calmly, but he was filled with a greater anger than he had ever experienced. After all the injustices he had suffered, after all he had done—crossing to the New World, learning the hard voyageur trade and how to read and write and cipher, working out a way to use the forest for his fortune, all the business connections he had made—these Maine vermin had come to steal his timber.

Forgeron brought their canoe up to the campsite while Duquet searched until he found the trespassers' pit sawmill. There were no sawed planks beside it, indicating they had been there only a few days, but with the clear intention of stealing his trees. The

stack of limbed and squared logs told him that. He wondered if
they had planned to build a fort. It was said that the English were
plotting to build forts along all the rivers.

"Let us put our mark on them," Duquet said, and he and Forgeron took possession of the logs with two deep hatchet slashes on
the butt ends. They talked of ways to move them. It seemed that
a raft floated to the nearest sawmill might be the best way, getting
what they could, and while Duquet stayed to guard the timber in
case the thieves returned, Forgeron went to Portsmouth to hire
raftsmen.

During the early evening the mildness went out of the weather.
The sky filled with clouds the color of dark grapes, torn by flailing
stems of lightning. An hour of rain moved along, and behind it
the temperature dived into winter. Duquet woke at dawn, shivering. There was not a breath of wind, but every twig and branch
bristled with spiky hoarfrost. In the distance wolves howled messages to one another, their cries filleting the morning. They had
likely scented the boy's blood and infection and would linger out
of sight, waiting for a chance. Duquet got up and piled more wood
on the fire. The wounded boy's eyes were closed, his face feverish
and swollen, cheeks wet with melting frost. Duquet thought that
he would be dead after one more cold night. Or he might not last
until nightfall.

With some urgency, Duquet prodded the boy awake and fired
questions at him: his name, his village, his family's house. But the
boy only croaked for water, which Duquet did not give him, and
then went silent. He still lived. Duquet spent the short day estimat-
ing the boardfeet of the felled pines.

The light faded early as the growing storm invaded the sky, the
wind and sleety snow rattling and hissing in the pines. While there
was still light enough to see clearly, Duquet walked over to the
prisoner. The boy lay on his back, his right leg bursting with infection, a yellow froth of pus oozing out from under the bandage,
the leg a little splayed, as though it were detaching itself. Nothing
could be done with this burden except wait for him to die—one
more cold night. The boy opened his eyes and stared at something
across the river. Duquet followed his gaze, expecting to see Indians
or perhaps one of the woodcutters returning. He saw only a wall of
pines until a blink of yellow showed him where to look. A tall gray

owl sat on a branch, seeing them. Its eyes were very small and set close together, like twin gimlets.

The boy spoke. "Help. Me," he said in English. "Help. Me."

Inside Duquet, something like a tightly closed pinecone licked by fire opened abruptly, and he exploded with insensate and uncontrollable fury, a lifetime's pent-up rage. "*J'en ai rien à foutre.* No one helped me!" he shrieked. "I did everything myself! I endured! I contended with powerful men. I suffered in the wilderness. I accepted the risk that I might die! No one helped me!" The boy's gaze shifted, the fever-boiled eyes following Duquet's rising arm, closing only when the tomahawk split his brain. Duquet struck the hatchet into the loam to clean it, and the owl lifted into the air.

In the flying snow, Duquet dismantled the saw-pit scaffolding and threw the boy into the pit hole, piled the scaffolding on top, and set it alight. The gibbous moon rose.

Hours later, when the burning ceased, he went to shovel in the half-frozen excavated soil, but before he hurled the first shovelful he glanced down and saw the black arm bones crooked up, as if reaching for a helping hand.

"*Foutu!*"

He shoveled.

Forgeron arrived four days later with six men, who began constructing a raft of the cut pines. Not seeing the wounded boy, Forgeron opened his mouth several times, as if to speak, but he did not say anything except that the war was making it very difficult to find able-bodied labor.

"What war is that?" Duquet asked.

"Has not Peter the Great invaded Persia? They spoke of nothing else in Portsmouth. That and the smallpox inoculations inflicted on Bostonians."

In the next years Duquet changed, reinventing himself. In Boston, Duquet et Fils became Duke and Sons. But although there were endless business opportunities in the English colonies, he kept his enterprise and some holdings in New France. He sat with Dred-Peacock in the taproom of the Pine Dog, a pleasant tavern with a sign showing an eponymous carved mastiff, now their favored meeting place, as the Sign of the Red Bottle had burned in a conflagration that took half the wharves and several ships.

"Do you know aught of that fellow McBogle?" Duquet asked, breaking the crust edge from his meat pasty with heavy fingers.

Dred-Peacock, bewigged and togged out, regarded his steaming coffee. "I have not made his acquaintance, but I've heard much deleterious talk concerning his ways. As we both know, Maine is full to the scuppers with woodland entrepreneurs, water-powered sawmills, surveyors, tree choppers, potash makers, turpentine distillers, and settlers, every man assaulting the free-to-all timberlands."

"They think as I do," Duquet said, "so I cannot fault them. But dealing with them is always a struggle."

"The settlers are hard men, right enough, but there are others even harder, mostly in New Hampshire. I mean those men of Scots lineage lately removed from Ulster, in Ireland."

"Surely they are as other mortal men?"

"No. They are different. They are damned strange cruel men, clannish and proud to a fault, thirsty for vengeance over imagined slights, hard-drinking, and inhumanly tough. The whoresons prefer to sleep outside in storms, rather than in the comfort of a house. They know the country as the poxy Indians know it, and to live free is their banner. They choose to live in the most remote places. And they are key fighters in the escalating antipathy between the French and the English." He paused and took up his coffee cup, stared into Duquet's eyes.

"Dud McBogle, his brothers, and his sons are among these men."

Duquet threw back his head and laughed. "Well, I have heard bugbear stories aplenty and I would class McBogle tales among them. No doubt he eats children as sweetmeats and wears a red fur cloak bespangled with their bones. What do you say when I tell you I consider taking this man on as a partner?"

For once Dred-Peacock had nothing to say.

In Boston one day, Dred-Peacock came to the Duke warehouse, a cavernous building near the docks, redolent of pine, oak, furs, and roots.

"I thought you might wish to know that that man you mentioned some time ago has been asking people about you. How many sawmills you own, how disgustingly large your fortune may be, what ships you have, what tracts of timber and townships you possess. He himself operates five or six more sawmills on the Penobscot and in New Hampshire. He begins to look like a serious rival."

"Who do you mean? Elisha Cooke?" Duquet said.

"His damned hard man, McBogle."

"Indeed," Duquet said. "I hear this sometimes. He asks questions, but we never see him. What is your own perception of this situation?"

"I think that he should be absorbed. I doubt we could buy him out, but a partnership may be attractive. He has friendly relations not only with Elisha Cooke and the Wentworths but with many judges and businessmen here and in New Hampshire. Yet he does not have our contacts across the Atlantic." It was Dred-Peacock, with his assortment of languages, who knew the invaluable English and European men of business.

"I think we must talk with him and see what might be arranged. Where do we find him?"

"He may be difficult to locate. He has a sawmill on a tributary of the Penobscot and a house nearby. He keeps very much to himself in this remote place. If we go to him, we must bring a few men with us, for I hear he has a band of ruffians at his beck. And of course he has other mills, other houses, other affairs. He could be at any of them. Still, I could accompany you a week from today. But no sooner."

"*Bien,*" Duquet said.

Yet within the hour Forgeron, who had led a crew of woodsmen to cut down one of Duquet's pine-heavy townships, arrived in Boston. His lean face was blotched with a red rash. He hesitated, as though he wished not to speak his news. When he did speak, he threw his words down like playing cards.

"We found the best trees taken. Most of them were mast pines. The stumps still oozed sap."

"Who?" Duquet said.

"*Sais pas.* But there is talk that McBogle last week shipped two great loads of masts to Spain. He will have made a fat profit."

"I plan to find this man in a week's time and see what can be arranged. I will let him know we suspect him of this theft. It will be our leverage. We will come to an agreement with him."

"He is not known for compliance."

"Nor am I. Dred-Peacock will accompany us on the Monday. You must come as well. It is necessary we go in a body, as we do not know the strength of McBogle's men."

In the last year Duquet's eyesight had begun to deteriorate, dimness alternating with flashes of light and tiny particles gliding through his field of vision, like birds in the sky. He said nothing to Forgeron of this, only, "What is wrong with your face that it shows so rough and crimson?" Forgeron shrugged.

The plan was ill-fated. Two days later a packet entered Boston Harbor with great sacks of mail. Among Dred-Peacock's mountain of letters was one from the family attorney informing him that his older brother and his nephew had both perished on the flanks of an Icelandic volcano and that he, Dred-Peacock, had succeeded to the title and to the family estate in Wiltshire. In seconds Dred-Peacock's talk of colonial liberty and rights evaporated, his self-definition as a man dedicated to New England self-rule shriveled.

"I must go," he said to Duquet. "It is my responsibility to my family and to the estate. I cannot evade the title. I leave at once."

"Yes," Duquet said. "I quite see." Scratch a New England colonist, he thought, and you find Old England — the way a tree's bark may hide the inner rot.

And as if that were not enough, word came that Forgeron was ill with a fiery skin inflammation and the quinsy, a putrid sore throat that forced him into his bed. Duquet decided that he would not delay. He would seek out McBogle alone.

Duquet had the kitchen woman make him a canteen of strong black coffee. He would ration it out, drink it cold, eschewing fires, as the forest was sown with skulking Indians and Frenchmen looking for scalp money or payments for captives. He hired a schooner to take him to the mouth of the Penobscot, and there on the riverbank began his solitary journey.

It was early spring, rafts of rotten ice riding the current in company with the first of thousands of logs. Where there were mills, crowds of woodsmen stood on the banks, snagging the logs with their outfit's mark of ownership. The work continued all night by the light of enormous bonfires, cat-footed men running out onto the heaving carpet of logs to hook and prod their property to shore. Impossible to put a canoe into that maelstrom. Duquet had ordered his timber crews to hold back his logs until the river

cleared of the floating forest. Now he set out on foot. And noticed two riverbank men turn away from the heaving river and cut
obliquely into the forest. He smiled. Did they imagine they were
not noticed?

Sometimes he was on dim Indian trails, following landmarks almost always obscured by the jagged skylines of conifers, but more
often he made his way through logging slash and blow-downs. Although timber cutters had worked the area along the river, a mile
or so inland was still *terre sauvage,* and like the ocean it breathed
wild grandeur; from it emanated a sense of great depth. The tree
limbs arched over the silent earth like the dark roof of a vaulted
tomb. Once from a distance he saw two men working a pit sawmill,
the top man bending and rising like an automaton, the man below
in a smother of woolly sawdust. Intent on their labor, they did not
see him. If they were industrious, he thought, they could cut a
thousand boardfeet in a day, but it was more likely that their work
would be interrupted by a scouting party out for captives or blood.
Or the two riverbank louts.

He skirted innumerable ponds, sinking to his knees in soggy
moss, and took an entire day to cross an autumn burn, the charred
trunks of the smaller trees with their own black limbs tangled
around their roots like dropped drawers, still-smoldering logs that
could not be quenched. The biggest trees stood lightly scorched
but unharmed. Winter snow had converted the ash to black muck.
On steep slopes it was the ancient wind-felled monsters that caused
the greatest hindrance; the branches on the lower side plunged
into the earth and supported the main trunk, which resembled
a multilegged monster, the remaining branches clawing out like
arms with a hundred crooked spears thrusting upward. There
must have been a strong windstorm to put down so many large
trees. Some had pulled their neighbors to the ground too. Often
Duquet had to crawl beneath these barriers, through leaf mold,
fern, toadshade, and viburnum, through slimed fungi, only to encounter another half-decayed giant within a few paces. He could
not count all the streams and bogs, the hellish thickets of close-
packed larch, the whipping red stems of osier willow. The treetops
dazzled. The flashing wings of hundreds of thousands of north-
ward-migrating birds beat above him. He saw snowy owls drifting
silently through the trees, for they had come into the Maine woods
by the thousand that winter, and with the turn of the season were

retreating to the cold lands. His eyes wearied of broken, wind-bent cedar fringing glinted swamp water. All one afternoon he had the feeling he was being watched, and as twilight thickened he saw a gray owl flutter to a branch stub and grip him with its gimlet eyes. Of all birds, it was this wretch he hated most.

After six days he cut back toward the Penobscot, following Moosegut Brook; McBogle's sawmill, sited on this tributary stream, could not be far distant. He listened for the sound of falls. He felt the mill through his feet before he saw it, the metal clank and rasp of the drive-shift gears and the pitman arm sending a mind-less thumping rhythm into the ground. His eyes troubled him, the flashes growing more frequent, tree branches and needles spark-ing. He walked along the stream and, abruptly, there was the mill-pond and the mill, a heavy log structure built to take the weight of the saw machinery. He walked around to the side of the mill. And there was Dud McBogle standing above him in a razzle of flinch-ing lights.

Recognition was instant. Dud McBogle was the ginger-whiskered timber thief who long ago had turned back and called something to the wounded boy. Duquet felt a red cloud of anger envelop him, a certainty that this man knew all that had happened those years ago on the riverbank. His blood instantly flowed back on itself. The teeth of the moving saw gnawed through a 20-foot-long squared log, sent up a spray of sawdust.

"I have been waiting for you these some years," McBogle said in an easy tone. "I went back, you see. I went back and dug up the pit where you burned my boy." Four men, two of them the riverbank men, stepped out of the mill gloom and stood beside him.

Duquet could smell the hot sawdust as the blade began a new cut, chewing through the log. He bucked and twisted as he was seized by McBogle's men and carried into the mill. Narrow rods of light pierced the interstices of the shingled roof. He could hear the relentless up-and-down grind of the saw, could see McBogle's hand near the lever that stopped the saw, could see the hand move away. What could not happen began to happen.

SCOTT LORING SANDERS

Pleasant Grove

FROM *Floyd County Moonshine*

THE SNOW HAD JUST BEGUN to really fall when Johnny's
mother reminded him for the third time that she had to have milk
and eggs. He'd been through fourteen winters in his lifetime, all
of them in that same Virginia farmhouse back in the woods near
McPeak Mountain, so he felt he had a pretty good feel for how bad
this storm might be. The way the sky hung heavy, the way everything turned gray, the way smoke chugged from the chimney, not
in a straight column but instead barely making it out before spilling and hovering over the roof like a witch's brew. And by Johnny's
calculations, this was going to be a whopper. He'd seen deer feeding in the neighboring field in the middle of the day while he'd
been splitting stove wood. Another sign.

"Johnny, I'm telling you, we have to have milk," said his mother.
"Henry's probably going to close early. If the babies don't have
their food, there'll be hell to pay. The truck isn't going to be able
to deliver in this snow. Not for a few days, most likely."

"I know," said Johnny, buttoning his mackintosh and securing a
wool toboggan on his head. "I'm going."

His mother reached into her coin purse and handed him four
quarters. "Get as much as you can carry, and at least a dozen eggs.
The hens aren't laying good in this cold."

"All right, Ma," said Johnny as he threw a canvas rucksack over
his shoulder and headed out the door.

Those babies. Those damn babies. They were enough to drive
him insane. What his mother meant, what his mother called her babies, were the eight or nine or maybe ten cats, Johnny wasn't even

sure anymore, that ruled his mother's life. They ate better than he did most of the time, and he resented them for it. There'd been many a day, while his mother was at work and he'd already gotten home from school, when he'd considered taking the twenty-gauge and culling the kitty population by a few. But he'd never mustered the courage. Not yet, anyway.

He cursed those cats as he headed down the road to Henry's General Store—the dirt and gravel already covered in a thin layer of snow—working his way through the Pleasant Grove section of McPeak Mountain. It was the only store on the mountain, and he knew his mother was right: Henry often closed shop early, for any reason he felt like, though usually it was because he'd run out of liquor and needed to get home before his throat got too dry. So a snowstorm was a perfect excuse for him to close, head home, sit around a fire, and get down to some proper drinking.

The temperature wasn't cold, barely freezing, and there was no wind to speak of. The flakes fell straight down, fat and heavy, as Johnny trudged along, his boots giving that comforting crunching sound as they marched through the absolute quiet. Johnny loved the silence that a snowstorm brought. No birds chirping, no cars straining to make it up the hill, no clopping of horse hooves or the creaking of wagon wheels from old-timey farmers who'd still stubbornly resisted the purchase of an automobile.

The road was narrow and hilly, twisting and turning through stands of oak and pine. Henry's was only a mile away, but in the snow everything took longer, and besides, Johnny wasn't in any hurry. During the walk home it would be a different story, wanting to get the weight of the glass bottles off his back, but at the moment he was in no rush. At the moment he was going to enjoy it.

He stopped at the little stone bridge crossing Oldfield Creek and stared downstream, seeing rounded mounds of white on the exposed stones in the middle of the water. He often came down here and set leg-holds for mink, raccoon, and muskrat, selling the hides to Henry for a little spending money. But he preferred using snares, which he set in the fields by his house, occasionally catching the ultimate prize: a red fox.

As the creek gurgled along, as the snow continued to fall, now catching on the overhanging sycamore limbs that curled over the water, he wondered if his daddy had ever trapped. He wondered if his love for the hunt was inherited. He thought about that often when he was in the woods, imagining what his dad had been like, fantasizing about how different his life would be if his father hadn't been killed during a training exercise in the army. His mother had told him she was still pregnant when his father died, at a barracks in South Carolina, never even getting the chance to go overseas and kill some Nazis. She only had one photo, a handsome man in uniform, his face turned to the side in profile. But he felt that he resembled his father, and hoped that when he was grown he'd have the same strong jawline, those same rugged features.

Johnny snapped out of his reverie when he heard the high whine of a pickup approaching. The engine raced and the truck moved fast, coming down the hill and heading toward the bridge, the back end fishtailing. It was an older model, probably a '50 or '51, and definitely a Ford, judging by the rounded roof and distinct eyeball headlights.

Johnny had to make a decision and make it fast. The truck now slid from side to side, out of control, the man frantically working his hands over the steering wheel, trying to right the ship. But it wasn't going to happen. That ship was going to sink.

Johnny hopped onto the stone wall and then leapt, dropping 8 feet before hitting the creek. He landed on his feet, but his momentum carried him forward. He put out his hands, catching himself in the icy water, and avoided falling flat on his face. At the same instant his hands hit, a terrific crash sounded above him. Johnny looked back, arching his midsection over the water to stay dry, and saw metal colliding with stone, then a horrible scraping as sparks showered over the bridge. Finally there was a deadening thud as the truck careened across the road and slammed into the trunk of a fat oak.

Johnny's boots sucked up the shallow creek water before he stepped out and climbed the gentle embankment toward the road. Steam hissed from the front of the truck, and the snow, which was hammering down now, disappeared as it hit the hot steel of the crumpled hood. The two tires on the driver's side were flat and shredded.

The driver's window was clouded over with fog, preventing Johnny from seeing inside. He looked around, hoping someone would magically appear who could help him. Could tell him what to do. But all he saw in either direction was a column of peaceful hemlocks, holding soft pillows of snow as they lined the road.

Johnny grabbed the handle and pulled, but the door, dented and now showing streaks of silver in the red paint, was stuck. He tugged harder, throwing his weight into it, and the door opened awkwardly, sending off a horrendous squeak and pop through the otherwise silent afternoon.

Inside, the man sat slumped over the bent steering wheel, the top of it nearly touching the dashboard, almost as if it had melted. The windshield was fractured like pond ice, the epicenter containing pieces of hair and skin and blood. Johnny had never seen a dead person before, and though he was scared, he was also surprisingly calm. He grabbed at the wool collar of the man's red-checked hunting jacket, pulling him back so he could sit properly. His head lolled, as if he had no neck muscles, finally resting against the cold rear window, his bloody chin pointing toward the roof.

Johnny hadn't recognized the truck as one he'd seen around town before, nor did he recognize the man. But he didn't figure anyone, not even a best friend or a wife, would have recognized him right then. His smashed nose had shifted to the left. A large piece of skin was absent from his forehead, presumably clinging to the windshield, and mashed wire from his glasses had wedged into his cheeks, though somehow the lenses had stayed intact. His entire face, from forehead to chin, was sopping with blood, and a pool of it stained the thighs of his dungarees.

But he was still breathing. At first Johnny thought for sure the man had to be dead, but then he heard a slow gurgling, similar to Oldfield Creek rolling over the rocks.

"Mister, can you hear me? Mister, you okay?"

There was no response, and Johnny hadn't expected one. He wasn't sure what to do but figured since he was about halfway between home and Henry's, the smartest thing would be to go on to the store. His mother didn't have a telephone, but Henry did, and he could call the police once he got there. Except just as Johnny was about to leave, he looked across the man's lap and saw something lying on the passenger's side floorboard. It was a beige gunnysack, and spilling from the top, where the drawstring had loosened, were gobs of twenty-dollar bills, fanned out like tail feathers.

He closed the door and ran around to the other side, where the passenger door opened easily. As quickly as he could, without forethought of repercussions, he snatched the gunnysack and stuffed it inside his rucksack. He also found a pistol, which he grabbed before thinking properly. As he was about to close the door the man said, "I see you, boy." The voice was strained, weak, gravelly. But he heard it all the same.

Johnny slammed the door, ran to the bridge, and tossed the pistol as far as he could downstream. Then he took off for home, shuffling through the snow—now boot-high and rising fast—practicing the words he'd tell his mother once he arrived. "Henry's was already closed, Ma. I'm sorry. I know I messed up."

That evening, once he was sure his mother had gone to sleep, he pulled the bag from the back corner of his closet, where he'd hidden it beneath empty shoe boxes and a mound of dusty quilts. He dumped the cash onto his bed and began stacking the crisp twenties into piles of ten. When he'd finished, he couldn't believe the tally. He counted it again, and then again, before he uttered the amount aloud. "Four thousand eight hundred dollars."

Johnny didn't sleep well, tossing and turning, wondering about the man. Wondering if he was still alive. Most importantly, wondering if he—Johnny—would get caught for what he'd done.

The next morning, when there was a pounding on the front door, his heart screamed. He scrambled out of bed, slapped on clothes in a mad dash, and tried to beat his mother to the door, not at all sure what he'd do once he got there. Especially if it was the man.

But it wasn't the man. Instead, standing on the front porch was the local sheriff, dressed in a heavy coat and Mountie hat. "Hey, son," said the sheriff. "Your mama at home?"

"Yes, sir," he said, his heart screaming louder still, his cheeks flushing as he turned to yell for her. But she was already there, directly behind him, wiping her wet hands on the bottom of an apron, her hair pulled up tightly in a bun. One of the cats walked a series of figure eights through her legs, arching its back as it brushed the hem of her dress.

"Hey, Bryson," said his mother. "What brings you here in such pretty weather?"

"Patricia," said the sheriff, pinching the edge of his hat and nodding. "Was wondering if I might talk to you for a minute."

"Come on in. Get out of the cold. You want some coffee?"

"No, I'm okay." He stamped his boots on the porch boards, knocking out clods of frozen snow.

Johnny looked out at the front yard before closing the door behind the sheriff. The morning was overcast, but the snow had stopped. He figured there was about a foot and a half on the ground; his tracks should have easily been covered. At least he hoped so.

The sheriff followed Patricia into the kitchen, where she pulled out a chair for him at the table. He took it while she grabbed the hot kettle from the stove. Johnny sat down at the far end, staring at the hulking figure of the sheriff. All he could think about was the load of money in his room, second-guessing whether he'd put it back in the closet or left it sitting out.

She poured two cups of coffee, despite the sheriff's refusal, and set one in front of him. He warmed his hands around the mug before taking a sip.

"Johnny, you need to go get your chores started," said Patricia as she sat down. "Sheriff needs to talk to me."

Before Johnny could rise, the sheriff said, "Actually, he ought to stay. He needs to hear this too."

Johnny's cheeks flushed; his breathing went short, figuring the sheriff must know everything. Figured he'd found the man, the man told him that some boy had stolen his money, and the sheriff followed the tracks right to the front door.

"Last night one of my deputies located a truck right by the bridge at Oldfield Creek. Crashed into a tree. Thing was torn up pretty good. Looks like the fella lost control coming down the hill. Not sure how long it'd been there, but the tire tracks were already covered by the time my man arrived."

Johnny discreetly exhaled.

"The driver okay?" asked Patricia, a look of mild interest on her face, but not overly so. Instead her expression seemed to say, *So why are you telling me this?*

"I don't know if he's okay or not. He wasn't in the truck. There were some faint boot prints in the snow, but they'd pretty much filled up already by the time I arrived. And a fair amount of blood. Looks like he went to the creek and cleaned himself up before he took off to wherever he was going. But here's the thing. The truck was stolen. It was used as the getaway vehicle in a robbery yesterday. The guy knocked off the bank over in Floyd. Got away with nearly five thousand dollars."

Patricia took a sip of her coffee, her eyes showing a little more interest. "And you think he might've come here?"

"I don't think so. I scouted around your place before I knocked. I didn't see any sign. But he's around here somewhere. We're trying to get some dogs from over in Christiansburg, but with the snow, everything's at a standstill. I just wanted to let you know. Make you aware. He's got a pistol. Used it to rob the bank. You got a gun, don't you? And a vehicle?"

Patricia glanced over at Johnny, suddenly showing more concern. "The alternator's gone bad on the car. Haven't had the money to fix it. We've got a shotgun."

"What about a phone?"

"No, no phone," she said, shaking her head. "You got any idea who you're looking for? A description or something thereabouts?"

The sheriff hesitated, took a sip of his coffee, then scratched his nails across the grooves in the table, trying to buy some time. "Well, here's the other thing, Patricia," he said, talking to the table instead of her. "We've got a pretty good notion that the fella, the fella we're looking for, is Martin."

And with that, for the first time, Johnny saw a look of true fear cover his mother's face. Her eyes widened. Her jaw went slack. Johnny reacted the same way because he recognized the name, though suddenly nothing made any sense to him.

"What . . . what do you mean?" she said.

"That's the real reason I'm here," said the sheriff, finally making eye contact. "Considering the truck is less than a mile away, we think he was probably coming here, looking for a place to hide. You probably didn't know, but for the past five years he's been locked up at Petersburg. For another robbery."

Patricia barely nodded. She said, almost a whisper now, "I heard something about it."

"Well, two days ago he escaped. Warden called and alerted us."

"Bryson, I haven't seen that man in nearly fifteen years." Her voice was suddenly sharp. Angry. "Why would he come here? If he does, I'll blast him to kingdom come. I swear to God I will."

"I know you will. I'm not accusing you."

"You can search the entire house if you don't believe me. I wouldn't put him up for nothing."

"Patricia," said the sheriff, showing both restraint and calm,

"I'm only here to warn you. You two need to be on your guard. We're going to run patrols, get a search party going. But again, with this snow, it's going to take time. From the looks of the accident and the blood we saw, he couldn't have made it too far. He's probably banged up pretty good. Could've frozen to death last night for all I know."

"That man's tougher than a pine knot. You know that, Bryson. He eats barbed-wire pie for breakfast and smiles while chewing it. If he's got a pile of money to keep him warm, he's not about to just crawl up and die."

"Soon as we catch him, you'll be the first to know. In the meantime, keep that shotgun handy."

Patricia walked the sheriff to the door while Johnny remained at the table. He had so many questions. So many thoughts. *What's going on? Who's Martin? That was my daddy's name.*

Patricia sat back down at the kitchen table after showing the sheriff out. She grabbed her coffee cup and raised it to her lips but couldn't steady her hands enough to take a sip. "Johnny, baby, we need to have a little talk. There's something I have to tell you."

His father, as it turned out, hadn't been killed in the army after all. Instead he'd been a cheating, lying scoundrel who'd left Patricia once he learned he'd swollen her belly. Disappeared, leaving her with nothing.

"And the picture of the soldier?" Johnny had asked. "Who was that?"

Patricia had tears in her eyes, her face filled with anguish. But also with relief, it seemed to Johnny. Her secret was a secret no more. "That was my brother. Your Uncle Bruno. He was the one killed in South Carolina."

Johnny hadn't known what to do with himself. He'd go to his room, check on the money, then wrap his mind around everything he'd learned. He decided that if his mother wanted to keep secrets from him, then he had a four-thousand-dollar secret he'd keep from her. But after stewing for a while, he'd become restless and unsatisfied, thinking of new questions, so he'd go back and grill his mother for more answers. By late afternoon they were both exhausted. Emotionally drained.

"Those chickens have got to be fed," his mother said as dusk settled in. "In fact, why don't you kill one and I'll make us a hot soup. They aren't laying for squat right now anyway. We could use a good meal."

"Okay," said Johnny, thinking that getting outside might do him some good.

"Take the gun with you."

"I'm only going to the coop. It'll take five minutes, tops."

"Take the gun," she repeated, and he knew enough not to argue.

With the shotgun slung over his shoulder, Johnny sloughed through the high snow until he entered the chicken coop behind the house. He let his eyes adjust, then scanned the shack before setting the gun down. He removed the lid of the feed barrel and tossed a few handfuls of grain out the door and into the fenced-in area where the chickens normally fed. The kibble sprinkled the snow like candies on cake frosting, and Johnny laughed for the first time that day as the chickens scrambled out the door, trying not to sink in the snow, flapping their wings furiously as they pecked at the grains.

For the next twenty minutes he kept himself occupied by sporadically tossing out handfuls, having a little fun with the chickens. He was in the process of sweeping the coop, his mind still abuzz with the events of yesterday, when he heard a commotion. Pots and pans clattered together, and at first he thought his mother had had an accident, probably dropping the soup pot on the floor. But then he heard her yell. Yell for him. And then a man's voice. An angry, agitated man's voice.

Johnny grabbed the twenty-gauge and ran toward the kitchen. When he entered, the man he'd seen the day before, his own father, stood near the stove, a knife in hand. His mother was backed into the corner by the cupboard, shivering as if cold, gripping a cast-iron skillet.

The man turned to face Johnny, looking better than the day before but still a complete mess. He'd fixed his glasses the best that he could manage, but they were bent and hung askew from the bridge of his mashed nose. The wide gash on his forehead was pink and raw but no longer bleeding, his clothes stained with crusty dried blood.

"Listen, boy, I just want my money. Tell me where it is and I'll leave you both alone." His voice was stronger than the day before, but rough, like he smoked cigars. His face hard, his eyes harder. He glanced at the barrel of the shotgun pointing at his chest but didn't seem concerned. He'd strategically positioned himself in front of Patricia, so that if Johnny pulled the trigger, she'd also be hit by the birdshot spray. Because of the skillet, which she wielded like a baseball bat, he couldn't grab her, but again he didn't seem concerned.

"He doesn't have your god-blessed money, Martin," she yelled, the tendons in her neck straining like taut piano wire.

"Yes, he does," he said calmly. He seemed to know that he was going to get his money back, regardless. It was only a matter of how much blood he'd have to shed before he got it. He shifted his eyes back and forth between Johnny and Patricia, squeezing the hilt of the knife. "I saw him when he stole it from my truck. Didn't even bother to help me, Patty. Just took the money and ran. But I recognized him right off. Had blood running down my face, dripping in my eyes, but even still, saw right off he was the spitting image of his mama."

Martin took a slow step away from Patricia and shuffled, with a subtle limp, a bit closer to Johnny. Johnny took a step back at the same time, performing some sort of awkward dance ritual, keeping the gun trained at Martin's chest.

"You saw the wrong boy," said Patricia, almost pleading. "Johnny was here with me all day yesterday. He doesn't have your money."

"Tell her, boy. *Johnny*, is it? Tell her how you took my sack of money," he said, smiling a little as he limped a step closer. "Tell her, *son*."

"It wasn't me," said Johnny. He wondered if Martin could see the end of the shotgun quivering. "I didn't take your money."

"Oh, but you did. You took it, and I want it back. Show me where it is, and I'll even give you some. A little reward. Put the gun down and lead me to it. Then I'll be gone."

"I didn't take it."

Martin took another step forward, now only a few feet from the tip of the barrel, his head on a swivel as he kept a bead on both Patricia and Johnny. "You wouldn't shoot your old man, now would you? Your dear old daddy?"

Quicker than Johnny thought possible, especially for a man in Martin's condition, he snatched for the end of the barrel like a striking snake. And then Johnny felt his own shoulder blades slam into the wall. The pleasant smell of cordite clouded the kitchen, and Johnny's ears rang from the explosion going off in such close quarters.

Martin lay curled in a ball on the slats of the pine floor, blood seeping into the cracks and meandering in different directions like raindrops dancing on a windshield. A couple of cats scurried away, taking cover. Patricia ran from her corner, the frying pan gripped in both hands above her head, and brought it down with all her weight on Martin's left ear. For good measure. It landed with a dull, solid thud but hadn't been necessary. It only caused the inevitable to happen a little quicker.

Johnny stood against the wall, the gun still pointed at his father, his shoulder aching from the kickback.

"You just killed your daddy, Johnny." She didn't say it in accusatory fashion. She didn't say it happily either. Just matter-of-fact.

"I'm sorry, Ma. I thought he was going to hurt you. Hurt me."

"That son of a bitch has been dead to me for years, baby." She kneeled over the body and surveyed it but still held the handle of the skillet at the ready. When she was satisfied, she looked up. "Now where'd you hide that money?"

Johnny hesitated, still holding the gun, now realizing it was pointed at his mother as much as it was at Martin.

"You're not in trouble," she said, her voice soothing. Calming. The same way she purred to the cats. "Just tell me."

He hesitated again. "It's in my room. In my closet."

"Good," said Patricia, nodding and smiling almost imperceptibly as she stood up and set the skillet on the stove. "Now let's find a better hiding spot. Then we'll figure out what we're going to do with him."

Len had been a young teenager when the huge snowstorm hit Mc-Peak Mountain shortly before Christmas. One morning, a day or two after the storm, he was told by his father that he needed to go cut down a Christmas tree for the family. Being the oldest of the three children and the only boy, he obliged and was thrilled to do so. It was his first time going out on his own with such an important job, and it made him feel like his father recognized that he was becoming a man. He relished that feeling, proud of the responsibility, and he didn't want to disappoint.

So he bundled himself up, took an apple-butter sandwich his

mother had made, and along with a canteen and an oiled crosscut saw he procured from the horse barn, he set off slogging through the deep snow. The sun was out, the sky a deep blue, telling Len that the front had indeed passed.

Len knew exactly where he was going. He often spent time in the woods, sometimes hunting, more often just hiking to see what he could see. But he knew that if he crossed the pasture behind the farm and then climbed the formidable wooded hill, there was a nice stand of white pine running along the ridgeline. The ridge that marked the end of his property line. The ridge that separated the land he lived on from several other families that were sparsely located in that little section of Pleasant Grove. Right on the other side of the ridge, and nestled down at the foot of McPeak Mountain, almost a direct shot as the crow flies, was another small farmhouse, where a mother and her son lived, the father having run off years ago.

By the time Len made it to the top of the ridge he'd already unbuttoned his jacket and let it flap open at his hips. He'd removed his watchman's cap and stuffed it into his back pocket as sweat trickled along his neck. He took a drink of water and then decided that he'd explore a little before he cut the tree down. It was going to be an all-day affair, what with the depth of the snow and having to drag the tree nearly a mile back to home, so he had no reason to rush. Besides, the longer he was gone, the more chores his sisters would have to do for him. Len was no fool.

There was an old, abandoned woodcutter's cabin that he frequented from time to time when he was out in the woods. A place he and his sisters would sometimes play. A place that Len thought of as his own. The foundation was made of granite, with a fireplace made from similar stone, while the structure itself had been built with roughly hewn poplar logs sometime around the turn of the century. When his sisters weren't around, Len still enjoyed going there by himself, mainly because he'd stashed a pile of girly magazines beneath some rotted floorboards. And they weren't just standard run-of-the-mill magazines, where women might be scantily clad but certainly didn't show any nipples. No, these were underground magazines, because they showed women in all their glory. And not only women, but men too. Men who were doing unspeakable things to these women. Things that Len and his school buddies had often talked about when they were far away from the ears of adults, but certainly not things that he'd ever seen or been a part of.

So that's where he was headed. It was an easy walk of about a half mile along the ridgeline. At least it was easy when there wasn't high snow to slog through. But a boy's urges are strong at that age, and an extra half mile of trudging through snow was a small price to pay.

He'd made it about halfway there, keeping his eyes down and following a set of deer tracks, when he heard something at the bottom of the slope. The slope that fell away from his house. Len had spent enough time in the forest to know the difference between the natural sounds of the woods and those that were manmade. And this sound was definitely human. He couldn't discern it exactly, but whatever it was, there was the distinct sound of metal occasionally glancing against something hard. Maybe it was another piece of metal, or rock perhaps. Regardless, Len knew it was a sound that wasn't supposed to be there, and it disappointed him because it might disrupt his plans.

With every step he took, the sound seemed to get louder. A rhythmic sound that kept an almost perfect cadence. Len slowed and walked as quietly as he could. Before long, by keeping his eyes trained down the mountainside, he was finally able to locate the noise. At the base of the hill, smack in the middle of the forest, were two figures. One was a hunched-over woman wrapped in a shawl, and the other was a thin young man, about the same size as Len, standing by her side as she worked at a bare patch of ground, dropping mounds of dirt onto the otherwise white blanket of the woods. The sound was slightly delayed as it carried up the hillside, but Len saw that the woman was diligently digging a hole. After a few more shovelfuls, she passed the handle off to the boy, and he took over.

Len stopped and kneeled in the snow, hiding behind the large trunk of a pine. He was thrilled and exhilarated, and it took no time before the cabin and magazines no longer mattered, because once he settled in, he realized that there was a third figure among the other two. But this third figure was slightly off to the side, lying in the snow, motionless and, from what Len could tell, facedown. It didn't take a genius to figure out what was going on down there. And of course Len knew exactly who the people were. At least, at that time he knew who the two people still *alive* were. It would take another week of reading the newspapers and asking innocent questions of his parents about what had ever happened to Johnny's father, over on the other side of the hill, before Len put it all together.

But at that moment he was mesmerized. A dead body. Two people, a mother and son, obviously trying to get rid of that body. Judging by the trough in the snow that ended at the man's feet, the trough that wound through the trees and back toward Johnny's farmhouse, the man certainly hadn't walked into those woods on his own. It wasn't like Johnny and his mother had found the man lying there while out looking for their own Christmas tree. No, he'd been dragged, and whatever they were up to, it was sinister.

Len watched the rest of the process with that same exhilaration. The pair struggled mightily to pull the body toward the hole, each grabbing an arm as if it were a heavy piece of furniture with no good holds, and finally rolled him into the rectangle they'd excavated. They both collapsed next to the grave once they'd dropped him in, not out of any grief, it seemed, but simply out of pure exhaustion. There was no telling how long they'd been working, but considering they'd dragged him through the snow a good half mile from the farmhouse — assuming that's where he'd died — then dug a deep hole in frozen ground, it was no surprise they were worn out.

They rested for only a few minutes, each of them taking snow and stuffing it into their mouths like handfuls of popcorn at the picture house. Len couldn't discern their words as they talked, but he imagined the conversation. Before too long they slowly got up and labored at refilling the hole. When they were close to finished, Johnny reached down and grabbed something about the size of a large cigar box. He opened the lid, took a peek inside, then carefully placed the box in the grave. He and his mother finished filling in the hole, then covered it with soggy leaves before finally tossing snow over top and smoothing it out as best they could. As if frosting a cake.

If Len hadn't witnessed it with his own eyes, he'd have never noticed the area looking strange or out of the ordinary, except maybe the trough of snow that snaked through the trees. But a little wind or another snowfall would take care of that in no time.

No, all things considered, Len thought they'd covered their tracks pretty well.

He waited until they'd both walked away and headed home before he left his perch behind the tree. He immediately dashed to cut a Christmas tree as quickly as he could. He'd learned early on that being privy to other people's secrets could work to his advantage. He'd used the method repeatedly when he had dirt on his sisters. Dirt that they didn't want their parents to know. So he could never be too sure when he might be able to use Johnny's secret, but he knew he'd keep his mouth shut. Having a secret as big as this one, he felt sure, was something he could certainly use someday. Not to mention, as soon as he felt it was safe, he planned on finding out what was in that buried box.

That winter had been an especially brutal one for Johnny and his mother. It seemed that every time the snow had almost melted away, another storm would dump another foot. Which wasn't necessarily a bad thing. With every storm, the fresh snow helped hide the secret.

Before they'd buried Martin, along with the money, Johnny's mother had decided to keep four hundred dollars, which they could use for expenses—unpaid bills, groceries, getting the car fixed. They had no idea if the money had been marked by the bank, but by using a twenty here or there down at Henry's General Store, they didn't figure they were in much jeopardy of getting caught. The sheriff had stopped by a couple of times—the first time only three days after Johnny had shot his father—to inform them that they hadn't been able to locate Martin. He said he imagined Martin had probably either frozen to death or bled to death (or a combination of both) and his body would most likely be found in the spring melt.

By mid-March the snow had indeed disappeared, but his mother advised that they leave the money where it was for the time being. They were in no need at the moment, and the longer they let things settle, the safer they'd be. But that all changed after the engine on the recently repaired car seized in late April. It had to be towed down the mountain to a mechanic in Floyd, who informed Patricia that the car was ruined and beyond repair. Since she had to have a car to get to and from work, the solution was obvious.

"You need to go out there and dig the box up," she informed him after he'd gotten home from school. "I think we're safe now anyway. Besides, I'd rather have it hidden in the house than all the way out there in the middle of the woods. Or maybe we could stash it under the chicken coop. Doesn't matter. We'll figure that out. What's important is that we have it nearby."

He grabbed a shovel from the shed, slung it over his shoulder like a hobo with a bindle, and set out through the woods. It was a perfect spring day, warm with blue skies and a bit of a breeze rustling the tops of the mostly leafless trees. The poplar leaves were as big as squirrels' ears, and the oaks had already formed their pollen-filled strings, reminding Johnny of pipe cleaners, which drifted to the ground when the wind gusted. Johnny enjoyed the walk, loving the woods as they came back to life after the winter. He even loved the mud and muck of a bog he had to tramp through to get to his father's burial site. The beginnings of skunk cabbage had sprouted, their little green heads starting to poke through the mud, and Johnny stamped on every one he saw, sending off a strong, pungent odor.

When he made it to a dumping ground where old-timers had tossed their steel beer cans, brown medicine bottles, and rusted appliances, Johnny took a left and headed toward the foot of the hill. He'd always been fascinated with the dumping ground, wondering who had put all that garbage there. There were no houses around, other than an abandoned cabin on the ridge, so he'd never been able to figure out why anyone would have chosen that place to dump their trash. Regardless, as a younger boy he'd enjoyed rummaging around the dump site, imagining in his boyhood fantasies that he might discover some sort of hidden treasure.

But today, as he left the dump behind, he was in search of an actual hidden treasure. He was excited to uncover the iron lockbox, open it, and run his fingers all over that beautiful cash. The cash that would buy him some decent clothes so he wouldn't get made fun of at school every day. The cash that would enable him to purchase candy bars and maybe even the occasional T-bone steak. The cash that would send him to Virginia Polytechnic Institute and get him out of the poor, depressed confines of Pleasant Grove. Confines that offered no sort of future. In short, the cash that would insure that he and his mother would escape poverty once and for all.

So he was excited to dig up the money, get back home, and count it. Over and over. Just sit there and stack each and every bill into little piles, the same as he'd done that day on his bed. The events of those few days, of the truck crashing, of him taking the money, of finding out the man's identity, of then blowing the guts out of that same man, his father, of dragging him through the snow and burying him in a makeshift grave, all of those events had haunted him. But it had gotten better with every passing week. The memories weren't quite as sharp, the guilt subsided, and there was always that pot of gold at the end of the rainbow. That's what really made it easier to deal with. That, and knowing that his father would have most likely killed him and his mother if he hadn't pulled the trigger. That's certainly the way his mother had rationalized it to him on those cold nights when they'd huddled around the woodstove and the subject had come up. They'd talked about it often for the first few weeks, until finally his mother had laid down an ultimatum, saying it was time to move forward. What was done was done and they had to try to forget about it. To be thankful that Johnny's sorry excuse for a father had at least been able to provide them with something before he died, especially considering that for the past fourteen years he'd never given them as much as a penny.

But as he neared the spot where he'd buried both his father and the money, his excitement turned to dread. The idea of being alone in the woods with the body of his dead father didn't seem so appealing. Yes, the day was beautiful, but deep in the woods it was almost impossible to see the sky. And every time the wind blew and the tree limbs slapped against one another, eerily clicking and clacking, he shuddered. Because of the wind, he realized he couldn't tell if other people might be shuffling around in the woods. Might be hiding, waiting to jump him and steal the money.

And even worse was the realization that he was about to dig up a grave. His father's grave. Yes, the iron box was right on top and he shouldn't come close to the decaying corpse, but what if the ground had shifted? What if the box had sunk during the snowmelt, when the soil had gotten soft and saturated? What if he glimpsed his father's dead face, the flesh rotting and peeling from the skull? What if there really was such a thing as ghosts?

At the foot of a steep hill, Johnny located the area where he and his mother had dug. He'd always been good in the woods, knew how to remember landmarks, and in this instance the landmark was a maple with a forked trunk. When he'd originally picked the spot, he'd stood with his back to the tree before walking six paces. Then he'd started digging.

But he didn't have to recount his paces this time because, much to his surprise, the dirt still looked relatively fresh. Dead, wind-blown leaves had covered the area, but if someone who was really an expert in the woods — like the sheriff, for example — had seen the partially exposed patch, they would have easily recognized that it wasn't natural. That something was off. Which bothered him. If the sheriff decided to get a search party together sometime soon, the grave might be detected.

These new thoughts, of getting caught, suddenly superseded his previous ideas about ghosts and rotting flesh, so he immediately stuck his shovel into the earth, amazed by how soft it was. How easy the digging was. He'd only been working for five minutes when he felt and heard the steel of his shovel clink against the lockbox. And what a beautiful sound it was. It was the sound of a cash register sliding open, offering up its riches.

Johnny dug around the perimeter of the box, then got on his knees, grabbed the edges, and shifted it back and forth as he loosed it from the rich, dark soil. He brushed away the dirt, then unstuck muddy clumps and clods attached to the hinges. When it was nearly clean, he blew across the top as if extinguishing a candle, removing the last tiny particles. He then lifted the clasp.

And that's when, as he raised the lid, he would have much rather seen ghosts and goblins and wicked spirits rise from the ground than what he saw instead. He would have rather smelled his father's decaying flesh, would have rather had witches creep from behind the trees and boil him in water. Because the box was empty. The cash, all of those crisp twenty-dollar bills, was gone. What he saw instead was a vacuum of empty space. Nothing. Absolutely nothing.

Johnny rapidly closed the box, then opened it again as if prying apart an oyster shell, hoping that he'd been mistaken and this time he'd find the pearl. But there was no pearl. He immediately tossed the box to the side and began digging around in the dirt with his hands. His fingers worked through the soil, spraying the surrounding dead leaves as he pawed at the ground like a dog after a bone. Maybe, he thought, somehow the money had fallen out when he'd dropped it in the hole. Maybe the money hadn't been in the box to begin with, though he was positive it had been. He remembered taking one last glance before carefully setting the box in place. He searched all around, digging deeper and deeper, not even caring if he ran into the remains of his father. He frantically slung dirt out of the hole, ripping earthworms in half, scratching his fingers against small stones until they bled. But it was no use. The money was gone.

He almost vomited as he dejectedly filled in the hole as best he could. But his effort was halfhearted. He knew he had to make the scene look perfect. Knew he couldn't afford to be lazy, but he simply didn't care. At that moment prison sounded like as good a place as any to spend the rest of his days. When he'd finished sprinkling the area with clumps of dead leaves, he grabbed the box and shovel and turned to go, his mind racing with various scenarios. But there was only one answer, and rage and anger grew as the idea became more and more of a reality. There was only one possibility. Only one person could have known about the money. Only one person could have taken it.

He gripped the handle of the shovel tightly as he stormed off back toward the house, feeling the weight of the spade as it hung over his shoulder behind him. It would make as good a weapon as any. And if his mother didn't 'fess up immediately, he decided, he might just bring the edge of that heavy blade down and across her neck. Because she'd betrayed him. He knew it for a fact. As the demons swirled in his brain, they convinced him that his mother had double-crossed him. They also convinced him that he'd be a fool if he let her get away with it.

NANCY PAULINE SIMPSON

Festered Wounds

FROM *Alfred Hitchcock's Mystery Magazine*

SHE DIDN'T FLINCH none. Gag neither. I'll give her that. But after looking flinty-eyed at the body for a minute or more, both of 'em still as stumps, she did stare me straight in the face while we talked, so as not to get another eyeful by accident. That staring was, I figure, more discomfiting for me than seeing a corpse was for her. Our county nurse, Miss Haseltine Polk, is as fine-looking a woman as you'll find anywheres. I'd never yet been close enough to see that her eyes are green and sparkly, like a bitters bottle. The wavy dark hair, mostly tucked under a poufy crocheted hat, I'd noticed more than I care to admit.

It had been a godsend she'd drove by within shouting distance while I was there. I was down in the creek bed under the trestle bridge, where some colored boys had come across the body an hour afore. The boys had been fishing and were so affrighted by what they found, they flagged down a passing farmer, showing themselves to be in no way responsible for whatever had took place or they'd have surely run away instead. The farmer found me at the railroad depot, buying a box lunch, and I ran right over to the livery to borrow a horse.

I was taking in first impressions of the nattily attired body when I saw her whipping by on the roadbed above me in that little two-wheeled pony trap she favored for unpaved roads. Her dog, a pink-nosed white bulldog she called Gumbo, for no good reason I could think of, rode in the trap beside her. He spotted me afore she did and barked to help me get her attention.

She hopped down that rocky red-clay bank light as a fairy, only stopping to gather up some excess skirt and tie together the ends of that long blue cape she wore when she was on official county-nurse business. Her dog whined and wriggled around in the pony cart where she'd ordered him to stay. The pony was indifferent.

I took off my hat and stationed myself between her and the body to give her time to steady herself on that slick, oozing creek bank before I revealed what I wanted her to see. Her job was mostly checking on the bedridden and the newborn, but I knew that upon occasion she assisted old Dr. McQuinney in some right gruesome undertakings. If what he was doing required four hands instead of two, and there weren't no man around with a strong stomach.

I was pretty sure she knowed who I was. But I hooked my thumb under my gunbelt, pushing my coat front aside to reveal my badge. I have to pin my badge into the thick leather of my gunbelt ever since the cheap safety catch on the badge back broke off. I can't pin it to my lapel no more without risking losing it or wounding myself. Might as well get used to it. I'll have my first set of false teeth afore the county buys me a new one.

"Good afternoon, Miss Polk. I'm terrible sorry to inconvenience you, but I need some assistance and you are just the person to help me. You might need to brace yourself for a disturbing sight."

She didn't say nothing, but if she'd been a pup, I'd of said her ears pricked up. I stepped aside. The man's body was half crumpled up and half flung out over a cluster of smooth flat boulders. A shallow but lively trickle of creek water had soaked the underside of the man's good-quality tweed suit and near-new pinstriped shirt. Looking up, I could see what was probably his hat wobbling in the breeze overhead, snagged by a bolt projecting from a trestle beam about 20 feet overhead. His head was stove in at the temple and his neck twisted enough to permit us to see most of his face and to conclude he'd suffered a broke neck.

"It appears, Miss Polk, that this unfortunate man either jumped or fell from the bridge. Would you happen to know who he is?"

"I'm sad to say I do. His name is Reynard Farley. A drummer. Haskell Pitt Shoe Company. 'Ten toes in heaven.'"

"Ma'am?"

"That's the motto of the Haskell Pitt Shoe Company, not an observation."

"I see. And you're sure this is Mr. Farley?"

"Oh, yes, I'm entirely certain, sheriff. Lord, what a pitiful sight!"

"*Deputy,* Miss Polk. Deputy Jervis Stickley. Farley, huh? I thought that's who it was. Lives at the hotel, don't he?"

"Yes. He and his wife are boarders." She got real quiet, thinking about them that was left behind and was going to have to make do without Mr. Reynard Farley.

"I was hoping you'd help me, Miss Polk, by breaking the sad news to Mrs. Farley about what has transpired and see, maybe, if there ain't some friends or kin we should communicate with on her behalf. I've got to get the body back to town and have the doctor pronounce him officially dead. I'd hate for Mrs. Farley to get such news accidental like. Those colored boys that found him might have recognized him too, and have already set the county grapevine afire."

She narrowed her eyes to fluttering quarter-moons and mulled things over. "I'll help you get him into my pony cart. We'll have to fold him up, but I've got some vulcanized rubber sheets we can wrap him in. Dr. McQuinney is in Moultrie visiting his nephew. In his absence, either the sheriff or I have the authority to pronounce a body dead. The sheriff is sleeping off the lancing of an axillary abscess."

I knowed that already. Our sheriff was susceptible to frequent armpit boils.

She knelt down by the body, pressed his neck and wrist, and draped a filmy handkerchief she drew from somewhere within that cape over Farley's nose. It lay motionless as them boulders.

"He's dead, all right. Not a doubt in my mind. And I'll sign the document to that effect. Wound still gelatinous. I'd estimate he's been dead no more than a couple of hours."

She stood up, brushed herself off, and glanced all around. "Where's his automobile?" I must have looked dumb as a barrel bung.

"What I mean to say, deputy, is how'd he get out here?"

"Had an automobile, did he?" My first thought was that Farley had been in a horse-drawn vehicle of some kind, which the horse had probably already towed home to stall and feedbag. I hadn't noticed any automobiles stopped alongside the road. More people had them every year, including yours truly, but they was still a whole lot less numerous than mules and still as likely to draw a crowd of excited little boys as the mules are to draw flies.

"Well, might be it's up there." She pointed to the trestle bridge. I should mention that the trestle bridge roadbed was wide enough on both sides of the track to serve as walkway or mule crossing, although it would be a mite foolish to attempt such a passage while an actual train was on the bridge. Flying cinders might scorch your clothes, and the side draft could knock a scrawny fella off his pegs.

A regular-sized dirt road extended beyond the bridge on both ends, running alongside the rail bed. On the east side that road made a sharp turn downhill, becoming a feeder to the county road. On the other side the road soon shrank to just tracks and enough rail bed for the train to follow into town.

Miss Haseltine Polk whistled for Gumbo to come on down and keep an eye on the deceased while we scouted the area. His hackles went up at the first close whiff, but he did as he was told. Miss Polk had a naturally commanding presence.

Sure enough, there, parked at the foot of that dirt road, occulted by hovering redbuds, was a Sears and Roebuck Model P, its trunk lid neatly tied down to secure all the shoe boxes stowed inside that kept the latch from catching like it was supposed to.

I pointed out to Miss Polk some deep scrambling-type footprints going up the road toward the trestle bridge. There was none coming back down.

"What in the world would lure him up onto that bridge in such a hurry?"

Me and her mused as one. Once onto the trestle bridge, we didn't see nothing out of the ordinary, until Miss Haseltine Polk found some tweedy wool threads trapped in the rivets and welded seams of a particular steel railing, about two-thirds of the way across.

"Must be where he pitched over," I concluded.

I was the one who spied what might be splatters of blood on a nearby upright.

"Don't seem likely he jumped, you know, intentional, now does it?"

She shook her head. "It wouldn't make sense even without the blood. He's got a load of orders to deliver and make a profit on. A real sweet wife waiting for him at home. He was wearing a watch and chain that were in no respect trinkets. Wouldn't you think he'd have left those behind for his wife if he intended to take his own life?"

She cleared her throat. "And to add to the conundrum, there's that peculiar injury to his face."

"Good God, I mean, good gracious, Miss Polk. The man fell off a bridge onto a pile of rocks. Can't hardly expect him to look like the Arrow collar man."

She gave me a look I would have described as fish-eyed, only nothing sporting gills ever had eyes made my mustache tingle like hers did.

"I know that perfectly well, Deputy Stickley. But those rocks he leapt or fell onto are mossy and humpbacked as a camel. That wound across Mr. Farley's eye and cheek looks like it was made with a hoe handle. Something elongated and shaped the same from one end of where it struck to the other. It appears he suffered an orbital . . . *eye socket* . . . fracture."

I hadn't paid much mind to that particular wound, but now that I recollected it, she was right. "Then you think he was struck in the face, up there on the bridge, afore he fell?"

"I do."

"But why? If somebody wanted to rob him, why'd they leave his watch? And all them spanking-new shoes in his automobile? Not to mention the automobile itself."

She shrugged.

"Say, how well *do* you know the Farleys? Anybody holding a grudge? Old enemies? Ever been accused of cheating anybody? His shoes give anybody one too many bunions?"

It wasn't fish eyes but daggers she was flashing my way now.

"Beg pardon, miss. My levity was uncalled for."

The wind gusts on the trestle liked to knock off both our hats. She wrapped her cape more snugly around her, to keep from getting airborne like one of them Wright brothers' flying machines. Meanwhile the wind continued to riffle her skirt above a pair of sturdy, lace-up shoes and dainty ankles. Her stockings were white as moonlight peeking through dark clouds. She let me cradle her elbow as we made our way off the bridge.

"I understand that Mr. Farley travels quite a bit," she told me, "but whenever he's in town, he seems to get along with everybody just fine. He moved here from Michigan, I believe. But he's not the least bit brash or irritating. His wife's from Clayton County. And his reputation as a businessman is spotless. That fusspot Lottie Kreuger just about wore out a pair of pumps before deciding they didn't fit and she wanted her money back. He gave it to her too."

I won't detail the events surrounding our getting Farley's body out of the creek bed and into the pony cart, all wrapped up in them vulcanized rubber sheets. Just let me say that Miss Haseltine Polk's strength in no way is a reflection of them dainty ankles. I swear, I think she could have done the job all by herself. We left the body with John Milton Penrose, the most respected embalmer and undertaker in the county. Penrose could make a ninety-year-old scrofula victim look like a Florodora girl.

Mrs. Farley was sitting on the front porch of the hotel stringing beans. She was a well-made young woman with yellow hair pulled back from a Kewpie-baby face. She was wearing a shirtwaist and one of them boiled-wool jackets women wear nowadays instead of a shawl. Her shoes were perfection, embossed black leather with gilt buttons. Her gold wedding ring was plain, but wide enough to reach her first knuckle. I pulled off my hat, introduced myself, and asked if there was somewheres me and Miss Polk might talk to her alone.

Mrs. Farley reacted to the news like somebody at the periphery of a coal mine explosion, stricken but not really grasping the situation. Which is why I'd wanted Miss Polk to stay with her awhile. I didn't want Mrs. Farley to be alone when she got to be fully cognizant of what had happened to her husband.

I left them in order to roust Edgar Fulton and have him go to Penrose's to take some camera pictures of the body for Dr. McQuinney and the sheriff to argue about. I told Fulton the county would make good on his expenses, but that was more wishful thinking on my part than anything else.

That evening Miss Haseltine Polk swept through a fiery sunset to tell me Mrs. Farley was unloading her grief on the Methodist preacher and his wife and that one or the other of them would be sending a telegram to Mrs. Farley's people in Valdosta, who were good Christians and would probably come to collect Mrs. Farley as soon as they could.

We were in my office, such as it is. It's really a tacked-on back room of the general mercantile. Half of a back room. The other half is where the post office stashes undeliverable letters and parcels. But I got my own desk and a rack for my hat and my overcoat.

My law-enforcement certificate hangs behind my chair, which swivels if the wheels are canted just right. And there's a sign on the door with type set by the same fella makes the posters when a tent revival or circus comes to town. It says: DEPUTY SHERIFF, CLAYTON COUNTY. No name. I'm a probationary hire until the county commissioners quit insulting each other long enough to put me on permanent.

I gave Miss Polk the chair and sat on the old church pew that serves as visitor seating.

"I think she finally grasped what had happened when I gave her Mr. Farley's watch and chain. It's a terrible thing for a woman to lose a husband she loves," Miss Polk said.

"Indeed it is." I cleared my throat. "I don't want to seem unfeeling, but I suppose we can ascertain that Mrs. Farley was at some distance from that trestle bridge when Mr. Farley was killed?"

She gave me a mildly reproving look, but the same thought must have passed through her own mind because she answered me right away.

"Gansy Washington, one of the hotel cooks, said Mrs. Farley spent the morning in the kitchen, learning how to make yeast rolls. Apparently Mrs. Farley is sufficiently skilled at biscuits but falls short of the mark when it comes to yeast rolls. Gansy is an exacting instructor, I guess, and Mrs. Farley had to go right upstairs for a rest afterwards."

"Mrs. Beasley lets guests have the run of her kitchen?"

Mrs. Beasley's was one of two hotels in town, but the only one you'd let your sister stay in. I'd already learnt that Miss Haseltine Polk and a lady tutor who preferred not to live with her pupils and a spinster living on her father's railroad pension and the Farleys boarded there in respectable comfort.

"Can't see why not. The Farleys have been staying in the Bullet Room for more than a year."

"The Bullet Room?"

"Oh, I keep forgetting you weren't brought up here. The Bullet Room is so named because of the evening a group of drummers decided to relieve the monotony of travel with some target practice, using a portrait of Solomon Beasley as the target. They fired off a regular fusillade before somebody got up the courage to intervene. But after everything calmed down, the drummers were properly ashamed of themselves. No one was hurt.

And their aim had been so godawful, Solomon Beasley didn't even get nicked. So Mrs. Hymenia Beasley decided not to make too much of it. Just set a rule that no more than two imbibing drummers can congregate upstairs after dinner. She patched the holes, of course, but it's been known as the Bullet Room ever since. It's more of a suite than a room, truth be told, with a side room to dress in and a big rosewood screen separating the sitting room part from the bed."

Truth be told, I was getting so tuckered out and hungry, I was starting to hallucinate about Miss Polk in one of them pink silk wrappers women are said to wear when they brush out their hair at night. I pushed open the door to let in some fresh air and skeeters.

"Was she able to tell you anything more about Farley?"

"Oh, once the dam broke, it was a regular flood." Miss Polk unhooked her cape and opened it to show me the damp spots on her bodice. I forced my gaze to be fleeting.

"She told me they met three years ago, at a Chautauqua in Michigan. She was there as part of a Methodist ladies' chorale and he was there lecturing on persuasive speech. Their eyes met during 'Glow, Little Glow Worm,' and a few lectures and refrains later, he persuaded her to marry him." Miss Polk sighed deeply, and her eyes welled up in sympathy but did not overflow. No breached dams for Miss Polk.

"And they decided to settle here instead of in Michigan?"

"The Haskell Pitt Shoe Company wanted to expand south and had offered Mr. Farley an exclusive sales territory. Having married into a southern family, he seemed like an ideal candidate. Mrs. Farley told me more than once that he's done quite well."

"Married three years, you say? And no children?"

She flushed. "I didn't ask her to explain *that*."

"Whys and wherefores aside, no young 'uns?"

She shook her head sadly. "I almost wish . . . That's to say, she'd have something, *someone,* to remember him by, if they had . . . if she were . . ."

I stood up and cracked my tired back. That pew was meaner than a bony mule. "On the other hand, all things considered, a young widow might fare better childless than otherwise."

Miss Polk jerked to her feet and gave me a look sharp as a crosscut saw. "Well, some people can find a silver lining in just about anything."

As admiring as I was of her, sharp look and all, I was not about to apologize for being sensible.

I accompanied her through the dim empty store to the main street door, not wanting to turn her out into the pitch-black alley my office door led into. She refused my offer to accompany her to the hotel, but she seemed to have softened a little toward me during our passage through the livestock feed section.

"It's been a trying day, Deputy Stickley, and I want you to know I think you handle your job beautifully. For the most part."

"Likewise, Miss Polk." I cleared my throat. "Might I impose on your kindness one more time?"

She looked a little wary, but curious.

"Since the Miss Wainwrights live closest to that trestle bridge, I'd like to pay them a call. And I'd like you to go with me. My little birdies tell me they think of you as a friend."

"I have no objections whatsoever. I was on my way there today when you waved me down. I'd be glad to help out."

"Wagon or automobile?"

"Your roadster?" She laughed. "Their dogs would have fits and their chickens would die from fright."

What with one thing and another, I didn't get myself out that way for two days. I'd spoke to the sheriff by telephone and he seemed inclined to think Farley was a victim of ungainliness, not mischief. Till I had evidence to the contrary, I was to look to that for the explanation. What I looked to even more keenly was the Miss Wainwrights, because I heared from my little birdies that one or both of 'em walked over that trestle bridge almost every day and might have seen something. Miss Haseltine Polk had a pressing obligation that morning but agreed to meet me at the millpond afterwards to help me analyze any developments and share a scenic picnic lunch.

I telephoned Miss Lucretia Wainwright beforehand to give her fair warning. By then there was almost a dozen telephones in town. Although the Miss Wainwrights had been among the last to get electrified, they were among the first to get a telephone. Their place was a little hard to get to and both ladies had some health problems, so it was interesting but not unreasonable that the oldest person in town had one of the newest gadgets. The house itself was the crumbling remains of the only plantation house in the county to survive the War Between the States and the turn of the century with the same family in residence. It appeared, however, to be about the end of the line for both.

I had to run a gauntlet of wheezing, nipping old dogs to get to the front porch, but the immediate yard was nicely tended and the steps swept. The colored woman who answered the door was lanky, pop-eyed, and, I'm guessing, somewhere in her forties. Her hair was completely hid by a mustard-yellow kerchief wrapped tight as a ball of twine, so I can't speak to how gray she was. She let me into a small side parlor, glaring at my insufficiently scraped boots like she wanted to chop 'em off with a ax.

A brisk little pitter-patter in the outer hall told me someone was on her way. I'd only seen the "old" Miss Wainwright from a distance in town. I was surprised to realize that the younger of the "old" sisters wasn't so very old at all. She had some white wisps at the hairline, where it ran up against a pink powdered face. And she wore her hair pulled back from a straight-razor center part in that antiquated style old ladies favor over a fringe. But the bun that gray hair fed into was still chestnut brown. And though she was plumped up in several directions, she had held on to most of her womanly shape. I speculate she wasn't much more than fifty. She introduced herself as Lucretia Wainwright and said her elderly sister, Beryl, had been so upset by the news of a death on the trestle bridge that she'd taken some "calming" syrup and was unlikely to be downstairs the rest of the day.

My little birdies had told me that Beryl Wainwright was something of a holy relic, being the oldest local survivor of the Lost Cause. There was an old man in town who might qualify as such a relic too, only nobody had knowed any of his people and his memory was so full of holes, it was hard to credit anything he said.

Lucretia was Beryl's half-sister, born of her father's postbellum second marriage to a woman hardly older than Beryl. The shortage of men after 1865 had led to some peculiar mismatches in age and social standing. The second wife didn't outlast Lucretia's arrival by much.

When they were younger, I hear, both sisters sang in the Methodist Church choir and held office in the local chapter of the DAR. But the past few years the sisters had kept to themselves for the most part because Beryl was now deaf as a fence post and Lucretia had nerves. But they got along, what with the colored woman and the telephone, which Dr. McQuinney used regularly to reassure Miss Lucretia that Miss Beryl could live forever. And they had occasional visits from other old ladies and whichever of the old ladies' grandchildren could be bribed to come along. The sisters took frequent walks into town, a distance of about three miles. I asked Miss Wainwright about their perambulations.

"I'm not so fond of walking as my sister is, Mr. Stickley. But Dr. McQuinney says the exercise is beneficial for us, so I occasionally accompany her. She sets a leisurely pace for herself, of course. I don't discourage her. Oh, I've mildly protested from time to time, on those days when her knee is stiff enough to require the aid of a walking cane. But she will have her way. Sometimes Iris—that's our colored girl—goes with her as far as the other side of the trestle bridge and lends her an arm to help her descend the path that leads from there to the county road. She *could* go directly down our drive, of course, but she admires the view from the bridge, with the willows and the creek and all."

"Nonetheless, Miss Wainwright, three miles to town and back seems right arduous for an elderly lady."

"Oh, it's not quite the expedition it sounds. When Big Sister gets to the main road, one of our kindly neighbors often stops to offer her a ride the rest of the way. And she never walks back. Why, the postal delivery man, Gus Murchison, practically considers her part of his route. Weather permitting, she goes to the train depot and checks the schedules to see if there are any changes."

She leaned toward me and lowered her voice—though I don't have no idea *why*, since we was talking about a sedated deaf woman. "She said something once that gave me the idea she thinks—only in passing, mind you—that she's checking the war casualty lists they used to post there when she was a girl. Oh, she's still sharp as a tack. I just mean that sometimes the very old can mix up the past and the present in equal parts. Time doesn't dilute old memories as much as we might expect, Mr. Stickley."

Or might hope, I thought.

"She checks that schedule religiously. I bought her a lovely little Gallet quarter-repeater pocket watch. She pushes a tiny button and the prettiest little chimes tell her the time. So even if she loses track of—oh my, I made a little joke, didn't I?—she can avoid being on that bridge if a train is almost due. She attaches the watch to her pince-nez chain."

"A chiming pocket watch? I understood she was hard of hearing."

Miss Wainwright laughed a not-displeasing laugh and patted my sleeve.

"*Hard* of hearing? I'd say impossible of hearing was a fitter description. No, I suppose she doesn't actually *hear* the chimes, but she can distinguish the vibrations that represent the hour and quarter hour. When one sense fails, the others compensate sometimes, they say."

"How do the two of you communicate, Miss Wainwright?"

"We communicate through hand gestures and little notes. And she is capable of some lip-reading if she puts her mind to it. But she can still talk, believe me, and makes her wishes known."

"And day before yesterday? The day of the unfortunate accident on the bridge?"

"Perfectly awful, wasn't it? I shudder just to think! Well, let's see. She set out as usual, about nine o'clock. I had wound her watch for her, same as always. By afternoon her fingers are fairly nimble, but they're not too cooperative in the morning. She went on her way, in a fine mood because her jonquils are starting to flaunt their pretty yellow frocks. The weather was lovely, if you recall."

"What time did she get home?"

"In time for lunch, same as always. About twelve-thirty. I think her appetite would keep her punctual even if the pocket watch failed."

"And did she make mention of seeing anything unusual when she come home?"

"Why, no. She did seem a bit more tuckered out than usual, but, Mr. Stickley, my poor sister is over eighty. I can hardly expect her to be lively as a cricket every day."

As if on cue, a specter in a rustling black dress crept into the doorway, a look of guarded surprise on a shriveled face pierced by two dark glaring eyes. Before Lucretia Wainwright could rise to greet her sister, the specter disappeared and could be heard rustling and mumbling her way down an unseen hall. But she'd been in view long enough for me to see the trembling, clawlike left hand gripping the door molding. A stump the size of a candle end held the space where a ring finger should be.

"Please forgive my sister, Mr. Stickley. She's not herself today and, frankly, doesn't enjoy making new acquaintances much anymore."

"Nothing to apologize for. I won't impose no further, Miss Wainwright. Excepting one thing. Did y'all know Mr. Farley, the, uh, victim?"

"I do seem to recall meeting him at the train depot one afternoon last fall. It must have been in connection with his business. Yes, that's it. A member of my Sunday school class, Beatrice McKay, had recommended Mr. Farley's shoes highly and took the opportunity to introduce us. But Big Sister and I special-order our shoes from Atlanta, as Mrs. McKay should know very well, so that was the extent of my association with Mr. Farley. A nice-looking young man, I do recall that. From the Great Lakes area, wasn't he? I've heard that those lakes freeze so solid in the winter that people can actually take horse-drawn sleigh rides all the way across."

Once I'd made my adieus and heard the door close at my back, I had the urge to fly down those steps like a schoolboy fleeing the truant officer. The millpond! But I stifled that impulse when I saw the colored woman, Iris, heading toward the house with a Baby Moses–sized basket of laundry riding on her hip.

She stopped but did not speak or smile when I blocked her path at a nonthreatening distance.

"Fine day, ain't it? Been with the Wainwrights long . . . Iris, is it?" I fished a fresh double square of Oceanic cut plug from my coat pocket and passed it to her. She palmed it in a flash and secreted it in the folds of her apron. Then she smiled.

"Yes, sir. Iris Washington. My people been with the Wainwrights for three generations. The others all died or moved away. Mr. Ellington Wainwright—*their* papa—was already an old man and Miss Beryl middle-aged when I come on to work regular."

"I was wondering, Iris. It's too delicate a thing to bring up to the ladies directly, but I am curious. How did Miss Beryl lose that finger?"

"Miss Beryl's life been one sorrow after another, the worst of it heaped on 'fore Miss Lucretia and me even knowed her. And it ain't really 'Miss.' She done married twice. One husband kilt in the first year of the war, one kilt in the last. Two babies too. One born already dead, and one dead from the whooping cough.

I never knowed any of their names. She be 'Mr. Wainwright's older daughter' so long, people forget she was ever *Missus* Somebody. After Mr. Ellington Wainwright died, people just slipped back into calling both of the sisters 'Miss.' As to that finger . . . Miss Lucretia told me, serious as judgment, that it was cut off by a renegade Yankee soldier when Miss Beryl couldn't pull off her diamond wedding ring quick enough to suit him."

I must have recoiled, first from the story itself, and then from the eerie cackle she followed it with.

"Folks can't believe everything they hear, Mr. Stickley. Seems like everywhere I go, I hear some variation of that old story 'bout a Yankee cutting off a lady's finger to get her ring. Sometimes a old lady. Sometimes a young lady. Makes me sorta ponder. I expect a lot of ladies who never held a ax afore in they life learned to chop wood the hard way during the war. Gutting a chicken can be tricky the first few times too."

"But she *is* missing a finger, Iris."

"That so. Sure is." She sighed and shifted Moses to her other hip. "More sad stories done come out of that war than come out of the Book of Job." A slow sweet smile brought a broken picket fence of teeth into view. "But she do all right, Mr. Stickley. They never hungry. And Miss Beryl, she got her flower garden and her Victrola. She can't hear it no more, but she still wind it up and hug it tight to feel the vibrations. Most days she need a cane to walk any distance, but she still get around pretty good. She got more to keep her content than some old folks."

"And Miss Lucretia? What's *she* got?"

"Why, I guess she got Miss Beryl to take care of. 'Fore that she had old Mr. Wainwright to take care of."

"Is Miss Lucretia really a 'Miss'?"

"Far as I know. Never heard nothing different."

"Thank you, Iris. One more thing. Were you here yesterday morning when Miss Beryl went out?"

"No, sir. Was helping my husband set out tobacco. All day. Same as every year."

She shifted the basket with a noisy groan, to indicate I was making a nuisance of myself, and I let her pass.

I half expected Miss Haseltine Polk not to put in an appearance at the millpond, but I'd come prepared. I'd bought two box lunches at the train depot from Mrs. Beasley's cousin Lydianna, who sold them every morning from a table set up on the platform for that purpose. Each box contained two pieces of fried chicken—one white meat, one dark—a biscuit; an apple; a hard-boiled egg; a slice of layer cake; and a little twist of paper that held a spoonful of salt. To be truthful, I oftentimes bought two box lunches and finished them both off by myself. I wasn't always sure I'd have more than a can of porky beans on hand for supper. My wild-hare work hours meant my meals were mostly movable feasts.

But there she was, her cape thrown back to reveal a green-striped dress with a dark green sailor collar and flyaway cuffs. Seeing her hatless hair was a revelation. Our picnic, laid out on a cloth as white as those memorable stockings, proved a banquet. Miss Haseltine Polk had brung homemade pimento cheese sandwiches on bread thin and translucent as magnolia petals. She'd brung pickled tomatoes and okra and boiled peanuts and squares of toasted pound cake spread with fig preserves. Instead of having to resort to the jug of stale water in my saddle kit, we were able to refresh ourselves from a washed-out vinegar jar she'd filled with delicious lip-puckering lemonade. Gumbo got a cow hock.

Afterwards, I come as close to trying to kiss that woman as I ever come to doing anything risky. But I reckoned, at that juncture, the odds of offending her were about equal to the odds of pleasing her and decided to wait for better odds.

We talked about all kinds of things. My one-armed grandfather coming down out of Missouri after the war. Me being one of five children, two of which was twins. We talked about her deciding to be a nurse after going with her suffragette aunt to hear Clara Barton talk on providing relief for refugees from the Galveston hurricane. I learned that she had three sisters and knowed how to ride a velocipede and had delivered a baby with six fingers on each hand. I ain't never been so captivated by the finer points of somebody else's life. Even without the kissing, I went home a happy man.

The next day I got a message that Miss Beryl Wainwright had died during the night and would I come over. I headed out there as soon as I could get a shave and put on a clean shirt. If I had expected Miss Lucretia to be beside herself with grief, I would have been mighty disappointed. I don't mean to say she was skipping around the yard exactly, but she had a demeanor more fitting for the undertaker, Mr. Penrose, than the grieving next of kin. Her black get-up—moiré taffeta trimmed in silk braid, Miss Polk told me afterwards—was so picture-perfect, I wondered if Miss Lucretia hadn't set it aside some time ago, anticipating the day she'd put it on.

She took me upstairs and gestured me into the room where Miss Beryl was laid out in bed, looking like an unconvincing waxwork. The little shriveled face peeked out of a ribbon-trimmed night bonnet. Both were propped up on a ruffled bolster. The rest of Miss Beryl was concealed by linens smooth as boiled frosting. Them piercing eyes would pierce no more.

I heared a creak and a rustle and a *thump, thump,* and realized Miss Haseltine Polk had beat me there or, from the tired circles under her eyes, had sat a deathwatch with Miss Lucretia most of the night. She was sitting in a rocking chair, nearly invisible in a gloomy corner. Gumbo was sprawled at her feet. That explained why the Wainwrights' elderly dogs was whining and laying low under the porch.

I nodded at Miss Polk, then turned back to the deceased, where I stood, head respectfully bowed, for several seconds. I hoped to give the impression I was meditating on the fleeting nature of mortal coils. I had no idea what to say or do next.

Miss Wainwright took the problem out of my hands by stepping between me and Miss Polk, blocking our view of Miss Beryl's frilly remains.

"I'm so glad y'all have been kind enough to come and offer me comfort. You see, there's something heavy on my heart and I wish to unburden myself." As Miss Lucretia looked about as heavy-hearted as a flying squirrel, I was curious as to what this burden might be. She waved for Miss Polk and me to follow her out of the room, touching her finger to her lips as if Miss Beryl's hearing had miraculously returned at her soul's passing. She led us downstairs to a more formal parlor than the one my muddy boots had been tolerated in earlier, and swooped her hand over the two pink velvet chairs me and Miss Polk was meant to sit in. She herself sat on a shiny horsehair loveseat.

Miss Lucretia arranged all that moiré taffeta in a black puddle around herself like she was fixing to sit for a portrait painting.

"I hardly know how to begin," she chirped. "You see, last night, before she fell into her final stupor, my sister confided in me a secret so terrible, I feel it is my duty to impart it to you, Mr. Stickley, as an official representative of the law, and to you, Miss Polk, as my sister's and my succoring angel and confidante this past year."

Terrible secret? A love child disposed of in the wishing well? A third crazy sister in the attic? Falsified DAR papers? I don't think even Diviner Dave could have guessed what was coming next.

"My sister was responsible for Mr. Farley's death."

I thought of the little ribbon-trimmed mummy lying in the bed upstairs and had to repress a smile.

"She struck him with her cane and she watched him fall off that bridge to his death and didn't regret it for one minute."

Miss Haseltine Polk found her vocal cords afore I found mine. "B-u-ut, why on earth would she do such a thing, Miss Wainwright?"

"Mr. Farley must have heard the train coming and seen my sister crossing the bridge, walking on the tracks. When she didn't respond to his shouts of warning, he ran up onto the bridge and tried to pull her to safety."

Miss Polk gave a little gasp of realization. "Oh, dear! Poor Miss Beryl! I guess she mistook Mr. Farley's intentions, running at her like that. Scared her out of her wits, like as not."

Miss Lucretia Wainwright smiled an unwholesome smile. "She knew what she was doing, all right."

"Beg pardon, ma'am?"

"Oh, she mightn't have meant to *kill* him. Although I wouldn't have put it past her."

"Kill Reynard Farley! But why? She hardly knew him!"

"She knew where he came from. That was enough. I'm not sure how she got wind of it. Maybe reading Beatrice McKay's lips. But she forbade me to take even the smallest peek at his shoes."

"Where he came from? Do you mean to say . . ." I felt a cold epiphany creeping up my neck like a big wolf spider. "*Michigan,* ma'am?"

Miss Lucretia shrugged off my simplemindedness. "Michigan, Pennsylvania, Maine. Take your pick. *Up north.*"

Miss Haseltine Polk seen where this was going too. She slumped down beside Miss Lucretia, half on the loveseat, half on the floor. She took Miss Lucretia's forearm in both her hands. Whether to shush her or to embolden her to keep on talking, I cannot say. But Miss Lucretia kept on talking.

"When Big Sister turned around and saw who it was had laid his hands on her, she struck out with her cane like she thought she was Nathan Bedford Forrest at Shiloh."

"Do you mean to say . . ."

"Mr. Stickley, you *do* repeat yourself! I'd never have guessed she was physically up to such a thing. She must have summoned every ounce of strength left in her poor, frail body. Knocked him right up against the trestle railing, she said. 'I'd rather be hit by a train,' she shrieked at him, 'than be touched by a Yankee.' Those were her very words.

"I suppose he was concussed. Stunned, at the very least. He lost his balance, she said, and then made the mistake of turning his back on her, trying to retrieve his hat, and she did him another. He went all rubbery and kind of slithered over the railing, she said. I always did contend those low railings were a safety hazard. When the train did finally cross the trestle bridge, Big Sister was holding on to an upright beam, barely out of harm's way, looking down at the creek bed where her eternal foe lay vanquished at last."

I don't mean Miss Lucretia no disrespect, but I sensed a kind of theatrical character to her recitation that was, well, in poor taste. She thought my dumbstruck expression meant I didn't believe her.

"I assure you, it's God's own truth. 'I've settled all my accounts,' she kept saying. 'I've settled all my accounts.' Those were her last words. Next thing I know, she falls into a comalike state—our poor father went the same way—and I sent word to Miss Polk to come sit with me until the end. Comforting as any angel, that's our dear Miss Polk!" Miss Lucretia rose, her languid movement accompanied by a sustained, three-note sigh.

"Would either of y'all like some coffee while we're waiting for Mr. Penrose? I've got with chicory and without."

I guess she took our being speechless as assent and started out of the room with an airy step. But she stopped in the doorframe and twirled around. "I feel I share her guilt, at least a teensy bit, because I forgot to wind her watch that morning. I thought about needing to do it, then I thought I *had* done it, instead of just thinking about needing to do it, and then she was out of the house. I didn't realize my oversight until later. If she hadn't been on that bridge when the train was coming, Mr. Farley wouldn't have rushed to her assistance and he'd still be alive. It's all so tragic, it's, well, *Shakespearean*."

I don't think I ever in my life took part in a conversation quite as peculiar as that one. If Iris hadn't arrived about then, I'd have been more than a little uneasy about going outside to answer a call of nature, leaving Miss Haseltine Polk alone with a corpse and a crazy woman. Iris's arrival meant I could escape to the outdoor privy for several forms of relief, including fresh air.

When I returned, Miss Polk was patting Miss Lucretia's hand and saying Miss Lucretia had no cause to torment herself.

"The last thing she required of me and I failed her." Miss Lucretia was sniffling into a little lacy wad. "That watch will haunt me!"

Miss Polk, gentle as May rain, tried to shift the conversation.

"You needn't stay in this big house by yourself, Miss Wainwright. Perhaps . . ."

Now, I expect Miss Polk was thinking about that particular day and the next, but Miss Lucretia had her eye set on a more distant object. I swear I thought I saw her toes start tapping under that long black skirt.

"Well, now that you broach the subject, I *have* always wanted to travel. The Holy Land, of course. And the Ziegfeld Follies."

"Ma'am?"

"Ever since I was a girl, I've wanted to go see that Broadway. Ziegfeld Follies. I know I sound foolish as all get-out, but before I die, I want, just once, to hear people telling naughty stories and laughing out loud and see women wearing spangled stockings and headdresses with plumes tall as Christmas trees."

Speaking of plumes, you could have just about knocked me over with a hummingbird feather. Miss Lucretia Wainwright must have noted the staggered expressions Miss Polk and I were exchanging.

"Oh, I have every intention of seeing my sister laid to rest with proper dignity and sacrament. Don't give that a moment's worry. But I must confess, after all these years, not even being able to utter the words *New York* without being accused of every perversity known to mankind, I do feel a certain iota of . . . release. I couldn't even look at Papa's stereoscope slides of Niagara Falls when she was in the room. I finally determined to put all thoughts of personal satisfaction out of my mind. It's amazing how quickly they're all popping out again."

Miss Polk and I climbed into the pony trap in silence, seating ourselves by necessity close to each other, going extra slow on account of my horse being tethered to a hitching eye at the back end. The silence continued until she suddenly swiveled toward me and gasped.

"Oh, Deputy Stickley! Something perfectly chilling just occurred to me."

I looked at her in mock disappointment. "We've shared two dead bodies and a box lunch. Can't you bring yourself to call me Jervis, leastwise when it's just the two of us?"

She didn't appear to hear me.

"It's the wickedest thought you could ever imagine."

"Share it and it'll be only half so wicked."

"All right. What if Miss Lucretia forgot to wind Miss Beryl's watch . . . *on purpose?* Miss Beryl knew that train schedule by heart. Checked at the depot almost every day for any changes. She knew she had to get it right, because she wouldn't hear the train coming. And Miss Lucretia knew the schedule too. What if she . . . *planned* for Miss Beryl to get hit by a train? What if all that caregiving had just gotten to be too much, what with Dr. McQuinney saying Miss Beryl could live forever? Plumes, my foot!"

I couldn't help myself. Her expression was so indignant and adorable, I had to slip my free arm around her waist. She didn't pay it no mind.

"But look here, Miss Polk. She didn't have to conjure up a plot fittin' for Edgar Poe in order to get away. If she was tired of being a nursemaid to her sister, she could have just divvied up their money, stole away on a Seaboard sleeper heading north, and spent the rest of her days chasing down bawdy jokes and spangles."

Miss Haseltine Polk cocked her head in my direction. It brought her face so near to mine, a strand of that fine dark hair skittered over my mustache. Did I detect a coquettish little gleam mixed in with all that bitters-bottle sparkle?

"Why, Jervis Stickley, you know better than that. There's some kind of devilish plotting goes on in the best of families. But abandonment?" She drew her dark-crescent eyebrows together. "There'd be no end of talk."

DENNIS TAFOYA

Satan's Kingdom

FROM *Needle*

LAROCQUE GOT A CALL when his father died. This was when he was living in the desert, in a trailer on the edge of Banning. He couldn't remember giving out the number, but one day in December the phone rang and it was his father's girlfriend, telling him that Henry had died of cancer. She said he had to come decide what to do about the property, the dogs. She was moving to Florida, to Del Ray. After he hung up the phone Larocque put a hand on his chest, feeling a tightness there as if she had called to tell him about a bill he owed.

He stood for a long time in the open door of the trailer, feeling the heat, watching the trucks go by on 10. After a while he began to carry his few possessions to the truck: the fan, the microwave with the taped door. He left a pile of things in the middle of the floor with a note for Jed and Marie thanking them for the use of the place and saying they should sell what they could. They were gone, visiting Jed's son in Kanab, and the two Mexican kids whose names he had never learned were working the station, so he just stood at the edge of the broken asphalt thinking about the difference between this place and Cheshire County. Here the bright yellow and red of the desert was everywhere, even when you closed your eyes, even in a dream. He remembered New Hampshire as a wilderness of dark blue and black so that even at noon it seemed like twilight and it was hard to feel that what was happening was real.

He had liked the trailer, the descending shelf of brown dust that led to the highway, the heat that he felt held him hard against the ground. Around the lot were scattered desert plants that gave off bright, medicinal smells. Marie said that each one could cure a specific disease and was always pushing some tea at Larocque that she said would clear up his cough or stop his nightmares. She made sweet, grainy cookies and bread from mesquite and sold them from a little display Jed built in front of the station to the families on their way to Palm Springs or Marines from Twentynine Palms. The young Marines were quick and lithe and seemed to Larocque tense with the coiled and watchful energy of people capable of great violence. He wondered what he looked like to these travelers and would take pains to smile at everyone, especially the cars full of young girls heading to weekends in the desert, to parties he'd imagine in night-lit casinos he'd never seen except on television.

Jed said he liked knowing Larocque was there by the station after hours in case something happened, though nothing ever did. Days he worked landscaping for Bermudez Triangle, and after dark he sat looking out at the highway through the trailer's open door as if from a cave and sipping White Horse. On his last night he watched a truck burning out on the highway, the police and fire trucks going by in showers of red light, and he realized that all the years he'd been in the California desert, he had been hiding.

It took him four days to get home. He stopped at a motel in Joplin off 44 and slept one night in a bed. He got breakfast in a diner and pulled a heavy coat off the rack as he was leaving. He was running out of money, wondered how fast he could sell the property, the furniture. His father had guns that would be worth something. A Lefever 10-gauge with a Damascus barrel, a prewar Marlin. He had kept them locked up against Larocque and his friends, would make a show of slapping the big padlock on the gun safe with an open hand to make it rattle.

He'd been running with Gifford Pelletier then, and would pass through his father's house at dawn, stinking of hash oil and beer after being out all night on the roads between Keene and Manchester. He'd been big early, Larocque, wide in the shoulders and more than 6 feet at fifteen. The old man would loom over him at the table, jerk back his arm as if to hit him with the open hand that had dogged him since he was small. Larocque would cut his initials into the soft, pale underside of the pine coffee table or throw pinecones at the blue heelers Henry had been raising then.

The old man's feints made him flinch for a while, and then one day they didn't. He and Gifford stole the sign from the park called Satan's Kingdom across the border in Northfield, and Larocque hung it in his room and waited for his father to say something. By then the old man was ignoring him, other than to snort like an animal at a watering hole when Larocque high-stepped through the living room with a drunk's exaggerated care at three in the morning, his eyes red as coals. The knowledge that he was beyond his father's control had made him feel weightless, almost nauseous, the way he thought an astronaut loosed from gravity must feel. That was one of his nightmares, flying away from the earth, the sky turning from deep blue to black at the edge of the void.

Lying in the back seat of the Le Mans in the parking lot of a Denny's just west of Wheeling, he remembered being sixteen and driving all night, him and Gifford making wider and wider circles, 202 south to 119, west to 10. Fitzwilliam to Richmond to Winchester and up to Marlborough in the dark, and a hard white rime on the windows that shed flakes of frost onto their shoulders. Pelletier had an Italian pistol not much bigger than a pack of cigarettes that he'd take out of the glove compartment and stick in his belt. They'd walk through gas stations and Dunkin' Donuts in the early hours, the Mr. Mike's on 202, Pelletier sticking candy in Larocque's pockets and flashing him the butt of the little .32, watching for the cameras. They'd try the locks on the doors of the bank in Jaffrey, a metals shop in Keene that somebody said processed gold. Pelletier would read him stories from the *Union Leader* about robberies in Boston, a double murder in Etna. Pelletier would put a CD in, some garage band he'd heard in Manchester, and they'd watch a young girl through the windows of a convenience store, her Wildcats hoodie riding up on her slim hips when she reached to get a pack of Marlboros. They had been trying to think of themselves a certain way. They had been working up to something.

When he got to his father's house, there was a card stuck in the frame of the screen, a woman's name and the seal of the county sheriff. He froze when he saw it, took it out and stuck it fast in his pocket and looked around him, as if a quarter mile down the dirt track off Peg Shop Road there was anybody watching. Behind the house the dogs keened and howled and wanted out of their pens. He went to a moldering planter at the corner of the porch and found an envelope from Henry's girlfriend and a key to the door. There were complicated instructions about the woodstove and phone numbers for a lawyer and for people his father had known.

The dogs watched him when he came out the back door, what looked to be two shepherds, one still a splay-footed puppy, and something else he didn't recognize with a blaze of white on its face and wolfish green eyes. They looked to his hands, his face, the house behind him. Larocque hefted a spade that had been leaning against the door of the shed and trapped it awkwardly against his neck while he picked through keys on the ring until he realized the locks hung open on the latches. He went to the youngest dog's pen first, feeling a little thrill of fear as he opened the door. He let each one out, the dogs standing patiently until all three had been released and then running in tight circles around the yard. After a minute he let the shovel go, realizing that he had seen the dogs not as things in themselves but as some wild extension of his father's dark will, spirits standing in for his anger and disapproval. Under his breath he said, *They're just dogs, you idiot.*

He found rags and bottles of pine cleaner and Simple Green, and threw away moldering food and swept out the first floor. The gun safe had stood empty when he came in, whatever had been in there taken by the girlfriend or his cousins from Vermont. The first night he ate a can of macaroni in red sauce he found in the cupboard and watched a tape in the ancient, whistling VCR about making lures, a man with thick glasses and tufts of gray hair at his ears carving and painting crankbait bodies. When the wind picked up, he went out and let the dogs out of their pens and brought them into the house, and from the way they settled companionably on the couch he figured it was something Henry had often done. He had scoured the cabinets and found nothing to drink but some old grape juice, and he sipped at that, watching the man on the tape work in near silence, stopping to show off a stripe of vivid red, a spray of green dots. Something in the hissing and popping of the dry wood in the stove reminded him of his father's voice.

The next morning Larocque came out of the shower and cracked a window against the steam. While he was standing there feeling the narrow blade of cold air on his arms, a sheriff's car pulled up outside and the dogs began barking and pawing at the windows. He got dressed fast and stepped outside, pulling at his shirt and wishing for something to carry, to have something to do with his hands. It was the woman who had left the card, Carrie Milgram, and she introduced herself and shook his hand and waved at the puppy that was pushing at the screen with one long paw. She pointed at the dog, asking permission, and he nodded, so she let her out and the dog danced and pantomimed joy and prodded her hand to be stroked, which the woman did, giving each dog in turn a treat from one of her pockets.

She told him their names, pointing to each in turn. "The Belgians are Masie and Poke, the border collie is Halley. I was helping Henry train them for the county." She explained that they paid Henry a little money to use the dogs for tracking. Search and rescue when hikers got lost on Mount Pisgah. The dogs watched her closely while she told Larocque about tracking, finding lost kids and old people who had wandered away from family outings by the lake in Otter Brook. Her face was wide and plain and open, like a girl's, and the brown parka and gunbelt obscured her shape.

"We were all real sorry about Henry," she said. "We took up a collection for the funeral. He was real well thought of." Larocque nodded, not knowing what to say. "He said you were out west? A contractor, he said?"

"Oh, you know. A little, you know, just small jobs." He had no idea what his father would have said about him, how he would have explained him, and he watched her face for some sign that she was lying or being polite, but she had the same open expression as the young dog and he thought she wasn't much given to hiding what she thought. He nodded as if she had made some comment and felt a little dizzy, as if he were impersonating somebody, creating an identity by just standing on his dead father's porch and having a civil conversation with somebody in authority. Somebody in a uniform. He wanted to say, *Don't you know who I am? What I've done?* But nobody knew, nobody but Gifford Pelletier, and he figured Gifford must have run even farther away than he had, must be locked up or dead.

Carrie began to come over after her shift with the sheriff's office. The dogs would stand up just before he heard her car, the young

Belgian throwing his head like a horse. The first few times Larocque had nodded from the porch, his hands in his pockets, and then he began to follow them down the trail behind the house where she ran them through the woods. There was always something in her pockets for the dogs, and they watched her hands, her eyes. One Monday afternoon she brought a short, round man in khaki overalls gobbed with pine sap out to the house, and Larocque felt a pang, a bright flash of jealousy, until she explained that the man was a contractor looking for a backhoe operator. He shook hands with the man and felt himself standing taller. When he left, Larocque asked Carrie to have a drink with him, and she said yes.

One night when he'd been back a month he went to pick up cigarettes at Jake's in Keene. He was standing by the glass doors looking at the beer when Gifford Pelletier walked in with a boy. Larocque watched them together, the boy a smaller, blonder version of Pelletier. His son, maybe. He could hear a conversation about ice cream, Pelletier saying it was winter and ice cream was for the summer. Larocque waited until the boy went to stand by the candy and then walked out, Pelletier turning to look at him and then back at the cashier. Larocque didn't know what to do with himself, so he kept walking, out to the parking lot, working his keys in his hand. He was standing by his father's pickup when a shadow fell on the truck and he turned to see Pelletier standing behind him. Larocque covered his eyes against the glare from the lights. His breath glowed white in the cold.

"I thought that was you."

Larocque nodded. "Was that your son? That boy?"

"Don't worry about him." His accent had thickened, it sounded like, and Larocque was conscious of how the years in California had softened and lengthened his own speech so that he sounded to himself as if he were drawling, floating his words on the open air like balloons. They stood for a minute, Larocque feeling the cold working into his clothes, up his sleeves and down his collar. There was something threatening in Pelletier's silence, the way he held his body canted to one side as if hiding something behind his hip. He said, "What are you doing home?"

Larocque lifted a shoulder. "Henry died."

"Okay," the other man said, as if that was an acceptable excuse. "Closing up the house? Selling out?"

"I don't know."

Pelletier nodded, his face shadowed and unreadable. "I see."

"I thought I would, you know. Come and go. That's what I thought when I started back."

"Yeah? What happened?"

"I don't know. It ain't the same. Maybe with the old man gone it's just a place."

"You should think about that." Pelletier was breathing heavily, like he was working up to doing something. Hitting him, maybe? He had on a parka that thickened his middle and a white hat with a wide brim. Larocque couldn't help thinking that the Pelletier he had known would have knocked a hat like that off a stranger just to see it roll in the dirt.

"I'm surprised you're still here, far as that goes. You got married?"

"Yeah, Jennifer Harrington."

"I remember her."

"Do you?"

He did remember her, as one of those high school girls with old-lady haircuts who seemed in all the particulars of their appearance and demeanor to be already in some henlike middle age.

Pelletier's chest moved in and out. "Why are you here?"

"I said. I'm here because my father died. I needed a place to live."

"Yeah? You should think about that."

Larocque thought they were somehow having two different conversations. When Pelletier turned, Larocque climbed into the cab of the truck and drove away. He drove a wide circle to the T-Bird on West Street to get the cigarettes he'd forgotten. As he walked through the dark lot to his car, his hands were shaking and he cradled the carton in his arms like a child. The wind picked at the hem of his jacket and he whirled in place, thinking he would find somebody behind him.

A week after that Larocque was coming out of the One Stop with a bag of dog food under his arm to find Pelletier standing next to the pickup looking at the dogs. Carrie was sitting in the open door while the Belgian puppy pushed her snout under Pelletier's stiff hand.

"I didn't know you kept dogs."

Carrie looked from Pelletier to Larocque, who nodded. "They were Henry's."

Carrie said, "They're trackers. Find anything. Lost kids, people." The young Belgian stood tall, looked from face to face, alert.

"Is that right," Pelletier said, and Larocque dropped the heavy bag in the truck bed and got in beside Carrie. To Larocque, Pelletier said, "You with the police now?"

Carrie smiled, "No, he's not, but he helps run the dogs when they're looking for someone."

"Looking for someone? For who?"

As he started the car, Larocque saw Pelletier's face change, grow purple as if a hand had closed on his throat. A white vein stood out on his neck. Larocque said, "We gotta go," and left Pelletier standing by Roxbury Street, his hands jammed in his pockets.

Carrie watched his face as they drove. "Who was that?"

Larocque shook his head. "Nobody. Don't talk to him."

She raised her eyebrows. "Is that so?"

He let his breath go in an agitated hiss. "He's just somebody I used to know. He's just . . ." He was conscious of her watching his face, and he felt heat spreading across his cheeks and up to his hairline. "He's not a good guy." He drove too fast until they reached the park around the reservoir and Carrie put her hand over his and he nodded and slowed down. He thought he'd feel safer under the white pines and balsam, but as the road narrowed he felt crowded by the looming trees. He wondered if he should have stayed in the desert, with nothing but the sky overhead, a ribbon of stars at night and sometimes the pale, bruised face of the moon.

A child disappeared, a ten-year-old girl who had been camping with her father on the Ashuelot River. He had gone to the store to get marshmallows and smokes and when he'd come back she was gone. Carrie took the dogs out, and Larocque waited with the man and a park ranger. The man told them her name, Allyson, and said they'd been driving around earlier and he'd shown the girl the covered bridge down in Winchester and he was afraid she was heading there, that she'd been fascinated by the fact of what seemed to be a house built right over the river, with a roof and a wooden floor. The man sat smoking at a picnic table and stole terrified glances at the river behind him. Larocque stood some distance away, trying to be respectful, but some secret part of him wondered if he would be blamed or accused. He said her name, Allyson Briese, to himself and wondered if that was a strong enough name to be the name of a survivor.

Carrie came back after an hour with a state trooper and said the dogs had made a wide circle back to Pine Street a half mile away. She stood with one hand on the man's shoulder but looked meaningfully at Larocque, and when they were alone in her cruiser she stroked the dogs with a gloved hand and said the girl must have gotten into somebody's car. She touched the dogs in turn and presented them each a piece of hot dog from a plastic bag, telling him (as she had before) about how frustrated dogs could get when they couldn't find the person they were searching for. The tracking dogs at the towers on 9/11, she said, had felt it was their fault when they couldn't find survivors in the collapsed buildings. A dog could take on the guilt of the people around it, she said.

That night he climbed through a confused welter of burning rubble and jutting steel, looking for the dogs. He woke up knowing he'd have the dream again, wondering what it meant that he was the one searching, digging through the ash, ruining his hands on the white-hot shards of steel looking for the dog that would save him.

Two days later Carrie met him at the house, the lights of her cruiser going and the dogs already leashed. He locked up his tools in the truck and jumped in and they were moving, the familiar landscape transformed by riding next to her, cars scattering at the intersections and people turning to watch them pass.

Carrie told him a state trooper had gone to question a man about the disappearance of Allyson Briese and they'd fought, the man struggling for the trooper's gun and running off into the state park north of Winchester.

"Did he get the gun?"

She motioned for him to be quiet and listened to the radio chatter, otherworldly metallic pips and shrieks, alien and indecipherable, that Carrie understood but that to Larocque seemed to announce some emergency so dire that there was no way to prepare for it or survive it when it came.

They got out on 119 south of the park and walked by state police cars, ambulances, news vans. There were circles of police in military dress, wearing combat boots and helmets. The breeze rose and he walked crabwise, trying to give it his back. Men and dogs squinted into the wind, and a helicopter moved overhead, rotors pounding. Carrie held a twelve-gauge Winchester in both hands. She went to stand with a group of men who had a map spread on the hood of a car, listening to a briefing. She was serious, somber, her mouth set in a way he hadn't seen before. Afterward she showed Larocque lines on a map and pointed into the woods, and he brought the dogs alongside the state trooper's car. There were black bullet holes punched in the metal of the door and the windshield was shattered.

Somebody brought a paper bag over to where the dogs stood ready, and Carrie reached in with a gloved hand and took out a wide-brim white hat. She looked at Larocque and he nodded yes.

The wind died as they walked, but the sky was woven with threads of blue and black. He tried to talk to Carrie about Gifford, couldn't think of a way to go at it. They were making their way uphill slowly through the hemlock and red oak, watching the dogs as they moved, tongues hanging. Masie was out front, running a zigzag course, and Carrie said, "She's quartering," showing Larocque a side-to-side motion with her hand that was the dog trying to find the scent trail. When they reached the firebreak, the radio at Carrie's hip crackled and a voice told them to wait where they were, so Carrie stopped and opened the pack she carried to get out a plastic bottle and let the dogs drink water from her hand. Larocque sat heavily on a cracked, blackened stump and breathed through his mouth. He saw Carrie looking at him, a question in her eyes.

He said, "I was a kid when I knew Gifford. I don't know. Not kids, but. Seventeen?" He looked into the woods ahead of them, the dark spaces between the trees. "We would drive around, talk all this crazy talk, all these things we were going to do." He dropped his head, unable to look at her while he talked about himself. "Henry, my father. I don't know what he ever said about me. I can't remember anymore if I acted wrong because he hated me or if I really did wear him down with the things I did. He was just angry all the time after my mother left. So what do you do when your father thinks you're no good? I guess I thought I'd be bad, be what he thought I was."

She put away the water and picked up the gun and stood wait-

ing by a mottled white rock that was like the back of some sea
creature buried in the hill. He said, "I think when you're a boy
that age, maybe you just need something to be, even if it isn't real.
Every minute you're play-acting, you know? We'd drive around
breaking things, sneaking into places." His voice got quiet. "And
we had a knife. Then we had a gun."

Carrie stood with the shotgun at port arms, as if ready to stand
him off. Her face was so pale in the cold light she looked almost
blue. She said, "Did you use them?"

"No, no, but . . ." The dogs went to stand by Carrie, and he sat
alone on his stump and felt something clench inside him, some
fist that grabbed his heart to be alone, separated from them just
that few feet. "I think I knew something was going on. I knew if we
kept going out something would happen."

"Did you want something to happen?"

He was still. "We took a girl, we brought her out here." He
thought about how that sounded. "We didn't *take* her, you know,
we just came out here. We were drinking. She was drinking a lot."

"You got her drunk."

"We were all drunk. We started at the Pub, and then we just . . ."

"Did you hurt her?"

"No." He shook his head, emphatic. His face was hot, sweat running from the hair at his collar though the day was cold and there
were circles of gray snow shaped to the shadows of the rocks.

He looked over finally at Carrie, but she faced away, holding
tight to Poke's collar. "Was she afraid?" Her voice was small, thin,
and it was strange how she seemed like a very young girl herself,
lost in her shapeless parka and holding the outsized shotgun in
her small hands.

"No. I don't think so. We were just kids, getting drunk in the
woods. She was older than us, I think. I don't think she thought, I
mean, maybe she thought we were going to fool around, all of us.
Hell, I don't know. But I could see he was thinking about it. Gifford." He got a flash of his friend standing in the dark, a few feet
away from where he and the girl sat with their backs against a tree.
The girl laughing, her teeth white. Gifford had been looking off
into the black woods and Larocque knew he was wondering if anybody knew where they were. "I couldn't drink like that, like they
were. I went back to the truck and passed out. When I woke up,
Gifford was driving me home. He said he'd dropped off the girl at

her place." He had the thought that this was the most he'd spoken to Carrie, the most he'd spoken out loud to anyone in years, and it was just this terrible thing that he thought he'd never tell anyone.

"A couple of days later it was all over the news, the girl. That she was missing. I hid for a few days, but I didn't know what to do. I was sitting in Lindy's and in comes Gifford and I could see in his eyes, I could just see it. I had the papers open in front of me and he just stood there looking at me. I never saw anybody look like that. I don't know how to say what it was like. Like his skull was coming through his skin. Like he wasn't a regular human being."

"Did the police talk to him?"

He had to stop looking at her, and turned to see only the trees and the rocks and the gunmetal sky. "I don't know. I don't know anything. I left. I moved out to California to work for my Uncle Ronnie hanging sheetrock. Ronnie went out of business and came home, but I just stayed out there and found work. If Henry hadn't died, I'd have never come back."

Carrie started to say something else, but then he heard her make a small noise, a grunt or cough, and turned to see Pelletier standing over her as she fell, the barrel of the pistol in his hands and the butt out, like the bell of a hammer, and one wrist clamped in a steel cuff. Larocque stumbled over the white rock to get to her and Pelletier had the Winchester pump out of her slack hands and he climbed awkwardly away onto the hump of boulder. The dogs whined and barked and the young Belgian made a noise low in his throat. Pelletier pointed the pump gun and Larocque grabbed the dog's collar and held him down, crouching by Carrie's body.

Pelletier said, "See? What did you think would happen?"

"You killed her."

"Maybe," he said. "Are you asking or telling?"

Larocque said, "That woman from the bar. And more, right? That girl at the campground, Allyson. Didn't you?" He wanted to touch Carrie's face but was afraid he would know then she was dead.

Gifford made a noise that might have been laughing, but his eyes were red and full. "You left. How do you know what I did?"

"I knew you. That's why I had to go. I knew even before it happened. The things we did, it wasn't enough for you. You were going to hurt somebody."

"Then why did you come back?"

"I told you. Henry died. I never thought you'd still be here."

Larocque watched Gifford's fingers twitch on the trigger and his head swivel crazily around, searching the hill around them. "I can't find her. The girl I took. I knew it was around here somewhere, but I can't find it anymore." He gestured drunkenly with the barrel of the gun. "There was the rock, the trees. Some kind of hollow where she was. It's all different."

It was getting darker. Gifford wiped at the sweat above his eyes and left a gritty smear. He pointed the gun at Larocque. "You can make those dogs find her."

"It doesn't work like that, Gifford."

"You left me here with these things in my head. You left me here." He lifted the gun barrel and awkwardly racked the slide, a bright green shell arcing out into the dirt. "Why didn't you stop me? You could see what I was going to do. How could you leave me alone with that?" He was crying now. "Wasn't you my friend?"

"I'm sorry." Larocque did feel a kind of sorrow in that second, and his breath caught in his throat. Pelletier brought the Winchester to his shoulder and tensed. Carrie jerked upright, her eyes wide and white bark stuck to her bloody hair, and brought her hand up with her service pistol in it. Pelletier started, opened his mouth to say something, but she shot him three times and he stepped back off the rock and collapsed into the dead leaves.

Three summers later a group of young kids from a college in Boston came to shoot a movie. One of the crew was a local girl, and she asked Carrie if they'd bring the dogs and let them be filmed. Larocque came with her to stand at the pickup and drink coffee, but when they saw him getting Masie out of the truck they asked if he'd be in the film. Carrie looked at him and lowered her head to smile, and he said sure and winked at her. The director, a short, skinny kid who wore a suit jacket and vest over faded jeans, told him the movie was called *Satan's Kingdom,* after the wilderness area down in Northfield, and Laroque said he knew all about it. They wanted him to stand with the dogs at the edge of the forest and pantomime fear when something came out of the woods, some horror that they would put in later through a process Larocque couldn't understand.

They asked him to walk the dogs up and down John Hill Road and introduced him to a girl, a small, slim girl holding a birch rod who would come through the woods at him. She'd tap the rod against the trees so he would know where to look, and he was supposed to throw his hands up and yell when she reached the tree line.

He ran the Belgians up and down the narrow verge of the road, and when the girl began to tap the stick, Poke came up short and peered into the woods. The kids in the crew looked at each other and nodded their heads, and the tapping got louder, and Larocque stepped close to the dogs and looked nervously past them into the dark trees.

The tapping seemed to come from everywhere, a hollow sound that echoed in the spaces between his ribs and made the hair stand up on his neck like the quills of some startled animal, and he ran his hand over the back of his head and felt sweat at his temples.

The sound grew louder and there was a distinct rustling from the pines. Larocque backed across the road, and the kid in the vest followed him with the camera, murmuring encouragement to Larocque, or maybe to himself. Larocque tripped backing up and went down hard on his haunches. The dogs whined.

When the girl's stick smacked the base of a telephone pole at the verge of the road, the long white rod poking from the shadow like a disembodied bone, Larocque screamed and covered his head with his hands. He dropped to his knees and sobbed, his mouth open. Masie howled, and Poke took it up, lifting his long head and closing his eyes to sing the man's grief. A minute went by, then two, and the director stopped filming and lifted the camera away. The girl, who had emerged from the woods with a red leaf stuck in her hair, dropped her stick and crossed the road and put one hand on Larocque's back. Without lifting his head, he put one hand on hers while his tears and spit darkened the asphalt.

After a minute Carrie reached him, helped him up, and guided him to the truck, where he sat in the passenger seat staring through the glass. No one said a word, and she gathered up the dogs and drove them home.

LAURA VAN DEN BERG

Antarctica

FROM *Glimmer Train*

I.

IN ANTARCTICA, there was nothing to identify because there
was nothing left. The Brazilian station at the tip of the Antarctic Peninsula had burned to the ground. All that remained of my
brother was a stainless steel watch. It was returned to me in a sealed
plastic bag, the inside smudged with soot. The rescue crew had
also uncovered an unidentified tibia, which might or might not
have belonged to him. This was explained in a cold, windowless
room at Belgrano II, the Argentinian station that had taken in the
survivors of the explosion. Luiz Cardoso, the head researcher at
the Brazilian base, had touched my shoulder as he spoke about the
bone, as though this was information intended to bring comfort.

Other explanations followed, less about the explosion and more
about the land itself. Antarctica was a desert. There was little snowfall or rain. Much of it was still unexplored. There were no cities.
The continent was ruled by no one; rather, it was an international
research zone. My brother had been visiting from McMurdo, an
American base on Ross Island, but since it was a Brazilian station
that had exploded, the situation would be investigated according
to their laws.

"Where is the bone now? The tibia?" I'd lost track of how long
it had been since I'd slept, or what time zone I was in. It felt very
strange not to know where I was in time.

"In Brazil." His English was accented but clear. It had been less than a week since the explosion. "It's not as though you could have recognized it."

We stood next to an aluminum table and two chairs. The space reminded me of an interrogation room. I hadn't wanted to sit down. I had never been to South America before, and as Luiz spoke, I pictured steamy Amazonian rivers and graveyards with huge stone crosses. It was hard to imagine their laws having sway over all this ice. It was equally hard to believe a place this big—an entire fucking continent, after all—had no ruler. I felt certain that it would only be a matter of time before there was a war over Antarctica.

"It's lucky the explosion happened in March." Luiz was tall, with deep-set eyes and the rough beginnings of a beard, a few clicks shy of handsome.

"How's that?" My brother was dead. Nothing about this situation seemed lucky.

"Soon it will be winter," he said. "It's dark all the time. It would have been impossible for you to come."

"I don't know how you stand it." The spaces underneath my eyes ached.

My husband hadn't wanted me to come to Antarctica at all, and when our son saw where I was going on a map, he cried. My husband had tried to convince me everything could be handled from afar. *You're a wife,* he'd reminded me as I packed. *A mother too.*

"Did you know about your brother's work?" Luiz said. "With the seismograph?"

"Of course." I listened to wind batter the building. "We were very close."

I couldn't stop thinking about him as a boy, many years before everything went wrong: tending to his ant farms and catching snowflakes in his mouth during winter. Peering into a telescope and quizzing me on the stars. Saying tongue twisters—*I wish to wish the wish you wish to wish*—to help his stutter. We had not spoken in over a year.

Luiz clapped his hands lightly. Even though we were indoors, he'd kept his gloves on. I had drifted away and was momentarily surprised to find myself still in the room.

"You have collected your brother's things, such as they are. There will be an official inquiry, but you shouldn't trouble yourself with that."

"I'm booked on a flight that leaves in a week. I plan to stay until then."

"The explosion was an accident," he said. "A leak in the machine room."

"I get it." Exhaustion was sinking into me. My voice sounded like it was coming from underwater. "Nobody's fault."

I had flown from JFK to New Zealand, where I picked up a charter plane to an airstrip in Coats Land. There had been gut-popping turbulence, and from the window I could see nothing but ice. Luiz had been the one to meet me on the tarmac and drive me to Belgrano II in a red snow tractor. I'd packed in a hurry and brought what would get me through winter in New Hampshire: a puffy coat that reached my knees, a knit hat with a tassel, leather gloves, suede hiking boots. I'd had to lobby hard to come to Antarctica; the stations weren't keen on civilians hanging around. When I spoke with the director of McMurdo, I'd threatened to release a letter that said details of the explosion, the very information needed to properly grieve, were being kept from the victims' families. I knew Luiz was looking me over and thinking that the best thing I could do for everyone, including my brother, including myself, was just to go on home.

"Are there polar bears here?" I felt oddly comforted by the idea of spotting a white bear lumbering across the ice.

"A common mistake." He drummed his fingers against the table. He had a little gray in his eyebrows and around his temples. "Polar bears are in the North Pole."

"My brother and I were very close," I said again.

There was a time when that statement would have been true. We had been close once. During our junior year of college, we rented a house in Davis Square, a blue two-story with a white front porch. Our parents had died in a car accident when we were in middle school—a late spring snowstorm, a collision on a bridge—leaving behind the grandparents who raised us and an inheritance. My brother was in the Earth Sciences Department at MIT, and I was studying astronomy at UMass Boston. (I was a year older, but he had been placed on an accelerated track.) Back then I thought I would never grow tired of looking at the sky.

When it was just the two of us, we did not rely on language. He would see me cleaning chicken breasts in the sink and take out breadcrumbs and butter for chicken Kiev, our grandmother's recipe. After dinner we watched whatever movie was on TV. *E.T.* played two nights in a row, and *Maybe it was just an iguana* became something we said when we didn't know what else to do, because even though we had been close, we never really learned how to talk to each other. Sometimes we didn't bother with clearing the table or washing dishes until morning. We went weeks without doing laundry. My brother wore the same striped polos and rumpled khakis; I showed up for class with unwashed hair and dirty socks. His interest in seismology was taking hold. He started talking about P-waves and S-waves. Fault lines and ruptures. He read biographies of Giuseppe Mercalli, who invented a scale for measuring volcanoes, and Frank Press, who had land named after him in Antarctica, a peak in the Ellsworth Mountains.

It was at MIT that he met Eve. She was a theater arts major. They dated for a semester and wed the same week they graduated, in the Somerville courthouse. I was their only guest. Eve wore a tea-length white dress and a daffodil behind her ear. She was lithe and elegant, with straight blond hair and freckles on the bridge of her nose. When the justice of the peace said "man and wife," she called out "wife and man!" and laughed, and then everyone started laughing, even the justice. I wasn't sure why we were laughing, but I was glad that we were.

There were three bedrooms in the house. It might have seemed strange, brother and sister and his new wife all living together, but it felt like the most natural thing. Our first summer we painted the walls colors called Muslin and Stonebriar and bought rocking chairs for the porch. We pulled the weeds that had sprung up around the front steps. All the bedrooms were upstairs. When I was alone in my room, I played music to give them privacy. At dinner I would watch my brother and Eve—their fingers intertwined under the table, oblivious—and wonder how long it would take them to have children. I liked the idea of the house slowly filling with people.

That fall my brother started his earth sciences PhD at MIT. He kept long hours in the labs, and when he was home, he was engrossed in textbooks. Eve and I spent more time together. She lived her life like an aria—jazz so loud I could hear it from the sidewalk; phone conversations that sprawled on for hours, during which she often spoke different languages; heels and silk dresses to the weekend farmers' market. She always wore a gold bracelet with a locket. I would stare at the oval dangling from her wrist and wonder if there were photos inside. I helped her rehearse for auditions in the living room, standing on a threadbare oriental rug. I got to be Williams's Stanley Kowalski and Pinter's Max, violent and dangerous men. I started carrying slim plays around in my purse, like Eve did, even though I had no plans to write or perform; the act alone felt purposeful. I learned that her father was an economics professor and she had majored in theater to enrage him, only to discover that she loved the stage. I'd never met anyone from her family before.

One afternoon I went to see her perform in *The Tempest* at a community theater in Medford. My brother had been too busy to come. She was cast as Miranda. Onstage she wore a blue silk dress with long sleeves and gold slippers. In one scene Miranda argued with her father during a storm; somewhere a sound machine simulated thunder. Everything about her carriage and voice worked to convey power and rage — "Had I been any great god of power, I would have sunk the sea within the earth . . ." — but for the first time I noticed that something was wrong with her eyes. Under the lights they looked more gray than blue, and her gaze was cold and flat.

Afterward we drank at the Burren. The bar was bright and crowded. A band was unpacking instruments from black cases. We jammed ourselves into a small table in the back with glasses of red wine. Eve was depressed about the production: the turnout, the quality of the lighting and the costumes.

"And the guy who played Prospero," she moaned. She had left a perfect lip print on the rim of her wineglass. "I would've rather had my own father up there."

When the waitress came around, she ordered another drink, a martini this time. She took an eyebrow pencil out of her purse and drew hearts on a cocktail napkin.

"What do squirrels give for Valentine's Day?" she asked.

I shook my head. My hands were wrapped around the stem of my glass.

"Forget-me-nuts." She twirled the pencil in her fingers and laughed the way she had during her wedding, only this time I caught the sadness in her voice that I'd missed before.

She put down the pencil and leaned closer. At the table next to ours, a couple was arguing. The band tuned their guitars. When she spoke, her voice was syrupy and low.

"Lee," she said. "I have a secret."

*

In Antarctica I shared a bedroom with a meteorologist from Buenos Aires. Her name was Annabelle and she talked in her sleep. Every morning I had a three-minute shower in the communal bathroom (it was important to conserve water). I took my meals in the mess hall, with its long tables and plastic trays and harsh overhead lights. I sat with the ten Argentinean scientists who worked at the base; we ate scrambled eggs and canned fruit and smoked fish. They spoke in Spanish, but I still nodded as if I could follow. The five scientists from the Brazilian station always sat at their own table, isolated by their tragedy, which I understood. After my parents died, it took me months before I could carry on a conversation with someone who had not known them, who expected me to be young and sparkling and untouched by grief.

Four of the Argentinean scientists were women. They had glossy dark hair and thick, rolling accents. In Antarctica I'd found that personalities tended to match the landscape, chilly and coarse, but these women were kind. There was a warmth between them, an intimacy, that made me miss being with Eve. They lent me the right clothes. They let me watch the launch of their meteorology balloon from the observation room, a glass dome affixed to the top of the station. The balloon was white and round and looked like a giant egg ascending into the sky. In broken English, they told me what it was like during the darkness of winter: *The sun,* they said. *One day it's just not there. There are no shadows. You have very strange dreams.* They included me in their movie nights in the recreation room, which had a TV, a small library of DVDs, a computer, and a phone. Once it was *Top Gun,* another time *E.T.* Everything was dubbed in Spanish, and when I didn't get to hear the iguana line, I started to cry. I didn't make a sound, didn't even realize it was happening until I felt moisture on my cheeks. The women pretended not to notice.

I started wearing my brother's watch. No matter how much I cleaned the metal, it kept leaving black rings around my wrist. With my calling card, I phoned McMurdo, only to be told that the scientists who worked with my brother had departed in anticipation of winter; all they could offer was the date he left and that their reports indicated he'd been in good health. I started pestering Luiz for a meeting with everyone from the Brazilian station, with the hope that they had more to tell.

"An interview?" he asked, frowning.

"No." By then I'd been in Antarctica for three days, though I felt it had been much longer. "A conversation."

The day of the meeting I dressed in thermals, snow pants, wool socks, fleece-lined boots, a hooded parka, and thick red gloves that turned my hands into paddles. I added a white ski mask that covered everything but my eyes. From Annabelle I'd learned it was called a balaclava. She had given me a laminated sheet with a drawing of a human body. Arrows pointed to what kind of layer should cover each part, to avoid frostbite.

When I first stepped onto the ice, I felt like an astronaut making contact with the surface of the moon. I wandered around the trio of heated research tents and the buzzing generators and the snow tractors. The sky was blue-black; the period of twilight, which seemed to grow smaller each day, would soon begin. By April, Antarctica would be deep into winter and there would be no relief from the dark.

I found all five of the Brazilians in the middle research tent, standing by a long white table covered with black rocks. With the snowsuits and the balaclavas, it was hard to tell who was who, though I always recognized Luiz by his height. Some of the rocks on the table were the size of a fist, others the size of a grapefruit. One was as large as a basketball.

"Meteorites," Luiz said when he saw me looking. Apparently the ice in Antarctica preserved meteorites better than any climate in the world. His team had discovered ones that were thousands of years old.

I touched the basketball-sized rock—it was the color of sand and banded with black—and remembered how much my brother had loved the moon rock collection at MIT.

"So what did you want to ask?" Luiz wore an orange snow suit. His goggles rested on top of his forehead.

I stopped touching the meteorite. Red heat lamps were clamped to the top of the tent. Standing before the other scientists, I suddenly felt like the one about to be questioned. It was hard to breathe through the balaclava.

"What do you remember about him?"

Not much, it turned out. One scientist volunteered that he often ate alone; another said he never participated in group activities like evening card games and Ping-Pong. He sang in the shower on occasion, an American song no one recognized. He had a stutter, though sometimes it was barely noticeable.

"What about the other times?" I asked.

"He could barely say his own name," Luiz said.

"How much longer was he supposed to stay with you?" I wished I had a notepad. I would remember everything, of course, but writing it down would have made me feel official and organized, like I was asking questions that might lead us somewhere.

"Two more weeks," Luiz said.

"And when did you last see him?"

There was silence, the shaking of heads. Someone thought they saw him the morning of the explosion, pouring a cup of coffee in the break room.

"Nothing else?" These weren't the questions I came with, not really, but maybe if we kept talking a door would open and I could ask something like *Did you know he had a sister?* or *Did he seem happy?* or *What did he love about being here?*

"I crawled out of the station." The words came from the woman in a sharp burst, like a gunshot. The hood of her parka was down and auburn hair peeked through the top of her balaclava. Bianca, that was her name.

"On my stomach, through fire, smoke. This is what I remember." She swept her hand toward the group. "No one was thinking about your brother. We barely knew him. We can't understand what you're doing here."

She pulled up her hood and walked out of the research tent. The other three scientists looked at Luiz, who shrugged and said something in Portuguese before following her.

I watched them go. The tent flapped open, revealing a pale wedge of sky. Already I was failing as a detective.

"I didn't mean for it to go like that," I said.

"You want to know the truth?" Luiz said. "Your brother was a beaker."

"A what?"

"A beaker. A scientist who can't get along with the others. It wasn't a privilege for him to be at our station. They were tired of him at McMurdo."

At breakfast Annabelle had bragged that she could teach me to say *asshole* in any language. If you spent enough time in Antarctica, you learned a little of everything.

"*Ojete.*" I picked up a meteorite the size of a grape and threw it at his feet. "*Ojete, Ojete.*"

Luiz looked down at the rock, unfazed. I left the tent and walked away from the station. I tried to run but kept slipping on the ice. When I finally stopped and looked back, the U-shaped building was minuscule against the vastness of the land. It was like standing in the middle of a white sea—ice in all directions, stretching into infinity. I pulled at the balaclava. I wanted to take it off but couldn't figure out how. The thought of venturing any farther was suddenly terrifying.

Annabelle had explained that most researchers came for short stints, a handful of months. Few stayed as long as a year, like my brother had. There was the feeling that nothing but the elements could touch you out here, and I understood that was something he would have appreciated. Since we had been close, I could make these kinds of calculations.

I turned in a circle, still looking. I imagined my brother trekking across the ice, fascinated by the world that existed beneath. My throat ached from the cold. My breath made white ghosts in the air. It was impossible to distinguish land from sky.

II.

It happened right after Eve's seventeenth birthday, in Concord, where she had grown up. She had been reading Jane Austen in a park and was just starting home. She remembered the soft yellow blanket rolled under her arm, the page she had dog-eared, the streaks of gold in the sky. She was on the edge of the park when she felt an arm wrap around her chest. For a moment she thought someone was giving her a hug, a classmate or a cousin. She had lots of cousins in Concord. But then there was the knife at her throat and the gray sedan with the passenger door flung open. She dropped the Jane Austen and the blanket on the sidewalk. Somewhere, she imagined, those things were in a collection of crime scene photos.

At the Burren, she stopped there. Her martini glass was empty. The band was playing a Bruce Springsteen cover. She balled up her cocktail napkin and asked if I wanted to dance. She was wearing a silk turquoise dress and T-strap heels. Her bracelet shone on her wrist. She took my hand and we dipped and twirled. Men watched us. One even tried to cut in.

Two days later I woke to the sound of my bedroom door opening. It was midnight. Eve stood in the doorway in a white nightgown. She got into bed with me and started telling me the rest,
or most of the rest. She lay on her back. I watched her lips move
in the darkness and wondered if my brother had noticed that his
wife was no longer next to him. Soon he would be departing for a
month-long research trip to study the Juan de Fuca Plate in Vancouver, leaving us in each other's care.

The man was a stranger. He was fat around the middle. He had
a brown beard and a straight white scar under his right eye. In the
car, he turned the radio to a sports station. He told her that if she
did anything—scream, jump out—he would stab her in the heart.
He drove them to a little house on a dirt road in Acton, where she
stayed for three days.

Her parents had money. She told herself that he was just going
to hold her for ransom; she didn't allow herself to consider that
maybe he had other things in mind. The thing she remembered
most vividly from the car ride was the radio, the sound of a crowd
cheering in a stadium.

"That and one of those green, tree-shaped things you hang
from the rearview mirror," she said. "To freshen the air." This explained why she hated Christmas trees, why the scent alone made
her lightheaded and queasy. On our first holiday together, she'd
told us she was allergic to pine and we'd gotten a plastic tree instead.

"How did you get away?" I asked.

"I didn't." She blinked. Her eyelashes were so pale they were
almost translucent. "I was rescued."

Eve had been half right about the man's intentions. After holding her for forty-eight hours, he placed a ransom demand; it didn't
take long for the authorities to figure out the rest. The police
found her in a basement. Her wrists were tied to a radiator with
twine. She was wearing a long white T-shirt with a pocket on the
front. She had no idea where it had come from or what had happened to her clothes. Right before she was rescued, she remembered tracking the beam of a flashlight as it moved down the wall.

In the months that followed, the man's attorney had him diag-
nosed with a dissociative disorder, something Eve had never heard
of before. He hadn't been himself when he had taken her, hadn't
been himself in Acton. That was their claim. He got seven years

and was out in five due to overcrowding. Her parents advised her to move on with her life. *He's been punished,* her father once said. *What else do you want to happen?* Now she just spoke to them on the phone every few months. They didn't even know she had gotten married.

"Where is he now?" I asked. "Do you know?"

"I've lost track of him." She tugged at the comforter. Her foot brushed against mine.

This was not a secret Eve had shared with my brother. I should have been thinking about him—how I couldn't believe he did not know about this, how he needed to know about this—but I wasn't. Instead I was trying to understand how anyone ever ventured into this world of head-on collisions and lunatic abductors and all the other things one had little hope of recovering from.

"I never went to therapy, but acting is having a therapeutic effect," she said next.

"How so?" During one of her epic phone conversations, I'd glimpsed her sprawled out on the living room sofa, painting her toenails and speaking in French. I'd picked up the landline in the kitchen, curious to know who she was talking to, but there had just been her voice and the buzz of the line. I'd wondered if it was some kind of acting exercise.

"Getting to disappear into different characters. Getting to not be myself."

I remembered her face on the stage in Medford. She was supposed to be Miranda, but her eyes had never stopped being Eve.

In time, I would learn it was possible to tell a secret but also keep a piece of it close to yourself. That was what happened with Eve, who never told me what, exactly, went on during those three days in Acton. The floor was damp concrete. He fed her water with a soupspoon. I never got much more than that.

Of course, I could only assume the worst.

The aurora australis was Luiz's idea of a peace offering. We met in the observation room after dinner. It had been dark for hours. Despite my studies in astronomy, I couldn't get over how clear the sky was in Antarctica. I'd never seen so many stars, and it was comforting to feel close to something I had once loved. Annabelle and the others had gone back to work. I still hadn't forgiven Luiz for calling my brother a beaker.

"I've had too much ice time," he said. "I've gotten too used to the way this place can swallow people up." In his first month in Antarctica, two of his colleagues hiked to a subglacial lake and fell through the ice into a cavern. By the time they were rescued, their bodies were eaten up with frostbite. One lost a hand, the other a leg.

"So it's Antarctica's fault you're an asshole?" I said.

"I blame everything on Antarctica," he said. "Just ask my ex-wife."

"Divorced!" I said. "What a surprise."

Luiz had arrived with two folded-up lounge chairs under his arms. They were made of white plastic, the kind of thing you'd expect to see at the beach. In the summer months, when there was no night, the scientists lounged on them in their snow pants and thermal shirts, a kind of Antarctic joke.

"I got them out of storage." He had arranged the chairs so they were side by side. "Just for you."

We reclined in our lounge chairs and stared through the glass. Since we were indoors, I was wearing my New Hampshire gear, the tassel hat and the leather gloves. A wisp of green light swirled above us.

"Tell me more about the explosion," I said, keeping my eyes on the sky.

The early word from the inspectors had confirmed his suspicions: a gas leak in the machine room. They were alleging questionable maintenance practices, because it was impossible to have a disaster without a cause. When the explosion happened, the three people working in the machine room were killed, along with two scientists in a nearby hallway. A researcher from Rio de Janeiro died from smoke inhalation; she and Bianca had worked together for many years. Others were hospitalized with third- and fourth-degree burns. But my brother, he should have made it out. His seismograph was on the opposite end. He'd been sleeping next to it, on a foam mattress, for God's sake. Everyone thought he was crazy.

The green light returned, brighter this time. It was halo-shaped and hovering above the observation room. I hadn't stayed with astronomy long enough to see the auroras in anything other than photos and slides. I thought back to a course in extragalactic astronomy, to the lectures on Hubble's law, and the quasars that radiated red light and the tidal pull of super-massive black holes, which terrified me. In college I had imagined myself working in remote observatories and seeing something new in the sky.

"He thought he'd found an undiscovered fault line," Luiz continued. "He was compiling his data. No one believed him. The peninsula isn't known for seismic activity. He was the only one with an office in that part of the building who didn't survive."

"Where were you during the explosion?" I watched the circle of light contract and expand.

"Outside. Scraping ice off our snow tractor."

So that was his guilt: he hadn't been close enough to believe he was going to die. He couldn't share in the trauma of having to save your own life, or the life of someone else; he could only report the facts. My brother had been too close, Luiz not close enough.

"We hadn't spoken in a long time." The halo dissolved and a sheet of luminous green spread across the horizon, at once beautiful and eerie.

"I asked him about family," Luiz said. "He didn't mention a sister."

I closed my eyes and thought about my brother in that hallway. I saw doorways alight with fire and black, curling smoke. His watch felt heavy on my wrist.

"Luiz," I said. "Do you have any secrets?"

"Too many to count." Silence fell over us in a way that made me think this was probably true. I pictured him tallying his secrets like coins. The sky hummed with green.

Later he explained the lights to me, the magnetic fields, the collision of electrons and atoms. I didn't tell him this was information I already knew. He reached for my hand and pulled off one of my gloves. He placed it on his chest and put his hand over it.

I sat up and took the glove back from him. He held on to it for a moment, smiling, before he let go.

"Of course," Luiz said. "You are married."

That afternoon I'd e-mailed my husband from the recreation room: *Still getting the lay of the land. Don't worry: polar bears are in the North Pole.* He was a real estate agent and always honest about his properties—what needed renovating, if there were difficult neighbors. He believed the truth was as easy to grasp as a baseball or a glass of water. That was why I had married him.

"Yes," I said. "But it doesn't have anything to do with that."

*

As it turned out, Eve had lied about losing track of the man who had taken her. After his release from prison, she had kept very careful track, aided by a cousin in Concord, a paralegal who had access to a private investigator. It was February when she came to me with news of him. We were sitting in a window seat and drinking tea and looking out at the snow-covered lawn. A girl passed on the sidewalk, carrying ice skates and a pink helmet.

"He's in a hospital," she said. "Down on the Cape. He might not get out. Something to do with his lungs." She sighed with her whole body.

"And?" I said.

"And I want to see him."

"Oh, Eve. I think that's a terrible idea."

"Probably." She blew on her tea. "Probably it is."

In the weeks that followed, she kept at it. She talked about it while we folded laundry and swept the front steps. She talked about it when I met her for drinks after her rehearsals—she was an understudy for a production of *Buried Child* at the American Repertory Theater—and while we rode the T, the train clacking over the tracks whenever we rose aboveground to cross the river. Eve explained that her parents had kept her from the court proceedings. She had wanted to visit him in prison, but that had been forbidden too. Now he was very sick. She was running out of chances.

"Chances for what?" We were waiting for the T in Central Square, on our way home from dinner. On the platform a man was playing a violin for change. Eve had been in rehearsals earlier and was still wearing the false eyelashes and heavy red lipstick.

"To tell him that I made it." She raised her hands. Her gold bracelet slid down her wrist. "That I'm an actress. That I got married. That he wasn't the end of me. That I won."

"How about a phone call?" I said. "Or a letter?"

The T came through the tunnel and ground to a stop. The doors opened. People spilled onto the platform. A woman carrying a sleeping child slipped between me and Eve. My brother had been in Vancouver for two weeks and called home on Sunday mornings.

"You don't understand," she said as we boarded the train. "It has to be done in person."

*

I missed the perfect chance to tell my brother everything. The day before he left for Vancouver, I went to see him at MIT. His department was housed in the Green Building, which had been constructed by a famous architect and was the tallest building in all of Cambridge. From the outside you could see a white radome on the roof. The basement level was connected to the MIT tunnel system. The first time I visited him on campus, he told me you could take the tunnels all the way to Kendall Square.

"How about some air?" I had found him hunched over a microscope. He was surprised to see me. I hadn't told him I was coming.

"I'm gone tomorrow." He gestured to the open laptops and the stacks of notebooks and the empty coffee mugs that surrounded him. Eve had been trimming his hair, and there was an unevenness to the cut that made him look like he was holding his head at a funny angle. The lenses of his glasses were smudged.

"I know," I said. "That's why I'm here."

We left campus and walked along Memorial Drive. By the river it was cold and windy. We pulled up the collars of our coats and tightened our scarves. We turned onto the Longfellow Bridge and kept going, until we were standing between two stone piers with domed roofs and tiny windows. They reminded me of medieval lookout towers. We leaned against the bridge and gazed out at the river and the city skyline beyond it.

I should have had a plan, but I didn't. Rather, the weight of Eve's secret had propelled me toward him, the way I imagined a current tugs at the objects that find their way into its waters.

"The house," my brother said. "Is everything okay there?"

Without him realizing, I felt he had become an anchor for me and Eve; we always knew he was there, in the background, and with his departure I could feel a shift looming: subtle as a change in the energy, the way the air gets damp and cool before a storm. But this was before Eve had brought up going to the Cape. I didn't know how to explain what I was feeling, or if I should even try. I couldn't imagine what the right words would be.

"Everything's fine."

"Eve says you've been like a sister," he said.

"We'll miss you," I said. "Don't forget to call."

A gust nearly carried away my hat. I pulled it down over my ears. Snow clouds were settling over the brownstones and high-rises. My brother put his arm around me and started talking about the Juan de Fuca Plate, his voice bright with excitement. I could only detect the slightest trace of a stutter. The plate was bursting with seismic activity, a hotbed of shifts and tremors. I wrapped my arms around his waist and leaned into him. With his free hand, he drew the different kinds of fault lines — listric, ring, strike-slip — in the air.

The near-constant darkness of Antarctica made my body confused about when to rest. At three in the morning I got out of bed and pulled fleece-lined boots over my flannel pajamas. I put on my gloves and hat. Annabelle was babbling in Spanish. At dinner, under the fluorescent lights of the mess hall, I'd noticed a scattering of freckles on her cheekbones and thought of Eve. I had to stop myself from reaching across the table and touching her face.

The station was quiet. The doorways were dark and shuttered. I peered through shadows at the end of hallways and around corners as if I were searching for something in particular — what that would be, I didn't know. I drifted to the front of the station. In the mud room I surveyed the red windbreakers hanging on the wall, the bundles of goggles and gloves, the rows of boots. The entrance was a large steel door with a porthole window. I thought about opening the door, just for a moment, even though the temperature outside would be deep in the negatives; I imagined my hair turning into icicles, my eyes to glass.

Through the window the station lights illuminated the outbuildings and the ice. The darkness was too thick, too absolute, to see anything more. When Luiz first told me that the rescue crew hadn't found any remains, there had been a moment when I'd thought my brother hadn't died in the explosion at all. Maybe he hadn't even been in the building. Maybe he had seen smoke rising from the land and realized this was his chance to vanish. I could picture him boarding an icebreaker and sailing to Uruguay or Cape Town. Standing on the deck of a ship and watching a new horizon emerge.

For a long time I kept watch through the window, willing myself to see a figure surface from the night. Who was to say he hadn't sailed to another land? Who was to say he wasn't somewhere in that darkness? For him, I would open the door. For him, I would endure the cold. But of course nothing was out there.

In the observation room, after the aurora australis had left the sky, I'd turned to Luiz and said, *Here's what I want.* The idea had come suddenly and with force. I wanted to go to the Brazilian station, to the site of the explosion. At first Luiz said it was impossible; it would involve chartering a helicopter, for one thing. I told him that if he could figure out a way to make this happen, I'd be on the next flight to New Zealand. I didn't care how much it cost. He promised to see what he could do.

I left the window and slipped back into the hallway. A light had been left on in the recreation room. I sat in the armchair next to the phone. I'd tucked my calling card into my pajama pocket, thinking I might phone my husband. Instead I dialed the number of the house in Davis Square, which I still knew by heart. The phone rang five times before someone answered. I'd thought a machine might come on and I could leave whoever lived there now a message about polar bears and green lights in the sky. For a moment I imagined my sister-in-law picking up. *Où avez-vous été?* she would say. *Where have you been?*

A woman answered. Her voice was high and uncertain, not at all like Eve's. I pressed the phone against my ear. I pulled on the cord and thought about fault lines. I could see a dark streak running down my ribs, a fissure in my sternum.

"Hello?" she said. Static flared on the line. "How can I help you?"

III.

It was a military hospital, just outside Barnstable. The morning we left, Eve talked to my brother on the phone and said we were going to see the glass museum in Sandwich. I drove. She was dressed in jeans and a gray sweatshirt, unadorned by jewelry, the plainest I'd ever seen her. She rested her socked feet on the dashboard and told me what her cousin had discovered about this man. He'd been in the military, dishonorably discharged. Years ago he'd been involved with a real estate scam involving fraudulent mortgages and the elderly, but pleaded out of jail time. He had two restraining orders in his file.

"I'm surprised someone hasn't killed him already." She cracked the window. The air was heavy with moisture and salt.

We drove through Plymouth and Sandwich. From the highway I saw a billboard ad for the glass museum. At the hospital—a labyrinthine gray building just off the highway—we learned he was in the ICU. We pretended to be family.

He was in a room with two other men. A thin curtain hung between each of the beds. Eve slowly walked from one to the other. The first patient was gazing at the TV bolted to the wall. The second was drinking orange juice from a straw. The third was asleep. He wore a white hospital gown. His gray hair was shorn close to the scalp. One hand rested on his stomach, the other on the mattress. I followed Eve to his bedside. His face was speckled with broken capillaries, his cheekbones sharp, his slender forearms bruised. He was on oxygen and attached to a heart monitor. I smelled something sour.

"Are you sure this is him?" I asked Eve, even though I could see the scar. It was just as she had described: a thin line of white under his eye.

"Don't say it." She walked over to the window and looked out at the parking lot.

"Say what?"

"That's he's old and frail and defenseless." Eve turned from the window. "He's not like that at all. Not on the inside." She pressed her fist against her chest.

She slumped down on the linoleum floor. A nurse was attending to the patient next to us. I watched her shadow through the curtain. She carried away a tray with an empty glass on it. She told the man who had been drinking the juice to have a nice day.

"So what do we do now?" I asked. "Wake him up?"

"I'm thinking," Eve said. "I'm thinking of what to do."

It took her a long time to do her thinking. I listened to the din of the TV. I thought a game show was on from the way people kept calling out numbers.

Finally Eve jumped up and started digging through her purse. She took out a tube of lipstick, the garish red color she wore onstage, and raised it like a prize.

"Okay," she said. "I have my first idea."

She uncapped the lipstick and went to the sleeping man. She smeared color across his mouth. I stood on the other side of his bed and stared down, trying to see the evil in him. Eve used the lipstick to rouge his cheeks before passing it to me. I drew red half-circles above his eyebrows. We waited for him to wake up, to cry for help, but he only made a faint gurgling sound. His hand twitched on his stomach. That was all.

"Now I have another idea," Eve said.

For this second thing she wanted to be alone. I looked at the clown's face we had given this man. My stomach felt strange. On the intercom, a doctor was being paged to surgery.

"Five minutes. Three hundred seconds." Her face was free of makeup, her freckles visible. She'd had her teeth bleached recently and they looked unnaturally white. "That's all I'm asking for, Lee."

After what had happened to her, wasn't she owed five minutes alone with him? That was my thinking at the time. On my way out of the ICU, the same nurse who had picked up the juice glass asked me if I'd had a pleasant visit.

I waited on the sidewalk. I watched people come and go through the automatic doors. An old man on crutches. An old man in a wheelchair. A nurse in lavender scrubs. What was the worst thing these people had done?

Eve stayed in the hospital for fifty-seven minutes. I couldn't bring myself to go back inside. I paced in the cold. I had forgotten my gloves and my hands were going numb. Even though I'd never smoked in my life, I asked a doctor smoking outside if I could bum a cigarette.

"These things will kill you." The doctor winked and flipped open his cigarette pack.

When Eve emerged from the hospital, she took my hand and pulled me toward the car. We drove in silence. She rested her head against the window. When I tried to turn on the radio, she touched my wrist. Her fingertips were waxy with lipstick.

"Please," she said.

After a half-hour on the road, I exited at Sagamore Beach. The silence felt like a pair of hands around my throat. Eve didn't object when I parked in the designated beach lot, empty on account of its being February, or when we climbed over dunes and through sea grass. Cold sand leaked into our shoes. I didn't stop until I reached water.

We were standing on the edge of Cape Cod Bay. The water was still and gray. Clusters of rock extended into the bay like fingers. A white mist hung over us. A freighter was visible in the distance.

"Why didn't you come out when you said you would?" The freighter was moving farther away. When it vanished from sight, it looked like it had gone into a cloud. "What were you doing in there?"

"We were talking." Her face was dewy from the mist. Her pale hair had frizzed. She picked up a white stone and threw it into the water.

"So he woke up?"

"Yes," she said. "He did and then he didn't."

She picked up another stone. It was gray with a black dot in the center. She held on to it for a little while, turning it over in her hands, before it went into the bay.

In Cambridge she wanted to be dropped at the Repertory Theater. She had to tell the director that she couldn't make rehearsal; she promised to come home soon. Her hair was still curled from being at the beach. Her cheeks and forehead were damp. I tried to determine if anything had shifted in her eyes.

I idled on Brattle Street until Eve had gone into the theater. Her purse swung from her shoulder, and somewhere inside it was that lipstick. I kept telling myself that the most dangerous part was over. We were home now. Everything would be the same as before.

But no. Nothing would be the same as before. Eve never talked to her director. She never returned to the house. I had to call my brother and tell him to come home from Vancouver. When I picked him up at the airport, it was late. I waited in baggage claim. Long before he noticed me, I spotted him coming down the escalator, a duffel bag slung over his shoulder. He had lost weight. His hair had grown out. I remember thinking that I wished I knew him better, that I wished we'd taken the time to learn how to talk to each other. When he finally saw me, he tried to call out, *Lee*, but his stutter was as bad as it had been in childhood. It took him three tries to say my name.

A report was filed. Eve's parents—a frail, bookish couple —came into town from Concord. An investigation went on for weeks. There was no sign of Eve, no sign of foul play. As gently as he could, the detective asked us to consider the possibility that she had run away. Apparently women—young mothers, young wives —did this more frequently than people might think. I told everyone I'd dropped Eve at the theater, but the truth stopped there. Every time I tried to say more, I felt like a stone was lodged in my throat.

Because I was his sister, because we had been close, my brother knew I was holding something back. He pressed me for information. Had she been taking an inordinate amount of calls? Had anything peculiar arrived in the mail? Was she having an affair with a castmate? Had we really gone to the glass museum in Sandwich? I submitted to these questions, even though I didn't—couldn't, I felt at the time—always tell the truth. And I knew he was confronting his own failing, the fact that he hadn't cared to know any of this until after his wife was gone.

We waited months before we packed up her belongings: the silk dresses, the shoes, the jewelry, the plays. Her possessions had always seemed rich and abundant, but only filled three cardboard boxes. My brother kept them stacked at the foot of his bed. When he moved, two boxes went to Eve's parents and he took the other one with him. I don't know what happened to her things after that.

The last time he asked me a question about Eve, we were on the front porch. It was late spring. The trees were blooming green and white. I was in a rocking chair. My brother was leaning against the porch railing, facing the street.

"Do you think you knew her better than I did?" he said.

"No." Once I had come upon them in the upstairs hallway: they were pressed against the wall, kissing, and he was twisting one of Eve's wrists behind her back. It was clear that the pleasure was mutual, which led me to believe that she might enjoy a degree of pain. Only my brother could say how much.

He stared out at the glowing streetlights. I could tell from the way he licked his lips and squeezed the railing that he did not believe me.

By summer we had moved into separate apartments: his on Beacon Hill, so he could be closer to MIT; mine in the North End, scrunched between a pastry shop and a butcher. I bounced from one entry-level lab job to another, my ambition dulled, while I watched my brother pull his own disappearing act: into his dissertation; into the conference circuit; into one far-flung expedition after another. The Philippines, Australia, Haiti. Antarctica. The phone calls and postcards turned from weekly to monthly to hardly at all.

I got married the year I turned thirty. My brother came, but left before the cake was served. It was too painful, watching the night unfold; I understood this without his ever saying so. I only told my husband that he had been married briefly and years ago we'd all lived together in Davis Square. Soon I had a child. I worked part-time as a lab assistant, sorting someone else's data, and cared for him, which was not the life I'd imagined for myself, but it seemed like a fair exchange: I hadn't kept sufficient watch over Eve, hadn't kept her from danger. This was my chance to make it up. I tried to tell myself she was someplace far away and happy. I tried to forget that she might have been in trouble, that she might have needed us. When I looked at my son, I tried not to think about all the things I could never tell him. I tried to shake the feeling that I was living someone else's life.

In the years to come I would start so many letters to my brother, each one beginning in a different way: *Eve was not who you thought,* and *I don't know how it all started,* and *How could you not have known?* I never got very far because I knew I was still lying. The letter I finally finished—addressed to the McMurdo station but never mailed—opened with *None of this was your fault.*

Another thing I never told him: before leaving the house in Davis Square, I cut open one of Eve's boxes and found her gold bracelet in a tiny plastic bag. The chain was tarnished. I popped open the locket; the frames were empty. I took the bracelet and resealed the box with packing tape. I held on to it—never wearing it, always hiding it away, even before there were people to hide it from. My husband found it once, and I said it had been a gift from my mother. I imagined other people discovering the bracelet through the years and telling each one a different story. I would carry it with me to Antarctica, tucked in the side pocket of my suitcase, though I was never able to bring it out into the open.

Not long after Eve's disappearance, I looked up the name of her abductor on a computer: Randall Smith. I'd only heard her say it aloud once, in the hospital. After a little searching, I found an obituary. He had died the day after our visit, survived by no one. The obituary said it was natural causes, which explained nothing.

It was twilight when we flew over Admiralty Bay. Luiz said that if I watched the water carefully, I might see leopard seals. The pilot was from the Netherlands, hired for a price that would horrify my husband when the check posted. Luiz's boss had gotten wind of our expedition and wasn't at all pleased; that morning he'd called from Brazil and told Luiz that he was not in the business of es-

corting tourists. Soon I would have to get on the plane to New
Zealand, as I had promised, but I wasn't completely out of time.

The landscape was different on the peninsula. The ice was
sparser, exposing the rocky peaks of mountains and patches of
black soil near the coastline. When the explosion site came into
view, it looked like a dark scar on the snow.

The helicopter touched down. Black headsets swallowed our
ears, muffling the sound of the propellers. The helicopter swayed
as it landed. I could feel the engine rumbling beneath us; it made
my skin vibrate inside my many layers of clothes. Luiz got out first,
then helped me onto the ice. The pilot shouted something in
Dutch, which Luiz translated: soon the twilight would be gone; he
didn't want to fly back in the dark.

Together we approached the wreckage. Luiz still had his headset on. I had taken mine off too soon and now my ears buzzed. Up
close, the site was smaller than I'd expected: a black rectangle the
size of the swimming pool I took my son to in the summer. Nothing of the structure remained except for metal beams jutting from
ridges of ash and debris. The sky was a golden haze.

"I told you there wasn't much to see." He slipped off his headset. His face was covered except for his eyes. I was wearing a balaclava too and knew I looked the same.

"Tell me what it was like before."

The station had been shaped like a horseshoe. He pointed to
the empty spaces where the mess hall used to be, the dormitories,
the bathroom, my brother's seismograph. Their base had been
smaller than Belgrano. They didn't have an observation room or
heated research tents. Everything had been contained under one
roof.

I stepped in the ash and listened to it crunch under my boots. I
passed black spears of wood and warped beams. One section of the
site was even more charred, the ground scooped in. I stood inside
the depression and looked at the bits of metal glinting in the ash.
I picked up something the size of a quarter. I wasn't sure what it
had been before; the fire had made it glossy and flat. I slipped it
into my pocket and kept walking. I told myself it was evidence; I
just didn't know what kind.

The wind blew flurries of ash around my legs. On the other end
of the site, I looked for some sign of my brother's seismograph. I
came across a spoon, the handle melted into a glob of metal, and

a lighter. I put those things in my pockets too. More evidence. Luiz was still on the edge of the site. By then I understood he was someone who had no desire to go searching for things. He didn't even collect the meteorites; his only concern was classifying them. The helicopter would be ready for us soon, but the sky still held a dull glow.

There were so many times when I wanted to tell my brother everything—when, in the middle of the night, I wanted to kneel by his bed and whisper, *I have a secret.* In Cambridge, I'd told myself these were Eve's secrets to keep or expose; it was her life to walk away from, if that's what she wanted. And the more time that passed, the more unimaginable the truth seemed. To admit one lie would mean admitting another and then another.

I imagined myself at home in New Hampshire, arranging everything on the living room floor. A map of Antarctica, with stars to mark the bases: McMurdo; here; Belgrano. My brother's watch. Eve's empty locket. The photo he mailed, without a note, when he first arrived in Antarctica. He was wearing a yellow snow suit and standing outside McMurdo, surrounded by bright white ice. Around these materials I would place the metals I had collected at the site and try to see something: a pattern, a sign. Or maybe I would just read aloud the last letter I wrote to him. Or maybe, in the helicopter, I would turn to Luiz and tell him everything.

The sky was almost dark. I was back inside the depression. I was sitting down in it and hugging my knees. I had no memory of walking over there and stepping into the hole; I had just done it automatically. Luiz was calling to me. The wind carried his voice away.

Maybe it was just an iguana, I heard my brother say.

In Antarctica, I did not know if he had denied himself the chance to get out of the burning building. I did not know what he believed I knew, or what would have changed if I'd given him the truth. I did not know if I would ever see Eve again. I did not know what had happened in that hospital room, or in Acton. Some of these things I did not know not because they were unknowable, but because I had turned away from the knowledge. In Antarctica, I decided that was the worst thing I'd ever done, that refusal.

The stars were coming out. Luiz was crossing the site, waving and calling my name. The temperature was dropping. My eyes watered. I sank deeper into the hole.

In Antarctica, I did not know that a month after I left, Luiz would become trapped in a whiteout and lose two fingers to frostbite. I did not know that the tibia would turn out to have belonged to my brother, that it would be shipped back to America in a metal box. I did not know if one day I would disappear and no one except a missing woman and a dead man would be able to tell the people who loved me why.

Contributors' Notes

Other Distinguished Mystery Stories of 2013

Contributors' Notes

Megan Abbott is the Edgar Award–winning author of seven novels, including *The Fever* and *Dare Me*. Her stories have appeared in collections including *Detroit Noir, Best Crime and Mystery Stories of the Year, Queens Noir, Wall Street Noir,* and *The Speed Chronicles*. She is also the author of *The Street Was Mine*, a study of hardboiled fiction and film noir, and *A Hell of a Woman*, a female crime fiction anthology. She has been nominated for awards including the Crime Writers Association's Steel Dagger, the *Los Angeles Times* Book Prize, the Pushcart Prize, and the Hammett Prize. She lives in Queens, New York.

  ▪ The idea for "My Heart Is Either Broken" came straight from the front page of the *New York Daily News*. The headline of the day was the acquittal of Casey Anthony, the Florida woman charged in the death of her two-year-old daughter. For months the tabloids had been writhing over the case, painting Anthony as a demonic party girl or a down-market femme fatale. The front-page photo that day depicted Anthony, hair pulled back in a prim ponytail, donning the pale pink buttoned-up shirt of a devout schoolgirl. The *News* editors, however, had clearly chosen the image for a reason, because for all the demure restraint of the outfit, Anthony had been snapped smiling in a way that, given the paper's coverage of her, can only be described as witchy. Dangerous. The actual facts of the case are complicated, the trial was troubled—but what interested me was how Anthony's behavior was the media focus. She did not "act" as a distraught mother should after her daughter's disappearance, and she wasn't performing the role of "unjustly accused" now. I began to think about how much our expectations of how grief, trauma, and maternal love are expressed rule the way we view guilt or innocence. And about the special fear we have of mothers who don't seem to love their children the way we want them to, or at least don't know how to play the part for us.

Daniel Alarcón's books include *War by Candlelight*, a finalist for the 2005
PEN/Hemingway Award, and *Lost City Radio*, named a Best Novel of the
Year by the *San Francisco Chronicle* and the *Washington Post*. He is executive
producer of Radio Ambulante.org, a Spanish-language narrative journalism podcast. In 2010 *The New Yorker* named him one of the twenty best writers under forty, and his most recent novel, *At Night We Walk in Circles*, was a
finalist for the 2014 PEN/Faulkner Award.

   ▪ This story came together after years visiting the prison known as Lu-
rigancho, on the outskirts of Lima. I went inside for the first time in 2007
and have been returning ever since, never quite knowing what I am doing
there or what keeps drawing me back to that place. In 2009 I taught a writing workshop there, and eventually, in 2011, I pitched a piece to *Harper's*
about life in the drug trafficking block. "Collectors" is based on the material gathered on that reporting trip. In this case, the spark was an offhand
comment by an inmate, who began musing about the prison's collection of
terrible odors. He said it half jokingly, and then mentioned the worst smell
of all: the smell of sex when you weren't having any. I asked him to explain,
and he did. The story was eye-opening. I knew I had to do something with
that.

Jim Allyn is a graduate of Alpena Community College and the University
of Michigan, where he earned a master's degree in journalism. While at
Michigan he won a Hopwood Creative Writing Award, Major Novel Division, and the Detroit Press Club Foundation Student Grant Award for
the best writing in a college newspaper or periodical. Upon graduation
he pursued a career in health-care marketing and communication. He
recently retired as vice president of marketing and community relations
at Elkhart General Healthcare System in Elkhart, Indiana. His first short
story, "The Tree Hugger," appeared in *Ellery Queen's Mystery Magazine* in
1995, and four others have been published by *EQMM* since then. He is
a U.S. Naval Air Force veteran, having served aboard the aircraft carrier
U.S.S. *Intrepid*.

   ▪ About 250 miles north of Detroit, on the shores of Lake Huron, sits
the tiny village of Black River, Michigan. The mouth of the river, not a
major artery but a narrow trout stream, is right there in the village. My
family's 200-acre wilderness retreat in the Great North Woods—known to
us simply as "Camp"—is situated about 2 miles upstream on the Black. On
the western edge of our property, on the river's highest bank, is a cemetery,
a rustic spot under a tall jack pine fenced off by cedar poles. It is the place
where for the past sixty years we have buried creatures with nobler hearts
than ours.

   An odd assortment of aging small wood and stone markers carry the
names of the buried friends, companions, and fellow hunters who made

the journey with us. Donda, the matriarch of a clan of blooded German shorthair pointers that we grew up with . . . Misty, Daisy Mae, Tiger Jones, Lady Mike. And other wonderful shorthairs . . . Zipper, Shoshone, Roadie, Bonnie Brown, Max. And there's Little Dog, aka Sweet Pea, a wonderfully affectionate Manchester toy terrier with a warrior's heart who waded among the giant shorthairs absolutely unafraid. There's Jeremy, a little mixed-breed who fiercely defended my son Brodie even if I was just trying to kiss him goodnight. The cemetery's patriarch is Smokey Joe, a Labrador retriever who romped with us in the big lake on the summer side of life.

But in this quiet resting place on Black River all are not here who should be here. Two are missing: Jenny Wren and McGill. I buried them on a restored farm near Ann Arbor about forty years ago. Sometimes life grabs you by the throat and it's all you can do just to hold on. McGill and Jenny died during such a time, and I just wasn't able to make the trip north to Camp. A white-collar nomad, I sold the house and was long gone to Illinois and then Indiana. Over the years I resolved that at some point I would return for Jenny Wren and McGill. That would involve knocking on the door, trying to explain myself to strangers, and, if allowed, seeing if I could even find the graves after all this time. As I contemplated this, it struck me that it was an unusual thing to do and could be a story. But if a beloved pet is really in the grave, it's not a mystery. So what if something else was buried there, something dark and sinister? What would it be and who would bury it?

The story I will eventually tell to the current occupants of my old farmhouse will resonate very strongly with the story that serial killer Lyle Collins spins out to Derek and Parveen Lane. The motives Collins lies about will be my real motives.

The story's title, emerging as it does at the end, is how it emerged in real life. I was doing my final edit — the story was done and entitled "Princess Jenny" — when I applied the standard of criminal behavior, which holds that you always look for patterns. Hence a second grave — "Princess Anne." The story for Jim Howard ends as he's walking back to his Jeep, parked at the church. The nonfiction story will end when Jenny Wren and McGill come home to Camp.

Jodi Angel is the author of two collections of short stories. Her first collection, *The History of Vegas,* was published in 2005 and was named a *San Francisco Chronicle* Best Book of 2005 as well as a *Los Angeles Times Book Review* Discovery. Her second collection, *You Only Get Letters from Jail,* which includes "Snuff," was named a Best Book of 2013 by *Esquire* and a Notable New Release by the *New York Times.* Angel's work has appeared in *Esquire, Tin House, One Story, Zoetrope: All-Story,* and *Byliner,* among other publications and anthologies. Her stories have received several Pushcart Prize nominations, and "A Good Deuce" was named as a distinguished story in

The Best American Short Stories 2012. Angel grew up in northern California —in a family of girls.

▪ I have always romanticized the 1970s, and one aspect of that decade that fascinated me was the urban legend that developed around snuff films and whether they are real. I wanted to write a story about a snuff film, but what came out was not really a story about a snuff film but a story about a brother and sister who are involved in a car accident on a deserted back-country road. Because my stories are from the point of view of teenage narrators, the journey from innocence to experience often takes place under the surface of everything else that goes on, but in "Snuff" I deviate from that a little bit by having the narrator come to the story as having already lost his innocence by watching the "could be" snuff film at his buddy Billy's house, so the character who actually makes the journey to experience during the story is the narrator's sister, Charlotte. "Snuff" is a story about sex and violence and appearances versus realities—much of what drives the snuff-film myth—and about how who Charlotte wants to be isn't who she is. It's going to take more than a pocket knife and a bad situation to change that fact, but in her innocence, she believes it could be just that easy. Charlotte loses her innocence by the end of the story, but like most losses, it's a painful process.

Russell Banks is the prizewinning author of seventeen books of fiction, including the novels *Continental Drift* and *Cloudsplitter*, both finalists for the Pulitzer Prize. Two of his novels, *Affliction* and *The Sweet Hereafter*, have been made into critically acclaimed, award-winning films. He has published six collections of short stories, most recently *A Permanent Member of the Family* (2013), which includes "Former Marine." His work is widely translated, and in 2010 he was made an Officier de l'Ordre des Arts et des Lettres by the minister of culture of France. He is the former president of the International Parliament of Writers and a member of the American Academy of Arts and Letters. He was the New York State Author from 2004 to 2008 and in 2014 was inducted into the New York Writers' Hall of Fame. He resides in upstate New York and Miami Beach, Florida.

▪ In the fall of 2011, after having written three novels in a row and no short stories, I decided to take a break from the long form while the well refilled (with the hope that it would indeed refill) and return to the short form for a while. I went back over my notebooks and culled a dozen sketches, ideas, notions, scraps, and yellowing newspaper articles I'd saved during the previous decade. Then I sat down and over the next year wrote the twelve stories that became *A Permanent Member of the Family*, which opens with "Former Marine." Among the notes and clippings that generated the stories was a one-paragraph news account of a man in his seventies who had gone on a bank-robbing spree in Illinois and had been caught and turned in by his son, who happened to be a police officer. There was nothing about why an old man would suddenly become a bank robber, and nothing about the moral crisis his son the cop must have faced on discovering that his dad had a secret life as a criminal. I wrote the story as a way of penetrating those twinned mysteries—maybe the only way I could penetrate them. Of course, it's in the nature of fiction, perhaps all art, that when you gain access to a mystery, you are inevitably led beyond it to a still deeper mystery. In this case, perhaps it's the mystery of a father's complex need for his sons' love and respect, something I've never experienced directly, having fathered only daughters (four of them). One of the many reasons we write and read stories and novels, I believe, is to experience what the narrow, happenstance circumstances of our lives have denied us. Though I've never robbed a bank, I've had secrets and been found out, like Connie, and I've accidentally uncovered a few of my parents' secrets, like Connie's sons, Jack and his two law-enforcement brothers. But I've never had to arrange my life so that it could be both forgiven by my sons and respected by them. Except in fiction.

James Lee Burke was born in 1936 and has published thirty-three novels and two collections of short stories. His most recent work is the novel *Wayfaring Stranger*, a story of the Great Depression and Bonnie and Clyde and Benny Siegel and the Battle of the Ardennes and the postwar oil boom along the Gulf Coast. He and his wife of fifty-four years, Pearl Burke, live on a ranch in western Montana. They have four children, one of whom is the novelist Alafair Burke.

▪ I wrote this story as a tribute to the migrant workers and drifters and roustabouts I knew many years ago in the Deep South and the American West. High school and college history books contain little if any information about bindlestiffs and the IWW and individuals such as Woody Guthrie and Cisco Houston and Emma Goldman and Elizabeth Flynn and Joe Hill and all those who fought the good fight for working people everywhere. The story was also meant as an allegory, and calls to mind Jesus' last statement to his followers, namely, to love one another. The story is set in a magical land, one where the stars look like a snow shower arching over the mountains and where rocks creak and murmur to one another under the water. I hope my story measures up. The story of the American West is an epic one. Kerouac caught it better than anyone I can think of. I'd like to think I caught at least a small piece of it.

Patricia Engel is the author of *It's Not Love, It's Just Paris* and *Vida*, which was a *New York Times* Notable Book of the Year and a finalist for the PEN/ Hemingway and Young Lions fiction awards. Her fiction has appeared in *The Atlantic, A Public Space, Boston Review, Harvard Review,* and numerous other publications and anthologies and has received various honors, including a fellowship from the National Endowment for the Arts. She lives in Miami.

▪ I was watching a documentary-style crime show on television about a girl who was kidnapped on her way home from a rock concert when I got the idea for "Aida." I was touched in particular by the expressions on the parents' faces as they spoke of their daughter, whose remains were eventually found. I was haunted by their words for a long time, and a series of images came to me, of a girl who'd been sheltered and protected from the world by her loving family, only to be stolen from her life forever. I was especially interested in showing how the brutal interruption of a tragedy, like an abduction, can affect a family whose emotional life already hangs in the balance, and how this particular family, which considered themselves a culture unto themselves, would respond to the loss. The voice of Salma, Aida's twin, came to me early on, and I knew that their bond would be crucial to the telling. For me, the focus was less on the details of Aida's disappearance and more on how the loss of a child can cause the family unit to disintegrate, and also how a small-town community responds or absolves itself of the crimes experienced by one of its own, or in this case by a family who were always considered outsiders.

Ernest Finney writes stories and novels. His short fiction has received a number of awards, among them an O. Henry first prize for "Peacocks." His books include four novels, *Winterchill, Lady with the Alligator Purse, Words of My Roaring,* and *California Time,* and three story collections, *Birds Landing, Flights in the Heavenlies,* and *Sequoia Gardens: California Stories.* He has just finished a novel with Dwight Smith of "The Wrecker" as its main character.

▪ I had nothing better to do, so when a friend asked if I wanted to take a ride, I got into the cab of his wrecker. For the next five hours I watched Jack work down some bank's list, repossessing eight cars, three pickup trucks, and one powerboat despite various attempts to thwart him: one guy with a machete but most with fists or fingernails. My story "The Wrecker" grew out of that afternoon. Jamie, the babe, was part fantasy, part good luck.

Roxane Gay is the author of three books, *Ayiti, An Untamed State,* and *Bad Feminist.* Her work has also appeared in *The Best American Short Stories 2012,* the *New York Times Book Review, Oxford American, West Branch,* and others. She lives and writes in the Midwest.

▪ My first novel, *An Untamed State,* is about a kidnapping, and when I wrote "I Will Follow You," the idea of people being stolen from their lives was still very much on my mind. This story began with thinking about two sisters with an uncanny bond, and as I imagined their relationship, I wanted to know more about how that bond had developed, what they had seen and endured together, and how they were trying to move forward. I live in a small town with a courthouse at the center of the town square. One afternoon I found myself standing in front of the courthouse, watching people trickle in and out of the building, and I knew that one of the sisters had been married in a courthouse like that, surrounded by such a strange swath of humanity. I'm also a movie buff, so I knew the other sister would be involved with a guy who was so obsessed with movies he couldn't really interact normally with anyone. I kept imagining the various elements of the story and the characters, and finally I put it all together.

Michelle Butler Hallett is the author of the novels *Deluded Your Sailors, Sky Waves, Double-blind,* and the short story collection *The Shadow Side of Grace.* Her short stories have been anthologized in *The Vagrant Revue of New Fiction, Hard Ol' Spot, Everything Is So Political,* and *Running the Whale's Back.* Her novel *Double-blind,* a study of complicity and love narrated by an American psychiatrist working under MK-Ultra protocol during the Cold War, was shortlisted for the 2007 Sunburst Award.

▪ I write about power and morality, and I often write about captivities. "Bush-Hammer Finish" took spark from the terrible death of Canadian poet Pat Lowther in 1975. Married to an increasingly unstable man, Lowther was just getting serious critical attention for her work when her husband killed her as she slept. He beat in her skull with a hammer and then dumped her body in a creek that she liked. I knew and greatly admired Lowther's work before I found out how she died. It haunts me. I've wanted to write about her somehow for years, but she was a real person who left behind children and friends who love and miss her. Writing about Pat Lowther as Pat Lowther felt like a terrible intrusion, something I had no right to do. Yet . . . yet the story did not free me. I know next to nothing about Vancouver in the early 1970s, but I do know a fair bit about present-day St. John's, so I tried approaching a similar storyline in a context I better understood.

The beginning of evil is the moment when one person dehumanizes another. The misogyny at work in Lowther's death, the idea that a woman can be a possession, something to be kept or thrown away, remains: a blight, a danger, a poison.

Charlaine Harris has been writing novels and short stories for thirty-five years. She has won numerous awards in several genres, but she considers mystery her home base. Her best-known work, the Sookie Stackhouse novels, were adapted by Alan Ball into the HBO series *True Blood.* Charlaine has one husband, three children, two grandchildren, and several dogs. She lives in a house on a cliff in Texas.

▪ When I was showering one morning, I noticed that I had developed a procedure for getting clean, without conscious planning. Left shoulder first, then face, then right shoulder, and so on. I became aware that my routine was so fixed that I'd never even recognized it. I began wondering what it would take to blast that routine to smithereens. Since I'm naturally prone to imagine the worst possible scenario, I thought, *What if someone tried to kill me while I was trimming my hair?* Of course I'd be totally thrown off base. But what if there was a woman who wasn't? What if the interruption was more of an annoyance than a complete surprise? What if she *expected* someone to try to kill her and she was quite capable of dealing with the situation? Anne DeWitt began to take shape in my mind. What kind of job would such a woman take, a job where she could exercise her formidable skills? Why, she'd be a high school principal, of course . . .

Joseph Heller (1923–1999) was an American novelist, short story writer, and playwright. He was neither a prolific nor a successful writer, with the notable exception of his satirical novel *Catch-22* (1961), which was an international bestseller and a popular motion picture. Its title has become part of the English language, referring to a perplexing circle in which the most logical decision is still an absurd, no-win choice. It tells the story of Captain Joseph Yossarian and his attempt to avoid serving in World War II by pretending to be insane. His plan is thwarted by the doctor's argument that if he were truly mad, he would risk his life and seek to fight additional missions. Alternatively, if he were sane, he would be able to follow orders, so he could be sent to fight more missions.

▪ *A note from Andrew Gulli, editor of* The Strand Magazine, *which first published this story:* Literary treasure hunts are glamorous and exciting— on the surface. I've gone on several, and whenever I'm asked what it's like to find an unpublished gem, I often leave out the frustrations and disappointments. You start by searching the archives of a legendary— though now departed—writer, and if you're lucky, you'll find an undiscovered one. Then a few things might happen: the work will be unreadable, the manuscript incomplete, the handwriting hard to decipher, or, after you bypass these hurdles, the literary estate will decide it doesn't want the gem (which you've dedicated weeks or months to searching for) ever to see the light of day. In the case of "Almost Like Christmas," I was fortunate. I chose the story over seven other unpublished pieces by Heller that I found; the manuscript was typo-free; and Heller's estate was so easygoing I thought I'd died and gone to editor's heaven. On top of that, it's classic Heller. Rich with the author's trademark cynicism about the dark recesses of human nature, it also creates an atmosphere of tension and suspense that had me quickly turning pages to the tragic denouement.

David H. Ingram's love of writing began early in his life in his hometown of Ontario, Canada, when he won two short story contests while still in high school. After a detour into the theater, where for a couple of decades he was an actor, director, and music composer for a touring company, he returned to writing. His first mystery story, "A Good Man of Business," was published in *Ellery Queen's Mystery Magazine* and won the Robert L. Fish Award for 2012. Since then he has had several short stories published, including one by the *Journal of Legal Education* in an online addition to its first fiction issue. Along with writing fiction, Ingram is a book reviewer for *Suspense Magazine*. He is currently marketing his first novel. He lives in Illinois with his wife, who is the minister of a church.

▪ I'm an eclectic history buff. My interests run from Alexander the Great and the Roman Caesars to current events. A subsection that has always fascinated me is how natural disasters and weather affect history. Having lived through a hurricane myself—a small one named David— I've read and researched historic storms, such as the Great New England Hurricane of 1938 and the Labor Day storm in the Florida Keys. The most devastating event was the 1900 Galveston hurricane, the deadliest storm in U.S. history. The death estimates vary widely, but the lowest estimate is six thousand, more than twice the toll of the next deadliest storm on record. In the storm's aftermath, newspapers reported at first that the death toll was five hundred—not because they didn't know that it was larger, but because they didn't think the public would believe the actual number.

Arrogance played a large part in increasing the number of people who were killed. Forecasters in Cuba, a country recently acquired by the United States in the Spanish-American War, correctly projected the hurricane's path. However, the U.S. Weather Service considered Cuba to be a backward nation, in spite of the Cubans' years of experience with hurricanes. The Weather Service projected that the storm would take an easterly track, and it clung to that forecast even as Galveston was being ravaged.

In a sense, the inhabitants of Galveston were like the passengers on the *Titanic.* At the beginning of the twentieth century, Galveston was the seat of financial power in Texas, rivaling New York City and Newport in the number of millionaires within its borders. People built homes only a few feet above sea level, confident that a low-pressure system off the coast would always turn away hurricanes. After the storm, Galveston never regained its prominence in financial dominance, losing that honor to Houston.

This was the first storm to have its devastation captured by motion pictures. A photographic team from Thomas Edison's film company was nearby and made its way to Galveston after the storm. The footage can be seen on YouTube. If you want to know more about what happened, I heartily recommend Eric Larson's wonderful book *Isaac's Storm.*

I have my wife to thank for planting the seed that grew into "The Covering Storm." While I was reading about the hurricane, she said, "Why don't you use it as the setting for a mystery?" Why not indeed? Before the storm there was no shortage of hubris among Galveston's upper crust. Its inhabitants were unaware of what was happening as the hurricane approached. I personalized these traits in the characters I created, and "The Covering Storm" is the result.

Ed Kurtz is the author of *A Wind of Knives*, *The Forty-Two*, and *Angel of the Abyss*. His short fiction has appeared in *Thuglit*, *Needle*, *Shotgun Honey*, and numerous anthologies. He lives in Texas, where he is at work on his next project. Visit him online at www.edkurtz.net.

▪ "A Good Marriage" is an exploration of the limits of sin and penance, in this case of the domestic variety. Its protagonist is not an innocent man, and as such is the recipient of tremendous mistrust and no small amount of grave disapproval—but these punishments come with a cost far greater than the misconducts they reprove. The husband's crime, however, is never acquitted, and indeed made worse in his failure to remain faithful (compounded by his fear to walk away from his wife's terrorizing efforts to force a patently bad marriage to at least appear like a good one). It is a story about broken people breaking each other, taken to extreme conclusions, but apart from that I think perhaps uncomfortably familiar to many. And despite its horrific elements, "A Good Marriage" is at its heart a noir tale—and what could be more noir than the precarious dichotomy of closeness and distance in a marriage? Particularly one in which such intimate personal information could be used so destructively by one entrusted with said knowledge. There is, perhaps, no more dangerous an enemy than one that a person has already let into the walls of his or her proverbial fortress. When Michael Corleone said, "Keep your friends close but your enemies closer," one wonders whether his own troubled marriage came to mind! Sin and penance can and perhaps do often ebb and flow over the course of a given relationship's years, should it endure enough of them. That was my starting point when writing this particular piece, and taken to the lengths it goes—well, perhaps take it as a gentle warning to sleep with one eye open, all you lovers out there.

Matthew Neill Null is a writer from West Virginia, a graduate of the Iowa Writers' Workshop, and a winner of the O. Henry Award and the Mary McCarthy Prize in short fiction. His stories have appeared in *Oxford American*, *Ploughshares*, *Mississippi Review*, *American Short Fiction*, *West Branch*, and *PEN/O. Henry Prize Stories 2011*. He has received writing fellowships from the Fine Arts Work Center, the University of Iowa, the Jentel Foundation, and the Michener-Copernicus Society of America, among others. His debut novel, *Honey in the Lion's Head,* is forthcoming in spring 2016. His story collection, *Aleghney Front,* which includes "Gauley Season," is also forthcoming in 2016.

▪ All great stories have a ghost in them—I've come to be convinced of that. Something to haunt the land, quicken the flesh, never appear. This story has two ghosts, the first one obvious. Beyond that, I was born in Summersville, West Virginia, in 1984. Rafting on the Gauley began about then, so you could say we grew up together. The use of water is fascinating—its manipulation, its political power, its final resistance to the plans of men. The lake beat me into the world by eighteen years. I'll take any excuse to write about Lyndon Johnson, certainly the most interesting president of the twentieth century, perhaps any century. "A genuine peace cannot be founded in a desert," he said. "A genuine peace cannot be founded among crowded nations that are starved for this elemental—yes, this divine—gift." Great thanks to G. C. Waldrep and *West Branch* for taking a chance on my work.

Annie Proulx has written short stories, novels, and essays. The work has been flattered with many awards, including the PEN/Faulkner Award, Irish Times International Fiction Prize, Dos Passos Prize, National Book Award, Pulitzer Prize, and more. Several of the stories have been made into films, including *The Shipping News* and *Brokeback Mountain.* Proulx wrote the libretto for the *Brokeback Mountain* opera. She is a member of the American Academy of Arts and Letters and currently lives in Washington State.

▪ "Rough Deeds" is a somewhat modified chapter from my novel in progress, *Barkskins.* The character Charles Duquet has come to the forests of North America from the slums of Paris. He has a driving, relentless need to become wealthy and respected at any cost. Among his rough deeds is the killing of a timber poacher's son. He gets as good as he gives in that no-holds-barred frontier world. His sons and grandsons become timber barons and forever wonder what happened to their ancestor, but only the reader knows the answer to the mystery of his disappearance.

Scott Loring Sanders was raised in New Jersey but has spent the past twenty-five years in the Blue Ridge Mountains of Virginia. He has published two young adult mystery novels, the first of which, *The Hanging Woods,* has found a small but loyal following among adult readers. He has been the writer in residence at the Camargo Foundation in Cassis, France, as well as a two-time fellow at the Virginia Center for the Creative Arts. His short stories and essays have appeared in magazines and journals ranging in scope from *Ellery Queen's Mystery Magazine* to *Creative Nonfiction* to *Appalachian Heritage.* He recently finished his first adult novel and is currently at work on a collection of mystery stories. He teaches creative writing at Virginia Tech.

▪ I'm often intrigued by how a story actually becomes a story and the journey it takes once it leaves my hands. "Pleasant Grove" is a prime example of this, mainly because it didn't start off as a short story at all. It was a piece of backstory for a novel I was working on (a failed novel, as it turns out) set in New Jersey. As the book dissolved, there were some scraps I liked and wanted to keep, including this one. I sent the story to a dozen or so of the usual suspects, all of whom promptly rejected it. I moved on to other things, and the story sat untouched for three years. When I learned of a small local literary magazine that had popped up in Floyd, Virginia, a town I'd once lived in, I revisited the piece with thoughts of sending it to them. I changed the setting from New Jersey to the rural mountains of Virginia, based Johnny's house and property on the old farmhouse in Floyd where my wife and I lived when our son was born, and things finally clicked. I sent the story off and it was accepted five days later. Being a part of *The Best American Mystery Stories* has been a goal of mine ever since I threw caution to the wind, quit my corporate job with a Fortune 500 company, and focused solely on writing, in 2003. I've never once looked back or regretted that decision.

Nancy Pauline Simpson describes herself as "a first-wave baby boomer who remembers both 'Duck and Cover' and the federal polio immunization program." Memorable moments of her youth include being part of a Beatles press conference, drinking Heineken aboard a Dutch submarine, and playing the lead in *Star-Spangled Girl* at the Cavalier Dinner Theater in Norfolk, Virginia. She was born in Louisiana and has lived as far north as Virginia, where she graduated from Old Dominion University ("It was a mercy admission"), and as far west as Okinawa, Japan. She benefited greatly from living in an Asian culture almost as ghost-filled as the American South ("But I still need a waitress to put a rubber band on my chopsticks"). In fact, the first fiction she sold, to *Alfred Hitchcock's Mystery Magazine,* featured malevolent Asian spirits and themes gothic enough to take place in New Orleans instead of Naha. It seemed only natural to segue to the southern version of uncanniness when she returned to the United States. "Anybody who thinks the South does not lend itself to imagining supernatural things has never driven the two-lane highway from Savannah to Beaufort on a breezy night with Spanish moss twitching over the top of the car."

Simpson is now the divorced mother of two grown daughters, one a physician and the other a pipeline engineer ("Yeah, I had to look it up too"). Her one marriage was to a career officer in the Marine Corps, who introduced her to Camp Lejeune, the setting for her first novel, *B.O.Q.,* a mystery that features a female NCIS special agent.

In addition to her stories, which have appeared in *Alfred Hitchcock's Mys-*

tery Magazine, she has written a true-crime book, *Tunnel Vision,* about an unsolved triple homicide that took place at Camp Lejeune in 1981. She has also worked as a foreign correspondent for *Off Duty* magazine, based in Hong Kong, as a reporter and editor for stateside newspapers, and as an ESL instructor for Wake Tech Community College in Raleigh, North Carolina ("This one's multiple choice: ESL means (a) Extra Sensory Lasciviousness (b) Eating and Surviving Lutefisk (c) English as a Second Language").

▪ Suspense, like passion, requires pacing, and the payoff shouldn't take so long that you start losing interest. That's why the short story may be the very best vehicle for suspense. I think their brevity partly explains the success of the Sherlock Holmes stories. They immediately grab you, throw you to the ground, then release you while your heart's still racing. Suspense (or passion) is just not as effective if the mood has been repeatedly interrupted by too many descriptions of scenery or, God forbid, moralizing.

Dennis Tafoya is the author of three novels, *Dope Thief, The Wolves of Fairmount Park,* and *The Poor Boy's Game,* and his short stories have appeared in various anthologies, including *Philadelphia Noir.*

▪ I love short stories, but I take almost as long to write a short story as a novel. I remember it was most of a year from when I first saw the sign for Satan's Kingdom in Franklin County until I sent the story off to Steve Weddle at *Needle.* I think, left to my own devices, I'd never send anything out but just tinker endlessly. And the stories would probably be better for it, because whenever I read one of them, I see opportunities I missed and places I'd like to push harder and get more. Isn't there always more to get?

It's not hard to imagine that for the Congregationalists of seventeenth-century New England, the dark woods of western Massachusetts were literally the devil's kingdom, a place for the banished and condemned. The story began to take shape when I learned that (according to local legend) authorities had been deliberately misspelling the name as Statan's Kingdom to try to deter stoner kids from stealing the signs.

The protagonist of "Satan's Kingdom" is the kind of character I most enjoy spending time with. He's done things he's ashamed of and no longer knows for sure whether he's essentially good or bad. I think that a lot of us fall into this trap—we long for some crisis to arise that will reveal our truest nature, but we're terrified that we'll find ourselves more frail and frightened than heroic. So I think most of us just wait and see, year in and year out, until, like Larocque, we realize we've been hiding a long time.

Laura van den Berg is the author of the story collections *What the World Will Look Like When All the Water Leaves Us,* which was a Barnes & Noble

"Discover Great New Writers" selection and shortlisted for the Frank O'Connor International Award, and *The Isle of Youth*. A *New York Times* Editors' Choice, *The Isle of Youth* was named a Best Book of 2013 by NPR, Amazon, the *Boston Globe,* the *New Republic,* and *O, The Oprah Magazine*. Van den Berg's first novel, *Find Me,* is forthcoming in 2015. She currently lives in the Boston area.

▪ In 2012, I heard about an explosion at the Comandante Ferraz research base in Admiralty Bay on the news. Two men were killed. The story stayed with me. A few weeks later a line got stuck in my head: "There was nothing to identify in Antarctica because there was nothing left." Right away I was flooded with questions. Why was this person in Antarctica? Who or what was she there to identify? Why was there nothing left? This line soon became the first line of a new story, and eventually two interlocking narratives emerged: a present thread set in Antarctica, where the narrator has come to investigate the mysterious death of her scientist brother, who perished in an explosion, and a past thread set in Cambridge, Massachusetts. I have never been to Antarctica, but I know Cambridge intimately, and it was the collision between the radically familiar and the radically foreign that helped this story take flight.

Other Distinguished Mystery Stories of 2014

ALLYN, DOUG
   Borrowed Time. *Ellery Queen's Mystery Magazine*, September/October

BOHEM, LES
   Remus. *Popcorn Fiction*, December/January

CHARYN, JEROME
   Marla. *The Southern Review*, Autumn
CHRISTENSEN, PAUL
   How Frank Died. *The Antioch Review*, Winter
COLEMAN, REED FARREL
   The Terminal. *Kwik Krimes*, ed. Otto Penzler (Thomas & Mercer)

DEAN, DAVID
   Jack and the Devil. *Ellery Queen's Mystery Magazine*, December
DERESKE, JO
   A Tree in Texas. *Kwik Krimes*, ed. Otto Penzler (Thomas & Mercer)
DOOLITTLE, SEAN
   Next Right. *Kwik Krimes*, ed. Otto Penzler (Thomas & Mercer)
DUBOIS, BRENDAN
   Small-Town Life. *Alfred Hitchcock's Mystery Magazine*, January/February

FINCH, DOC
   Prompt Watts. *Alfred Hitchcock's Mystery Magazine*, September

GILSTRAP, JOHN
   In the After. *The Strand Magazine*, February-May
GREEN, BRAD
   The Moans of Bill February. *Needle*, Summer

HAMILTON, STEVE
    The Weight. *Ellery Queen's Mystery Magazine,* August
HAMMETT, DASHIELL
    The Hunter. *The Hunter and Other Stories,* by Dashiell Hammett (Mysterious)
HENION, ANDY
    Liability. *Grift Magazine,* Spring

KENYON, JOHN
    Countdown. *Kwik Krimes,* ed. Otto Penzler (Thomas & Mercer)

LEOPOLD, BRIAN
    With One Stone. *Thuglit,* no. 5

MACHNIK, JUSTIN
    Marquette. *Midwestern Gothic: A Literary Journal,* Spring
MALLORY, MICHAEL
    Dirty Cop. *Death and the Detective,* ed. Jess Faraday (Elm Books)
MCGORAN, JONATHAN
    Bad Debt. *Grift Magazine,* Spring
MCKENNA, JOHN DWAIN
    The Emerald Pearl Witch. *Colorado Noir: Stories from the Dark Side,* by John
    Dwain McKenna (Rhyolite)
MCLEOD, CHARLES
    Dog. *Kwik Krimes,* ed. Otto Penzler (Thomas & Mercer)
MILES, SCOTT
    Erwin's Main Attraction. *Needle,* Summer
MINER, MIKE
    The Little Outlaw. *Plan B Magazine,* vol. 1, March

RABB, JONATHAN
    A Game Played. *The Strand Magazine,* June-September
REDWOOD, JAMES
    The Angel of the Tenderloin. *Notre Dame Review,* Summer/Fall
ROBINSON, TODD
    Good Dogs. *All Due Respect,* no. 1
ROSS, JAMES L.
    The Gypsy Ring. *Alfred Hitchcock's Mystery Magazine,* October

WILLIAMS, TIM L.
    Promissory Notes. *Ellery Queen's Mystery Magazine,* February

ZELVIN, ELIZABETH
    A Breach of Trust. *Mysterical-E,* Fall

THE BEST AMERICAN SERIES®

FIRST, BEST, AND BEST-SELLING

The Best American series is the premier annual showcase for the country's finest short fiction and nonfiction. Each volume's series editor selects notable works from hundreds of magazines, journals, and websites. A special guest editor, a leading writer in the field, then chooses the best twenty or so pieces to publish. This unique system has made the Best American series the most respected—and most popular—of its kind.

Look for these best-selling titles in the Best American series:

The Best American Comics

The Best American Essays

The Best American Infographics

The Best American Mystery Stories

The Best American Nonrequired Reading

The Best American Science and Nature Writing

The Best American Short Stories

The Best American Sports Writing

The Best American Travel Writing

Available in print and e-book wherever books are sold.
Visit our website: *www.hmhbooks.com/hmh/site/bas*